MW00512408

Henry James OM (15 April 1843 – 28 February 1916) was an American-British author regarded as a key transitional figure between literary realism and literary modernism, and is considered by many to be among the greatest novelists in the English language. He was the son of Henry James Sr. and the brother of renowned philosopher and psychologist William James and diarist Alice James.

He is best known for a number of novels dealing with the social and marital interplay between émigré Americans, English people, and continental Europeans. Examples of such novels include The Portrait of a Lady, The Ambassadors, and The Wings of the Dove. His later works were increasingly experimental. In describing the internal states of mind and social dynamics of his characters, James often made use of a style in which ambiguous or contradictory motives and impressions were overlaid or juxtaposed in the discussion of a character's psyche.(Source: Wikipedia)

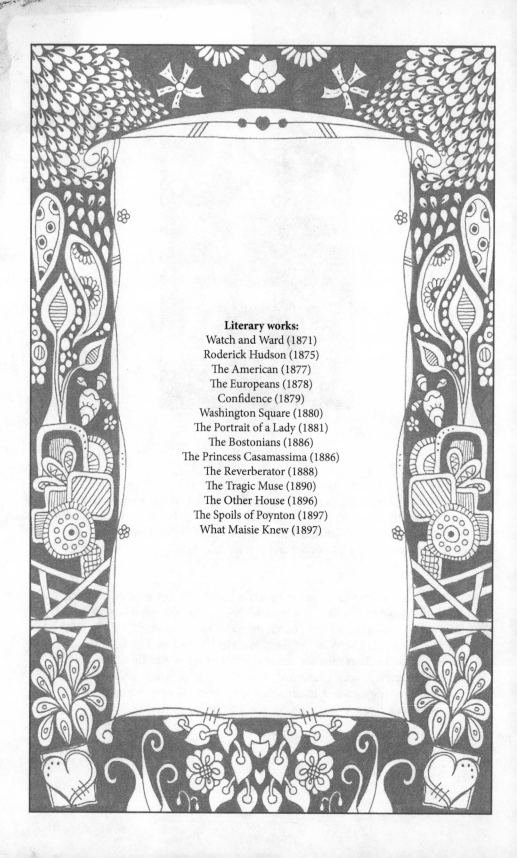

Literary works:
Watch and Ward (1871)
Roderick Hudson (1875)
The American (1877)
The Europeans (1878)
Confidence (1879)
Washington Square (1880)
The Portrait of a Lady (1881)
The Bostonians (1886)
The Princess Casamassima (1886)
The Reverberator (1888)
The Tragic Muse (1890)
The Other House (1896)
The Spoils of Poynton (1897)
What Maisie Knew (1897)

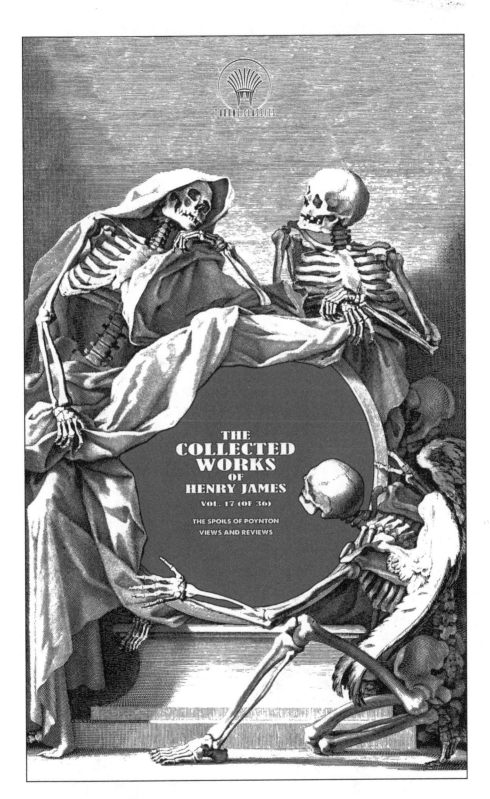

TUDOR CLASSICS

THE
COLLECTED
WORKS
OF
HENRY JAMES
VOL. 17 (OF 36)

THE SPOILS OF POYNTON
VIEWS AND REVIEWS

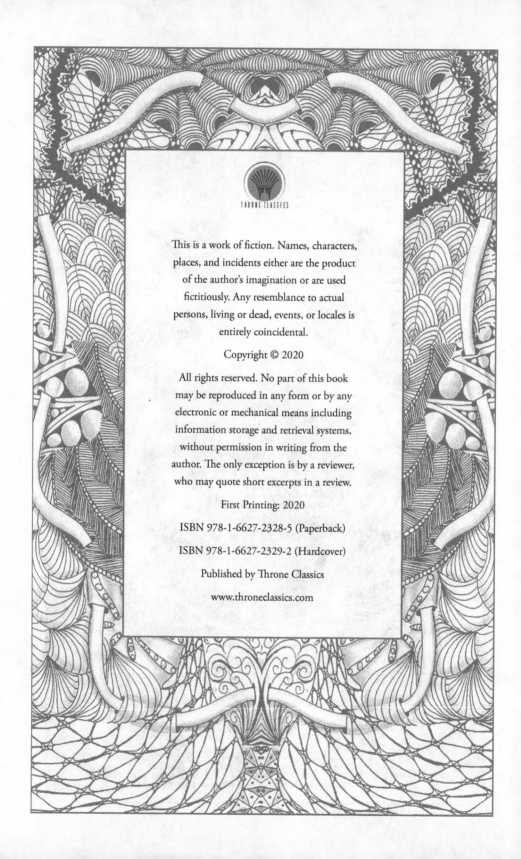

First Printing: 2020

ISBN 978-1-6627-2328-5 (Paperback)

ISBN 978-1-6627-2329-2 (Hardcover)

Published by Throne Classics

www.throneclassics.com

Contents

THE
COLLECTED
WORKS
OF
HENRY JAMES
VOL. 17 (OF 36)

THE SPOILS OF POYNTON

I

Mrs. Gereth had said she would go with the rest to church, but suddenly it seemed to her that she should not be able to wait even till church-time for relief: breakfast, at Waterbath, was a punctual meal, and she had still nearly an hour on her hands. Knowing the church to be near, she prepared in her room for the little rural walk, and on her way down again, passing through corridors and observing imbecilities of decoration, the æsthetic misery of the big commodious house, she felt a return of the tide of last night's irritation, a renewal of everything she could secretly suffer from ugliness and stupidity. Why did she consent to such contacts, why did she so rashly expose herself? She had had, heaven knew, her reasons, but the whole experience was to be sharper than she had feared. To get away from it and out into the air, into the presence of sky and trees, flowers and birds, was a necessity of every nerve. The flowers at Waterbath would probably go wrong in color and the nightingales sing out of tune; but she remembered to have heard the place described as possessing those advantages that are usually spoken of as natural. There were advantages enough it clearly didn't possess. It was hard for her to believe that a woman could look presentable who had been kept awake for hours by the wall-paper in her room; yet none the less, as in her fresh widow's weeds she rustled across the hall, she was sustained by the consciousness, which always added to the unction of her social Sundays, that she was, as usual, the only person in the house incapable of wearing in her preparation the horrible stamp of the same exceptional smartness that would be conspicuous in a grocer's wife. She would rather have perished than have looked *endimanchée*.

She was fortunately not challenged, the hall being empty of the other women, who were engaged precisely in arraying themselves to that dire end. Once in the grounds, she recognized that, with a site, a view that struck the note, set an example to its inmates, Waterbath ought to have been charming. How she herself, with such elements to handle, would have taken the fine hint of nature! Suddenly, at the turn of a walk, she came on a member of the party, a young lady seated on a bench in deep and lonely meditation. She had observed the girl at dinner and afterwards: she was always looking at girls with an apprehensive or speculative reference to her son. Deep in her heart was a conviction that Owen would, in spite of all her spells, marry at last a frump; and this from no evidence that she could have represented as adequate, but simply from her deep uneasiness, her belief that such a special sensibility as her own could have been inflicted on a woman only as a source of anguish. It would be her fate, her discipline, her cross, to have a frump brought hideously home to her. This girl, one of the two Vetches, had no beauty, but Mrs. Gereth, scanning the dullness for a sign of life, had been straightway able to classify such a figure as the least, for the moment, of her afflictions. Fleda Vetch was dressed with an idea, though perhaps with not much else; and that made a bond when there was none other, especially as in this case the idea was real, not imitation. Mrs. Gereth had long ago generalized the truth that the temperament of the frump is amply consistent with a certain usual prettiness. There were five girls in the party, and the prettiness of this one, slim, pale, and black-haired, was less likely than that of the others ever to occasion an exchange of platitudes. The two less developed Brigstocks, daughters of the house, were in particular tiresomely "lovely." A second glance, this morning, at the young lady before her conveyed to Mrs. Gereth the soothing assurance that she also was guiltless of looking hot and fine. They had had no talk as yet, but this was a note that would effectually introduce them if the girl should show herself in the least conscious of their community. She got up from her seat with a smile that but partly dissipated the prostration Mrs. Gereth had recognized in her attitude. The elder woman drew her down again, and for a minute, as they sat together, their eyes met and sent out mutual soundings. "Are you safe? Can I utter it?" each of them said to the other, quickly recognizing, almost proclaiming, their common need to escape. The tremendous fancy, as it came to be called, that Mrs. Gereth was destined to take to Fleda Vetch virtually began with this discovery that the poor child had been moved to flight even more promptly than herself. That the poor child no less quickly perceived how far she could now go was proved by the immense friendliness with which she instantly broke out: "Isn't it too dreadful?"

"Horrible—horrible!" cried Mrs. Gereth, with a laugh, "and it's really a comfort to be able to say it." She had an idea, for it was her ambition, that she successfully made a secret of that awkward oddity, her proneness to be rendered unhappy by the presence of the dreadful. Her passion for the exquisite was the cause of this, but it was a passion she considered that she never advertised nor gloried in, contenting herself with letting it regulate her steps and show quietly in her life, remembering at all times that there are few things more soundless than a deep devotion. She was therefore struck with the acuteness of the little girl who had already put a finger on her hidden spring. What was dreadful now, what was horrible, was the intimate ugliness of Waterbath, and it was of that phenomenon these ladies talked while they sat in the shade and drew refreshment from the great tranquil sky, from which no blue saucers were suspended. It was an ugliness fundamental and systematic, the result of the abnormal nature of the Brigstocks, from whose composition the principle of taste had been extravagantly omitted. In the arrangement of their home some other principle, remarkably active, but uncanny and obscure, had operated instead, with consequences depressing to behold, consequences that took the form of a universal futility. The house was bad in all conscience, but it might have passed if they had only let it alone. This saving mercy was beyond them; they had smothered it with trumpery ornament and scrapbook art, with strange excrescences and bunchy draperies, with gimcracks that might have been keepsakes for maid-servants and nondescript conveniences that might have been prizes for the blind. They had gone wildly astray over carpets and curtains; they had an infallible instinct for disaster, and were so cruelly doom-ridden that it rendered them almost tragic. Their drawing-room, Mrs. Gereth lowered her voice to mention, caused her face to burn, and each of the new friends confided to the other that in her own apartment she had given way to tears. There was in the elder lady's a set of comic water-colors, a family joke by a family genius, and in the younger's a souvenir from some centennial or other Exhibition, that they shudderingly alluded to. The house was perversely full of souvenirs of places even more ugly than itself and of things it would have been a pious duty to forget. The worst horror was the acres of varnish, something advertised and smelly, with which everything was smeared; it was Fleda Vetch's conviction that the application of it, by their own hands and hilariously shoving each other, was the amusement of the Brigstocks on rainy days.

When, as criticism deepened, Fleda dropped the suggestion that some people would perhaps see something in Mona, Mrs. Gereth caught her up with a groan of protest, a smothered familiar cry of "Oh, my dear!" Mona was the eldest of the three, the one Mrs. Gereth most suspected. She confided to her young friend that it was her suspicion that had brought her to Waterbath; and this was going very far, for on the spot, as a refuge, a remedy, she had clutched at the idea that something might be done with the girl before her. It was her fancied exposure at any rate that had sharpened the shock; made her ask herself with a terrible chill if fate could really be plotting to saddle her with a daughter-in-law brought up in such a place. She had seen Mona in her appropriate setting and she had seen Owen, handsome and heavy, dangle beside her; but the effect of these first hours had happily not been to darken the prospect. It was clearer to her that she could never accept Mona, but it was after all by no means certain that Owen would ask her to. He had sat by somebody else at dinner, and afterwards he had talked to Mrs. Firmin, who was as dreadful as all the rest, but redeemingly married. His heaviness, which in her need of expansion she freely named, had two aspects: one of them his monstrous lack of taste, the other his exaggerated prudence. If it should come to a question of carrying Mona with a high hand there would be no need to worry, for that was rarely his manner of proceeding.

15

Invited by her companion, who had asked if it weren't wonderful, Mrs. Gereth had begun to say a word about Poynton; but she heard a sound of voices that made her stop short. The next moment she rose to her feet, and Fleda could see that her alarm was by no means quenched. Behind the place where they had been sitting the ground dropped with a certain steepness, forming a long grassy bank, up which Owen Gereth and Mona Brigstock, dressed for church but making a familiar joke of it, were in the act of scrambling and helping each other. When they had reached the even ground Fleda was able to read the meaning of the exclamation in which Mrs. Gereth had expressed her reserves on the subject of Miss Brigstock's personality. Miss Brigstock had been laughing and even romping, but the circumstance hadn't contributed the ghost of an expression to her countenance. Tall, straight and fair, long-limbed and strangely festooned, she stood there without a look in her eye or any perceptible intention of any sort in any other feature. She belonged to the type in which speech is an unaided emission of sound and the secret of being is impenetrably and incorruptibly kept. Her expression would probably have been beautiful if she had had one, but whatever she communicated she communicated, in a manner best known to herself, without signs. This was not the case with Owen Gereth, who had plenty of them, and all very simple and immediate. Robust and artless, eminently natural, yet perfectly correct, he looked pointlessly active and pleasantly dull. Like his mother and like Fleda Vetch, but not for the same reason, this young pair had come out to take a turn before church.

The meeting of the two couples was sensibly awkward, and Fleda, who was sagacious, took the measure of the shock inflicted on Mrs. Gereth. There had been intimacy—oh yes, intimacy as well as puerility—in the horse-play of which they had just had a glimpse. The party began to stroll together to the house, and Fleda had again a sense of Mrs. Gereth's quick management in the way the lovers, or whatever they were, found themselves separated. She strolled behind with Mona, the mother possessing herself of her son, her exchange of remarks with whom, however, remained, as they went, suggestively inaudible. That member of the party in whose intenser consciousness we shall most profitably seek a reflection of the little drama with which we are concerned received an even livelier impression of Mrs. Gereth's intervention from the fact that ten minutes later, on the way to church, still another pairing had been effected. Owen walked with Fleda, and it was an amusement to the girl to feel sure that this was by his mother's direction. Fleda had other amusements as well: such as noting that Mrs. Gereth was now with Mona Brigstock; such as observing that she was all affability to that young woman; such as reflecting that, masterful and clever, with a great bright spirit, she was one of those who impose themselves as an influence;

such as feeling finally that Owen Gereth was absolutely beautiful and delightfully dense. This young person had even from herself wonderful secrets of delicacy and pride; but she came as near distinctness as in the consideration of such matters she had ever come at all in now surrendering herself to the idea that it was of a pleasant effect and rather remarkable to be stupid without offense—of a pleasanter effect and more remarkable indeed than to be clever and horrid. Owen Gereth at any rate, with his inches, his features, and his lapses, was neither of these latter things. She herself was prepared, if she should ever marry, to contribute all the cleverness, and she liked to think that her husband would be a force grateful for direction. She was in her small way a spirit of the same family as Mrs. Gereth. On that flushed and huddled Sunday a great matter occurred; her little life became aware of a singular quickening. Her meagre past fell away from her like a garment of the wrong fashion, and as she came up to town on the Monday what she stared at in the suburban fields from the train was a future full of the things she particularly loved.

II

These were neither more nor less than the things with which she had had time to
learn from Mrs. Gereth that Poynton overflowed. Poynton, in the south of England,
was this lady's established, or rather her disestablished home, having recently passed
into the possession of her son. The father of the boy, an only child, had died two years
before, and in London, with his mother, Owen was occupying for May and June a
house good-naturedly lent them by Colonel Gereth, their uncle and brother-in-law.
His mother had laid her hand so engagingly on Fleda Vetch that in a very few days
the girl knew it was possible they should suffer together in Cadogan Place almost as
much as they had suffered together at Waterbath. The kind colonel's house was also
an ordeal, but the two women, for the ensuing month, had at least the relief of their
confessions. The great drawback of Mrs. Gereth's situation was that, thanks to the rare
perfection of Poynton, she was condemned to wince wherever she turned. She had
lived for a quarter of a century in such warm closeness with the beautiful that, as she
frankly admitted, life had become for her a kind of fool's paradise. She couldn't leave
her own house without peril of exposure. She didn't say it in so many words, but Fleda
could see she held that there was nothing in England really to compare to Poynton.
There were places much grander and richer, but there was no such complete work of
art, nothing that would appeal so to those who were really informed. In putting such
elements into her hand fortune had given her an inestimable chance; she knew how
rarely well things had gone with her and that she had tasted a happiness altogether
rare.

There had been in the first place the exquisite old house itself, early Jacobean,
supreme in every part: it was a provocation, an inspiration, a matchless canvas for the
picture. Then there had been her husband's sympathy and generosity, his knowledge
and love, their perfect accord and beautiful life together, twenty-six years of planning
and seeking, a long, sunny harvest of taste and curiosity. Lastly, she never denied, there
had been her personal gift, the genius, the passion, the patience of the collector—a
patience, an almost infernal cunning, that had enabled her to do it all with a limited
command of money. There wouldn't have been money enough for any one else, she
said with pride, but there had been money enough for her. They had saved on lots of
things in life, and there were lots of things they hadn't had, but they had had in every
corner of Europe their swing among the Jews. It was fascinating to poor Fleda, who
hadn't a penny in the world nor anything nice at home, and whose only treasure was

her subtle mind, to hear this genuine English lady, fresh and fair, young in the fifties, declare with gayety and conviction that she was herself the greatest Jew who had ever tracked a victim. Fleda, with her mother dead, hadn't so much even as a home, and her nearest chance of one was that there was some appearance her sister would become engaged to a curate whose eldest brother was supposed to have property and would perhaps allow him something. Her father paid some of her bills, but he didn't like her to live with him; and she had lately, in Paris, with several hundred other young women, spent a year in a studio, arming herself for the battle of life by a course with an impressionist painter. She was determined to work, but her impressions, or somebody's else, were as yet her only material. Mrs. Gereth had told her she liked her because she had an extraordinary *flair*; but under the circumstances a *flair* was a questionable boon: in the dry places in which she had mainly moved she could have borne a chronic catarrh. She was constantly summoned to Cadogan Place, and before the month was out was kept to stay, to pay a visit of which the end, it was agreed, should have nothing to do with the beginning. She had a sense, partly exultant and partly alarmed, of having quickly become necessary to her imperious friend, who indeed gave a reason quite sufficient for it in telling her there was nobody else who understood. From Mrs. Gereth there was in these days an immense deal to understand, though it might be freely summed up in the circumstance that she was wretched. She told Fleda that she couldn't completely know why till she should have seen the things at Poynton. Fleda could perfectly grasp this connection, which was exactly one of the matters that, in their inner mystery, were a blank to everybody else.

The girl had a promise that the wonderful house should be shown her early in July, when Mrs. Gereth would return to it as to her home; but even before this initiation she put her finger on the spot that in the poor lady's troubled soul ached hardest. This was the misery that haunted her, the dread of the inevitable surrender. What Fleda had to sit up to was the confirmed appearance that Owen Gereth would marry Mona Brigstock, marry her in his mother's teeth, and that such an act would have incalculable bearings. They were present to Mrs. Gereth, her companion could see, with a vividness that at moments almost ceased to be that of sanity. She would have to give up Poynton, and give it up to a product of Waterbath—that was the wrong that rankled, the humiliation at which Fleda would be able adequately to shudder only when she should know the place. She did know Waterbath, and she despised it—she had that qualification for sympathy. Her sympathy was intelligent, for she read deep into the matter; she stared, aghast, as it came home to her for the first time, at the cruel English custom of the expropriation of the lonely mother. Mr. Gereth had apparently been a very amiable man, but Mr. Gereth had left things in a way that made the girl marvel. The house and its contents had been treated as a single splendid object; everything was to go straight to his son, and his widow was to have a maintenance and a cottage in another county. No account whatever had been taken of her relation to her treasures, of the passion with which she had waited for them, worked for them, picked them over, made them worthy of each other and the house, watched them, loved them, lived with them. He appeared to have assumed that she would settle questions with her son, that he could depend upon Owen's affection. And in truth, as poor Mrs. Gereth inquired, how could he possibly have had a prevision—he who turned his eyes instinctively from everything repulsive—of anything so abnormal as a Waterbath Brigstock? He had been in ugly houses enough, but had escaped that particular nightmare. Nothing so perverse could have been expected to happen as that the heir to the loveliest thing in England should be inspired to hand it over to a girl so exceptionally tainted. Mrs. Gereth spoke of poor Mona's taint as if to mention it were almost a violation of decency, and a person who had listened without enlightenment would have wondered of what fault the girl had been or had indeed not been guilty. But Owen had from a boy never cared, had never had the least pride or pleasure in his home.

"Well, then, if he doesn't care!"—Fleda exclaimed, with some impetuosity; stopping short, however, before she completed her sentence.

Mrs. Gereth looked at her rather hard. "If he doesn't care?"

Fleda hesitated; she had not quite had a definite idea. "Well—he'll give them up."

"Give what up?"

"Why, those beautiful things."

"Give them up to whom?" Mrs. Gereth more boldly stared.

"To you, of course—to enjoy, to keep for yourself."

"And leave his house as bare as your hand? There's nothing in it that isn't precious."

Fleda considered; her friend had taken her up with a smothered ferocity by which she was slightly disconcerted. "I don't mean of course that he should surrender everything; but he might let you pick out the things to which you're most attached."

"I think he would if he were free," said Mrs. Gereth.

"And do you mean, as it is, that *she*'ll prevent him?" Mona Brigstock, between these ladies, was now nothing but "she."

"By every means in her power."

"But surely not because she understands and appreciates them?"

"No," Mrs. Gereth replied, "but because they belong to the house and the house belongs to Owen. If I should wish to take anything, she would simply say, with that motionless mask: 'It goes with the house.' And day after day, in the face of every argument, of every consideration of generosity, she would repeat, without winking, in that voice like the squeeze of a doll's stomach: 'It goes with the house—it goes with the house.' In that attitude they'll shut themselves up."

Fleda was struck, was even a little startled with the way Mrs. Gereth had turned this over—had faced, if indeed only to recognize its futility, the notion of a battle with her only son. These words led her to make an inquiry which she had not thought it discreet to make before; she brought out the idea of the possibility, after all, of her friend's continuing to live at Poynton. Would they really wish to proceed to extremities? Was no good-humored, graceful compromise to be imagined or brought about? Couldn't the same roof cover them? Was it so very inconceivable that a married son should, for the rest of her days, share with so charming a mother the home she had devoted more than a score of years to making beautiful for him? Mrs. Gereth hailed this question with a wan, compassionate smile; she replied that a common household, in such a case, was exactly so inconceivable that Fleda had only to glance over the fair face of the English land to see how few people had ever conceived it. It was always thought a wonder, a "mistake," a piece of overstrained sentiment; and she confessed that she was as little capable of a flight of that sort as Owen himself. Even if they both had been capable, they would still have Mona's hatred to reckon with. Fleda's breath was sometimes taken away by the great bounds and elisions which, on Mrs. Gereth's lips, the course of discussion could take. This was the first she had heard of Mona's hatred, though she certainly had not needed Mrs. Gereth to tell her that in close quarters that young lady would prove secretly mulish. Later Fleda perceived indeed that perhaps almost any girl would hate a person who should be so markedly averse to having anything to do with her. Before this, however, in conversation with her young friend, Mrs. Gereth furnished a more vivid motive for her despair by asking how she could possibly be expected to sit there with the new proprietors and accept—or call it, for a day, endure—the horrors they would perpetrate in the house. Fleda reasoned that they wouldn't after all smash things nor burn them up; and Mrs. Gereth admitted when pushed that she didn't quite suppose they would. What she meant was that they would neglect them, ignore them, leave them to clumsy servants (there wasn't an object of them all but should be handled with perfect love), and in many cases probably wish to replace them by pieces answerable to some vulgar modern notion of the convenient. Above all, she saw in advance, with dilated eyes, the abominations they would inevitably mix up with them—the maddening relics of Waterbath, the little brackets and pink vases, the sweepings of bazaars, the family photographs and illuminated texts, the "household art" and household piety of Mona's hideous home. Wasn't it enough simply to contend that Mona would approach Poynton in the spirit of a Brigstock, and that in the spirit of a Brigstock she would deal with her acquisition? Did Fleda really see *her*, Mrs. Gereth demanded, spending the remainder of her days with such a creature's elbow in her eye?

Fleda had to declare that she certainly didn't, and that Waterbath had been a warning it would be frivolous to overlook. At the same time she privately reflected that they were taking a great deal for granted, and that, inasmuch as to her knowledge Owen Gereth had positively denied his betrothal, the ground of their speculations was by no means firm. It seemed to our young lady that in a difficult position Owen conducted himself with some natural art; treating this domesticated confidant of his mother's wrongs with a simple civility that almost troubled her conscience, so deeply she felt that she might have had for him the air of siding with that lady against him. She wondered if he would ever know how little really she did this, and that she was there, since Mrs. Gereth had insisted, not to betray, but essentially to confirm and protect. The fact that his mother disliked Mona Brigstock might have made him dislike the object of her preference, and it was detestable to Fleda to remember that she might have appeared to him to offer herself as an exemplary contrast. It was clear enough, however, that the happy youth had no more sense for a motive than a deaf man for a tune, a limitation by which, after all, she could gain as well as lose. He came and went very freely on the business with which London abundantly furnished him, but he found time more than once to say to her, "It's awfully nice of you to look after poor Mummy." As well as his quick speech, which shyness made obscure—it was usually as desperate as a "rush" at some violent game—his child's eyes in his man's face put it to her that, you know, this really meant a good deal for him and that he hoped she would stay on. With a person in the house who, like herself, was clever, poor Mummy was conveniently occupied; and Fleda found a beauty in the candor and even in the modesty which apparently kept him from suspecting that two such wiseheads could possibly be occupied with Owen Gereth.

III

They went at last, the wiseheads, down to Poynton, where the palpitating girl had the full revelation. "*Now* do you know how I feel?" Mrs. Gereth asked when in the wonderful hall, three minutes after their arrival, her pretty associate dropped on a seat with a soft gasp and a roll of dilated eyes. The answer came clearly enough, and in the rapture of that first walk through the house Fleda took a prodigious span. She perfectly understood how Mrs. Gereth felt—she had understood but meagrely before; and the two women embraced with tears over the tightening of their bond—tears which on the younger one's part were the natural and usual sign of her submission to perfect beauty. It was not the first time she had cried for the joy of admiration, but it was the first time the mistress of Poynton, often as she had shown her house, had been present at such an exhibition. She exulted in it; it quickened her own tears; she assured her companion that such an occasion made the poor old place fresh to her again and more precious than ever. Yes, nobody had ever, that way, felt what she had achieved: people were so grossly ignorant, and everybody, even the knowing ones, as they thought themselves, more or less dense. What Mrs. Gereth had achieved was indeed an exquisite work; and in such an art of the treasure-hunter, in selection and comparison refined to that point, there was an element of creation, of personality. She had commended Fleda's *flair*, and Fleda now gave herself up to satiety. Preoccupations and scruples fell away from her; she had never known a greater happiness than the week she passed in this initiation.

Wandering through clear chambers where the general effect made preferences almost as impossible as if they had been shocks, pausing at open doors where vistas were long and bland, she would, even if she had not already known, have discovered for herself that Poynton was the record of a life. It was written in great syllables of color and form, the tongues of other countries and the hands of rare artists. It was all France and Italy, with their ages composed to rest. For England you looked out of old windows—it was England that was the wide embrace. While outside, on the low terraces, she contradicted gardeners and refined on nature, Mrs. Gereth left her guest to finger fondly the brasses that Louis Quinze might have thumbed, to sit with Venetian velvets just held in a loving palm, to hang over cases of enamels and pass and repass before cabinets. There were not many pictures—the panels and the stuffs were themselves the picture; and in all the great wainscoted house there was not an inch of pasted paper. What struck Fleda most in it was the high pride of her friend's taste, a fine arrogance, a sense of style which, however amused and amusing, never compromised nor stooped. She felt indeed, as this lady had intimated to her that she would, both a respect and a compassion that she had not known before; the vision of the coming surrender filled her with an equal pain. To give it all up, to die to it—that thought ached in her breast. She herself could imagine clinging there with a closeness separate from dignity. To have created such a place was to have had dignity enough; when there was a question of defending it the fiercest attitude was the right one. After so intense a taking of possession she too was to give it up; for she reflected that if Mrs. Gereth's remaining there would have offered her a sort of future—stretching away in safe years on the other side of a gulf—the advent of the others could only be, by the same law, a great vague menace, the ruffling of a still water. Such were the emotions of a hungry girl whose sensibility was almost as great as her opportunities for comparison had been small. The museums had done something for her, but nature had done more.

If Owen had not come down with them nor joined them later, it was because he still found London jolly; yet the question remained of whether the jollity of London was not merely the only name his small vocabulary yielded for the jollity of Mona Brigstock. There was indeed in his conduct another ambiguity—something that required explaining so long as his motive didn't come to the surface. If he was in love, what was the matter? And what was the matter still more if he wasn't? The mystery was at last cleared up: this Fleda gathered from the tone in which, one morning at breakfast, a letter just opened made Mrs. Gereth cry out. Her dismay was almost a shriek: "Why, he's bringing her down—he wants her to see the house!" They flew, the two women, into each other's arms and, with their heads together, soon made out that the reason, the baffling reason why nothing had yet happened, was that Mona didn't know, or Owen didn't, whether Poynton would really please her. She was coming down to judge; and could anything in the world be more like poor Owen than the ponderous probity which had kept him from pressing her for a reply till she should have learned whether she approved what he had to offer her? That was a scruple it had naturally been impossible to impute. If only they might fondly hope, Mrs. Gereth wailed, that the girl's expectations would be dashed! There was a fine consistency, a sincerity quite affecting, in her arguing that the better the place should happen to look and to express the conceptions to which it owed its origin, the less it would speak to an intelligence so primitive. How could a Brigstock possibly understand what it was all about? How, really, could a Brigstock logically do anything but hate it? Mrs. Gereth, even as she whisked away linen shrouds, persuaded herself of the possibility on Mona's part of some bewildered blankness, some collapse of admiration that would prove disconcerting to her swain—a hope of which Fleda at least could see the absurdity and which gave the measure of the poor lady's strange, almost maniacal disposition to thrust in everywhere the question of "things," to read all behavior in the light of some fancied relation to them. "Things" were of course the sum of the world; only, for Mrs. Gereth, the sum of the world was rare French furniture and Oriental china. She could at a stretch imagine people's not having, but she couldn't imagine their not wanting and not missing.

The young couple were to be accompanied by Mrs. Brigstock, and with a prevision of how fiercely they would be watched Fleda became conscious, before the party arrived, of an amused, diplomatic pity for them. Almost as much as Mrs. Gereth's her taste was her life, but her life was somehow the larger for it. Besides, she had another care now: there was some one she wouldn't have liked to see humiliated even in the form of a young lady who would contribute to his never suspecting so much delicacy. When this young lady appeared Fleda tried, so far as the wish to efface herself allowed, to be mainly the person to take her about, show her the house, and cover up her ignorance. Owen's announcement had been that, as trains made it convenient, they would present themselves for luncheon and depart before dinner; but Mrs. Gereth, true to her system of glaring civility, proposed and obtained an extension, a dining and spending of the night. She made her young friend wonder against what rebellion of fact she was sacrificing in advance so profusely to form. Fleda was appalled, after the first hour, by the rash innocence with which Mona had accepted the responsibility of observation, and indeed by the large levity with which, sitting there like a bored tourist in fine scenery, she exercised it. She felt in her nerves the effect of such a manner on her companion's, and it was this that made her want to entice the girl away, give her some merciful warning or some jocular cue. Mona met intense looks, however, with eyes that might have been blue beads, the only ones she had—eyes into which Fleda thought it strange Owen Gereth should have to plunge for his fate and his mother for a confession of whether Poynton was a success. She made no remark that helped to supply this light; her impression at any rate had nothing in common with the feeling that, as the beauty of the place throbbed out like music, had caused Fleda Vetch to burst into tears. She was as content to say nothing as if, Mrs. Gereth afterwards exclaimed, she had been keeping her mouth shut in a railway-tunnel. Mrs. Gereth contrived at the end of an hour to convey to Fleda that it was plain she was brutally ignorant; but Fleda more subtly discovered that her ignorance was obscurely active.

She was not so stupid as not to see that something, though she scarcely knew what, was expected of her that she couldn't give; and the only mode her intelligence suggested of meeting the expectation was to plant her big feet and pull another way. Mrs. Gereth wanted her to rise, somehow or somewhere, and was prepared to hate her if she didn't: very well, she couldn't, she wouldn't rise; she already moved at the altitude that suited her, and was able to see that, since she was exposed to the hatred, she might at least enjoy the calm. The smallest trouble, for a girl with no nonsense about her, was to earn what she incurred; so that, a dim instinct teaching her she would earn it best by not being effusive, and combining with the conviction that she now held Owen, and therefore the place, she had the pleasure of her honesty as well as of her security. Didn't her very honesty lead her to be belligerently blank about Poynton, inasmuch as it was just Poynton that was forced upon her as a subject for effusiveness? Such subjects, to Mona Brigstock, had an air almost of indecency, and the house became uncanny to her through such an appeal—an appeal that, somewhere in the twilight of her being, as Fleda was sure, she thanked heaven she *was* the girl stiffly to draw back from. She was a person whom pressure at a given point infallibly caused to expand in the wrong place instead of, as it is usually administered in the hope of doing, the right one. Her mother, to make up for this, broke out universally, pronounced everything "most striking," and was visibly happy that Owen's captor should be so far on the way to strike: but she jarred upon Mrs. Gereth by her formula of admiration, which was that anything she looked at was "in the style" of something else. This was to show how much she had seen, but it only showed she had seen nothing; everything at Poynton was in the style of Poynton, and poor Mrs. Brigstock, who at least was determined to rise, and had brought with her a trophy of her journey, a "lady's magazine" purchased at the station, a horrible thing with patterns for antimacassars, which, as it was quite new, the first number, and seemed so clever, she kindly offered to leave for the house, was in the style of a vulgar old woman who wore silver jewelry and tried to pass off a gross avidity as a sense of the beautiful.

By the day's end it was clear to Fleda Vetch that, however Mona judged, the day had been determinant; whether or no she felt the charm, she felt the challenge: at an early moment Owen Gereth would be able to tell his mother the worst. Nevertheless, when the elder lady, at bedtime, coming in a dressing-gown and a high fever to the younger one's room, cried out, "She hates it; but what will she do?" Fleda pretended vagueness, played at obscurity and assented disingenuously to the proposition that they at least had a respite. The future was dark to her, but there was a silken thread she could clutch in the gloom—she would never give Owen away. He might give himself—he even certainly would; but that was his own affair, and his blunders, his innocence, only added to the appeal he made to her. She would cover him, she would protect him, and beyond thinking her a cheerful inmate he would never guess her intention, any more than, beyond thinking her clever enough for anything, his acute mother would discover it. From this hour, with Mrs. Gereth, there was a flaw in her frankness: her admirable friend continued to know everything she did; what was to remain unknown was the general motive.

From the window of her room, the next morning before breakfast, the girl saw Owen in the garden with Mona, who strolled beside him with a listening parasol, but without a visible look for the great florid picture that had been hung there by Mrs. Gereth's hand. Mona kept dropping her eyes, as she walked, to catch the sheen of her patent-leather shoes, which resembled a man's and which she kicked forward a little—it gave her an odd movement—to help her see what she thought of them. When Fleda came down Mrs. Gereth was in the breakfast-room; and at that moment Owen, through a long window, passed in alone from the terrace and very endearingly kissed his mother. It immediately struck the girl that she was in their way, for hadn't he been borne on a wave of joy exactly to announce, before the Brigstocks departed, that Mona had at last faltered out the sweet word he had been waiting for? He shook hands with his friendly violence, but Fleda contrived not to look into his face: what she liked most to see in it was not the reflection of Mona's big boot-toes. She could bear well enough that young lady herself, but she couldn't bear Owen's opinion of her. She was on the point of slipping into the garden when the movement was checked by Mrs. Gereth's suddenly drawing her close, as if for the morning embrace, and then, while she kept her there with the bravery of the night's repose, breaking out: "Well, my dear boy, what *does* your young friend there make of our odds and ends?"

"Oh, she thinks they're all right!"

Fleda immediately guessed from his tone that he had not come in to say what she supposed; there was even something in it to confirm Mrs. Gereth's belief that their danger had dropped. She was sure, moreover, that his tribute to Mona's taste was a repetition of the eloquent words in which the girl had herself recorded it; she could indeed hear, with all vividness, the pretty passage between the pair. "Don't you think it's rather jolly, the old shop?" "Oh, it's all right!" Mona had graciously remarked; and then they had probably, with a slap on a back, run another race up or down a green bank. Fleda knew Mrs. Gereth had not yet uttered a word to her son that would have shown him how much she feared; but it was impossible to feel her friend's arm round her and not become aware that this friend was now throbbing with a strange intention. Owen's reply had scarcely been of a nature to usher in a discussion of Mona's sensibilities; but Mrs. Gereth went on, in a moment, with an innocence of which Fleda could measure the cold hypocrisy: "Has she any sort of feeling for nice old things?" The question was as fresh as the morning light.

"Oh, of course she likes everything that's nice." And Owen, who constitutionally disliked questions—an answer was almost as hateful to him as a "trick" to a big dog— smiled kindly at Fleda and conveyed that she would understand what he meant even if his mother didn't. Fleda, however, mainly understood that Mrs. Gereth, with an odd, wild laugh, held her so hard that she hurt her.

"I could give up everything without a pang, I think, to a person I could trust, I could respect." The girl heard her voice tremble under the effort to show nothing but what she wanted to show, and felt the sincerity of her implication that the piety most real to her was to be on one's knees before one's high standard. "The best things here, as you know, are the things your father and I collected, things all that we worked for and waited for and suffered for. Yes," cried Mrs. Gereth, with a fine freedom of fancy, "there are things in the house that we almost starved for! They were our religion, they were our life, they were *us*! And now they're only *me*—except that they're also *you*, thank God, a little, you dear!" she continued, suddenly inflicting on Fleda a kiss apparently intended to knock her into position. "There isn't one of them I don't know and love—yes, as one remembers and cherishes the happiest moments of one's life. Blindfold, in the dark, with the brush of a finger, I could tell one from another. They're living things to me; they know me, they return the touch of my hand. But I could let them all go, since I have to, so strangely, to another affection, another conscience. There's a care they want, there's a sympathy that draws out their beauty. Rather than make them over to a woman ignorant and vulgar, I think I'd deface them with my own hands. Can't you see me, Fleda, and wouldn't you do it yourself?"—she appealed to her companion with glittering eyes. "I couldn't bear the thought of such a woman here—I *couldn't*. I don't know what she'd do; she'd be sure to invent some deviltry, if it should be only to bring in her own little belongings and horrors. The world is full of cheap gimcracks, in this awful age, and they're thrust in at one at every turn. They'd be thrust in here, on top of my treasures, my own. Who would save *them* for me—I ask you who *would*?" and she turned again to Fleda with a dry, strained smile. Her handsome, high-nosed, excited face might have been that of Don Quixote tilting at a windmill. Drawn into the eddy of this outpouring, the girl, scared and embarrassed, laughed off her exposure; but only to feel herself more passionately caught up and, as it seemed to her, thrust down the fine open mouth (it showed such perfect teeth) with which poor Owen's slow cerebration gaped. "*You* would, of course—only you, in all the world, because you know, you feel, as I do myself, what's good and true and pure." No severity of the moral law could have taken a higher tone in this implication of the young lady who had not the only virtue Mrs. Gereth actively esteemed. "*You* would replace me, *you* would watch over them, *you* would keep the place right," she austerely pursued, "and with you here—yes, with you, I believe I might rest, at last, in my grave!" She threw herself on Fleda's neck, and before Fleda, horribly shamed, could shake her off, had burst into tears which couldn't have been explained, but which might perhaps have been understood.

IV

A week later Owen Gereth came down to inform his mother that he had settled with Mona Brigstock; but it was not at all a joy to Fleda, conscious how much to himself it would be a surprise, that he should find her still in the house. That dreadful scene before breakfast had made her position false and odious; it had been followed, after they were left alone, by a scene of her own making with her extravagant friend. She notified Mrs. Gereth of her instant departure: she couldn't possibly remain after being offered to Owen, that way, before his very face, as his mother's candidate for the honor of his hand. That was all he could have seen in such an outbreak and in the indecency of her standing there to enjoy it. Fleda had on the prior occasion dashed out of the room by the shortest course and in her confusion had fallen upon Mona in the garden. She had taken an aimless turn with her, and they had had some talk, rendered at first difficult and almost disagreeable by Mona's apparent suspicion that she had been sent out to spy, as Mrs. Gereth had tried to spy, into her opinions. Fleda was sagacious enough to treat these opinions as a mystery almost awful; which had an effect so much more than reassuring that at the end of five minutes the young lady from Waterbath suddenly and perversely said: "Why has she never had a winter garden thrown out? If ever I have a place of my own I mean to have one." Fleda, dismayed, could see the thing—something glazed and piped, on iron pillars, with untidy plants and cane sofas; a shiny excrescence on the noble face of Poynton. She remembered at Waterbath a conservatory where she had caught a bad cold in the company of a stuffed cockatoo fastened to a tropical bough and a waterless fountain composed of shells stuck into some hardened paste. She asked Mona if her idea would be to make something like this conservatory; to which Mona replied: "Oh no, much finer; we haven't got a winter garden at Waterbath." Fleda wondered if she meant to convey that it was the only grandeur they lacked, and in a moment Mona went on: "But we have got a billiard-room—that I will say for us!" There was no billiard-room at Poynton, but there would evidently be one, and it would have, hung on its walls, framed at the "Stores," caricature-portraits of celebrities, taken from a "society-paper."

When the two girls had gone in to breakfast it was for Fleda to see at a glance that there had been a further passage, of some high color, between Owen and his mother; and she had turned pale in guessing to what extremity, at her expense, Mrs. Gereth had found occasion to proceed. Hadn't she, after her clumsy flight, been pressed upon Owen in still clearer terms? Mrs. Gereth would practically have said to him: "If you'll take *her*, I'll move away without a sound. But if you take any one else, any one I'm not sure of, as I am of her—heaven help me, I'll fight to the death!" Breakfast, this morning, at Poynton, had been a meal singularly silent, in spite of the vague little cries with which Mrs. Brigstock turned up the underside of plates and the knowing but alarming raps administered by her big knuckles to porcelain cups. Some one had to respond to her, and the duty assigned itself to Fleda, who, while pretending to meet her on the ground of explanation, wondered what Owen thought of a girl still indelicately anxious, after she had been grossly hurled at him, to prove by exhibitions of her fine taste that she was really what his mother pretended. This time, at any rate, their fate was sealed: Owen, as soon as he should get out of the house, would describe to Mona that lady's extraordinary conduct, and if anything more had been wanted to "fetch" Mona, as he would call it, the deficiency was now made up. Mrs. Gereth in fact took care of that—took care of it by the way, at the last, on the threshold, she said to the younger of her departing guests, with an irony of which the sting was wholly in the sense, not at all in the sound: "We haven't had the talk we might have had, have we? You'll feel that I've neglected you, and you'll treasure it up against me. *Don't*, because really, you know, it has been quite an accident, and I've all sorts of information at your disposal. If you should come down again (only you won't, ever,—I feel that!) I should give you plenty of time to worry it out of me. Indeed there are some things I should quite insist on your learning; not permit you at all, in any settled way, *not* to learn. Yes indeed, you'd put me through, and I should put you, my dear! We should have each other to reckon with, and you would see me as I really am. I'm not a bit the vague, mooning, easy creature I dare say you think. However, if you won't come, you won't; *n'en parlons plus*. It *is* stupid here after what you're accustomed to. We can only, all round, do what we can, eh? For heaven's sake, don't let your mother forget her precious publication, the female magazine, with the what-do-you-call-'em?—the grease-catchers. There!"

Mrs. Gereth, delivering herself from the doorstep, had tossed the periodical higher in air than was absolutely needful—tossed it toward the carriage the retreating party was about to enter. Mona, from the force of habit, the reflex action of the custom of sport, had popped out, with a little spring, a long arm and intercepted the missile as easily as she would have caused a tennis-ball to rebound from a racket. "Good catch!" Owen had cried, so genuinely pleased that practically no notice was taken of his mother's impressive remarks. It was to the accompaniment of romping laughter, as Mrs. Gereth afterwards said, that the carriage had rolled away; but it was while that laughter was still in the air that Fleda Vetch, white and terrible, had turned

31

upon her hostess with her scorching "How *could* you? Great God, how *could* you?" This lady's perfect blankness was from the first a sign of her serene conscience, and the fact that till indoctrinated she didn't even know what Fleda meant by resenting her late offense to every susceptibility gave our young woman a sore, scared perception that her own value in the house was just the value, as one might say, of a good agent. Mrs. Gereth was generously sorry, but she was still more surprised—surprised at Fleda's not having liked to be shown off to Owen as the right sort of wife for him. Why not, in the name of wonder, if she absolutely *was* the right sort? She had admitted on explanation that she could see what her young friend meant by having been laid, as Fleda called it, at his feet; but it struck the girl that the admission was only made to please her, and that Mrs. Gereth was secretly surprised at her not being as happy to be sacrificed to the supremacy of a high standard as she was happy to sacrifice her. She had taken a tremendous fancy to her, but that was on account of the fancy—to Poynton of course—Fleda herself had taken. Wasn't this latter fancy then so great after all? Fleda felt that she could declare it to be great indeed when really for the sake of it she could forgive what she had suffered and, after reproaches and tears, asseverations and kisses, after learning that she was cared for only as a priestess of the altar and a view of her bruised dignity which left no alternative to flight, could accept the shame with the balm, consent not to depart, take refuge in the thin comfort of at least knowing the truth. The truth was simply that all Mrs. Gereth's scruples were on one side and that her ruling passion had in a manner despoiled her of her humanity. On the second day, after the tide of emotion had somewhat ebbed, she said soothingly to her companion: "But you *would*, after all, marry him, you know, darling, wouldn't you, if that girl were not there? I mean of course if he were to ask you," Mrs. Gereth had thoughtfully added.

"Marry him if he were to ask me? Most distinctly not!"

The question had not come up with this definiteness before, and Mrs. Gereth was clearly more surprised than ever. She marveled a moment. "Not even to have Poynton?"

"Not even to have Poynton."

"But why on earth?" Mrs. Gereth's sad eyes were fixed on her.

Fleda colored; she hesitated. "Because he's too stupid!" Save on one other occasion, at which we shall in time arrive, little as the reader may believe it, she never came nearer to betraying to Mrs. Gereth that she was in love with Owen. She found a dim amusement in reflecting that if Mona had not been there and he had not been too stupid and he verily had asked her, she might, should she have wished to keep her secret, have found it possible to pass off the motive of her action as a mere passion for Poynton.

Mrs. Gereth evidently thought in these days of little but things hymeneal; for she broke out with sudden rapture, in the middle of the week: "I know what they'll do: they *will* marry, but they'll go and live at Waterbath!" There was positive joy in that form of the idea, which she embroidered and developed: it seemed so much the safest thing that could happen. "Yes, I'll have you, but I won't go *there*!" Mona would have said with a vicious nod at the southern horizon: "we'll leave your horrid mother alone there for life." It would be an ideal solution, this ingress the lively pair, with their spiritual need of a warmer medium, would playfully punch in the ribs of her ancestral home; for it would not only prevent recurring panic at Poynton—it would offer them, as in one of their gimcrack baskets or other vessels of ugliness, a definite daily felicity that Poynton could never give. Owen might manage his estate just as he managed it now, and Mrs. Gereth would manage everything else. When, in the hall, on the unforgettable day of his return, she had heard his voice ring out like a call to a terrier, she had still, as Fleda afterwards learned, clutched frantically at the conceit that he had come, at the worst, to announce some compromise; to tell her she would have to put up with the girl, yes, but that some way would be arrived at of leaving her in personal possession. Fleda Vetch, whom from the first hour no illusion had brushed with its wing, now held her breath, went on tiptoe, wandered in outlying parts of the house and through delicate, muffled rooms, while the mother and son faced each other below. From time to time she stopped to listen; but all was so quiet she was almost frightened: she had vaguely expected a sound of contention. It lasted longer than she would have supposed, whatever it was they were doing; and when finally, from a window, she saw Owen stroll out of the house, stop and light a cigarette and then pensively lose himself in the plantations, she found other matter for trepidation in the fact that Mrs. Gereth didn't immediately come rushing up into her arms. She wondered whether she oughtn't to go down to her, and measured the gravity of what had occurred by the circumstance, which she presently ascertained, that the poor lady had retired to her room and wished not to be disturbed. This admonition had been for her maid, with whom Fleda conferred as at the door of a death-chamber; but the girl, without either fatuity or resentment, judged that, since it could render Mrs. Gereth indifferent even to the ministrations of disinterested attachment, the scene had been tremendous.

She was absent from luncheon, where indeed Fleda had enough to do to look Owen in the face; there would be so much to make that hateful in their common memory of the passage in which his last visit had terminated. This had been her apprehension at least; but as soon as he stood there she was constrained to wonder at the practical simplicity of the ordeal—a simplicity which was really just his own simplicity, the particular thing that, for Fleda Vetch, some other things of course aiding, made almost any direct relation with him pleasant. He had neither wit, nor tact, nor inspiration: all she could say was that when they were together the alienation these charms were usually depended on to allay didn't occur. On this occasion, for instance, he did so much better than "carry off" an awkward remembrance: he simply didn't have it. He had clean forgotten that she was the girl his mother would have fobbed off on him; he was conscious only that she was there in a manner for service—conscious of the dumb instinct that from the first had made him regard her not as complicating his intercourse with that personage, but as simplifying it. Fleda found beautiful that this theory should have survived the incident of the other day; found exquisite that whereas she was conscious, through faint reverberations, that for her kind little circle at large, whom it didn't concern, her tendency had begun to define itself as parasitical, this strong young man, who had a right to judge and even a reason to loathe her, didn't judge and didn't loathe, let her down gently, treated her as if she pleased him, and in fact evidently liked her to be just where she was. She asked herself what he did when Mona denounced her, and the only answer to the question was that perhaps Mona didn't denounce her. If Mona was inarticulate he wasn't such a fool, then, to marry her. That he was glad Fleda was there was at any rate sufficiently shown by the domestic familiarity with which he said to her: "I must tell you I've been having an awful row with my mother. I'm engaged to be married to Miss Brigstock."

"Ah, really?" cried Fleda, achieving a radiance of which she was secretly proud. "How very exciting!"

"Too exciting for poor Mummy. She won't hear of it. She has been slating her fearfully. She says she's a 'barbarian.'"

"Why, she's lovely!" Fleda exclaimed.

"Oh, she's all right. Mother must come round."

"Only give her time," said Fleda. She had advanced to the threshold of the door thus thrown open to her and, without exactly crossing it, she threw in an appreciative glance. She asked Owen when his marriage would take place, and in the light of his reply read that Mrs. Gereth's wretched attitude would have no influence at all on the event, absolutely fixed when he came down, and distant by only three months. He liked Fleda's seeming to be on his side, though that was a secondary matter, for what really most concerned him now was the line his mother took about Poynton, her declared unwillingness to give it up.

"Naturally I want my own house, you know," he said, "and my father made every arrangement for me to have it. But she may make it devilish awkward. What in the world's a fellow to do?" This it was that Owen wanted to know, and there could be no better proof of his friendliness than his air of depending on Fleda Vetch to tell him. She questioned him, they spent an hour together, and, as he gave her the scale of the concussion from which he had rebounded, she found herself saddened and frightened by the material he seemed to offer her to deal with. It *was* devilish awkward, and it was so in part because Owen had no imagination. It had lodged itself in that empty chamber that his mother hated the surrender because she hated Mona. He didn't of course understand why she hated Mona, but this belonged to an order of mysteries that never troubled him: there were lots of things, especially in people's minds, that a fellow didn't understand. Poor Owen went through life with a frank dread of people's minds: there were explanations he would have been almost as shy of receiving as of giving. There was therefore nothing that accounted for anything, though in its way it was vivid enough, in his picture to Fleda of his mother's virtual refusal to move. That was simply what it was; for didn't she refuse to move when she as good as declared that she would move only with the furniture? It was the furniture she wouldn't give up; and what was the good of Poynton without the furniture? Besides, the furniture happened to be his, just as everything else happened to be. The furniture—the word, on his lips, had somehow, for Fleda, the sound of washing-stands and copious bedding, and she could well imagine the note it might have struck for Mrs. Gereth. The girl, in this interview with him, spoke of the contents of the house only as "the works of art." It didn't, however, in the least matter to Owen what they were called; what did matter, she easily guessed, was that it had been laid upon him by Mona, been made in effect a condition of her consent, that he should hold his mother to the strictest accountability for them. Mona had already entered upon the enjoyment of her rights. She had made him feel that Mrs. Gereth had been liberally provided for, and had asked him cogently what room there would be at Ricks for the innumerable treasures of the big house. Ricks, the sweet little place offered to the mistress of Poynton as the refuge of her declining years, had been left to the late Mr. Gereth, a considerable time before his death, by an old maternal aunt, a good lady who had spent most of her life there. The house had in recent times been let, but it was amply furnished, it contained all the defunct aunt's possessions. Owen had lately inspected it, and he communicated to Fleda that he had quietly taken Mona to see it. It wasn't a place like Poynton—what dower-house ever was?—but it was an awfully jolly little place, and Mona had taken a tremendous fancy to it. If there were a few things at Poynton that were Mrs. Gereth's peculiar property, of course she must take them away with her; but one of the matters that became clear to Fleda was that this transfer would be immediately subject to Miss Brigstock's approval. The special business that she herself now became aware of being charged with was that of seeing Mrs. Gereth safely and singly off the premises.

Her heart failed her, after Owen had returned to London, with the ugliness of this duty—with the ugliness, indeed, of the whole close conflict. She saw nothing of Mrs. Gereth that day; she spent it in roaming with sick sighs, in feeling, as she passed from room to room, that what was expected of her companion was really dreadful. It would have been better never to have had such a place than to have had it and lose it. It was odious to *her* to have to look for solutions: what a strange relation between mother and son when there was no fundamental tenderness out of which a solution would irrepressibly spring! Was it Owen who was mainly responsible for that poverty? Fleda couldn't think so when she remembered that, so far as he was concerned, Mrs. Gereth would still have been welcome to have her seat by the Poynton fire. The fact that from the moment one accepted his marrying one saw no very different course for Owen to take made her all the rest of that aching day find her best relief in the mercy of not having yet to face her hostess. She dodged and dreamed and romanced away the time; instead of inventing a remedy or a compromise, instead of preparing a plan by which a scandal might be averted, she gave herself, in her sentient solitude, up to a mere fairy tale, up to the very taste of the beautiful peace with which she would have filled the air if only something might have been that could never have been.

V

"I'll give up the house if they'll let me take what I require!" That, on the morrow, was what Mrs. Gereth's stifled night had qualified her to say, with a tragic face, at breakfast. Fleda reflected that what she "required" was simply every object that surrounded them. The poor woman would have admitted this truth and accepted the conclusion to be drawn from it, the reduction to the absurd of her attitude, the exaltation of her revolt. The girl's dread of a scandal, of spectators and critics, diminished the more she saw how little vulgar avidity had to do with this rigor. It was not the crude love of possession; it was the need to be faithful to a trust and loyal to an idea. The idea was surely noble: it was that of the beauty Mrs. Gereth had so patiently and consummately wrought. Pale but radiant, with her back to the wall, she rose there like a heroine guarding a treasure. To give up the ship was to flinch from her duty; there was something in her eyes that declared she would die at her post. If their difference should become public the shame would be all for the others. If Waterbath thought it could afford to expose itself, then Waterbath was welcome to the folly. Her fanaticism gave her a new distinction, and Fleda perceived almost with awe that she had never carried herself so well. She trod the place like a reigning queen or a proud usurper; full as it was of splendid pieces, it could show in these days no ornament so effective as its menaced mistress.

Our young lady's spirit was strangely divided; she had a tenderness for Owen which she deeply concealed, yet it left her occasion to marvel at the way a man was made who could care in any relation for a creature like Mona Brigstock when he had known in any relation a creature like Adela Gereth. With such a mother to give him the pitch, how could he take it so low? She wondered that she didn't despise him for this, but there was something that kept her from it. If there had been nothing else it would have sufficed that she really found herself from this moment the medium of communication with him.

"He'll come back to assert himself," Mrs. Gereth had said; and the following week Owen in fact reappeared. He might merely have written, Fleda could see, but he had come in person because it was at once "nicer" for his mother and stronger for his cause. He didn't like the row, though Mona probably did; if he hadn't a sense of beauty he had after all a sense of justice; but it was inevitable he should clearly announce at Poynton the date at which he must look to find the house vacant. "You don't think

I'm rough or hard, do you?" he asked of Fleda, his impatience shining in his idle eyes as the dining-hour shines in club-windows. "The place at Ricks stands there with open arms. And then I give her lots of time. Tell her she can remove everything that belongs to her." Fleda recognized the elements of what the newspapers call a deadlock in the circumstance that nothing at Poynton belonged to Mrs. Gereth either more or less than anything else. She must either take everything or nothing, and the girl's suggestion was that it might perhaps be an inspiration to do the latter and begin again on a clean page. What, however, was the poor woman, in that case, to begin with? What was she to do at all, on her meagre income, but make the best of the *objets d'art* of Ricks, the treasures collected by Mr. Gereth's maiden aunt? She had never been near the place: for long years it had been let to strangers, and after that the foreboding that it would be her doom had kept her from the abasement of it. She had felt that she should see it soon enough, but Fleda (who was careful not to betray to her that Mona had seen it and had been gratified) knew her reasons for believing that the maiden aunt's principles had had much in common with the principles of Waterbath. The only thing, in short, that she would ever have to do with the objets d'art of Ricks would be to turn them out into the road. What belonged to her at Poynton, as Owen said, would conveniently mitigate the void resulting from that demonstration.

The exchange of observations between the friends had grown very direct by the time Fleda asked Mrs. Gereth whether she literally meant to shut herself up and stand a siege, or whether it was her idea to expose herself, more informally, to be dragged out of the house by constables. "Oh, I prefer the constables and the dragging!" the heroine of Poynton had answered. "I want to make Owen and Mona do everything that will be most publicly odious." She gave it out that it was her one thought now to force them to a line that would dishonor them and dishonor the tradition they embodied, though Fleda was privately sure that she had visions of an alternative policy. The strange thing was that, proud and fastidious all her life, she now showed so little distaste for the world's hearing of the squabble. What had taken place in her above all was that a long resentment had ripened. She hated the effacement to which English usage reduced the widowed mother: she had discoursed of it passionately to Fleda; contrasted it with the beautiful homage paid in other countries to women in that position, women no better than herself, whom she had seen acclaimed and enthroned, whom she had known and envied; made in short as little as possible a secret of the injury, the bitterness she found in it. The great wrong Owen had done her was not his "taking up" with Mona—that was disgusting, but it was a detail, an accidental form: it was his failure from the first to understand what it was to have a mother at all, to appreciate the beauty and sanctity of the character. She was just his mother as his nose was just his nose, and he had never had the least imagination or tenderness or gallantry about her. One's mother, gracious heaven, if one were the kind of fine young man one ought to be, the only kind Mrs. Gereth cared for, was a subject for poetry, for idolatry. Hadn't she often told Fleda of her friend Madame de Jaume, the wittiest of women, but a small, black, crooked person, each of whose three boys, when absent, wrote to her every day of their lives? She had the house in Paris, she had the house in Poitou, she had more than in the lifetime of her husband (to whom, in spite of her appearance, she had afforded repeated cause for jealousy), because she had to the end of her days the supreme word about everything. It was easy to see that Mrs. Gereth would have given again and again her complexion, her figure, and even perhaps the spotless virtue she had still more successfully retained, to have been the consecrated Madame de Jaume. She wasn't, alas, and this was what she had at present a magnificent occasion to protest against. She was of course fully aware of Owen's concession, his willingness to let her take away with her the few things she liked best; but as yet she only declared that to meet him on this ground would be to give him a triumph, to put him impossibly in the right. "Liked best"? There wasn't a thing in the house that she didn't like best, and what she liked better still was to be left where she was. How could Owen use such an expression without being conscious of his hypocrisy? Mrs. Gereth, whose criticism was often gay, dilated with sardonic humor on the happy look a dozen objects from Poynton would wear and the charming effect they would conduce to when interspersed with the peculiar features of Ricks. What had her whole life been but an effort toward completeness and perfection? Better Waterbath at once, in its cynical unity, than the ignominy of such a mixture!

All this was of no great help to Fleda, in so far as Fleda tried to rise to her mission of finding a way out. When at the end of a fortnight Owen came down once more, it was ostensibly to tackle a farmer whose proceedings had been irregular; the girl was sure, however, that he had really come, on the instance of Mona, to see what his mother was doing. He wished to satisfy himself that she was preparing her departure, and he wished to perform a duty, distinct but not less imperative, in regard to the question of the perquisites with which she would retreat. The tension between them was now such that he had to perpetrate these offenses without meeting his adversary. Mrs. Gereth was as willing as himself that he should address to Fleda Vetch whatever cruel remarks he might have to make: she only pitied her poor young friend for repeated encounters with a person as to whom she perfectly understood the girl's repulsion. Fleda thought it nice of Owen not to have expected her to write to him; he wouldn't have wished any more than herself that she should have the air of spying on his mother in his interest. What made it comfortable to deal with him in this more familiar way was the sense that she understood so perfectly how poor Mrs. Gereth suffered, and that she measured so adequately the sacrifice the other side did take rather monstrously for granted. She understood equally how Owen himself suffered, now that Mona had already begun to make him do things he didn't like. Vividly Fleda apprehended how *she* would have first made him like anything she would have made him do; anything even as disagreeable as this appearing there to state, virtually on Mona's behalf, that of course there must be a definite limit to the number of articles appropriated. She took a longish stroll with him in order to talk the matter over; to say if she didn't think a dozen pieces, chosen absolutely at will, would be a handsome allowance; and above all to consider the very delicate question of whether the advantage enjoyed by Mrs. Gereth mightn't be left to her honor. To leave it so was what Owen wished; but there was plainly a young lady at Waterbath to whom, on his side, he already had to render an account. He was as touching in his offhand annoyance as his mother was tragic in her intensity; for if he couldn't help having a sense of propriety about the whole matter, so he could as little help hating it. It was for his hating it, Fleda reasoned, that she liked him so, and her insistence to his mother on the hatred perilously resembled, on one or two occasions, a revelation of the liking. There were moments when, in conscience, that revelation pressed her; inasmuch as it was just on the ground of her not liking him that Mrs. Gereth trusted her so much. Mrs. Gereth herself didn't in these days like him at all, and she was of course and always on Mrs. Gereth's side. He ended really, while the preparations for his marriage went on, by quite a little custom of coming and going; but on no one of these occasions would his mother receive him. He talked only with Fleda and strolled with Fleda; and when he asked her, in regard to the great matter, if Mrs. Gereth were really doing nothing, the girl usually replied: "She pretends not to be, if I may say so; but I think she's really thinking over what she'll take." When her friend asked her what Owen was doing, she could have but one answer: "He's waiting, dear lady, to see what *you* do!"

Mrs. Gereth, a month after she had received her great shock, did something abrupt and extraordinary: she caught up her companion and went to have a look at Ricks. They had come to London first and taken a train from Liverpool Street, and the least of the sufferings they were armed against was that of passing the night. Fleda's admirable dressing-bag had been given her by her friend. "Why, it's charming!" she exclaimed a few hours later, turning back again into the small prim parlor from a friendly advance to the single plate of the window. Mrs. Gereth hated such windows, the one flat glass, sliding up and down, especially when they enjoyed a view of four iron pots on pedestals, painted white and containing ugly geraniums, ranged on the edge of a gravel-path and doing their best to give it the air of a terrace. Fleda had instantly averted her eyes from these ornaments, but Mrs. Gereth grimly gazed, wondering of course how a place in the deepest depths of Essex and three miles from a small station could contrive to look so suburban. The room was practically a shallow box, with the junction of the walls and ceiling guiltless of curve or cornice and marked merely by the little band of crimson paper glued round the top of the other paper, a turbid gray sprigged with silver flowers. This decoration was rather new and quite fresh; and there was in the centre of the ceiling a big square beam papered over in white, as to which Fleda hesitated about venturing to remark that it was rather picturesque. She recognized in time that this remark would be weak and that, throughout, she should be able to say nothing either for the mantelpieces or for the doors, of which she saw her companion become sensible with a soundless moan. On the subject of doors especially Mrs. Gereth had the finest views: the thing in the world she most despised was the meanness of the single flap. From end to end, at Poynton, there were high double leaves. At Ricks the entrances to the rooms were like the holes of rabbit-hutches.

It was all, none the less, not so bad as Fleda had feared; it was faded and melancholy, whereas there had been a danger that it would be contradictious and positive, cheerful and loud. The house was crowded with objects of which the aggregation somehow made a thinness and the futility a grace; things that told her they had been gathered as slowly and as lovingly as the golden flowers of Poynton. She too, for a home, could have lived with them: they made her fond of the old maiden-aunt; they made her even wonder if it didn't work more for happiness not to have tasted, as she herself had done, of knowledge. Without resources, without a stick, as she said, of her own, Fleda was moved, after all, to some secret surprise at the pretensions of a shipwrecked woman who could hold such an asylum cheap. The more she looked about the surer she felt of the character of the maiden-aunt, the sense of whose dim presence urged her to pacification: the maiden-aunt had been a dear; she would have adored the maiden-aunt. The poor lady had had some tender little story; she had been sensitive and ignorant and exquisite: that too was a sort of origin, a sort of atmosphere for relics and rarities, though different from the sorts most prized at Poynton. Mrs. Gereth had of course more than once said that one of the deepest mysteries of life was the way that, by certain natures, hideous objects could be loved; but it wasn't a question of love, now, for these: it was only a question of a certain practical patience. Perhaps some thought of that kind had stolen over Mrs. Gereth when, at the end of a brooding hour, she exclaimed, taking in the house with a strenuous sigh: "Well, something can be done with it!" Fleda had repeated to her more than once the indulgent fancy about the maiden-aunt—she was so sure she had deeply suffered. "I'm sure I hope she did!" was, however, all that Mrs. Gereth had replied.

VI

It was a great relief to the girl at last to perceive that the dreadful move would really be made. What might happen if it shouldn't had been from the first indefinite. It was absurd to pretend that any violence was probable—a tussel, dishevelment, shrieks; yet Fleda had an imagination of a drama, a "great scene," a thing, somehow, of indignity and misery, of wounds inflicted and received, in which indeed, though Mrs. Gereth's presence, with movements and sounds, loomed large to her, Owen remained indistinct and on the whole unaggressive. He wouldn't be there with a cigarette in his teeth, very handsome and insolently quiet: that was only the way he would be in a novel, across whose interesting page some such figure, as she half closed her eyes, seemed to her to walk. Fleda had rather, and indeed with shame, a confused, pitying vision of Mrs. Gereth with her great scene left in a manner on her hands, Mrs. Gereth missing her effect and having to appear merely hot and injured and in the wrong. The symptoms that she would be spared even that spectacle resided not so much, through the chambers of Poynton, in an air of concentration as in the hum of buzzing alternatives. There was no common preparation, but one day, at the turn of a corridor, she found her hostess standing very still, with the hanging hands of an invalid and the active eyes of an adventurer. These eyes appeared to Fleda to meet her own with a strange, dim bravado, and there was a silence, almost awkward, before either of the friends spoke. The girl afterwards thought of the moment as one in which her hostess mutely accused her of an accusation, meeting it, however, at the same time, by a kind of defiant acceptance. Yet it was with mere melancholy candor that Mrs. Gereth at last sighingly exclaimed: "I'm thinking over what I had better take!" Fleda could have embraced her for this virtual promise of a concession, the announcement that she had finally accepted the problem of knocking together a shelter with the small salvage of the wreck.

Fleda had a depressed sense of not, after all, helping her much: this was lightened indeed by the fact that Mrs. Gereth, letting her off easily, didn't now seem to expect it. Her sympathy, her interest, her feeling for everything for which Mrs. Gereth felt, were a force that really worked to prolong the deadlock. "I only wish I bored you and my possessions bored you," that lady, with some humor, declared; "then you'd make short work with me, bundle me off, tell me just to pile certain things into a cart and have done." Fleda's sharpest difficulty was in having to act up to the character of thinking Owen a brute, or at least to carry off the inconsistency of seeing him when he came down. By good fortune it was her duty, her function, as well as a protection to Mrs. Gereth. She thought of him perpetually, and her eyes had come to rejoice in his manly magnificence more even than they rejoiced in the royal cabinets of the red saloon. She wondered, very faintly at first, why he came so often; but of course she knew nothing about the business he had in hand, over which, with men red-faced and leather-legged, he was sometimes closeted for an hour in a room of his own that was the one monstrosity of Poynton: all tobacco-pots and bootjacks, his mother had said—such an array of arms of aggression and castigation that he himself had confessed to eighteen rifles and forty whips. He was arranging for settlements on his wife, he was doing things that would meet the views of the Brigstocks. Considering the house was his own, Fleda thought it nice of him to keep himself in the background while his mother remained; making his visits, at some cost of ingenuity about trains from town, only between meals, doing everything to let it press lightly upon her that he was there. This was rather a stoppage to her meeting Mrs. Gereth on the ground of his being a brute; the most she really at last could do was not to contradict her when she repeated that he was watching—just insultingly watching. He *was* watching, no doubt; but he watched somehow with his head turned away. He knew that Fleda knew at present what he wanted of her, so that it would be gross of him to say it over and over. It existed as a confidence between them, and made him sometimes, with his wandering stare, meet her eyes as if a silence so pleasant could only unite them the more. He had no great flow of speech, certainly, and at first the girl took for granted that this was all there was to be said about the matter. Little by little she speculated as to whether, with a person who, like herself, could put him, after all, at a sort of domestic ease, it was not supposable that he would have more conversation if he were not keeping some of it back for Mona.

From the moment she suspected he might be thinking what Mona would say to his chattering so to an underhand "companion," who was all but paid, this young lady's repressed emotion began to require still more repression. She grew impatient of her situation at Poynton; she privately pronounced it false and horrid. She said to herself that she had let Owen know that she had, to the best of her power, directed his mother in the general sense he desired; that he quite understood it and that he also understood how unworthy it was of either of them to stand over the good lady with a notebook and a lash. Wasn't this practical unanimity just practical success? Fleda became aware of a sudden desire, as well as of pressing reasons, to bring her stay at Poynton to a close. She had not, on the one hand, like a minion of the law, undertaken to see Mrs. Gereth down to the train and locked, in sign of her abdication, into a compartment; neither had she on the other committed herself to hold Owen indefinitely in dalliance while his mother gained time or dug a counter-mine. Besides, people *were* saying that she fastened like a leech on other people—people who had houses where something was to be picked up: this revelation was frankly made her by her sister, now distinctly doomed to the curate and in view of whose nuptials she had almost finished, as a present, a wonderful piece of embroidery, suggested, at Poynton, by an old Spanish altar-cloth. She would have to exert herself still further for the intended recipient of this offering, turn her out for her marriage with more than that drapery. She would go up to town, in short, to dress Maggie; and their father, in lodgings at West Kensington, would stretch a point and take them in. He, to do him justice, never reproached her with profitable devotions; so far as they existed he consciously profited by them. Mrs. Gereth gave her up as heroically as if she had been a great bargain, and Fleda knew that she wouldn't at present miss any visit of Owen's, for Owen was shooting at Waterbath. Owen shooting was Owen lost, and there was scant sport at Poynton.

The first news she had from Mrs. Gereth was news of that lady's having accomplished, in form at least, her migration. The letter was dated from Ricks, to which place she had been transported by an impulse apparently as sudden as the inspiration she had obeyed before. "Yes, I've literally come," she wrote, "with a bandbox and a kitchen-maid; I've crossed the Rubicon, I've taken possession. It has been like plumping into cold water: I saw the only thing was to do it, not to stand shivering. I shall have warmed the place a little by simply being here for a week; when I come back the ice will have been broken. I didn't write to you to meet me on my way through town, because I know how busy you are and because, besides, I'm too savage and odious to be fit company even for you. You'd say I really go too far, and there's no doubt whatever I do. I'm here, at any rate, just to look round once more, to see that certain things are done before I enter in force. I shall probably be at Poynton all next week. There's more room than I quite measured the other day, and a rather good set of old Worcester. But what are space and time, what's even old Worcester, to your wretched and affectionate A. G.?"

The day after Fleda received this letter she had occasion to go into a big shop in Oxford Street—a journey that she achieved circuitously, first on foot and then by the aid of two omnibuses. The second of these vehicles put her down on the side of the street opposite her shop, and while, on the curbstone, she humbly waited, with a parcel, an umbrella, and a tucked-up frock, to cross in security, she became aware that, close beside her, a hansom had pulled up short, in obedience to the brandished stick of a demonstrative occupant. This occupant was Owen Gereth, who had caught sight of her as he rattled along and who, with an exhibition of white teeth that, from under the hood of the cab, had almost flashed through the fog, now alighted to ask her if he couldn't give her a lift. On finding that her destination was only over the way he dismissed his vehicle and joined her, not only piloting her to the shop, but taking her in; with the assurance that his errands didn't matter, that it amused him to be concerned with hers. She told him she had come to buy a trimming for her sister's frock, and he expressed an hilarious interest in the purchase. His hilarity was almost always out of proportion to the case, but it struck her at present as more so than ever; especially when she had suggested that he might find it a good time to buy a garnishment of some sort for Mona. After wondering an instant whether he gave the full satiric meaning, such as it was, to this remark, Fleda dismissed the possibility as inconceivable. He stammered out that it was for *her* he would like to buy something, something "ripping," and that she must give him the pleasure of telling him what would best please her: he couldn't have a better opportunity for making her a present—the present, in recognition of all she had done for Mummy, that he had had in his head for weeks.

Fleda had more than one small errand in the big bazaar, and he went up and down with her, pointedly patient, pretending to be interested in questions of tape and of change. She had now not the least hesitation in wondering what Mona would think of such proceedings. But they were not her doing—they were Owen's; and Owen, inconsequent and even extravagant, was unlike anything she had ever seen him before. He broke off, he came back, he repeated questions without heeding answers, he made vague, abrupt remarks about the resemblances of shopgirls and the uses of chiffon. He unduly prolonged their business together, giving Fleda a sense that he was putting off something particular that he had to face. If she had ever dreamed of Owen Gereth as nervous she would have seen him with some such manner as this. But why should he be nervous? Even at the height of the crisis his mother hadn't made him so, and at present he was satisfied about his mother. The one idea he stuck to was that Fleda should mention something she would let him give her: there was everything in the world in the wonderful place, and he made her incongruous offers—a traveling-rug, a massive clock, a table for breakfast in bed, and above all, in a resplendent binding, a set of somebody's "works." His notion was a testimonial, a tribute, and the "works" would be a graceful intimation that it was her cleverness he wished above all to commemorate. He was immensely in earnest, but the articles he pressed upon her betrayed a delicacy that went to her heart: what he would really have liked, as he saw them tumbled about, was one of the splendid stuffs for a gown—a choice proscribed by his fear of seeming to patronize her, to refer to her small means and her deficiencies. Fleda found it easy to chaff him about his exaggeration of her deserts; she gave the just measure of them in consenting to accept a small pin-cushion, costing sixpence, in which the letter F was marked out with pins. A sense of loyalty to Mona was not needed to enforce this discretion, and after that first allusion to her she never sounded her name. She noticed on this occasion more things in Owen Gereth than she had ever noticed before, but what she noticed most was that he said no word of his intended. She asked herself what he had done, in so long a parenthesis, with his loyalty or at least his "form;" and then reflected that even if he had done something very good with them the situation in which such a question could come up was already a little strange. Of course he wasn't doing anything so vulgar as making love to her; but there was a kind of punctilio for a man who was engaged.

That punctilio didn't prevent Owen from remaining with her after they had left the shop, from hoping she had a lot more to do, and from pressing her to look with him, for a possible glimpse of something she might really let him give her, into the windows of other establishments. There was a moment when, under this pressure, she made up her mind that his tribute would be, if analyzed, a tribute to her insignificance. But all the same he wanted her to come somewhere and have luncheon with him: what was that a tribute to? She must have counted very little if she didn't count too much for a romp in a restaurant. She had to get home with her trimming, and the most, in his company, she was amenable to was a retracing of her steps to the Marble Arch and then, after a discussion when they had reached it, a walk with him across the Park. She knew Mona would have considered that she ought to take the omnibus again; but she had now to think for Owen as well as for herself—she couldn't think for Mona. Even in the Park the autumn air was thick, and as they moved westward over the grass, which was what Owen preferred, the cool grayness made their words soft, made them at last rare and everything else dim. He wanted to stay with her—he wanted not to leave her: he had dropped into complete silence, but that was what his silence said. What was it he had postponed? What was it he wanted still to postpone? She grew a little scared as they strolled together and she thought. It was too confused to be believed, but it was as if somehow he felt differently. Fleda Vetch didn't suspect him at first of feeling differently to *her*, but only of feeling differently to Mona; yet she was not unconscious that this latter difference would have had something to do with his being on the grass beside her. She had read in novels about gentlemen who on the eve of marriage, winding up the past, had surrendered themselves for the occasion to the influence of a former tie; and there was something in Owen's behavior now, something in his very face, that suggested a resemblance to one of those gentlemen. But whom and what, in that case, would Fleda herself resemble? She wasn't a former tie, she wasn't any tie at all; she was only a deep little person for whom happiness was a kind of pearl-diving plunge. It was down at the very bottom of all that had lately happened; for all that had lately happened was that Owen Gereth had come and gone at Poynton. That was the small sum of her experience, and what it had made for her was her own affair, quite consistent with her not having dreamed it had made a tie— at least what *she* called one—for Owen. The old one, at any rate, was Mona—Mona whom he had known so very much longer.

They walked far, to the southwest corner of the great Gardens, where, by the old round pond and the old red palace, when she had put out her hand to him in farewell, declaring that from the gate she must positively take a conveyance, it seemed suddenly to rise between them that this was a real separation. She was on his mother's side, she belonged to his mother's life, and his mother, in the future, would never come to Poynton. After what had passed she wouldn't even be at his wedding, and it was not possible now that Mrs. Gereth should mention that ceremony to the girl, much less express a wish that the girl should be present at it. Mona, from decorum and with reference less to the bridegroom than to the bridegroom's mother, would of course not invite any such girl as Fleda. Everything therefore was ended; they would go their different ways; this was the last time they would stand face to face. They looked at each other with the fuller sense of it and, on Owen's part, with an expression of dumb trouble, the intensification of his usual appeal to any interlocutor to add the right thing to what he said. To Fleda, at this moment, it appeared that the right thing might easily be the wrong. He only said, at any rate: "I want you to understand, you know—I want you to understand."

What did he want her to understand? He seemed unable to bring it out, and this understanding was moreover exactly what she wished not to arrive at. Bewildered as she was, she had already taken in as much as she should know what to do with; the blood also was rushing into her face. He liked her—it was stupefying—more than he really ought: that was what was the matter with him and what he desired her to assimilate; so that she was suddenly as frightened as some thoughtless girl who finds herself the object of an overture from a married man.

"Good-bye, Mr. Gereth—I *must* get on!" she declared with a cheerfulness that she felt to be an unnatural grimace. She broke away from him sharply, smiling, backing across the grass and then turning altogether and moving as fast as she could. "Good-bye, good-bye!" she threw off again as she went, wondering if he would overtake her before she reached the gate; conscious with a red disgust that her movement was almost a run; conscious too of just the confused, handsome face with which he would look after her. She felt as if she had answered a kindness with a great flouncing snub, but at any rate she had got away, though the distance to the gate, her ugly gallop down the Broad Walk, every graceless jerk of which hurt her, seemed endless. She signed from afar to a cab on the stand in the Kensington Road and scrambled into it, glad of the encompassment of the four-wheeler that had officiously obeyed her summons and that, at the end of twenty yards, when she had violently pulled up a glass, permitted her to recognize the fact that she was on the point of bursting into tears.

VII

As soon as her sister was married she went down to Mrs. Gereth at Ricks—a promise to this effect having been promptly exacted and given; and her inner vision was much more fixed on the alterations there, complete now, as she understood, than on the success of her plotting and pinching for Maggie's happiness. Her imagination, in the interval, had indeed had plenty to do and numerous scenes to visit; for when on the summons just mentioned it had taken a flight from West Kensington to Ricks, it had hung but an hour over the terrace of painted pots and then yielded to a current of the upper air that swept it straight off to Poynton and to Waterbath. Not a sound had reached her of any supreme clash, and Mrs. Gereth had communicated next to nothing; giving out that, as was easily conceivable, she was too busy, too bitter, and too tired for vain civilities. All she had written was that she had got the new place well in hand and that Fleda would be surprised at the way it was turning out. Everything was even yet upside down; nevertheless, in the sense of having passed the threshold of Poynton for the last time, the amputation, as she called it, had been performed. Her leg had come off—she had now begun to stump along with the lovely wooden substitute; she would stump for life, and what her young friend was to come and admire was the beauty of her movement and the noise she made about the house. The reserve of Poynton and Waterbath had been matched by the austerity of Fleda's own secret, under the discipline of which she had repeated to herself a hundred times a day that she rejoiced at having cares that excluded all thought of it. She had lavished herself, in act, on Maggie and the curate, and had opposed to her father's selfishness a sweetness quite ecstatic. The young couple wondered why they had waited so long, since everything was after all so easy. She had thought of everything, even to how the "quietness" of the wedding should be relieved by champagne and her father kept brilliant on a single bottle. Fleda knew, in short, and liked the knowledge, that for several weeks she had appeared exemplary in every relation of life.

She had been perfectly prepared to be surprised at Ricks, for Mrs. Gereth was a wonder-working wizard, with a command, when all was said, of good material; but the impression in wait for her on the threshold made her catch her breath and falter. Dusk had fallen when she arrived, and in the plain square hall, one of the few good features, the glow of a Venetian lamp just showed, on either wall, the richness of an admirable tapestry. This instant perception that the place had been dressed at the expense of Poynton was a shock: it was as if she had abruptly seen herself in the light of an accomplice. The next moment, folded in Mrs. Gereth's arms, her eyes were diverted; but she had already had, in a flash, the vision of the great gaps in the other house. The two tapestries, not the largest, but those most splendidly toned by time, had been on the whole its most uplifted pride. When she could really see again she was on a sofa in the drawing-room, staring with intensity at an object soon distinct as the great Italian cabinet that, at Poynton, had been in the red saloon. Without looking, she was sure the room was occupied with other objects like it, stuffed with as many as it could hold of the trophies of her friend's struggle. By this time the very fingers of her glove, resting on the seat of the sofa, had thrilled at the touch of an old velvet brocade, a wondrous texture that she could recognize, would have recognized among a thousand, without dropping her eyes on it. They stuck to the cabinet with a kind of dissimulated dread, while she painfully asked herself whether she should notice it, notice everything, or just pretend not to be affected. How could she pretend not to be affected, with the very pendants of the lustres tinkling at her and with Mrs. Gereth, beside her and staring at her even as she herself stared at the cabinet, hunching up a back like Atlas under his globe? She was appalled at this image of what Mrs. Gereth had on her shoulders. That lady was waiting and watching her, bracing herself, and preparing the same face of confession and defiance she had shown the day, at Poynton, she had been surprised in the corridor. It was farcical not to speak; and yet to exclaim, to participate, would give one a bad sense of being mixed up with a theft. This ugly word sounded, for herself, in Fleda's silence, and the very violence of it jarred her into a scared glance, as of a creature detected, to right and left. But what again the full picture most showed her was the far-away empty sockets, a scandal of nakedness in high, bare walls. She at last uttered something formal and incoherent—she didn't know what: it had no relation to either house. Then she felt Mrs. Gereth's hand once more on her arm. "I've arranged a charming room for you—it's really lovely. You'll be very happy there." This was spoken with extraordinary sweetness and with a smile that meant, "Oh, I know what you're thinking; but what does it matter when you're so loyally on my side?" It had come indeed to a question of "sides," Fleda thought, for the whole place was in battle array. In the soft lamplight, with one fine feature after another looming up into sombre richness, it defied her not to pronounce it a triumph of taste. Her passion for beauty leaped back into life; and was not what now most appealed to it a certain gorgeous audacity? Mrs. Gereth's high hand was, as mere great effect, the climax of the impression.

"It's too wonderful, what you've done with the house!"—the visitor met her friend's eyes. They lighted up with joy—that friend herself so pleased with what she had done. This was not at all, in its accidental air of enthusiasm, what Fleda wanted to have said: it offered her as stupidly announcing from the first minute on whose side she was. Such was clearly the way Mrs. Gereth took it: she threw herself upon the delightful girl and tenderly embraced her again; so that Fleda soon went on, with a studied difference and a cooler inspection: "Why, you brought away absolutely everything!"

"Oh no, not everything; I saw how little I could get into this scrap of a house. I only brought away what I required."

Fleda had got up; she took a turn round the room. "You 'required' the very best pieces—the *morceaux de musée*, the individual gems!"

"I certainly didn't want the rubbish, if that's what you mean." Mrs. Gereth, on the sofa, followed the direction of her companion's eyes; with the light of her satisfaction still in her face, she slowly rubbed her large, handsome hands. Wherever she was, she was herself the great piece in the gallery. It was the first Fleda had heard of there being "rubbish" at Poynton, but she didn't for the moment take up this insincerity; she only, from where she stood in the room, called out, one after the other, as if she had had a list in her hand, the pieces that in the great house had been scattered and that now, if they had a fault, were too much like a minuet danced on a hearth-rug. She knew them each, in every chink and charm—knew them by the personal name their distinctive sign or story had given them; and a second time she felt how, against her intention, this uttered knowledge struck her hostess as so much free approval. Mrs. Gereth was never indifferent to approval, and there was nothing she could so love you for as for doing justice to her deep morality. There was a particular gleam in her eyes when Fleda exclaimed at last, dazzled by the display: "And even the Maltese cross!" That description, though technically incorrect, had always been applied, at Poynton, to a small but marvelous crucifix of ivory, a masterpiece of delicacy, of expression, and of the great Spanish period, the existence and precarious accessibility of which she had heard of at Malta, years before, by an odd and romantic chance—a clue followed through mazes of secrecy till the treasure was at last unearthed.

"'Even' the Maltese cross?" Mrs. Gereth rose as she sharply echoed the words. "My dear child, you don't suppose I'd have sacrificed *that*! For what in the world would you have taken me?"

"A *bibelot* the more or the less," Fleda said, "could have made little difference in this grand general view of you. I take you simply for the greatest of all conjurers.

You've operated with a quickness—and with a quietness!" Her voice trembled a little as she spoke, for the plain meaning of her words was that what her friend had achieved belonged to the class of operation essentially involving the protection of darkness. Fleda felt she really could say nothing at all if she couldn't say that she knew what the danger had been. She completed her thought by a resolute and perfectly candid question: "How in the world did you get off with them?"

Mrs. Gereth confessed to the fact of danger with a cynicism that surprised the girl. "By calculating, by choosing my time. I *was* quiet, and I *was* quick. I manœuvred; then at the last rushed!" Fleda drew a long breath: she saw in the poor woman something much better than sophistical ease, a crude elation that was a comparatively simple state to deal with. Her elation, it was true, was not so much from what she had done as from the way she had done it—by as brilliant a stroke as any commemorated in the annals of crime. "I succeeded because I had thought it all out and left nothing to chance: the whole process was organized in advance, so that the mere carrying it into effect took but a few hours. It was largely a matter of money: oh, I was horribly extravagant—I had to turn on so many people. But they were all to be had—a little army of workers, the packers, the porters, the helpers of every sort, the men with the mighty vans. It was a question of arranging in Tottenham Court Road and of paying the price. I haven't paid it yet; there'll be a horrid bill; but at least the thing's done! Expedition pure and simple was the essence of the bargain. 'I can give you two days,' I said; 'I can't give you another second.' They undertook the job, and the two days saw them through. The people came down on a Tuesday morning; they were off on the Thursday. I admit that some of them worked all Wednesday night. I had thought it all out; I stood over them; I showed them how. Yes, I coaxed them, I made love to them. Oh, I was inspired—they found me wonderful. I neither ate nor slept, but I was as calm as I am now. I didn't know what was in me; it was worth finding out. I'm very remarkable, my dear: I lifted tons with my own arms. I'm tired, very, very tired; but there's neither a scratch nor a nick, there isn't a teacup missing." Magnificent both in her exhaustion and in her triumph, Mrs. Gereth sank on the sofa again, the sweep of her eyes a rich synthesis and the restless friction of her hands a clear betrayal. "Upon my word," she laughed, "they really look better here!"

Fleda had listened in awe. "And no one at Poynton said anything? There was no alarm?"

"What alarm should there have been? Owen left me almost defiantly alone: I had taken a time that I had reason to believe was safe from a descent." Fleda had another wonder, which she hesitated to express: it would scarcely do to ask Mrs. Gereth if she hadn't stood in fear of her servants. She knew, moreover, some of the secrets of her humorous household rule, all made up of shocks to shyness and provocations to curiosity—a diplomacy so artful that several of the maids quite yearned to accompany her to Ricks. Mrs. Gereth, reading sharply the whole of her visitor's thought, caught it up with fine frankness. "You mean that I was watched—that he had his myrmidons, pledged to wire him if they should see what I was 'up to'? Precisely. I know the three persons you have in mind: I had them in mind myself. Well, I took a line with them—I settled them."

Fleda had had no one in particular in mind; she had never believed in the myrmidons; but the tone in which Mrs. Gereth spoke added to her suspense. "What did you do to them?"

"I took hold of them hard—I put them in the forefront. I made them work."

"To move the furniture?"

"To help, and to help so as to please me. That was the way to take them; it was what they had least expected. I marched up to them and looked each straight in the eye, giving him the chance to choose if he'd gratify me or gratify my son. He gratified *me*. They were too stupid!"

Mrs. Gereth massed herself there more and more as an immoral woman, but Fleda had to recognize that she too would have been stupid and she too would have gratified her. "And when did all this take place?"

"Only last week; it seems a hundred years. We've worked here as fast as we worked there, but I'm not settled yet: you'll see in the rest of the house. However, the worst is over."

"Do you really think so?" Fleda presently inquired. "I mean, does he, after the fact, as it were, accept it?"

"Owen—what I've done? I haven't the least idea," said Mrs. Gereth.

"Does Mona?"

"You mean that she'll be the soul of the row?"

"I hardly see Mona as the 'soul' of anything," the girl replied. "But have they made no sound? Have you heard nothing at all?"

"Not a whisper, not a step, in all the eight days. Perhaps they don't know. Perhaps they're crouching for a leap."

"But wouldn't they have gone down as soon as you left?"

"They may not have known of my leaving." Fleda wondered afresh; it struck her as scarcely supposable that some sign shouldn't have flashed from Poynton to London. If the storm was taking this term of silence to gather, even in Mona's breast, it would probably discharge itself in some startling form. The great hush of every one concerned was strange; but when she pressed Mrs. Gereth for some explanation of it, that lady only replied, with her brave irony: "Oh, I took their breath away!" She had no illusions, however; she was still prepared to fight. What indeed was her spoliation of Poynton but the first engagement of a campaign?

All this was exciting, but Fleda's spirit dropped, at bedtime, in the chamber embellished for her pleasure, where she found several of the objects that in her earlier room she had most admired. These had been reinforced by other pieces from other rooms, so that the quiet air of it was a harmony without a break, the finished picture of a maiden's bower. It was the sweetest Louis Seize, all assorted and combined—old chastened, figured, faded France. Fleda was impressed anew with her friend's genius for composition. She could say to herself that no girl in England, that night, went to rest with so picked a guard; but there was no joy for her in her privilege, no sleep even for the tired hours that made the place, in the embers of the fire and the winter dawn, look gray, somehow, and loveless. She couldn't care for such things when they came to her in such ways; there was a wrong about them all that turned them to ugliness. In the watches of the night she saw Poynton dishonored; she had cared for it as a happy whole, she reasoned, and the parts of it now around her seemed to suffer like chopped limbs. Before going to bed she had walked about with Mrs. Gereth and seen at whose expense the whole house had been furnished. At poor Owen's, from top to bottom—there wasn't a chair he hadn't sat upon. The maiden aunt had been exterminated—no trace of her to tell her tale. Fleda tried to think of some of the things at Poynton still unappropriated, but her memory was a blank about them, and in trying to focus the old combinations she saw again nothing but gaps and scars, a vacancy that gathered at moments into something worse. This concrete image was her greatest trouble, for it was Owen Gereth's face, his sad, strange eyes, fixed upon her now as they had never been. They stared at her out of the darkness, and their expression was more than she could bear: it seemed to say that he was in pain and that it was somehow her fault. He had looked to her to help him, and this was what her help had been. He had done her the honor to ask her to exert herself in his interest, confiding to her a task of difficulty, but of the highest delicacy. Hadn't that been exactly the sort of service she longed to render him? Well, her way of rendering it had been simply to betray him and hand him over to his enemy. Shame, pity, resentment oppressed her in turn; in the last of these feelings the others were quickly submerged. Mrs. Gereth had imprisoned her in that torment of taste; but it was clear to her for an hour at least that she might hate Mrs. Gereth.

Something else, however, when morning came, was even more intensely definite: the most odious thing in the world for her would be ever again to meet Owen. She took on the spot a resolve to neglect no precaution that could lead to her going through life without that accident. After this, while she dressed, she took still another. Her position had become, in a few hours, intolerably false; in as few more hours as possible she would therefore put an end to it. The way to put an end to it would be to inform Mrs. Gereth that, to her great regret, she couldn't be with her now, couldn't cleave to her to the point that everything about her so plainly urged. She dressed with a sort of violence, a symbol of the manner in which this purpose was precipitated. The more they parted company the less likely she was to come across Owen; for Owen would be drawn closer to his mother now by the very necessity of bringing her down. Fleda, in the inconsequence of distress, wished to have nothing to do with her fall; she had had too much to do with everything. She was well aware of the importance, before breakfast and in view of any light they might shed on the question of motive, of not suffering her invidious expression of a difference to be accompanied by the traces of tears; but it none the less came to pass, downstairs, that after she had subtly put her back to the window, to make a mystery of the state of her eyes, she stupidly let a rich sob escape her before she could properly meet the consequences of being asked if she wasn't delighted with her room. This accident struck her on the spot as so grave that she felt the only refuge to be instant hypocrisy, some graceful impulse that would charge her emotion to the quickened sense of her friend's generosity—a demonstration entailing a flutter round the table and a renewed embrace, and not so successfully improvised but that Fleda fancied Mrs. Gereth to have been only half reassured. She had been startled, at any rate, and she might remain suspicious: this reflection interposed by the time, after breakfast, the girl had recovered sufficiently to say what was in her heart. She accordingly didn't say it that morning at all: she had absurdly veered about; she had encountered the shock of the fear that Mrs. Gereth, with sharpened eyes, might wonder why the deuce (she often wondered in that phrase) she had grown so warm about Owen's rights. She would doubtless, at a pinch, be able to defend them on abstract grounds, but that would involve a discussion, and the idea of a discussion made her nervous for her secret. Until in some way Poynton should return the blow and give her a cue, she must keep nervousness down; and she called herself a fool for having forgotten, however briefly, that her one safety was in silence.

Directly after luncheon Mrs. Gereth took her into the garden for a glimpse of the revolution—or at least, said the mistress of Ricks, of the great row—that had been decreed there; but the ladies had scarcely placed themselves for this view before the younger one found herself embracing a prospect that opened in quite another quarter. Her attention was called to it, oddly, by the streamers of the parlor-maid's cap, which, flying straight behind the neat young woman who unexpectedly burst from the house and showed a long red face as she ambled over the grass, seemed to articulate in their flutter the name that Fleda lived at present only to catch. "Poynton—Poynton!" said the morsels of muslin; so that the parlor-maid became on the instant an actress in the drama, and Fleda, assuming pusillanimously that she herself was only a spectator, looked across the footlights at the exponent of the principal part. The manner in which this artist returned her look showed that she was equally preoccupied. Both were haunted alike by possibilities, but the apprehension of neither, before the announcement was made, took the form of the arrival at Ricks, in the flesh, of Mrs. Gereth's victim. When the messenger informed them that Mr. Gereth was in the drawing-room, the blank "Oh!" emitted by Fleda was quite as precipitate as the sound on her hostess's lips, besides being, as she felt, much less pertinent. "I thought it would be somebody," that lady afterwards said; "but I expected on the whole a solicitor's clerk." Fleda didn't mention that she herself had expected on the whole a pair of constables. She was surprised by Mrs. Gereth's question to the parlor-maid.

"For whom did he ask?"

"Why, for *you*, of course, dearest friend!" Fleda interjected, falling instinctively into the address that embodied the intensest pressure. She wanted to put Mrs. Gereth between her and her danger.

"He asked for Miss Vetch, mum," the girl replied, with a face that brought startlingly to Fleda's ear the muffled chorus of the kitchen.

"Quite proper," said Mrs. Gereth austerely. Then to Fleda: "Please go to him."

"But what to do?"

"What you always do—to see what he wants." Mrs. Gereth dismissed the maid. "Tell him Miss Vetch will come." Fleda saw that nothing was in the mother's imagination at this moment but the desire not to meet her son. She had completely broken with him, and there was little in what had just happened to repair the rupture. It would now take more to do so than his presenting himself uninvited at her door. "He's right in asking for you—he's aware that you're still our communicator; nothing has occurred to alter that. To what he wishes to transmit through you I'm ready, as I've been ready before, to listen. As far as *I*'m concerned, if I couldn't meet him a month ago, how am I to meet him to-day? If he has come to say, 'My dear mother, you're here, in the hovel into which I've flung you, with consolations that give me pleasure,' I'll listen to him; but on no other footing. That's what you're to ascertain, please. You'll oblige me as you've obliged me before. There!" Mrs. Gereth turned her back and, with a fine imitation of superiority, began to redress the miseries immediately before her. Fleda meanwhile hesitated, lingered for some minutes where she had been left, feeling secretly that her fate still had her in hand. It had put her face to face with Owen Gereth, and it evidently meant to keep her so. She was reminded afresh of two things: one of which was that, though she judged her friend's rigor, she had never really had the story of the scene enacted in the great awestricken house between the mother and the son weeks before—the day the former took to her bed in her over-throw; the other was, that at Ricks as at Poynton, it was before all things her place to accept thankfully a usefulness not, she must remember, universally acknowledged. What determined her at the last, while Mrs. Gereth disappeared in the shrubbery, was that, though she was at a distance from the house and the drawing-room was turned the other way, she could absolutely see the young man alone there with the sources of his pain. She saw his simple stare at his tapestries, heard his heavy tread on his carpets and the hard breath of his sense of unfairness. At this she went to him fast.

VIII

"I asked for you," he said when she stood there, "because I heard from the flyman who drove me from the station to the inn that he had brought you here yesterday. We had some talk, and he mentioned it."

"You didn't know I was here?"

"No. I knew only that you had had, in London, all that you told me, that day, to do; and it was Mona's idea that after your sister's marriage you were staying on with your father. So I thought you were with him still."

"I am," Fleda replied, idealizing a little the fact. "I'm here only for a moment. But do you mean," she went on, "that if you had known I was with your mother you wouldn't have come down?"

The way Owen hung fire at this question made it sound more playful than she had intended. She had, in fact, no consciousness of any intention but that of confining herself rigidly to her function. She could already see that, in whatever he had now braced himself for, she was an element he had not reckoned with. His preparation had been of a different sort—the sort congruous with his having been careful to go first and lunch solidly at the inn. He had not been forced to ask for her, but she became aware, in his presence, of a particular desire to make him feel that no harm could really come to him. She might upset him, as people called it, but she would take no advantage of having done so. She had never seen a person with whom she wished more to be light and easy, to be exceptionally human. The account he presently gave of the matter was that he indeed wouldn't have come if he had known she was on the spot; because then, didn't she see? he could have written to her. He would have had her there to let fly at his mother.

"That would have saved me—well, it would have saved me a lot. Of course I would rather see you than her," he somewhat awkwardly added. "When the fellow spoke of you, I assure you I quite jumped at you. In fact I've no real desire to see Mummy at all. If she thinks I *like* it—!" He sighed disgustedly. "I only came down because it seemed better than any other way. I didn't want her to be able to say I hadn't been all right. I dare say you know she has taken everything; or if not quite everything, why, a lot more than one ever dreamed. You can see for yourself—she has got half the place down. She has got them crammed—you can see for yourself!" He had his old trick of artless repetition, his helpless iteration of the obvious; but he was sensibly different, for Fleda, if only by the difference of his clear face, mottled over and almost disfigured by little points of pain. He might have been a fine young man with a bad toothache; with the first even of his life. What ailed him above all, she felt, was that trouble was new to him: he had never known a difficulty; he had taken all his fences, his world wholly the world of the personally possible, rounded indeed by a gray suburb into which he had never had occasion to stray. In this vulgar and ill-lighted region he had evidently now lost himself. "We left it quite to her honor, you know," he said ruefully.

"Perhaps you've a right to say that you left it a little to mine." Mixed up with the spoils there, rising before him as if she were in a manner their keeper, she felt that she must absolutely dissociate herself. Mrs. Gereth had made it impossible to do anything but give her away. "I can only tell you that, on my side, I left it to her. I never dreamed either that she would pick out so many things."

"And you don't really think it's fair, do you? You *don't*!" He spoke very quickly; he really seemed to plead.

Fleda faltered a moment. "I think she has gone too far." Then she added: "I shall immediately tell her that I've said that to you."

He appeared puzzled by this statement, but he presently rejoined: "You haven't then said to mamma what you think?"

"Not yet; remember that I only got here last night." She appeared to herself ignobly weak. "I had had no idea what she was doing; I was taken completely by surprise. She managed it wonderfully."

"It's the sharpest thing I ever saw in *my* life!" They looked at each other with intelligence, in appreciation of the sharpness, and Owen quickly broke into a loud laugh. The laugh was in itself natural, but the occasion of it strange; and stranger still, to Fleda, so that she too almost laughed, the inconsequent charity with which he added: "Poor dear old Mummy! That's one of the reasons I asked for you," he went on—"to see if you'd back her up."

Whatever he said or did, she somehow liked him the better for it. "How can I back her up, Mr. Gereth, when I think, as I tell you, that she has made a great mistake?"

"A great mistake! That's all right." He spoke—it wasn't clear to her why—as if this declaration were a great point gained.

"Of course there are many things she hasn't taken," Fleda continued.

"Oh yes, a lot of things. But you wouldn't know the place, all the same." He looked about the room with his discolored, swindled face, which deepened Fleda's compassion for him, conjuring away any smile at so candid an image of the dupe. "You'd know this one soon enough, wouldn't you? These are just the things she ought to have left. Is the whole house full of them?"

"The whole house," said Fleda uncompromisingly. She thought of her lovely room.

"I never knew how much I cared for them. They're awfully valuable, aren't they?" Owen's manner mystified her; she was conscious of a return of the agitation he had produced in her on that last bewildering day, and she reminded herself that, now she was warned, it would be inexcusable of her to allow him to justify the fear that had dropped on her. "Mother thinks I never took any notice, but I assure you I was awfully proud of everything. Upon my honor, I *was* proud, Miss Vetch."

There was an oddity in his helplessness; he appeared to wish to persuade her and to satisfy himself that she sincerely felt how worthy he really was to treat what had happened as an injury. She could only exclaim, almost as helplessly as himself: "Of course you did justice! It's all most painful. I shall instantly let your mother know," she again declared, "the way I've spoken of her to you." She clung to that idea as to the sign of her straightness.

"You'll tell her what you think she ought to do?" he asked with some eagerness.

"What she ought to do?"

"*Don't* you think it—I mean that she ought to give them up?"

"To give them up?" Fleda hesitated again.

"To send them back—to keep it quiet." The girl had not felt the impulse to ask him to sit down among the monuments of his wrong, so that, nervously, awkwardly, he fidgeted about the room with his hands in his pockets and an effect of returning a little into possession through the formulation of his view. "To have them packed and dispatched again, since she knows so well how. She does it beautifully"—he looked close at two or three precious pieces. "What's sauce for the goose is sauce for the gander!"

61

He had laughed at his way of putting it, but Fleda remained grave. "Is that what you came to say to her?"

"Not exactly those words. But I did come to say"—he stammered, then brought it out—"I did come to say we must have them right back."

"And did you think your mother would see you?"

"I wasn't sure, but I thought it right to try—to put it to her kindly, don't you see? If she won't see me, then she has herself to thank. The only other way would have been to set the lawyers at her."

"I'm glad you didn't do that."

"I'm dashed if I want to!" Owen honestly declared. "But what's a fellow to do if she won't meet a fellow?"

"What do you call meeting a fellow?" Fleda asked, with a smile.

"Why, letting *me* tell her a dozen things she can have."

This was a transaction that Fleda, after a moment, had to give up trying to represent to herself. "If she won't do that—?" she went on.

"I'll leave it all to my solicitor. *He* won't let her off: by Jove, I know the fellow!"

"That's horrible!" said Fleda, looking at him in woe.

"It's utterly beastly!"

His want of logic as well as his vehemence startled her; and with her eyes still on his she considered before asking him the question these things suggested. At last she asked it. "Is Mona very angry?"

"Oh dear, yes!" said Owen.

She had perceived that he wouldn't speak of Mona without her beginning. After waiting fruitlessly now for him to say more, she continued: "She has been there again? She has seen the state of the house?"

"Oh dear, yes!" Owen repeated.

Fleda disliked to appear not to take account of his brevity, but it was just because she was struck by it that she felt the pressure of the desire to know more. What it suggested was simply what her intelligence supplied, for he was incapable of any art of insinuation. Wasn't it at all events the rule of communication with him to say for him what he couldn't say? This truth was present to the girl as she inquired if Mona greatly resented what Mrs. Gereth had done. He satisfied her promptly; he was standing before the fire, his back to it, his long legs apart, his hands, behind him, rather violently jiggling his gloves. "She hates it awfully. In fact, she refuses to put up with it at all. Don't you see?—she saw the place with all the things."

"So that of course she misses them."

"Misses them—rather! She was awfully sweet on them." Fleda remembered how sweet Mona had been, and reflected that if that was the sort of plea he had prepared it was indeed as well he shouldn't see his mother. This was not all she wanted to know, but it came over her that it was all she needed. "You see it puts me in the position of not carrying out what I promised," Owen said. "As she says herself"—he hesitated an instant—"it's just as if I had obtained her under false pretenses." Just before, when he spoke with more drollery than he knew, it had left Fleda serious; but now his own clear gravity had the effect of exciting her mirth. She laughed out, and he looked surprised, but went on: "She regards it as a regular sell."

Fleda was silent; but finally, as he added nothing, she exclaimed: "Of course it makes a great difference!" She knew all she needed, but none the less she risked, after another pause, an interrogative remark. "I forget when it is that your marriage takes place?"

Owen came away from the fire and, apparently at a loss where to turn, ended by directing himself to one of the windows. "It's a little uncertain; the date isn't quite fixed."

"Oh, I thought I remembered that at Poynton you had told me a day, and that it was near at hand."

"I dare say I did; it was for the 19th. But we've altered that—she wants to shift it." He looked out of the window; then he said: "In fact, it won't come off till Mummy has come round."

"Come round?"

"Put the place as it was." In his offhand way he added: "You know what I mean!"

He spoke not impatiently, but with a kind of intimate familiarity, the sweetness of which made her feel a pang for having forced him to tell her what was embarrassing to him, what was even humiliating. Yes indeed, she knew all she needed: all she needed was that Mona had proved apt at putting down that wonderful patent-leather foot. Her type was misleading only to the superficial, and no one in the world was less superficial than Fleda. She had guessed the truth at Waterbath and she had suffered from it at Poynton; at Ricks the only thing she could do was to accept it with the dumb exaltation that she felt rising. Mona had been prompt with her exercise of the member in question, for it might be called prompt to do that sort of thing before marriage. That she had indeed been premature who should say save those who should have read the matter in the full light of results? Neither at Waterbath nor at Poynton had even Fleda's thoroughness discovered all that there was—or rather, all that there was not—in Owen Gereth. "Of course it makes all the difference!" she said in answer to his last words. She pursued, after considering: "What you wish me to say from you then to your mother is that you demand immediate and practically complete restitution?"

"Yes, please. It's tremendously good of you."

"Very well, then. Will you wait?"

"For Mummy's answer?" Owen stared and looked perplexed; he was more and more fevered with so much vivid expression of his case. "Don't you think that if I'm here she may hate it worse—think I may want to make her reply bang off?"

Fleda thought. "You don't, then?"

"I want to take her in the right way, don't you know?—treat her as if I gave her more than just an hour or two."

"I see," said Fleda. "Then, if you don't wait—good-bye."

This again seemed not what he wanted. "Must *you* do it bang off?"

"I'm only thinking she'll be impatient—I mean, you know, to learn what will have passed between us."

"I see," said Owen, looking at his gloves. "I can give her a day or two, you know. Of course I didn't come down to sleep," he went on. "The inn seems a horrid hole. I know all about the trains—having no idea you were here." Almost as soon as his interlocutress he was struck with the absence of the visible, in this, as between effect and cause. "I mean because in that case I should have felt I could stop over. I should have felt I could talk with you a blessed sight longer than with Mummy."

"We've already talked a long time," smiled Fleda.

"Awfully, haven't we?" He spoke with the stupidity she didn't object to. Inarticulate as he was, he had more to say; he lingered perhaps because he was vaguely aware of the want of sincerity in her encouragement to him to go. "There's one thing, please," he mentioned, as if there might be a great many others too. "Please don't say anything about Mona."

She didn't understand. "About Mona?"

"About its being *her* that thinks she has gone too far." This was still slightly obscure, but now Fleda understood. "It mustn't seem to come from *her* at all, don't you know? That would only make Mummy worse."

Fleda knew exactly how much worse, but she felt a delicacy about explicitly assenting: she was already immersed moreover in the deep consideration of what might make "Mummy" better. She couldn't see as yet at all; she could only clutch at the hope of some inspiration after he should go. Oh, there was a remedy, to be sure, but it was out of the question; in spite of which, in the strong light of Owen's troubled presence, of his anxious face and restless step, it hung there before her for some minutes. She felt that, remarkably, beneath the decent rigor of his errand, the poor young man, for reasons, for weariness, for disgust, would have been ready not to insist. His fitness to fight his mother had left him—he wasn't in fighting trim. He had no natural avidity and even no special wrath; he had none that had not been taught him, and it was doing his best to learn the lesson that had made him so sick. He had his delicacies, but he hid them away like presents before Christmas. He was hollow, perfunctory, pathetic; he had been girded by another hand. That hand had naturally been Mona's, and it was heavy even now on his strong, broad back. Why then had he originally rejoiced so in its touch? Fleda dashed aside this question, for it had nothing to do with her problem. Her problem was to help him to live as a gentleman and carry through what he had undertaken; her problem was to reinstate him in his rights. It was quite irrelevant that Mona had no intelligence of what she had lost—quite irrelevant that she was moved not by the privation, but by the insult: she had every reason to be moved, though she was so much more movable, in the vindictive way, at any rate, than one might have supposed—assuredly more than Owen himself had imagined.

"Certainly I shall not mention Mona," Fleda said, "and there won't be the slightest necessity for it. The wrong's quite sufficiently yours, and the demand you make is perfectly justified by it."

"I can't tell you what it is to me to feel you on my side!" Owen exclaimed.

"Up to this time," said Fleda, after a pause, "your mother has had no doubt of my being on hers."

"Then of course she won't like your changing."

"I dare say she won't like it at all."

"Do you mean to say you'll have a regular kick-up with her?"

"I don't exactly know what you mean by a regular kick-up. We shall naturally have a great deal of discussion—if she consents to discuss the matter at all. That's why you must decidedly give her two or three days."

"I see you think she *may* refuse to discuss it at all," said Owen.

"I'm only trying to be prepared for the worst. You must remember that to have to withdraw from the ground she has taken, to make a public surrender of what she has publicly appropriated, will go uncommonly hard with her pride."

Owen considered; his face seemed to broaden, but not into a smile. "I suppose she's tremendously proud, isn't she?" This might have been the first time it had occurred to him.

"You know better than I," said Fleda, speaking with high extravagance.

"I don't know anything in the world half so well as you. If I were as clever as you I might hope to get round her." Owen hesitated; then he went on: "In fact I don't quite see what even you can say or do that will really fetch her."

"Neither do I, as yet. I must think—I must pray!" the girl pursued, smiling. "I can only say to you that I'll try. I *want* to try, you know—I want to help you." He stood looking at her so long on this that she added with much distinctness: "So you must leave me, please, quite alone with her. You must go straight back."

"Back to the inn?"

"Oh no, back to town. I'll write to you to-morrow."

He turned about vaguely for his hat.

"There's the chance, of course, that she may be afraid."

"Afraid, you mean, of the legal steps you may take?"

"I've got a perfect case—I could have her up. The Brigstocks say it's simple stealing."

"I can easily fancy what the Brigstocks say!" Fleda permitted herself to remark without solemnity.

"It's none of their business, is it?" was Owen's unexpected rejoinder. Fleda had already noted that no one so slow could ever have had such rapid transitions.

She showed her amusement. "They've a much better right to say it's none of mine."

"Well, at any rate, you don't call her names."

Fleda wondered whether Mona did; and this made it all the finer of her to exclaim in a moment: "You don't know what I shall call her if she holds out!"

Owen gave her a gloomy glance; then he blew a speck off the crown of his hat. "But if you do have a set-to with her?"

He paused so long for a reply that Fleda said: "I don't think I know what you mean by a set-to."

"Well, if she calls *you* names."

"I don't think she'll do that."

"What I mean to say is, if she's angry at your backing me up—what will you do then? She can't possibly like it, you know."

"She may very well not like it; but everything depends. I must see what I shall do. You mustn't worry about me."

She spoke with decision, but Owen seemed still unsatisfied. "You won't go away, I hope?"

"Go away?"

"If she does take it ill of you."

Fleda moved to the door and opened it. "I'm not prepared to say. You must have patience and see."

"Of course I must," said Owen—"of course, of course." But he took no more advantage of the open door than to say: "You want me to be off, and I'm off in a

67

minute. Only, before I go, please answer me a question. If you *should* leave my mother, where would you go?"

Fleda smiled again. "I haven't the least idea."

"I suppose you'd go back to London."

"I haven't the least idea," Fleda repeated.

"You don't—a—live anywhere in particular, do you?" the young man went on. He looked conscious as soon as he had spoken; she could see that he felt himself to have alluded more grossly than he meant to the circumstance of her having, if one were plain about it, no home of her own. He had meant it as an allusion of a tender sort to all that she would sacrifice in the case of a quarrel with his mother; but there was indeed no graceful way of touching on that. One just couldn't be plain about it.

Fleda, wound up as she was, shrank from any treatment at all of the matter, and she made no answer to his question. "I *won't* leave your mother," she said. "I'll produce an effect on her; I'll convince her absolutely."

"I believe you will, if you look at her like that!"

She was wound up to such a height that there might well be a light in her pale, fine little face—a light that, while, for all return, at first, she simply shone back at him, was intensely reflected in his own. "I'll make her see it—I'll make her see it!" She rang out like a silver bell. She had at that moment a perfect faith that she should succeed; but it passed into something else when, the next instant, she became aware that Owen, quickly getting between her and the door she had opened, was sharply closing it, as might be said, in her face. He had done this before she could stop him, and he stood there with his hand on the knob and smiled at her strangely. Clearer than he could have spoken it was the sense of those seconds of silence.

"When I got into this I didn't know you, and now that I know you how can I tell you the difference? And *she's* so different, so ugly and vulgar, in the light of this squabble. No, like *you* I've never known one. It's another thing, it's a new thing altogether. Listen to me a little: can't something be done?" It was what had been in the air in those moments at Kensington, and it only wanted words to be a committed act. The more reason, to the girl's excited mind, why it shouldn't have words; her one thought was not to hear, to keep the act uncommitted. She would do this if she had to be horrid.

"Please let me out, Mr. Gereth," she said; on which he opened the door with an hesitation so very brief that in thinking of these things afterwards—for she was to think of them forever—she wondered in what tone she could have spoken. They went into the hall, where she encountered the parlor-maid, of whom she inquired whether Mrs. Gereth had come in.

"No, miss; and I think she has left the garden. She has gone up the back road." In other words, they had the whole place to themselves. It would have been a pleasure, in a different mood, to converse with that parlor-maid.

"Please open the house-door," said Fleda.

Owen, as if in quest of his umbrella, looked vaguely about the hall—looked even wistfully up the staircase—while the neat young woman complied with Fleda's request. Owen's eyes then wandered out of the open door. "I think it's awfully nice here," he observed; "I assure you I could do with it myself."

"I should think you might, with half your things here! It's Poynton itself—almost. Good-bye, Mr. Gereth," Fleda added. Her intention had naturally been that the neat young woman, opening the front door, should remain to close it on the departing guest. That functionary, however, had acutely vanished behind a stiff flap of green baize which Mrs. Gereth had not yet had time to abolish. Fleda put out her hand, but Owen turned away—he couldn't find his umbrella. She passed into the open air—she was determined to get him out; and in a moment he joined her in the little plastered portico which had small resemblance to any feature of Poynton. It was, as Mrs. Gereth had said, like the portico of a house in Brompton.

"Oh, I don't mean with all the things here," he explained in regard to the opinion he had just expressed. "I mean I could put up with it just as it was; it had a lot of good things, don't you think? I mean if everything was back at Poynton, if everything was all right." He brought out these last words with a sort of smothered sigh. Fleda didn't understand his explanation unless it had reference to another and more wonderful exchange—the restoration to the great house not only of its tables and chairs, but of its alienated mistress. This would imply the installation of his own life at Ricks, and obviously that of another person. Such another person could scarcely be Mona Brigstock. He put out his hand now; and once more she heard his unsounded words: "With everything patched up at the other place, I could live here with *you*. Don't you see what I mean?"

Fleda saw perfectly, and, with a face in which she flattered herself that nothing of this vision appeared, gave him her hand and said: "Good-bye, good-bye."

Owen held her hand very firmly and kept it even after an effort made by her to recover it—an effort not repeated, as she felt it best not to show she was flurried. That solution—of her living with him at Ricks—disposed of him beautifully, and disposed not less so of herself; it disposed admirably too of Mrs. Gereth. Fleda could only vainly wonder how it provided for poor Mona. While he looked at her, grasping her hand, she felt that now indeed she was paying for his mother's extravagance at Poynton—the vividness of that lady's public plea that little Fleda Vetch was the person to insure the general peace. It was to that vividness poor Owen had come back, and if Mrs. Gereth had had more discretion little Fleda Vetch wouldn't have been in a predicament. She saw that Owen had at this moment his sharpest necessity of speech, and so long as he didn't release her hand she could only submit to him. Her defense would be perhaps to look blank and hard; so she looked as blank and as hard as she could, with the reward of an immediate sense that this was not a bit what he wanted. It even made him hang fire, as if he were suddenly ashamed of himself, were recalled to some idea of duty and of honor. Yet he none the less brought it out. "There's one thing I dare say I ought to tell you, if you're going so kindly to act for me; though of course you'll see for yourself it's a thing it won't do to tell *her*." What was it? He made her wait for it again, and while she waited, under firm coercion, she had the extraordinary impression that Owen's simplicity was in eclipse. His natural honesty was like the scent of a flower, and she felt at this moment as if her nose had been brushed by the bloom without the odor. The allusion was undoubtedly to his mother; and was not what he meant about the matter in question the opposite of what he said—that it just *would* do to tell her? It would have been the first time he had said the opposite of what he meant, and there was certainly a fascination in the phenomenon, as well as a challenge to suspense in the ambiguity. "It's just that I understand from Mona, you know," he stammered; "it's just that she has made no bones about bringing home to me—" He tried to laugh, and in the effort he faltered again.

"About bringing home to you?"—Fleda encouraged him.

He was sensible of it, he achieved his performance. "Why, that if I don't get the things back—every blessed one of them except a few *she*'ll pick out—she won't have anything more to say to me."

Fleda, after an instant, encouraged him again. "To say to you?"

"Why, she simply won't marry me, don't you see?"

Owen's legs, not to mention his voice, had wavered while he spoke, and she felt his possession of her hand loosen so that she was free again. Her stare of perception broke into a lively laugh. "Oh, you're all right, for you *will* get them. You will; you're quite safe; don't worry!" She fell back into the house with her hand on the door. "Good-bye, good-bye." She repeated it several times, laughing bravely, quite waving him away and, as he didn't move and save that he was on the other side of it, closing the door in his face quite as he had closed that of the drawing-room in hers. Never had a face, never at least had such a handsome one, been so presented to that offense. She even held the door a minute, lest he should try to come in again. At last, as she heard nothing, she made a dash for the stairs and ran up.

IX

In knowing a while before all she needed, Fleda had been far from knowing as much as that; so that once upstairs, where, in her room, with her sense of danger and trouble, the age of Louis Seize suddenly struck her as wanting in taste and point, she felt that she now for the first time knew her temptation. Owen had put it before her with an art beyond his own dream. Mona would cast him off if he didn't proceed to extremities; if his negotiation with his mother should fail he would be completely free. That negotiation depended on a young lady to whom he had pressingly suggested the condition of his freedom; and as if to aggravate the young lady's predicament designing fate had sent Mrs. Gereth, as the parlor-maid said, "up the back road." This would give the young lady more time to make up her mind that nothing should come of the negotiation. There would be different ways of putting the question to Mrs. Gereth, and Fleda might profitably devote the moments before her return to a selection of the way that would most surely be tantamount to failure. This selection indeed required no great adroitness; it was so conspicuous that failure would be the reward of an effective introduction of Mona. If that abhorred name should be properly invoked Mrs. Gereth would resist to the death, and before envenomed resistance Owen would certainly retire. His retirement would be into single life, and Fleda reflected that he had now gone away conscious of having practically told her so. She could only say, as she waited for the back road to disgorge, that she hoped it was a consciousness he enjoyed. There was something *she* enjoyed; but that was a very different matter. To know that she had become to him an object of desire gave her wings that she felt herself flutter in the air: it was like the rush of a flood into her own accumulations. These stored depths had been fathomless and still, but now, for half an hour, in the empty house, they spread till they overflowed. He seemed to have made it right for her to confess to herself her secret. Strange then there should be for him in return nothing that such a confession could make right! How could it make right that he should give up Mona for another woman? His attitude was a sorry appeal to Fleda to legitimate that. But he didn't believe it himself, and he had none of the courage of his suggestion. She could easily see how wrong everything must be when a man so made to be manly was wanting in courage. She had upset him, as people called it, and he had spoken out from the force of the jar of finding her there. He had upset her too, heaven knew, but she was one of those who could pick themselves up. She had the real advantage, she considered, of having kept him from seeing that she had been overthrown.

She had moreover at present completely recovered her feet, though there was in the intensity of the effort required to do so a vibration which throbbed away into an immense allowance for the young man. How could she after all know what, in the disturbance wrought by his mother, Mona's relations with him might have become? If he had been able to keep his wits, such as they were, more about him he would probably have felt—as sharply as she felt on his behalf—that so long as those relations were not ended he had no right to say even the little he had said. He had no right to appear to wish to draw in another girl to help him to an escape. If he was in a plight he must get out of the plight himself, he must get out of it first, and anything he should have to say to any one else must be deferred and detached. She herself, at any rate—it was her own case that was in question—couldn't dream of assisting him save in the sense of their common honor. She could never be the girl to be drawn in, she could never lift her finger against Mona. There was something in her that would make it a shame to her forever to have owed her happiness to an interference. It would seem intolerably vulgar to her to have "ousted" the daughter of the Brigstocks; and merely to have abstained even wouldn't assure her that she had been straight. Nothing was really straight but to justify her little pensioned presence by her use; and now, won over as she was to heroism, she could see her use only as some high and delicate deed. She couldn't do anything at all, in short, unless she could do it with a kind of pride, and there would be nothing to be proud of in having arranged for poor Owen to get off easily. Nobody had a right to get off easily from pledges so deep, so sacred. How could Fleda doubt they had been tremendous when she knew so well what any pledge of her own would be? If Mona was so formed that she could hold such vows light, that was Mona's peculiar business. To have loved Owen apparently, and yet to have loved him only so much, only to the extent of a few tables and chairs, was not a thing she could so much as try to grasp. Of a different way of loving him she was herself ready to give an instance, an instance of which the beauty indeed would not be generally known. It would not perhaps if revealed be generally understood, inasmuch as the effect of the particular pressure she proposed to exercise would be, should success attend it, to keep him tied to an affection that had died a sudden and violent death. Even in the ardor of her meditation Fleda remained in sight of the truth that it would be an odd result of her magnanimity to prevent her friend's shaking off a woman he disliked. If he didn't dislike Mona, what was the matter with him? And if he did, Fleda asked, what was the matter with her own silly self?

Our young lady met this branch of the temptation it pleased her frankly to recognize by declaring that to encourage any such cruelty would be tortuous and base.

She had nothing to do with his dislikes; she had only to do with his good-nature and his good name. She had joy of him just as he was, but it was of these things she had the greatest. The worst aversion and the liveliest reaction moreover wouldn't alter the fact—since one was facing facts—that but the other day his strong arms must have clasped a remarkably handsome girl as close as she had permitted. Fleda's emotion at this time was a wondrous mixture, in which Mona's permissions and Mona's beauty figured powerfully as aids to reflection. She herself had no beauty, and *her* permissions were the stony stares she had just practiced in the drawing-room—a consciousness of a kind appreciably to add to the particular sense of triumph that made her generous. I may not perhaps too much diminish the merit of that generosity if I mention that it could take the flight we are considering just because really, with the telescope of her long thought, Fleda saw what might bring her out of the wood. Mona herself would bring her out; at the least Mona possibly might. Deep down plunged the idea that even should she achieve what she had promised Owen, there was still the contingency of Mona's independent action. She might by that time, under stress of temper or of whatever it was that was now moving her, have said or done the things there is no patching up. If the rupture should come from Waterbath they might all be happy yet. This was a calculation that Fleda wouldn't have committed to paper, but it affected the total of her sentiments. She was meanwhile so remarkably constituted that while she refused to profit by Owen's mistake, even while she judged it and hastened to cover it up, she could drink a sweetness from it that consorted little with her wishing it mightn't have been made. There was no harm done, because he had instinctively known, poor dear, with whom to make it, and it was a compensation for seeing him worried that he hadn't made it with some horrid mean girl who would immediately have dished him by making a still bigger one. Their protected error (for she indulged a fancy that it was hers too) was like some dangerous, lovely living thing that she had caught and could keep—keep vivid and helpless in the cage of her own passion and look at and talk to all day long. She had got it well locked up there by the time that, from an upper window, she saw Mrs. Gereth again in the garden. At this she went down to meet her.

X

Fleda's line had been taken, her word was quite ready; on the terrace of the painted pots she broke out before her interlocutress could put a question. "His errand was perfectly simple: he came to demand that you shall pack everything straight up again and send it back as fast as the railway will carry it."

The back road had apparently been fatiguing to Mrs. Gereth; she rose there rather white and wan with her walk. A certain sharp thinness was in her ejaculation of "Oh!"—after which she glanced about her for a place to sit down. The movement was a criticism of the order of events that offered such a piece of news to a lady coming in tired; but Fleda could see that in turning over the possibilities this particular peril was the one that during the last hour her friend had turned up oftenest. At the end of the short, gray day, which had been moist and mild, the sun was out; the terrace looked to the south, and a bench, formed as to legs and arms of iron representing knotted boughs, stood against the warmest wall of the house. The mistress of Ricks sank upon it and presented to her companion the handsome face she had composed to hear everything. Strangely enough, it was just this fine vessel of her attention that made the girl most nervous about what she must drop in. "Quite a 'demand,' dear, is it?" asked Mrs. Gereth, drawing in her cloak.

"Oh, that's what I should call it!" Fleda laughed, to her own surprise.

"I mean with the threat of enforcement and that sort of thing."

"Distinctly with the threat of enforcement—what would be called, I suppose, coercion."

"What sort of coercion?" said Mrs. Gereth.

"Why, legal, don't you know?—what he calls setting the lawyers at you."

"Is that what he calls it?" She seemed to speak with disinterested curiosity.

"That's what he calls it," said Fleda.

Mrs. Gereth considered an instant. "Oh, the lawyers!" she exclaimed lightly. Seated there almost cosily in the reddening winter sunset, only with her shoulders raised a little and her mantle tightened as if from a slight chill, she had never yet looked to Fleda so much in possession nor so far from meeting unsuspectedness halfway. "Is he going to send them down here?"

"I dare say he thinks it may come to that."

"The lawyers can scarcely do the packing," Mrs. Gereth humorously remarked.

"I suppose he means them—in the first place, at least—to try to talk you over."

"In the first place, eh? And what does he mean in the second?"

Fleda hesitated; she had not foreseen that so simple an inquiry could disconcert her. "I'm afraid I don't know."

"Didn't you ask?" Mrs. Gereth spoke as if she might have said, "What then were you doing all the while?"

"I didn't ask very much," said her companion. "He has been gone some time. The great thing seemed to be to understand clearly that he wouldn't be content with anything less than what he mentioned."

"My just giving everything back?"

"Your just giving everything back."

"Well, darling, what did you tell him?" Mrs. Gereth blandly inquired.

Fleda faltered again, wincing at the term of endearment, at what the words took for granted, charged with the confidence she had now committed herself to betray. "I told him I would tell you!" She smiled, but she felt that her smile was rather hollow and even that Mrs. Gereth had begun to look at her with some fixedness.

"Did he seem very angry?"

"He seemed very sad. He takes it very hard," Fleda added.

"And how does *she* take it?"

"Ah, that—that I felt a delicacy about asking."

"So you didn't ask?" The words had the note of surprise.

Fleda was embarrassed; she had not made up her mind definitely to lie. "I didn't think you'd care." That small untruth she would risk.

"Well—I don't!" Mrs. Gereth declared; and Fleda felt less guilty to hear her, for the statement was as inexact as her own. "Didn't you say anything in return?" Mrs. Gereth presently continued.

"Do you mean in the way of justifying you?"

"I didn't mean to trouble you to do that. My justification," said Mrs. Gereth, sitting there warmly and, in the lucidity of her thought, which nevertheless hung back a little, dropping her eyes on the gravel—"my justification was all the past. My justification was the cruelty—" But at this, with a short, sharp gesture, she checked herself. "It's too good of me to talk—now." She produced these sentences with a cold patience, as if addressing Fleda in the girl's virtual and actual character of Owen's representative. Our young lady crept to and fro before the bench, combating the sense that it was occupied by a judge, looking at her boot-toes, reminding herself in doing so of Mona, and lightly crunching the pebbles as she walked. She moved about because she was afraid, putting off from moment to moment the exercise of the courage she had been sure she possessed. That courage would all come to her if she could only be equally sure that what she should be called upon to do for Owen would be to suffer. She had wondered, while Mrs. Gereth spoke, how that lady would describe her justification. She had described it as if to be irreproachably fair, give her adversary the benefit of every doubt, and then dismiss the question forever. "Of course," Mrs. Gereth went on, "if we didn't succeed in showing him at Poynton the ground we took, it's simply that he shuts his eyes. What I supposed was that you would have given him your opinion that if I was the woman so signally to assert myself, I'm also the woman to rest upon it imperturbably enough."

Fleda stopped in front of her hostess. "I gave him my opinion that you're very logical, very obstinate, and very proud."

"Quite right, my dear: I'm a rank bigot—about that sort of thing!" and Mrs. Gereth jerked her head at the contents of the house. "I've never denied it. I'd kidnap— to save them, to convert them—the children of heretics. When I know I'm right I go to the stake. Oh, he may burn me alive!" she cried with a happy face. "Did he abuse me?" she then demanded.

Fleda had remained there, gathering in her purpose. "How little you know him!"

Mrs. Gereth stared, then broke into a laugh that her companion had not expected. "Ah, my dear, certainly not so well as you!" The girl, at this, turned away again—she felt she looked too conscious; and she was aware that, during a pause, Mrs. Gereth's eyes watched her as she went. She faced about afresh to meet them, but what she met was a question that reinforced them. "Why had you a 'delicacy' as to speaking of Mona?"

She stopped again before the bench, and an inspiration came to her. "I should think *you* would know," she said with proper dignity.

Blankness was for a moment on Mrs. Gereth's brow; then light broke—she visibly remembered the scene in the breakfast-room after Mona's night at Poynton. "Because I contrasted you—told him *you* were the one?" Her eyes looked deep. "You were—you are still!"

Fleda gave a bold dramatic laugh. "Thank you, my love—with all the best things at Ricks!"

Mrs. Gereth considered, trying to penetrate, as it seemed; but at last she brought out roundly: "For you, you know, I'd send them back!"

The girl's heart gave a tremendous bound; the right way dawned upon her in a flash. Obscurity indeed the next moment engulfed this course, but for a few thrilled seconds she had understood. To send the things back "for her" meant of course to send them back if there were even a dim chance that she might become mistress of them. Fleda's palpitation was not allayed as she asked herself what portent Mrs. Gereth had suddenly perceived of such a chance: that perception could come only from a sudden suspicion of her secret. This suspicion, in turn, was a tolerably straight consequence of that implied view of the propriety of surrender from which, she was well aware, she could say nothing to dissociate herself. What she first felt was that if she wished to rescue the spoils she wished also to rescue her secret. So she looked as innocent as she could and said as quickly as possible: "For me? Why in the world for me?"

"Because you're so awfully keen."

"Am I? Do I strike you so? You know I hate him," Fleda went on.

She had the sense for a while of Mrs. Gereth's regarding her with the detachment of some stern, clever stranger. "Then what's the matter with you? Why do you want me to give in?"

Fleda hesitated; she felt herself reddening. "I've only said your son wants it. I haven't said *I* do."

"Then say it and have done with it!"

This was more peremptory than any word her friend, though often speaking in her presence with much point, had ever yet directly addressed to her. It affected her like the crack of a whip, but she confined herself, with an effort, to taking it as a reminder that she must keep her head. "I know he has his engagement to carry out."

"His engagement to marry? Why, it's just that engagement we loathe!"

"Why should *I* loathe it?" Fleda asked with a strained smile. Then, before Mrs. Gereth could reply, she pursued: "I'm thinking of his general undertaking—to give her the house as she originally saw it."

"To give her the house!" Mrs. Gereth brought up the words from the depth of the unspeakable. The effort was like the moan of an autumn wind; it was in the power of such an image to make her turn pale.

"I'm thinking," Fleda continued, "of the simple question of his keeping faith on an important clause of his contract: it doesn't matter whether it's with a stupid girl or with a monster of cleverness. I'm thinking of his honor and his good name."

"The honor and good name of a man you hate?"

"Certainly," the girl resolutely answered. "I don't see why you should talk as if one had a petty mind. You don't think so. It's not on that assumption you've ever dealt with me. I can do your son justice, as he put his case to me."

"Ah, then he did put his case to you!" Mrs. Gereth exclaimed, with an accent of triumph. "You seemed to speak just now as if really nothing of any consequence had passed between you."

"Something always passes when one has a little imagination," our young lady declared.

"I take it you don't mean that Owen has any!" Mrs. Gereth cried with her large laugh.

Fleda was silent a moment. "No, I don't mean that Owen has any," she returned at last.

"Why is it you hate him so?" her hostess abruptly inquired.

"Should I love him for all he has made you suffer?"

Mrs. Gereth slowly rose at this and, coming across the walk, took her young friend in her arms and kissed her. She then passed into one of Fleda's an arm perversely and imperiously sociable. "Let us move a little," she said, holding her close and giving a slight shiver. They strolled along the terrace, and she brought out another question. "He *was* eloquent, then, poor dear—he poured forth the story of his wrongs?"

Fleda smiled down at her companion, who, cloaked and perceptibly bowed, leaned on her heavily and gave her an odd, unwonted sense of age and cunning. She took refuge in an evasion. "He couldn't tell me anything that I didn't know pretty well already."

"It's very true that you know everything. No, dear, you haven't a petty mind; you've a lovely imagination and you're the nicest creature in the world. If you were inane, like most girls—like every one, in fact—I would have insulted you, I would have outraged you, and then you would have fled from me in terror. No, now that I think of it," Mrs. Gereth went on, "you wouldn't have fled from me; nothing, on the contrary, would have made you budge. You would have cuddled into your warm corner, but you would have been wounded and weeping and martyrized, and you would have taken every opportunity to tell people I'm a brute—as indeed I should have been!" They went to and fro, and she would not allow Fleda, who laughed and protested, to attenuate with any light civility this spirited picture. She praised her cleverness and her patience; then she said it was getting cold and dark and they must go in to tea. She delayed quitting the place, however, and reverted instead to Owen's ultimatum, about which she asked another question or two; in particular whether it had struck Fleda that he really believed she would comply with such a summons.

"I think he really believes that if I try hard enough I can make you:" after uttering which words our young lady stopped short and emulated the embrace she had received a few moments before.

"And you've promised to try: I see. You didn't tell me that, either," Mrs. Gereth added as they went on. "But you're rascal enough for anything!" While Fleda was occupied in thinking in what terms she could explain why she had indeed been rascal enough for the reticence thus denounced, her companion broke out with an inquiry somewhat irrelevant and even in form somewhat profane. "Why the devil, at any rate, doesn't it come off?"

Fleda hesitated. "You mean their marriage?"

"Of course I mean their marriage!" Fleda hesitated again. "I haven't the least idea."

"You didn't ask him?"

"Oh, how in the world can you fancy?" She spoke in a shocked tone.

"Fancy your putting a question so indelicate? *I* should have put it—I mean in your place; but I'm quite coarse, thank God!" Fleda felt privately that she herself was coarse, or at any rate would presently have to be; and Mrs. Gereth, with a purpose that struck the girl as increasing, continued: "What, then, *was* the day to be? Wasn't it just one of these?"

"I'm sure I don't remember."

It was part of the great rupture and an effect of Mrs. Gereth's character that up to this moment she had been completely and haughtily indifferent to that detail. Now, however, she had a visible reason for being clear about it. She bethought herself and she broke out—"Isn't the day past?" Then, stopping short, she added: "Upon my word, they must have put it off!" As Fleda made no answer to this she sharply went on: "*Have* they put it off?"

"I haven't the least idea," said the girl.

Her hostess was looking at her hard again. "Didn't he tell you—didn't he say anything about it?"

Fleda, meanwhile, had had time to make her reflections, which were moreover the continued throb of those that had occupied the interval between Owen's departure and his mother's return. If she should now repeat his words, this wouldn't at all play the game of her definite vow; it would only play the game of her little gagged and blinded desire. She could calculate well enough the effect of telling Mrs. Gereth how she had had it from Owen's troubled lips that Mona was only waiting for the restitution and would do nothing without it. The thing was to obtain the restitution without imparting that knowledge. The only way, also, not to impart it was not to tell any truth at all about it; and the only way to meet this last condition was to reply to her companion, as she presently did: "He told me nothing whatever: he didn't touch on the subject."

"Not in any way?"

"Not in any way."

Mrs. Gereth watched Fleda and considered. "You haven't any idea if they are waiting for the things?"

"How should I have? I'm not in their counsels."

"I dare say they are—or that Mona is." Mrs. Gereth reflected again; she had a bright idea. "If I don't give in, I'll be hanged if she'll not break off."

"She'll never, never break off!" said Fleda.

"Are you sure?"

"I can't be sure, but it's my belief."

"Derived from *him?*"

The girl hung fire a few seconds. "Derived from him."

Mrs. Gereth gave her a long last look, then turned abruptly away. "It's an awful bore you didn't really get it out of him! Well, come to tea," she added rather dryly, passing straight into the house.

XI

The sense of her adversary's dryness, which was ominous of something she couldn't read, made Fleda, before complying, linger a little on the terrace; she felt the need moreover of taking breath after such a flight into the cold air of denial. When at last she rejoined Mrs. Gereth she found her erect before the drawing-room fire. Their tea had been set out in the same quarter, and the mistress of the house, for whom the preparation of it was in general a high and undelegated function, was in an attitude to which the hissing urn made no appeal. This omission, for Fleda, was such a further sign of something to come that, to disguise her apprehension, she immediately and without an apology took the duty in hand; only, however, to be promptly reminded that she was performing it confusedly and not counting the journeys of the little silver shovel she emptied into the pot. "Not *five*, my dear—the usual three," said her hostess, with the same dryness; watching her then in silence while she clumsily corrected her mistake. The tea took some minutes to draw, and Mrs. Gereth availed herself of them suddenly to exclaim: "You haven't yet told me, you know, how it is you propose to 'make' me!"

"Give everything back?" Fleda looked into the pot again and uttered her question with a briskness that she felt to be a little overdone. "Why, by putting the question well before you; by being so eloquent that I shall persuade you, shall act upon you; by making you sorry for having gone so far," she said boldly; "by simply and earnestly asking it of you, in short; and by reminding you at the same time that it's the first thing I ever have so asked. Oh, you've done things for me—endless and beautiful things," she exclaimed; "but you've done them all from your own generous impulse. I've never so much as hinted to you to lend me a postage-stamp."

"Give me a cup of tea," said Mrs. Gereth. A moment later, taking the cup, she replied: "No, you've never asked me for a postage-stamp."

"That gives me a pull!" Fleda returned, smiling.

"Puts you in the situation of expecting that I shall do this thing just simply to oblige you?"

The girl hesitated. "You said a while ago that for me you *would* do it."

"For you, but not for your eloquence. Do you understand what I mean by the difference?" Mrs. Gereth asked as she stood stirring her tea.

Fleda, to postpone answering, looked round, while she drank it, at the beautiful room. "I don't in the least like, you know, your having taken so much. It was a great shock to me, on my arrival here, to find you had done so."

"Give me some more tea," said Mrs. Gereth; and there was a moment's silence as Fleda poured out another cup. "If you were shocked, my dear, I'm bound to say you concealed your shock."

"I know I did. I was afraid to show it."

Mrs. Gereth drank off her second cup. "And you're not afraid now?"

"No, I'm not afraid now."

"What has made the difference?"

"I've pulled myself together." Fleda paused; then she added: "And I've seen Mr. Owen."

"You've seen Mr. Owen"—Mrs. Gereth concurred. She put down her cup and sank into a chair, in which she leaned back, resting her head and gazing at her young friend. "Yes, I did tell you a while ago that for you I'd do it. But you haven't told me yet what you'll do in return."

Fleda thought an instant. "Anything in the wide world you may require."

"Oh, 'anything' is nothing at all! That's too easily said." Mrs. Gereth, reclining more completely, closed her eyes with an air of disgust, an air indeed of inviting slumber.

Fleda looked at her quiet face, which the appearance of slumber always made particularly handsome; she noted how much the ordeal of the last few weeks had added to its indications of age. "Well then, try me with something. What is it you demand?"

At this, opening her eyes, Mrs. Gereth sprang straight up. "Get him away from her!"

Fleda marveled: her companion had in an instant become young again. "Away from Mona? How in the world—?"

"By not looking like a fool!" cried Mrs. Gereth very sharply. She kissed her, however, on the spot, to make up for this roughness, and summarily took off her hat, which, on coming into the house, our young lady had not removed. She applied a friendly touch to the girl's hair and gave a businesslike pull to her jacket. "I say don't look like an idiot, because you happen not to be one, not the least bit. *I'm* idiotic; I've been so, I've just discovered, ever since our first days together. I've been a precious donkey; but that's another affair."

Fleda, as if she humbly assented, went through no form of controverting this; she simply stood passive to her companion's sudden refreshment of her appearance. "How *can* I get him away from her?" she presently demanded.

"By letting yourself go."

"By letting myself go?" She spoke mechanically, still more like an idiot, and felt as if her face flamed out the insincerity of her question. It was vividly back again, the vision of the real way to act upon Mrs. Gereth. This lady's movements were now rapid; she turned off from her as quickly as she had seized her, and Fleda sat down to steady herself for full responsibility.

Her hostess, without taking up her ejaculation, gave a violent poke at the fire and then faced her again. "You've done two things, then, to-day—haven't you?—that you've never done before. One has been asking me the service, or favor, or concession—whatever you call it—that you just mentioned; the other has been telling me—certainly too for the first time—an immense little fib."

"An immense little fib?" Fleda felt weak; she was glad of the support of her seat.

"An immense big one, then!" said Mrs. Gereth irritatedly. "You don't in the least 'hate' Owen, my darling. You care for him very much. In fact, my own, you're in love with him—there! Don't tell me any more lies!" cried Mrs. Gereth with a voice and a face in the presence of which Fleda recognized that there was nothing for her but to hold herself and take them. When once the truth was out, it was out, and she could see more and more every instant that it would be the only way. She accepted therefore what had to come; she leaned back her head and closed her eyes as her companion had done just before. She would have covered her face with her hands but for the still greater shame. "Oh, you're a wonder, a wonder," said Mrs. Gereth; "you're magnificent, and I was right, as soon as I saw you, to pick you out and trust you!" Fleda closed her eyes tighter at this last word, but her friend kept it up. "I never dreamed of it till a while ago, when, after he had come and gone, we were face to face.

Then something stuck out of you; it strongly impressed me, and I didn't know at first quite what to make of it. It was that you had just been with him and that you were not natural. Not natural to *me*," she added with a smile. "I pricked up my ears, and all that this might mean dawned upon me when you said you had asked nothing about Mona. It put me on the scent, but I didn't show you, did I? I felt it was *in* you, deep down, and that I must draw it out. Well, I *have* drawn it, and it's a blessing. Yesterday, when you shed tears at breakfast, I was awfully puzzled. What has been the matter with you all the while? Why, Fleda, it isn't a crime, don't you know that?" cried the delighted woman. "When I was a girl I was always in love, and not always with such nice people as Owen. I didn't behave as well as you; compared with you I think I must have been horrid. But if you're proud and reserved, it's your own affair; I'm proud too, though I'm not reserved—that's what spoils it. I'm stupid, above all—that's what I am; so dense that I really blush for it. However, no one but you could have deceived me. If I trusted you, moreover, it was exactly to be cleverer than myself. You must be so now more than ever!" Suddenly Fleda felt her hands grasped: Mrs. Gereth had plumped down at her feet and was leaning on her knees. "Save him—save him: you *can*!" she passionately pleaded. "How could you *not* like him, when he's such a dear? He *is* a dear, darling; there's no harm in my own boy! You can do what you will with him— you know you can! What else does he give us all this time for? Get him away from her; it's as if he besought you to, poor wretch! Don't abandon him to such a fate, and I'll never abandon *you*. Think of him with that creature, that future! If you'll take him I'll give up everything. There, it's a solemn promise, the most sacred of my life! Get the better of her, and he shall have every stick I removed. Give me your word, and I'll accept it. I'll write for the packers to-night!"

Fleda, before this, had fallen forward on her companion's neck, and the two women, clinging together, had got up while the younger wailed on the other's bosom. "You smooth it down because you see more in it than there can ever be; but after my hideous double game how will you be able to believe in me again?"

"I see in it simply what *must* be, if you've a single spark of pity. Where on earth was the double game, when you've behaved like such a saint? You've been beautiful, you've been exquisite, and all our trouble is over."

Fleda, drying her eyes, shook her head ever so sadly. "No, Mrs. Gereth, it isn't over. I can't do what you ask—I can't meet your condition."

Mrs. Gereth stared; the cloud gathered in her face again. "Why, in the name of goodness, when you adore him? I know what you see in him," she declared in another tone. "You're right!"

Fleda gave a faint, stubborn smile. "He cares for her too much."

"Then why doesn't he marry her? He's giving you an extraordinary chance."

"He doesn't dream I've ever thought of him," said Fleda. "Why should he, if you didn't?"

"It wasn't with me you were in love, my duck." Then Mrs. Gereth added: "I'll go and tell him."

"If you do any such thing, you shall never see me again,—absolutely, literally never!"

Mrs. Gereth looked hard at her young friend, showing she saw she must believe her. "Then you're perverse, you're wicked. Will you swear he doesn't know?"

"Of course he doesn't know!" cried Fleda indignantly.

Her interlocutress was silent a little. "And that he has no feeling on *his* side?"

"For me?" Fleda stared. "Before he has even married her?"

Mrs. Gereth gave a sharp laugh at this. "He ought at least to appreciate your wit. Oh, my dear, you *are* a treasure! Doesn't he appreciate anything? Has he given you absolutely no symptom—not looked a look, not breathed a sigh?"

"The case," said Fleda coldly, "is as I've had the honor to state it."

"Then he's as big a donkey as his mother! But you know you must account for their delay," Mrs. Gereth remarked.

"Why must I?" Fleda asked after a moment.

"Because you were closeted with him here so long. You can't pretend at present, you know, not to have any art."

The girl hesitated an instant; she was conscious that she must choose between two risks. She had had a secret and the secret was gone. Owen had one, which was still unbruised, and the greater risk now was that his mother should lay her formidable hand upon it. All Fleda's tenderness for him moved her to protect it; so she faced the smaller peril. "Their delay," she brought herself to reply, "may perhaps be Mona's doing. I mean because he has lost her the things."

Mrs. Gereth jumped at this. "So that she'll break altogether if I keep them?"

Fleda winced. "I've told you what I believe about that. She'll make scenes and conditions; she'll worry him. But she'll hold him fast; she'll never give him up."

Mrs. Gereth turned it over. "Well, I'll keep them, to try her," she finally pronounced; at which Fleda felt quite sick, as if she had given everything and got nothing.

XII

"I must in common decency let him know that I've talked of the matter with you," she said to her hostess that evening. "What answer do you wish me to write to him?"

"Write to him that you must see him again," said Mrs. Gereth.

Fleda looked very blank. "What on earth am I to see him for?"

"For anything you like."

The girl would have been struck with the levity of this had she not already, in an hour, felt the extent of the change suddenly wrought in her commerce with her friend—wrought above all, to that friend's view, in her relation to the great issue. The effect of what had followed Owen's visit was to make that relation the very key of the crisis. Pressed upon her, goodness knew, the crisis had been, but it now seemed to put forth big, encircling arms—arms that squeezed till they hurt and she must cry out. It was as if everything at Ricks had been poured into a common receptacle, a public ferment of emotion and zeal, out of which it was ladled up to be tasted and talked about; everything at least but the one little treasure of knowledge that she kept back. She ought to have liked this, she reflected, because it meant sympathy, meant a closer union with the source of so much in her life that had been beautiful and renovating; but there were fine instincts in her that stood off. She had had—and it was not merely at this time—to recognize that there were things for which Mrs. Gereth's *flair* was not so happy as for bargains and "marks." It wouldn't be happy now as to the best action on the knowledge she had just gained; yet as from this moment they were still more intimately together, so a person deeply in her debt would simply have to stand and meet what was to come. There were ways in which she could sharply incommode such a person, and not only with the best conscience in the world, but with a sort of brutality of good intentions. One of the straightest of these strokes, Fleda saw, would be the dance of delight over the mystery Mrs. Gereth had laid bare—the loud, lawful, tactless joy of the explorer leaping upon the strand. Like any other lucky discoverer, she would take possession of the fortunate island. She was nothing if not practical: almost the only thing she took account of in her young friend's soft secret was the excellent use she could make of it—a use so much to her taste that she refused to feel a hindrance in the quality of the material. Fleda put into Mrs. Gereth's answer to her question a good deal more meaning than it would have occurred to her a few hours before that she was prepared to put, but she had on the spot a foreboding that even so broad a hint would live to be bettered.

"Do you suggest that I shall propose to him to come down here again?" she presently inquired.

"Dear, no; say that you'll go up to town and meet him." It *was* bettered, the broad hint; and Fleda felt this to be still more the case when, returning to the subject before they went to bed, her companion said: "I make him over to you wholly, you know—to do what you please with. Deal with him in your own clever way—I ask no questions. All I ask is that you succeed."

"That's charming," Fleda replied, "but it doesn't tell me a bit, you'll be so good as to consider, in what terms to write to him. It's not an answer from you to the message I was to give you."

"The answer to his message is perfectly distinct: he shall have everything in the place the minute he'll say he'll marry you."

"You really pretend," Fleda asked, "to think me capable of transmitting him that news?"

"What else can I really pretend when you threaten so to cast me off if I speak the word myself?"

"Oh, if *you* speak the word!" the girl murmured very gravely, but happy at least to know that in this direction Mrs. Gereth confessed herself warned and helpless. Then she added: "How can I go on living with you on a footing of which I so deeply disapprove? Thinking as I do that you've despoiled him far more than is just or merciful—for if I expected you to take something, I didn't in the least expect you to take everything—how can I stay here without a sense that I'm backing you up in your cruelty and participating in your ill-gotten gains?" Fleda was determined that if she had the chill of her exposed and investigated state she would also have the convenience of it, and that if Mrs. Gereth popped in and out of the chamber of her soul she would at least return the freedom. "I shall quite hate, you know, in a day or two, every object that surrounds you—become blind to all the beauty and rarity that I formerly delighted in. Don't think me harsh; there's no use in my not being frank now. If I leave you, everything's at an end."

90

Mrs. Gereth, however, was imperturbable: Fleda had to recognize that her advantage had become too real. "It's too beautiful, the way you care for him; it's music in my ears. Nothing else but such a passion could make you say such things; that's the way I should have been too, my dear. Why didn't you tell me sooner? I'd have gone right in for you; I never would have moved a candlestick. Don't stay with me if it torments you; don't, if you suffer, be where you see the old rubbish. Go up to town—go back for a little to your father's. It need be only for a little; two or three weeks will see us through. Your father will take you and be glad, if you only will make him understand what it's a question of—of your getting yourself off his hands forever. I'll make him understand, you know, if you feel shy. I'd take you up myself, I'd go with you, to spare your being bored; we'd put up at an hotel and we might amuse ourselves a bit. We haven't had much pleasure since we met, have we? But of course that wouldn't suit our book. I should be a bugaboo to Owen—I should be fatally in the way. Your chance is there—your chance is to be alone; for God's sake, use it to the right end. If you're in want of money I've a little I can give you. But I ask no questions—not a question as small as your shoe!"

She asked no questions, but she took the most extraordinary things for granted. Fleda felt this still more at the end of a couple of days. On the second of these our young lady wrote to Owen; her emotion had to a certain degree cleared itself—there was something she could say briefly. If she had given everything to Mrs. Gereth and as yet got nothing, so she had on the other hand quickly reacted—it took but a night—against the discouragement of her first check. Her desire to serve him was too passionate, the sense that he counted upon her too sweet: these things caught her up again and gave her a new patience and a new subtlety. It shouldn't really be for nothing that she had given so much; deep within her burned again the resolve to get something back. So what she wrote to Owen was simply that she had had a great scene with his mother, but that he must be patient and give her time. It was difficult, as they both had expected, but she was working her hardest for him. She had made an impression—she would do everything to follow it up. Meanwhile he must keep intensely quiet and take no other steps; he must only trust her and pray for her and believe in her perfect loyalty. She made no allusion whatever to Mona's attitude, nor to his not being, as regarded that young lady, master of the situation; but she said in a postscript, in reference to his mother, "Of course she wonders a good deal why your marriage doesn't take place." After the letter had gone she regretted having used the word "loyalty;" there were two or three milder terms which she might as well have employed. The answer she immediately received from Owen was a little note of which she met all the deficiencies by describing it to herself as pathetically simple, but which, to prove that Mrs. Gereth might ask as many questions as she liked, she at once made his mother read. He had no art with his pen, he had not even a good hand, and his letter, a short profession of friendly confidence, consisted of but a few familiar and colorless words of acknowledgment and assent. The gist of it was that he would certainly, since Miss Vetch recommended it, not hurry mamma too much. He would not for the present cause her to be approached by any one else, but he would nevertheless continue to hope that she would see she *must* come round. "Of course, you know," he added, "she can't keep me waiting indefinitely. Please give her my love and tell her that. If it can be done peaceably I know you're just the one to do it."

Fleda had awaited his rejoinder in deep suspense; such was her imagination of the possibility of his having, as she tacitly phrased it, let himself go on paper that when it arrived she was at first almost afraid to open it. There was indeed a distinct danger, for if he should take it into his head to write her love-letters the whole chance of aiding him would drop: she would have to return them, she would have to decline all further communication with him: it would be quite the end of the business. This imagination of Fleda's was a faculty that easily embraced all the heights and depths and extremities of things; that made a single mouthful, in particular, of any tragic or desperate necessity. She was perhaps at first just a trifle disappointed not to find in the note in question a syllable that strayed from the text; but the next moment she had risen to a point of view from which it presented itself as a production almost inspired in its simplicity. It was simple even for Owen, and she wondered what had given him the cue to be more so than usual. Then she saw how natures that are right just do the things that are right. He wasn't clever—his manner of writing showed it; but the cleverest man in England couldn't have had more the instinct that, under the circumstances, was the supremely happy one, the instinct of giving her something that would do beautifully to be shown to Mrs. Gereth. This was a kind of divination, for naturally he couldn't know the line Mrs. Gereth was taking. It was furthermore explained—and that was the most touching part of all—by his wish that she herself should notice how awfully well he was behaving. His very bareness called her attention to his virtue; and these were the exact fruits of her beautiful and terrible admonition. He was cleaving to Mona; he was doing his duty; he was making tremendously sure he should be without reproach.

If Fleda handed this communication to her friend as a triumphant gage of the innocence of the young man's heart, her elation lived but a moment after Mrs. Gereth had pounced upon the tell-tale spot in it. "Why in the world, then," that lady cried, "does he still not breathe a breath about the day, the *day*, the day?" She repeated the word with a crescendo of superior acuteness; she proclaimed that nothing could be more marked than its absence—an absence that simply spoke volumes. What did it prove in fine but that she was producing the effect she had toiled for—that she had settled or was rapidly settling Mona?

Such a challenge Fleda was obliged in some manner to take up. "You may be settling Mona," she returned with a smile, "but I can hardly regard it as sufficient evidence that you're settling Mona's lover."

"Why not, with such a studied omission on his part to gloss over in any manner the painful tension existing between them—the painful tension that, under providence, I've been the means of bringing about? He gives you by his silence clear notice that his marriage is practically off."

"He speaks to me of the only thing that concerns me. He gives me clear notice that he abates not one jot of his demand."

"Well, then, let him take the only way to get it satisfied."

Fleda had no need to ask again what such a way might be, nor was her support removed by the fine assurance with which Mrs. Gereth could make her argument wait upon her wish. These days, which dragged their length into a strange, uncomfortable fortnight, had already borne more testimony to that element than all the other time the two women had passed together. Our young lady had been at first far from measuring the whole of a feature that Owen himself would probably have described as her companion's "cheek." She lived now in a kind of bath of boldness, felt as if a fierce light poured in upon her from windows opened wide; and the singular part of the ordeal was that she couldn't protest against it fully without incurring, even to her own mind, some reproach of ingratitude, some charge of smallness. If Mrs. Gereth's apparent determination to hustle her into Owen's arms was accompanied with an air of holding her dignity rather cheap, this was after all only as a consequence of her being held in respect to some other attributes rather dear. It was a new version of the old story of being kicked upstairs. The wonderful woman was the same woman who, in the summer, at Poynton, had been so puzzled to conceive why a good-natured girl shouldn't have contributed more to the personal rout of the Brigstocks—shouldn't have been grateful even for the handsome puff of Fleda Vetch. Only her passion was keener now and her scruple more absent; the fight made a demand upon her, and her pugnacity had become one with her constant habit of using such weapons as she could pick up. She had no imagination about anybody's life save on the side she bumped against. Fleda was quite aware that she would have otherwise been a rare creature; but a rare creature was originally just what she had struck her as being. Mrs. Gereth had really no perception of anybody's nature—had only one question about persons: were they clever or stupid? To be clever meant to know the marks. Fleda knew them by direct inspiration, and a warm recognition of this had been her friend's tribute to her character. The girl had hours, now, of sombre wishing that she might never see anything good again: that kind of experience was evidently not an infallible source of peace. She would be more at peace in some vulgar little place that should owe its *cachet* to Tottenham Court Road. There were nice strong horrors in West Kensington; it was as if they beckoned her and wooed her back to them. She had a relaxed recollection of Waterbath; and of her reasons for staying on at Ricks the force was rapidly ebbing. One of these was her pledge to Owen—her vow to press his mother close; the other was the fact that of the two discomforts, that of being prodded by Mrs. Gereth and that of appearing to run after somebody else, the former remained for a while the more endurable.

As the days passed, however, it became plainer to Fleda that her only chance of success would be in lending herself to this low appearance. Then, moreover, at last, her nerves settling the question, the choice was simply imposed by the violence done to her taste—to whatever was left of that high principle, at least, after the free and reckless meeting, for months, of great drafts and appeals. It was all very well to try to evade discussion: Owen Gereth was looking to her for a struggle, and it wasn't a bit of a struggle to be disgusted and dumb. She was on too strange a footing—that of having presented an ultimatum and having had it torn up in her face. In such a case as that the envoy always departed; he never sat gaping and dawdling before the city. Mrs. Gereth, every morning, looked publicly into "The Morning Post," the only newspaper she received; and every morning she treated the blankness of that journal as fresh evidence that everything was "off." What did the Post exist for but to tell you your children were wretchedly married?—so that if such a source of misery was dry, what could you do but infer that for once you had miraculously escaped? She almost taunted Fleda with supineness in not getting something out of somebody—in the same breath indeed in which she drenched her with a kind of appreciation more onerous to the girl than blame. Mrs. Gereth herself had of course washed her hands of the matter; but Fleda knew people who knew Mona and would be sure to be in her confidence—inconceivable people who admired her and had the privilege of Waterbath. What was the use therefore of being the most natural and the easiest of letter-writers, if no sort of side-light—in some pretext for correspondence—was, by a brilliant creature, to be got out of such barbarians? Fleda was not only a brilliant creature, but she heard herself commended in these days for new and strange attractions; she figured suddenly, in the queer conversations of Ricks, as a distinguished, almost as a dangerous beauty. That retouching of her hair and dress in which her friend had impulsively indulged on a first glimpse of her secret was by implication very frequently repeated. She had the sense not only of being advertised and offered, but of being counseled and enlightened in ways that she scarcely understood—arts obscure even to a poor girl who had had, in good society and motherless poverty, to look straight at realities and fill out blanks.

These arts, when Mrs. Gereth's spirits were high, were handled with a brave and cynical humor with which Fleda's fancy could keep no step: they left our young lady wondering what on earth her companion wanted her to do. "I want you to cut in!"—that was Mrs. Gereth's familiar and comprehensive phrase for the course she prescribed. She challenged again and again Fleda's picture, as she called it (though the sketch was too slight to deserve the name), of the indifference to which a prior attachment had committed the proprietor of Poynton. "Do you mean to say that, Mona or no Mona, he could see you that way, day after day, and not have the ordinary feelings of a man?" This was the sort of interrogation to which Fleda was fitfully and irrelevantly treated. She had grown almost used to the refrain. "Do you mean to say that when, the other day, one had quite made you over to him, the great gawk, and he was, on this very spot, utterly alone with you—?" The poor girl at this point never left any doubt of what she meant to say, but Mrs. Gereth could be trusted to break out in another place and at another time. At last Fleda wrote to her father that he must take her in for a while; and when, to her companion's delight, she returned to London, that lady went with her to the station and wafted her on her way. "The Morning Post" had been delivered as they left the house, and Mrs. Gereth had brought it with her for the traveler, who never spent a penny on a newspaper. On the platform, however, when this young person was ticketed, labeled, and seated, she opened it at the window of the carriage, exclaiming as usual, after looking into it a moment: "Nothing—nothing—nothing: don't tell *me*!" Every day that there was nothing was a nail in the coffin of the marriage. An instant later the train was off, but, moving quickly beside it, while Fleda leaned inscrutably forth, Mrs. Gereth grasped her friend's hand and looked up with wonderful eyes. "Only let yourself go, darling—only let yourself go!"

XIII

That she desired to ask no questions Mrs. Gereth conscientiously proved by closing her lips tight after Fleda had gone to London. No letter from Ricks arrived at West Kensington, and Fleda, with nothing to communicate that could be to the taste of either party, forbore to open a correspondence. If her heart had been less heavy she might have been amused to perceive how much rope this reticence of Ricks seemed to signify to her that she could take. She had at all events no good news for her friend save in the sense that her silence was not bad news. She was not yet in a position to write that she had "cut in;" but neither, on the other hand, had she gathered material for announcing that Mona was undisseverable from her prey. She had made no use of the pen so glorified by Mrs. Gereth to wake up the echoes of Waterbath; she had sedulously abstained from inquiring what in any quarter, far or near, was said or suggested or supposed. She only spent a matutinal penny on "The Morning Post;" she only saw, on each occasion, that that inspired sheet had as little to say about the imminence as about the abandonment of certain nuptials. It was at the same time obvious that Mrs. Gereth triumphed on these occasions much more than she trembled, and that with a few such triumphs repeated she would cease to tremble at all. What was most manifest, however, was that she had had a rare preconception of the circumstances that would have ministered, had Fleda been disposed, to the girl's cutting in. It was brought home to Fleda that these circumstances would have particularly favored intervention; she was quickly forced to do them a secret justice. One of the effects of her intimacy with Mrs. Gereth was that she had quite lost all sense of intimacy with any one else. The lady of Ricks had made a desert around her, possessing and absorbing her so utterly that other partakers had fallen away. Hadn't she been admonished, months before, that people considered they had lost her and were reconciled on the whole to the privation? Her present position in the great unconscious town defined itself as obscure: she regarded it at any rate with eyes suspicious of that lesson. She neither wrote notes nor received them; she indulged in no reminders nor knocked at any doors; she wandered vaguely in the western wilderness or cultivated shy forms of that "household art" for which she had had a respect before tasting the bitter tree of knowledge. Her only plan was to be as quiet as a mouse, and when she failed in the attempt to lose herself in the flat suburb she felt like a lonely fly crawling over a dusty chart.

How had Mrs. Gereth known in advance that if she had chosen to be "vile" (that was what Fleda called it) everything would happen to help her?—especially the way her poor father, after breakfast, doddered off to his club, showing seventy when he was really fifty-seven, and leaving her richly alone for the day. He came back about midnight, looking at her very hard and not risking long words—only making her feel by inimitable touches that the presence of his family compelled him to alter all his hours. She had in their common sitting-room the company of the objects he was fond of saying that he had collected—objects, shabby and battered, of a sort that appealed little to his daughter: old brandy-flasks and match-boxes, old calendars and hand-books, intermixed with an assortment of pen-wipers and ash-trays, a harvest he had gathered in from penny bazaars. He was blandly unconscious of that side of Fleda's nature which had endeared her to Mrs. Gereth, and she had often heard him wish to goodness there was something striking she cared for. Why didn't she try collecting something?—it didn't matter what. She would find it gave an interest to life, and there was no end of little curiosities one could easily pick up. He was conscious of having a taste for fine things which his children had unfortunately not inherited. This indicated the limits of their acquaintance with him—limits which, as Fleda was now sharply aware, could only leave him to wonder what the mischief she was there for. As she herself echoed this question to the letter she was not in a position to clear up the mystery. She couldn't have given a name to her errand in town or explained it save by saying that she had had to get away from Ricks. It was intensely provisional, but what was to come next? Nothing could come next but a deeper anxiety. She had neither a home nor an outlook—nothing in all the wide world but a feeling of suspense.

Of course she had her duty—her duty to Owen—a definite undertaking, reaffirmed, after his visit to Ricks, under her hand and seal; but there was no sense of possession attached to that; there was only a horrible sense of privation. She had quite moved from under Mrs. Gereth's wide wing; and now that she was really among the pen-wipers and ash-trays she was swept, at the thought of all the beauty she had forsworn, by short, wild gusts of despair. If her friend should really keep the spoils she would never return to her. If that friend should on the other hand part with them, what on earth would there be to return to? The chill struck deep as Fleda thought of the mistress of Ricks reduced, in vulgar parlance, to what she had on her back: there was nothing to which she could compare such an image but her idea of Marie Antoinette in the Conciergerie, or perhaps the vision of some tropical bird, the creature of hot, dense forests, dropped on a frozen moor to pick up a living. The mind's eye could see Mrs. Gereth, indeed, only in her thick, colored air; it took all the light of her treasures to make her concrete and distinct. She loomed for a moment, in any mere house, gaunt and unnatural; then she vanished as if she had suddenly sunk into a quicksand. Fleda lost herself in the rich fancy of how, if *she* were mistress of Poynton, a whole province, as an abode, should be assigned there to the august queen-mother. She would have returned from her campaign with her baggage-train and her loot, and the palace would unbar its shutters and the morning flash back from its halls. In the event of a surrender the poor woman would never again be able to begin to collect: she was now too old and too moneyless, and times were altered and good things impossibly dear. A surrender, furthermore, to any daughter-in-law save an oddity like Mona needn't at all be an abdication in fact; any other fairly nice girl whom Owen should have taken it into his head to marry would have been positively glad to have, for the museum, a custodian who was a walking catalogue and who understood beyond any one in England the hygiene and temperament of rare pieces. A fairly nice girl would somehow be away a good deal and would at such times count it a blessing to feel Mrs. Gereth at her post.

Fleda had fully recognized, the first days, that, quite apart from any question of letting Owen know where she was, it would be a charity to give him some sign: it would be weak, it would be ugly, to be diverted from that kindness by the fact that Mrs. Gereth had attached a tinkling bell to it. A frank relation with him was only superficially discredited: she ought for his own sake to send him a word of cheer. So she repeatedly reasoned, but she as repeatedly delayed performance: if her general plan had been to be as still as a mouse, an interview like the interview at Ricks would be an odd contribution to that ideal. Therefore with a confused preference of practice to theory she let the days go by; she felt that nothing was so imperative as the gain of precious time. She shouldn't be able to stay with her father forever, but she might now reap the benefit of having married her sister. Maggie's union had been built up round a small spare room. Concealed in this apartment she might try to paint again, and abetted by the grateful Maggie—for Maggie at least was grateful—she might try to dispose of her work. She had not indeed struggled with a brush since her visit to Waterbath, where the sight of the family splotches had put her immensely on her guard. Poynton moreover had been an impossible place for producing; no active art could flourish there but a Buddhistic contemplation. It had stripped its mistress clean of all feeble accomplishments; her hands were imbrued neither with ink nor with water-color. Close to Fleda's present abode was the little shop of a man who mounted and framed pictures and desolately dealt in artists' materials. She sometimes paused before it to look at a couple of shy experiments for which its dull window constituted publicity, small studies placed there for sale and full of warning to a young lady without fortune and without talent. Some such young lady had brought them forth in sorrow; some such young lady, to see if they had been snapped up, had passed and repassed as helplessly as she herself was doing. They never had been, they never would be, snapped up; yet they were quite above the actual attainment of some other young ladies. It was a matter of discipline with Fleda to take an occasional lesson from them; besides which, when she now quitted the house, she had to look for reasons after she was out. The only place to find them was in the shop-windows. They made her feel like a servant-girl taking her "afternoon," but that didn't signify: perhaps some day she would resemble such a person still more closely. This continued a fortnight, at the end of which the feeling was suddenly dissipated. She had stopped as usual in the presence of the little pictures; then, as she turned away, she had found herself face to face with Owen Gereth.

At the sight of him two fresh waves passed quickly across her heart, one at the heels of the other. The first was an instant perception that this encounter was not an accident; the second a consciousness as prompt that the best place for it was the street. She knew before he told her that he had been to see her, and the next thing she knew was that he had had information from his mother. Her mind grasped these things while he said with a smile: "I saw only your back, but I was sure. I was over the way. I've been at your house."

"How came you to know my house?" Fleda asked.

"I like that!" he laughed. "How came you not to let me know that you were there?"

Fleda, at this, thought it best also to laugh. "Since I didn't let you know, why did you come?"

"Oh, I say!" cried Owen. "Don't add insult to injury. Why in the world didn't you let me know? I came because I want awfully to see you." He hesitated, then he added: "I got the tip from mother: she has written to me—fancy!"

They still stood where they had met. Fleda's instinct was to keep him there; the more so that she could already see him take for granted that they would immediately proceed together to her door. He rose before her with a different air: he looked less ruffled and bruised than he had done at Ricks, he showed a recovered freshness. Perhaps, however, this was only because she had scarcely seen him at all as yet in London form, as he would have called it—"turned out" as he was turned out in town.

In the country, heated with the chase and splashed with the mire, he had always rather reminded her of a picturesque peasant in national costume. This costume, as Owen wore it, varied from day to day; it was as copious as the wardrobe of an actor; but it never failed of suggestions of the earth and the weather, the hedges and the ditches, the beasts and the birds. There had been days when it struck her as all nature in one pair of boots. It didn't make him now another person that he was delicately dressed, shining and splendid—that he had a higher hat and light gloves with black seams, and a spearlike umbrella; but it made him, she soon decided, really handsomer, and that in turn gave him—for she never could think of him, or indeed of some other things, without the aid of his vocabulary—a tremendous pull. Yes, this was for the moment, as he looked at her, the great fact of their situation—his pull was tremendous. She tried to keep the acknowledgement of it from trembling in her voice as she said to him with more surprise than she really felt: "You've then reopened relations with her?"

"It's she who has reopened them with me. I got her letter this morning. She told me you were here and that she wished me to know it. She didn't say much; she just gave me your address. I wrote her back, you know, 'Thanks no end. Shall go to-day.' So we *are* in correspondence again, aren't we? She means of course that you've something to tell me from her, eh? But if you have, why haven't you let a fellow know?" He waited for no answer to this, he had so much to say. "At your house, just now, they told me how long you've been here. Haven't you known all the while that I'm counting the hours? I left a word for you—that I would be back at six; but I'm awfully glad to have caught you so much sooner. You don't mean to say you're not going home!" he exclaimed in dismay. "The young woman there told me you went out early."

"I've been out a very short time," said Fleda, who had hung back with the general purpose of making things difficult for him. The street would make them difficult; she could trust the street. She reflected in time, however, that to betray to him she was afraid to admit him would give him more a feeling of facility than of anything else. She moved on with him after a moment, letting him direct their course to her door, which was only round a corner: she considered as they went that it might not prove such a stroke to have been in London so long and yet not to have called him. She desired he should feel she was perfectly simple with him, and there was no simplicity in that. None the less, on the steps of the house, though she had a key, she rang the bell; and while they waited together and she averted her face she looked straight into the depths of what Mrs. Gereth had meant by giving him the "tip." This had been perfidious, had been monstrous of Mrs. Gereth, and Fleda wondered if her letter had contained only what Owen repeated.

XIV

When Owen and Fleda were in her father's little place and, among the brandy-flasks and pen-wipers, still more disconcerted and divided, the girl—to do something, though it would make him stay—had ordered tea, he put the letter before her quite as if he had guessed her thought. "She's still a bit nasty—fancy!" He handed her the scrap of a note which he had pulled out of his pocket and from its envelope. "Fleda Vetch," it ran, "is at 10 Raphael Road, West Kensington. Go to see her, and try, for God's sake, to cultivate a glimmer of intelligence." When in handing it back to him she took in his face she saw that its heightened color was the effect of his watching her read such an allusion to his want of wit. Fleda knew what it was an allusion to, and his pathetic air of having received this buffet, tall and fine and kind as he stood there, made her conscious of not quite concealing her knowledge. For a minute she was kept silent by an angered sense of the trick that had been played her. It was a trick because Fleda considered there had been a covenant; and the trick consisted of Mrs. Gereth's having broken the spirit of their agreement while conforming in a fashion to the letter. Under the girl's menace of a complete rupture she had been afraid to make of her secret the use she itched to make; but in the course of these days of separation she had gathered pluck to hazard an indirect betrayal. Fleda measured her hesitations and the impulse which she had finally obeyed and which the continued procrastination of Waterbath had encouraged, had at last made irresistible. If in her high-handed manner of playing their game she had not named the thing hidden, she had named the hiding-place. It was over the sense of this wrong that Fleda's lips closed tight: she was afraid of aggravating her case by some ejaculation that would make Owen prick up his ears. A great, quick effort, however, helped her to avoid the danger; with her constant idea of keeping cool and repressing a visible flutter, she found herself able to choose her words. Meanwhile he had exclaimed with his uncomfortable laugh: "That's a good one for me, Miss Vetch, isn't it?"

"Of course you know by this time that your mother's very sharp," said Fleda.

"I think I can understand well enough when I know what's to be understood," the young man asserted. "But I hope you won't mind my saying that you've kept me pretty well in the dark about that. I've been waiting, waiting, waiting; so much has depended on your news. If you've been working for me I'm afraid it has been a thankless job. Can't she say what she'll do, one way or the other? I can't tell in the least where I am, you know. I haven't really learnt from you, since I saw you there, where *she* is. You wrote me to be patient, and upon my soul I have been. But I'm afraid you don't quite realize what I'm to be patient with. At Waterbath, don't you know? I've simply to account and answer for the damned things. Mona looks at me and waits, and I, hang it, I look at you and do the same." Fleda had gathered fuller confidence as he continued; so plain was it that she had succeeded in not dropping into his mind the spark that might produce the glimmer invoked by his mother. But even this fine assurance gave a start when, after an appealing pause, he went on: "I hope, you know, that after all you're not keeping anything back from me."

In the full face of what she was keeping back such a hope could only make her wince; but she was prompt with her explanations in proportion as she felt they failed to meet him. The smutty maid came in with tea-things, and Fleda, moving several objects, eagerly accepted the diversion of arranging a place for them on one of the tables. "I've been trying to break your mother down because it has seemed there may be some chance of it. That's why I've let you go on expecting it. She's too proud to veer round all at once, but I think I speak correctly in saying that I've made an impression."

In spite of ordering tea she had not invited him to sit down; she herself made a point of standing. He hovered by the window that looked into Raphael Road; she kept at the other side of the room; the stunted slavey, gazing wide-eyed at the beautiful gentleman and either stupidly or cunningly bringing but one thing at a time, came and went between the tea-tray and the open door.

"You pegged at her so hard?" Owen asked.

"I explained to her fully your position and put before her much more strongly than she liked what seemed to me her absolute duty."

Owen waited a little. "And having done that, you departed?"

Fleda felt the full need of giving a reason for her departure; but at first she only said with cheerful frankness: "I departed."

Her companion again looked at her in silence. "I thought you had gone to her for several months."

"Well," Fleda replied, "I couldn't stay. I didn't like it. I didn't like it at all—I couldn't bear it," she went on. "In the midst of those trophies of Poynton, living with them, touching them, using them, I felt as if I were backing her up. As I was not a bit of an accomplice, as I hate what she has done, I didn't want to be, even to the extent of the mere look of it—what is it you call such people?—an accessory after the fact." There was something she kept back so rigidly that the joy of uttering the rest was double. She felt the sharpest need of giving him all the other truth. There was a matter as to which she had deceived him, and there was a matter as to which she had deceived Mrs. Gereth, but her lack of pleasure in deception as such came home to her now. She busied herself with the tea and, to extend the occupation, cleared the table still more, spreading out the coarse cups and saucers and the vulgar little plates. She was aware that she produced more confusion than symmetry, but she was also aware that she was violently nervous. Owen tried to help her with something: this made rather for disorder. "My reason for not writing to you," she pursued, "was simply that I was hoping to hear more from Ricks. I've waited from day to day for that."

"But you've heard nothing?"

"Not a word."

"Then what I understand," said Owen, "is that, practically, you and Mummy have quarreled. And you've done it—I mean you personally—for *me*."

"Oh no, we haven't quarreled a bit!" Then with a smile: "We've only diverged."

"You've diverged uncommonly far!"—Owen laughed back. Fleda, with her hideous crockery and her father's collections, could conceive that these objects, to her visitor's perception even more strongly than to her own, measured the length of the swing from Poynton and Ricks; she was aware too that her high standards figured vividly enough even to Owen's simplicity to make him reflect that West Kensington was a tremendous fall. If she had fallen it was because she had acted for him. She was all the more content he should thus see she *had* acted, as the cost of it, in his eyes, was none of her own showing. "What seems to have happened," he exclaimed, "is that you've had a row with her and yet not moved her!"

Fleda considered a moment; she was full of the impression that, notwithstanding her scant help, he saw his way clearer than he had seen it at Ricks. He might mean many things; and what if the many should mean in their turn only one? "The difficulty is, you understand, that she doesn't really see into your situation." She hesitated. "She doesn't comprehend why your marriage hasn't yet taken place."

Owen stared. "Why, for the reason I told you: that Mona won't take another step till mother has given full satisfaction. Everything must be there. You see, everything *was* there the day of that fatal visit."

"Yes, that's what I understood from you at Ricks," said Fleda; "but I haven't repeated it to your mother." She had hated, at Ricks, to talk with him about Mona, but now that scruple was swept away. If he could speak of Mona's visit as fatal, she need at least not pretend not to notice it. It made all the difference that she had tried to assist him and had failed: to give him any faith in her service she must give him all her reasons but one. She must give him, in other words, with a corresponding omission, all Mrs. Gereth's. "You can easily see that, as she dislikes your marriage, anything that may seem to make it less certain works in her favor. Without my telling her, she has suspicions and views that are simply suggested by your delay. Therefore it didn't seem to me right to make them worse. By holding off long enough, she thinks she may put an end to your engagement. If Mona's waiting, she believes she may at last tire Mona out." That, in all conscience, Fleda felt was lucid enough.

So the young man, following her attentively, appeared equally to feel. "So far as that goes," he promptly declared, "she *has* at last tired Mona out." He uttered the words with a strange approach to hilarity.

Fleda's surprise at this aberration left her a moment looking at him. "Do you mean your marriage is off?"

Owen answered with a kind of gay despair. "God knows, Miss Vetch, where or when or what my marriage is! If it isn't 'off,' it certainly, at the point things have reached, isn't *on*. I haven't seen Mona for ten days, and for a week I haven't heard from her. She used to write me every week, don't you know? She won't budge from Waterbath, and I haven't budged from town." Then he suddenly broke out: "If she *does* chuck me, will mother come round?"

Fleda, at this, felt that her heroism had come to its real test—felt that in telling him the truth she should effectively raise a hand to push his impediment out of the way. Was the knowledge that such a motion would probably dispose forever of Mona capable of yielding to the conception of still giving her every chance she was entitled to? That conception was heroic, but at the same moment it reminded Fleda of the place it had held in her plan, she was also reminded of the not less urgent claim of the truth. Ah, the truth—there was a limit to the impunity with which one could juggle with it! Wasn't what she had most to remember the fact that Owen had a right to his property and that he had also her vow to stand by him in the effort to recover it? How did she stand by him if she hid from him the single way to recover it of which she was quite sure? For an instant that seemed to her the fullest of her life she debated. "Yes," she said at last, "if your marriage is really abandoned, she will give up everything she has taken."

"That's just what makes Mona hesitate!" Owen honestly exclaimed. "I mean the idea that I shall get back the things only if she gives me up."

Fleda thought an instant. "You mean makes her hesitate to keep you—not hesitate to renounce you?"

Owen looked a trifle bewildered. "She doesn't see the use of hanging on, as I haven't even yet put the matter into legal hands. She's awfully keen about that, and awfully disgusted that I don't. She says it's the only real way, and she thinks I'm afraid to take it. She has given me time and then has given me again more. She says I give Mummy too much. She says I'm a muff to go pottering on. That's why she's drawing off so hard, don't you see?"

"I don't see very clearly. Of course you must give her what you offered her; of course you must keep your word. There must be no mistake about *that*!" the girl declared.

Owen's bewilderment visibly increased. "You think, then, as she does, that I *must* send down the police?"

The mixture of reluctance and dependence in this made her feel how much she was failing him. She had the sense of "chucking" him too. "No, no, not yet!" she said, though she had really no other and no better course to prescribe. "Doesn't it occur to you," she asked in a moment, "that if Mona is, as you say, drawing away, she may have, in doing so, a very high motive? She knows the immense value of all the objects detained by your mother, and to restore the spoils of Poynton she is ready—is that it!—to make a sacrifice. The sacrifice is that of an engagement she had entered upon with joy."

Owen had been blank a moment before, but he followed this argument with success—a success so immediate that it enabled him to produce with decision: "Ah, she's not that sort! She wants them herself," he added; "she wants to feel they're hers; she doesn't care whether I have them or not! And if she can't get them she doesn't want *me*. If she can't get them she doesn't want anything at all."

This was categoric; Fleda drank it in. "She takes such an interest in them?"

"So it appears."

"So much that they're *all*, and that she can let everything else absolutely depend upon them?"

Owen weighed her question as if he felt the responsibility of his answer. But that answer came in a moment, and, as Fleda could see, out of a wealth of memory. "She never wanted them particularly till they seemed to be in danger. Now she has an idea about them; and when she gets hold of an idea—Oh dear me!" He broke off, pausing and looking away as with a sense of the futility of expression: it was the first time Fleda had ever heard him explain a matter so pointedly or embark at all on a generalization. It was striking, it was touching to her, as he faltered, that he appeared but half capable of floating his generalization to the end. The girl, however, was so far competent to fill up his blank as that she had divined, on the occasion of Mona's visit to Poynton, what would happen in the event of the accident at which he glanced. She had there with her own eyes seen Owen's betrothed get hold of an idea. "I say, you know, *do* give me some tea!" he went on irrelevantly and familiarly.

Her profuse preparations had all this time had no sequel, and, with a laugh that she felt to be awkward, she hastily complied with his request. "It's sure to be horrid," she said; "we don't have at all good things." She offered him also bread and butter, of which he partook, holding his cup and saucer in his other hand and moving slowly about the room. She poured herself a cup, but not to take it; after which, without wanting it, she began to eat a small stale biscuit. She was struck with the extinction of the unwillingness she had felt at Ricks to contribute to the bandying between them of poor Mona's name; and under this influence she presently resumed: "Am I to understand that she engaged herself to marry you without caring for you?"

Owen looked out into Raphael Road. "She *did* care for me awfully. But she can't stand the strain."

"The strain of what?"

"Why, of the whole wretched thing."

"The whole thing has indeed been wretched, and I can easily conceive its effect upon her," Fleda said.

Her visitor turned sharp round. "You *can*?" There was a light in his strong stare. "You can understand it's spoiling her temper and making her come down on *me*? She behaves as if I were of no use to her at all!"

Fleda hesitated. "She's rankling under the sense of her wrong."

"Well, was it *I*, pray, who perpetrated the wrong? Ain't I doing what I can to get the thing arranged?"

The ring of his question made his anger at Mona almost resemble for a minute an anger at Fleda; and this resemblance in turn caused our young lady to observe how handsome he looked when he spoke, for the first time in her hearing, with that degree of heat, and used, also for the first time, such a term as "perpetrated." In addition, his challenge rendered still more vivid to her the mere flimsiness of her own aid. "Yes, you've been perfect," she said. "You've had a most difficult part. You've *had* to show tact and patience, as well as firmness, with your mother, and you've strikingly shown them. It's I who, quite unintentionally, have deceived you. I haven't helped you at all to your remedy."

"Well, you wouldn't at all events have ceased to like me, would you?" Owen demanded. It evidently mattered to him to know if she really justified Mona. "I mean of course if you *had* liked me—liked me as *she* liked me," he explained.

Fleda looked this inquiry in the face only long enough to recognize that, in her embarrassment, she must take instant refuge in a superior one. "I can answer that better if I know how kind to her you've been. *Have* you been kind to her?" she asked as simply as she could.

"Why, rather, Miss Vetch!" Owen declared. "I've done every blessed thing she wished. I rushed down to Ricks, as you saw, with fire and sword, and the day after that I went to see her at Waterbath." At this point he checked himself, though it was just the point at which her interest deepened. A different look had come into his face as he put down his empty teacup. "But why should I tell you such things, for any good it does me? I gather that you've no suggestion to make me now except that I shall request my solicitor to act. *Shall* I request him to act?"

Fleda scarcely heard his words; something new had suddenly come into her mind. "When you went to Waterbath after seeing me," she asked, "did you tell her all about that?"

Owen looked conscious. "All about it?"

"That you had had a long talk with me, without seeing your mother at all?"

"Oh yes, I told her exactly, and that you had been most awfully kind, and that I had placed the whole thing in your hands."

Fleda was silent a moment. "Perhaps that displeased her," she at last suggested.

"It displeased her fearfully," said Owen, looking very queer.

"Fearfully?" broke from the girl. Somehow, at the word, she was startled.

"She wanted to know what right you had to meddle. She said you were not honest."

"Oh!" Fleda cried, with a long wail. Then she controlled herself. "I see."

"She abused you, and I defended you. She denounced you—"

She checked him with a gesture. "Don't tell me what she did!" She had colored up to her eyes, where, as with the effect of a blow in the face, she quickly felt the tears gathering. It was a sudden drop in her great flight, a shock to her attempt to watch over what Mona was entitled to. While she had been straining her very soul in this attempt, the object of her magnanimity had been pronouncing her "not honest." She took it all in, however, and after an instant was able to speak with a smile. She would not have been surprised to learn, indeed, that her smile was strange. "You had said a while ago that your mother and I quarreled about you. It's much more true that you and Mona have quarreled about *me*."

Owen hesitated, but at last he brought it out. "What I mean to say is, don't you know, that Mona, if you don't mind my saying so, has taken it into her head to be jealous."

"I see," said Fleda. "Well, I dare say our conferences have looked very odd."

"They've looked very beautiful, and they've been very beautiful. Oh, I've told her the sort you are!" the young man pursued.

"That of course hasn't made her love me better."

"No, nor love me," said Owen. "Of course, you know, she says she loves me."

"And do you say you love her?"

"I say nothing else—I say it all the while. I said it the other day a dozen times." Fleda made no immediate rejoinder to this, and before she could choose one he repeated his question of a moment before. "*Am* I to tell my solicitor to act?"

She had at that moment turned away from this solution, precisely because she saw in it the great chance of her secret. If she should determine him to adopt it she might put out her hand and take him. It would shut in Mrs. Gereth's face the open door of surrender: she would flare up and fight, flying the flag of a passionate, an heroic defense. The case would obviously go against her, but the proceedings would last longer than Mona's patience or Owen's propriety. With a formal rupture he would be at large; and she had only to tighten her fingers round the string that would raise the curtain on that scene. "You tell me you 'say' you love her, but is there nothing more in it than your saying so? You wouldn't say so, would you, if it's not true? What in the world has become, in so short a time, of the affection that led to your engagement?"

"The deuce knows what has become of it, Miss Vetch!" Owen cried. "It seemed all to go to pot as this horrid struggle came on." He was close to her now, and, with his face lighted again by the relief of it, he looked all his helpless history into her eyes. "As I saw you and noticed you more, as I knew you better and better, I felt less and less—I couldn't help it—about anything or any one else. I wished I had known you sooner—I knew I should have liked you better than any one in the world. But it wasn't you who made the difference," he eagerly continued, "and I was awfully determined to stick to Mona to the death. It was she herself who made it, upon my soul, by the state she got into, the way she sulked, the way she took things, and the way she let me have it! She destroyed our prospects and our happiness, upon my honor. She made just the same smash of them as if she had kicked over that tea-table. She wanted to know all the while what was passing between us, between you and me; and she wouldn't take my solemn assurance that nothing was passing but what might have directly passed between me and old Mummy. She said a pretty girl like you was a nice old Mummy for me, and, if you'll believe it, she never called you anything else but that. I'll be hanged if I haven't been good, haven't I? I haven't breathed a breath of any sort to you, have I? You'd have been down on me hard if I had, wouldn't you? You're down on me pretty hard as it is, I think, aren't you? But I don't care what you say now, or what Mona says, either, or a single rap what any one says: she has given me at last, by her confounded behavior, a right to speak out, to utter the way I feel about it. The way I feel about it, don't you know, is that it had all better come to an end. You ask me if I don't love her, and I suppose it's natural enough you should. But you ask it at the very moment I'm half mad to say to you that there's only one person on the whole earth I *really* love, and that that person—" Here Owen pulled up short, and Fleda wondered if it was from the effect of his perceiving, through the closed door, the sound of steps and voices on the landing of the stairs. She had caught this sound herself with surprise and a vague uneasiness: it was not an hour at which her father ever came in, and there was no present reason why she should have a visitor. She had a fear, which after a few seconds deepened: a visitor was at hand; the visitor would be simply Mrs. Gereth. That lady wished for a near view of the consequence of her note to Owen. Fleda straightened herself with the instant thought that if this was what Mrs. Gereth desired Mrs. Gereth should have it in a form not to be mistaken. Owen's pause was the matter of a moment, but during that moment our young couple stood with their eyes holding each other's eyes and their ears catching the suggestion, still through the door, of a murmured conference in the hall. Fleda had begun to make the movement to cut it short when Owen stopped her with a grasp of her arm. "You're surely able to guess," he said, with his voice dropped and her arm pressed as she had never known such a drop or such a pressure—"you're surely able to guess the one person on earth I love?"

The handle of the door turned, and Fleda had only time to jerk at him: "Your mother!"

The door opened, and the smutty maid, edging in, announced "Mrs. Brigstock!"

XV

Mrs. Brigstock, in the doorway, stood looking from one of the occupants of the room to the other; then they saw her eyes attach themselves to a small object that had lain hitherto unnoticed on the carpet. This was the biscuit of which, on giving Owen his tea, Fleda had taken a perfunctory nibble: she had immediately laid it on the table, and that subsequently, in some precipitate movement, she should have brushed it off was doubtless a sign of the agitation that possessed her. For Mrs. Brigstock there was apparently more in it than met the eye. Owen at any rate picked it up, and Fleda felt as if he were removing the traces of some scene that the newspapers would have characterized as lively. Mrs. Brigstock clearly took in also the sprawling tea-things and the mark as of high water in the full faces of her young friends. These elements made the little place a vivid picture of intimacy. A minute was filled by Fleda's relief at finding her visitor not to be Mrs. Gereth, and a longer space by the ensuing sense of what was really more compromising in the actual apparition. It dimly occurred to her that the lady of Ricks had also written to Waterbath. Not only had Mrs. Brigstock never paid her a call, but Fleda would have been unable to figure her so employed. A year before the girl had spent a day under her roof, but never feeling that Mrs. Brigstock regarded this as constituting a bond. She had never stayed in any house but Poynton where the imagination of a bond, one way or the other, prevailed. After the first astonishment she dashed gayly at her guest, emphasizing her welcome and wondering how her whereabouts had become known at Waterbath. Had not Mrs. Brigstock quitted that residence for the very purpose of laying her hand on the associate of Mrs. Gereth's misconduct? The spirit in which this hand was to be laid our young lady was yet to ascertain; but she was a person who could think ten thoughts at once—a circumstance which, even putting her present plight at its worst, gave her a great advantage over a person who required easy conditions for dealing even with one. The very vibration of the air, however, told her that whatever Mrs. Brigstock's spirit might originally have been, it had been sharply affected by the sight of Owen. He was essentially a surprise: she had reckoned with everything that concerned him but his presence. With that, in awkward silence, she was reckoning now, as Fleda could see, while she effected with friendly aid an embarrassed transit to the sofa. Owen would be useless, would be deplorable: that aspect of the case Fleda had taken in as well. Another aspect was that he would admire her, adore her, exactly in proportion as she herself should rise gracefully superior. Fleda felt for the first time free to let herself "go," as Mrs. Gereth had said, and she was full of the sense that to "go" meant now to aim straight at the effect of moving Owen to rapture at her simplicity and tact. It was her impression that he had no positive dislike of Mona's mother; but she couldn't entertain that notion without a glimpse of the implication that he had a positive dislike of Mrs. Brigstock's daughter. Mona's mother declined tea, declined a better seat, declined a cushion, declined to remove her boa: Fleda guessed that she had not come on purpose to be dry, but that the voice of the invaded room had itself given her the hint.

"I just came on the mere chance," she said. "Mona found yesterday, somewhere, the card of invitation to your sister's marriage that you sent us, or your father sent us, some time ago. We couldn't be present—it was impossible; but as it had this address on it I said to myself that I might find you here."

"I'm very glad to be at home," Fleda responded.

"Yes, that doesn't happen very often, does it?" Mrs. Brigstock looked round afresh at Fleda's home.

"Oh, I came back from Ricks last week. I shall be here now till I don't know when."

"We thought it very likely you would have come back. We knew of course of your having been at Ricks. If I didn't find you I thought I might perhaps find Mr. Vetch," Mrs. Brigstock went on.

"I'm sorry he's out. He's always out—all day long."

Mrs. Brigstock's round eyes grew rounder. "All day long?"

"All day long," Fleda smiled.

"Leaving you quite to yourself?"

"A good deal to myself, but a little, to-day, as you see, to Mr. Gereth,—" and the girl looked at Owen to draw him into their sociability. For Mrs. Brigstock he had immediately sat down; but the movement had not corrected the sombre stiffness taking possession of him at the sight of her. Before he found a response to the appeal addressed to him Fleda turned again to her other visitor. "Is there any purpose for which you would like my father to call on you?"

Mrs. Brigstock received this question as if it were not to be unguardedly answered; upon which Owen intervened with pale irrelevance: "I wrote to Mona this morning of Miss Vetch's being in town; but of course the letter hadn't arrived when you left home."

"No, it hadn't arrived. I came up for the night—I've several matters to attend to." Then looking with an intention of fixedness from one of her companions to the other, "I'm afraid I've interrupted your conversation," Mrs. Brigstock said. She spoke without effectual point, had the air of merely announcing the fact. Fleda had not yet been confronted with the question of the sort of person Mrs. Brigstock was; she had only been confronted with the question of the sort of person Mrs. Gereth scorned her for being. She was really, somehow, no sort of person at all, and it came home to Fleda that if Mrs. Gereth could see her at this moment she would scorn her more than ever. She had a face of which it was impossible to say anything but that it was pink, and a mind that it would be possible to describe only if one had been able to mark it in a similar fashion. As nature had made this organ neither green nor blue nor yellow, there was nothing to know it by: it strayed and bleated like an unbranded sheep. Fleda felt for it at this moment much of the kindness of compassion, since Mrs. Brigstock had brought it with her to do something for her that she regarded as delicate. Fleda was quite prepared to help it to perform, if she should be able to gather what it wanted to do. What she gathered, however, more and more, was that it wanted to do something different from what it had wanted to do in leaving Waterbath. There was still nothing to enlighten her more specifically in the way her visitor continued: "You must be very much taken up. I believe you quite espouse his dreadful quarrel."

Fleda vaguely demurred. "His dreadful quarrel?"

"About the contents of the house. Aren't you looking after them for him?"

"She knows how awfully kind you've been to me," Owen said. He showed such discomfiture that he really gave away their situation; and Fleda found herself divided between the hope that he would take leave and the wish that he should see the whole of what the occasion might enable her to bring to pass for him.

She explained to Mrs. Brigstock. "Mrs. Gereth, at Ricks, the other day, asked me particularly to see him for her."

"And did she ask you also particularly to see him here in town?" Mrs. Brigstock's hideous bonnet seemed to argue for the unsophisticated truth; and it was on Fleda's lips to reply that such had indeed been Mrs. Gereth's request. But she checked herself, and before she could say anything else Owen had addressed their companion.

"I made a point of letting Mona know that I should be here, don't you see? That's exactly what I wrote her this morning."

"She would have had no doubt you would be here, if you had a chance," Mrs. Brigstock returned. "If your letter had arrived it might have prepared me for finding you here at tea. In that case I certainly wouldn't have come."

"I'm glad, then, it didn't arrive. Shouldn't you like him to go?" Fleda asked.

Mrs. Brigstock looked at Owen and considered: nothing showed in her face but that it turned a deeper pink. "I should like him to go with *me*." There was no menace in her tone, but she evidently knew what she wanted. As Owen made no response to this Fleda glanced at him to invite him to assent; then, for fear that he wouldn't, and would thereby make his case worse, she took upon herself to declare that she was sure he would be very glad to meet such a wish. She had no sooner spoken than she felt that the words had a bad effect of intimacy: she had answered for him as if she had been his wife. Mrs. Brigstock continued to regard him as if she had observed nothing, and she continued to address Fleda: "I've not seen him for a long time—I've particular things to say to him."

"So have I things to say to you, Mrs. Brigstock!" Owen interjected. With this he took up his hat as if for an immediate departure.

The other visitor meanwhile turned to Fleda. "What is Mrs. Gereth going to do?"

"Is that what you came to ask me?" Fleda demanded.

"That and several other things."

"Then you had much better let Mr. Gereth go, and stay by yourself and make me a pleasant visit. You can talk with him when you like, but it is the first time you've been to see me."

This appeal had evidently a certain effect; Mrs. Brigstock visibly wavered. "I can't talk with him whenever I like," she returned; "he hasn't been near us since I don't know when. But there are things that have brought me here."

"They are not things of any importance," Owen, to Fleda's surprise, suddenly asserted. He had not at first taken up Mrs. Brigstock's expression of a wish to carry him off: Fleda could see that the instinct at the bottom of this was that of standing by her, of seeming not to abandon her. But abruptly, all his soreness working within him, it had struck him that he should abandon her still more if he should leave her to be dealt with by her other visitor. "You must allow me to say, you know, Mrs. Brigstock, that I don't think you should come down on Miss Vetch about anything. It's very good of her to take the smallest interest in us and our horrid little squabble. If you want to talk about it, talk about it with *me*." He was flushed with the idea of protecting Fleda, of exhibiting his consideration for her. "I don't like your cross-questioning her, don't you see? She's as straight as a die: *I'll* tell you all about her!" he declared with an excited laugh. "Please come off with me and let her alone."

Mrs. Brigstock, at this, became vivid at once; Fleda thought she looked most peculiar. She stood straight up, with a queer distention of her whole person and of everything in her face but her mouth, which she gathered into a small, tight orifice. Fleda was painfully divided; her joy was deep within, but it was more relevant to the situation that she should not appear to associate herself with the tone of familiarity in which Owen addressed a lady who had been, and was perhaps still, about to become his mother-in-law. She laid on Mrs. Brigstock's arm a repressive hand. Mrs. Brigstock, however, had already exclaimed on her having so wonderful a defender. "He speaks, upon my word, as if I had come here to be rude to you!"

At this, grasping her hard, Fleda laughed; then she achieved the exploit of delicately kissing her. "I'm not in the least afraid to be alone with you, or of your tearing me to pieces. I'll answer any question that you can possibly dream of putting to me."

"I'm the proper person to answer Mrs. Brigstock's questions," Owen broke in again, "and I'm not a bit less ready to meet them than you are." He was firmer than she had ever seen him: it was as if she had not known he could be so firm.

"But she'll only have been here a few minutes. What sort of a visit is that?" Fleda cried.

"It has lasted long enough for my purpose. There was something I wanted to know, but I think I know it now."

"Anything you don't know I dare say I can tell you!" Owen observed as he impatiently smoothed his hat with the cuff of his coat.

Fleda by this time desired immensely to keep his companion, but she saw she could do so only at the cost of provoking on his part a further exhibition of the sheltering attitude, which he exaggerated precisely because it was the first thing, since he had begun to "like" her, that he had been able frankly to do for her. It was not in her interest that Mrs. Brigstock should be more struck than she already was with that benevolence. "There may be things you know that I don't," she presently said to her, with a smile. "But I've a sort of sense that you're laboring under some great mistake."

Mrs. Brigstock, at this, looked into her eyes more deeply and yearningly than she had supposed Mrs. Brigstock could look; it was the flicker of a certain willingness to give her a chance. Owen, however, quickly spoiled everything. "Nothing is more probable than that Mrs. Brigstock is doing what you say; but there's no one in the world to whom you owe an explanation. I may owe somebody one—I dare say I do; but not you, no!"

"But what if there's one that it's no difficulty at all for me to give?" Fleda inquired. "I'm sure that's the only one Mrs. Brigstock came to ask, if she came to ask any at all."

Again the good lady looked hard at her young hostess. "I came, I believe, Fleda, just, you know, to plead with you."

Fleda, with a bright face, hesitated a moment. "As if I were one of those bad women in a play?"

The remark was disastrous. Mrs. Brigstock, on whom her brightness was lost, evidently thought it singularly free. She turned away, as from a presence that had really defined itself as objectionable, and Fleda had a vain sense that her good humor, in which there was an idea, was taken for impertinence, or at least for levity. Her allusion was improper, even if she herself wasn't; Mrs. Brigstock's emotion simplified: it came to the same thing. "I'm quite ready," that lady said to Owen rather mildly and woundedly. "I do want to speak to you very much."

"I'm completely at your service." Owen held out his hand to Fleda. "Good-bye, Miss Vetch. I hope to see you again to-morrow." He opened the door for Mrs. Brigstock, who passed before the girl with an oblique, averted salutation. Owen and Fleda, while he stood at the door, then faced each other darkly and without speaking. Their eyes met once more for a long moment, and she was conscious there was something in hers that the darkness didn't quench, that he had never seen before and that he was perhaps never to see again. He stayed long enough to take it—to take it with a sombre stare that just showed the dawn of wonder; then he followed Mrs. Brigstock out of the house.

XVI

He had uttered the hope that he should see her the next day, but Fleda could easily reflect that he wouldn't see her if she were not there to be seen. If there was a thing in the world she desired at that moment, it was that the next day should have no point of resemblance with the day that had just elapsed. She accordingly aspired to an absence: she would go immediately down to Maggie. She ran out that evening and telegraphed to her sister, and in the morning she quitted London by an early train. She required for this step no reason but the sense of necessity. It was a strong personal need; she wished to interpose something, and there was nothing she could interpose but distance, but time. If Mrs. Brigstock had to deal with Owen she would allow Mrs. Brigstock the chance. To be there, to be in the midst of it, was the reverse of what she craved: she had already been more in the midst of it than had ever entered into her plan. At any rate she had renounced her plan; she had no plan now but the plan of separation. This was to abandon Owen, to give up the fine office of helping him back to his own; but when she had undertaken that office she had not foreseen that Mrs. Gereth would defeat it by a manœuvre so simple. The scene at her father's rooms had extinguished all offices, and the scene at her father's rooms was of Mrs. Gereth's producing. Owen, at all events, must now act for himself: he had obligations to meet, he had satisfactions to give, and Fleda fairly ached with the wish that he might be equal to them. She never knew the extent of her tenderness for him till she became conscious of the present force of her desire that he should be superior, be perhaps even sublime. She obscurely made out that superiority, that sublimity, mightn't after all be fatal. She closed her eyes and lived for a day or two in the mere beauty of confidence. It was with her on the short journey; it was with her at Maggie's; it glorified the mean little house in the stupid little town. Owen had grown larger to her: he would do, like a man, whatever he should have to do. He wouldn't be weak—not as she was: she herself was weak exceedingly.

Arranging her few possessions in Maggie's fewer receptacles, she caught a glimpse of the bright side of the fact that her old things were not such a problem as Mrs. Gereth's. Picking her way with Maggie through the local puddles, diving with her into smelly cottages and supporting her, at smellier shops, in firmness over the weight of joints and the taste of cheese, it was still her own secret that was universally inter-woven In the puddles, the cottages, the shops she was comfortably alone with it; that comfort prevailed even while, at the evening meal, her brother-in-law invited her attention to a diagram, drawn with a fork on too soiled a tablecloth, of the scandalous drains of the Convalescent Home. To be alone with it she had come away from Ricks; and now she knew that to be alone with it she had come away from London. This advantage was of course menaced, but not immediately destroyed, by the arrival, on the second day, of the note she had been sure she should receive from Owen. He had gone to West Kensington and found her flown, but he had got her address from the little maid and then hurried to a club and written to her. "Why have you left me just when I want you most?" he demanded. The next words, it was true, were more reassuring on the question of his steadiness. "I don't know what your reason may be," they went on, "nor why you've not left a line for me; but I don't think you can feel that I did anything yesterday that it wasn't right for me to do. As regards Mrs. Brigstock, certainly, I just felt what was right and I did it. She had no business whatever to attack you that way, and I should have been ashamed if I had left her there to worry you. I won't have you worried by any one; no one shall be disagreeable to you but me. I didn't mean to be so yesterday, and I don't to-day; but I'm perfectly free now to want you, and I want you much more than you've allowed me to explain. You'll see if I'm not all right, if you'll let me come to you. Don't be afraid—I'll not hurt you nor trouble you. I give you my honor I'll not hurt any one. Only I *must* see you, on what I had to say to Mrs. B. She was nastier than I thought she could be, but I'm behaving like an angel. I assure you I'm all right—that's exactly what I want you to see. You owe me something, you know, for what you said you would do and haven't done; what your departure without a word gives me to understand—doesn't it?—that you definitely can't do. Don't simply forsake me. See me, if you only see me once. I shan't wait for any leave—I shall come down to-morrow. I've been looking into trains and find there's something that will bring me down just after lunch and something very good for getting me back. I won't stop long. For God's sake, be there."

This communication arrived in the morning, but Fleda would still have had time to wire a protest. She debated on that alternative; then she read the note over and found in one phrase an exact statement of her duty. Owen's simplicity had expressed it, and her subtlety had nothing to answer. She owed him something for her obvious failure, and what she owed him was to receive him. If indeed she had known he would make this attempt she might have been held to have gained nothing by her flight. Well, she had gained what she had gained—she had gained the interval. She had no compunction for the greater trouble she should give the young man; it was now doubtless right that he should have as much trouble as possible. Maggie, who thought she was in her confidence, but was immensely not, had reproached her for having left Mrs. Gereth, and Maggie was just in this proportion gratified to hear of the visitor with whom, early in the afternoon, she would have to ask to be left alone. Maggie liked to see far, and now she could sit upstairs and rake the whole future. She had known that, as she familiarly said, there was something the matter with Fleda, and the value of that knowledge was augmented by the fact that there was apparently also something the matter with Mr. Gereth.

Fleda, downstairs, learned soon enough what this was. It was simply that, as he announced the moment he stood before her, he was now all right. When she asked him what he meant by that state he replied that he meant he could practically regard himself henceforth as a free man: he had had at West Kensington, as soon as they got into the street, such a horrid scene with Mrs. Brigstock.

"I knew what she wanted to say to me: that's why I was determined to get her off. I knew I shouldn't like it, but I was perfectly prepared," said Owen. "She brought it out as soon as we got round the corner; she asked me point-blank if I was in love with you."

"And what did you say to that?"

"That it was none of her business."

"Ah," said Fleda, "I'm not so sure!"

"Well, *I* am, and I'm the person most concerned. Of course I didn't use just those words: I was perfectly civil, quite as civil as she. But I told her I didn't consider she had a right to put me any such question. I said I wasn't sure that even Mona had, with the extraordinary line, you know, that Mona has taken. At any rate the whole thing, the way *I* put it, was between Mona and me; and between Mona and me, if she didn't mind, it would just have to remain."

Fleda was silent a little. "All that didn't answer her question."

"Then you think I ought to have told her?"

Again our young lady reflected. "I think I'm rather glad you didn't."

"I knew what I was about," said Owen. "It didn't strike me that she had the least right to come down on us that way and ask for explanations."

Fleda looked very grave, weighing the whole matter. "I dare say that when she started, when she arrived, she didn't mean to 'come down.'"

"What then did she mean to do?"

"What she said to me just before she went: she meant to plead with me."

"Oh, I heard her!" said Owen. "But plead with you for what?"

"For you, of course—to entreat me to give you up. She thinks me awfully designing—that I've taken some sort of possession of you."

Owen stared. "You haven't lifted a finger! It's I who have taken possession."

"Very true, you've done it all yourself." Fleda spoke gravely and gently, without a breath of coquetry. "But those are shades between which she's probably not obliged to distinguish. It's enough for her that we're singularly intimate."

"I am, but you're not!" Owen exclaimed.

Fleda gave a dim smile. "You make me at least feel that I'm learning to know you very well when I hear you say such a thing as that. Mrs. Brigstock came to get round me, to supplicate me," she went on; "but to find you there, looking so much at home, paying me a friendly call and shoving the tea-things about—that was too much for her patience. She doesn't know, you see, that I'm after all a decent girl. She simply made up her mind on the spot that I'm a very bad case."

"I couldn't stand the way she treated you, and that was what I had to say to her," Owen returned.

"She's simple and slow, but she's not a fool: I think she treated me, on the whole, very well." Fleda remembered how Mrs. Gereth had treated Mona when the Brigstocks came down to Poynton.

Owen evidently thought her painfully perverse. "It was you who carried it off; you behaved like a brick. And so did I, I consider. If you only knew the difficulty I had! I told her you were the noblest and straightest of women."

"That can hardly have removed her impression that there are things I put you up to."

"It didn't," Owen replied with candor. "She said our relation, yours and mine, isn't innocent."

"What did she mean by that?"

"As you may suppose, I particularly inquired. Do you know what she had the cheek to tell me?" Owen asked. "She didn't better it much: she said she meant that it's excessively unnatural."

Fleda considered afresh. "Well, it is!" she brought out at last.

"Then, upon my honor, it's only you who make it so!" Her perversity was distinctly too much for him. "I mean you make it so by the way you keep me off."

"Have I kept you off to-day?" Fleda sadly shook her head, raising her arms a little and dropping them.

Her gesture of resignation gave him a pretext for catching at her hand, but before he could take it she had put it behind her. They had been seated together on Maggie's single sofa, and her movement brought her to her feet, while Owen, looking at her reproachfully, leaned back in discouragement. "What good does it do me to be here when I find you only a stone?"

She met his eyes with all the tenderness she had not yet uttered, and she had not known till this moment how great was the accumulation. "Perhaps, after all," she risked, "there may be even in a stone still some little help for you."

Owen sat there a minute staring at her. "Ah, you're beautiful, more beautiful than any one," he broke out, "but I'll be hanged if I can ever understand you! On Tuesday, at your father's, you were beautiful—as beautiful, just before I left, as you are at this instant. But the next day, when I went back, I found it had apparently meant nothing; and now, again, that you let me come here and you shine at me like an angel, it doesn't bring you an inch nearer to saying what I want you to say." He remained a moment longer in the same position; then he jerked himself up. "What I want you to say is that you like me—what I want you to say is that you pity me." He sprang up and came to her. "What I want you to say is that you'll *save* me!"

Fleda hesitated. "Why do you need saving, when you announced to me just now that you're a free man?"

He too hesitated, but he was not checked. "It's just for the reason that I'm free. Don't you know what I mean, Miss Vetch? I want you to marry me."

Fleda, at this, put out her hand in charity; she held his own, which quickly grasped it a moment, and if he had described her as shining at him it may be assumed that she shone all the more in her deep, still smile. "Let me hear a little more about your freedom first," she said. "I gather that Mrs. Brigstock was not wholly satisfied with the way you disposed of her question."

"I dare say she wasn't. But the less she's satisfied the more I'm free."

"What bearing have *her* feelings, pray?" Fleda asked.

"Why, Mona's much worse than her mother. She wants much more to give me up."

"Then why doesn't she do it?"

"She will, as soon as her mother gets home and tells her."

"Tells her what?" Fleda inquired.

"Why, that I'm in love with *you*!"

Fleda debated. "Are you so very sure she will?"

"Certainly I'm sure, with all the evidence I already have. That will finish her!" Owen declared.

This made his companion thoughtful again. "Can you take such pleasure in her being 'finished'—a poor girl you've once loved?"

Owen waited long enough to take in the question; then with a serenity startling even to her knowledge of his nature, "I don't think I can have *really* loved her, you know," he replied.

Fleda broke into a laugh which gave him a surprise as visible as the emotion it testified to. "Then how am I to know that you 'really' love—anybody else?"

"Oh, I'll show you that!" said Owen.

"I must take it on trust," the girl pursued. "And what if Mona doesn't give you up?" she added.

Owen was baffled but a few seconds; he had thought of everything. "Why, that's just where you come in."

"To save you? I see. You mean I must get rid of her for you." His blankness showed for a little that he felt the chill of her cold logic; but as she waited for his rejoinder she knew to which of them it cost most. He gasped a minute, and that gave her time to say: "You see, Mr. Owen, how impossible it is to talk of such things yet!"

Like lightning he had grasped her arm. "You mean you *will* talk of them?" Then as he began to take the flood of assent from her eyes: "You *will* listen to me? Oh, you dear, you dear—when, when?"

"Ah, when it isn't mere misery!" The words had broken from her in a sudden loud cry, and what next happened was that the very sound of her pain upset her. She heard her own true note; she turned short away from him; in a moment she had burst into sobs; in another his arms were round her; the next she had let herself go so far that even Mrs. Gereth might have seen it. He clasped her, and she gave herself—she poured out her tears on his breast; something prisoned and pent throbbed and gushed; something deep and sweet surged up—something that came from far within and far off, that had begun with the sight of him in his indifference and had never had rest since then. The surrender was short, but the relief was long: she felt his lips upon her face and his arms tighten with his full divination. What she did, what she *had* done, she scarcely knew: she only was aware, as she broke from him again, of what had taken place in his own quick breast. What had taken place was that, with the click of a spring, he saw. He had cleared the high wall at a bound; they were together without a veil. She had not a shred of a secret left; it was as if a whirlwind had come and gone, laying low the great false front that she had built up stone by stone. The strangest thing of all was the momentary sense of desolation.

"Ah, all the while you *cared?*" Owen read the truth with a wonder so great that it was visibly almost a sadness, a terror caused by his sudden perception of where the impossibility was not. That made it all perhaps elsewhere.

"I cared, I cared, I cared!" Fleda moaned it as defiantly as if she were confessing a misdeed. "How couldn't I care? But you mustn't, you must never, never ask! It isn't for us to talk about!" she insisted. "Don't speak of it, don't speak!"

It was easy indeed not to speak when the difficulty was to find words. He clasped his hands before her as he might have clasped them at an altar; his pressed palms shook together while he held his breath and while she stilled herself in the effort to come round again to the real and the right. He helped this effort, soothing her into a seat with a touch as light as if she had really been something sacred. She sank into a chair and he dropped before her on his knees; she fell back with closed eyes and he buried his face in her lap. There was no way to thank her but this act of prostration, which lasted, in silence, till she laid consenting hands on him, touched his head and stroked it, held it in her tenderness till he acknowledged his long density. He made the avowal seem only his—made her, when she rose again, raise him at last, softly, as if from the abasement of shame. If in each other's eyes now, however, they saw the truth, this truth, to Fleda, looked harder even than before—all the harder that when, at the very moment she recognized it, he murmured to her ecstatically, in fresh possession of her hands, which he drew up to his breast, holding them tight there with both his own: "I'm saved, I'm saved,—I *am*! I'm ready for anything. I have your word. Come!" he cried, as if from the sight of a response slower than he needed, and in the tone he so often had of a great boy at a great game.

She had once more disengaged herself, with the private vow that he shouldn't yet touch her again. It was all too horribly soon—her sense of this was rapidly surging back. "We mustn't talk, we mustn't talk; we must *wait*!" she intensely insisted. "I don't know what you mean by your freedom; I don't see it, I don't feel it. Where is it yet, where, your freedom? If it's real there's plenty of time, and if it isn't there's more than enough. I hate myself," she protested, "for having anything to say about her: it's like waiting for dead men's shoes! What business is it of mine what she does? She has her own trouble and her own plan. It's too hideous to watch her and count on her!"

Owen's face, at this, showed a reviving dread, the fear of some darksome process of her mind. "If you speak for yourself I can understand, but why is it hideous for *me*?"

"Oh, I mean for myself!" Fleda said impatiently.

"*I* watch her, *I* count on her: how can I do anything else? If I count on her to let me definitely know how we stand, I do nothing in life but what she herself has led straight up to. I never thought of asking you to 'get rid of her' for me, and I never would have spoken to you if I hadn't held that I *am* rid of her, that she has backed out of the whole thing. Didn't she do so from the moment she began to put it off? I had already applied for the license; the very invitations were half addressed. Who but she, all of a sudden, demanded an unnatural wait? It was none of *my* doing; I had never dreamed of anything but coming up to the scratch." Owen grew more and more lucid, and more confident of the effect of his lucidity. "She called it 'taking a stand,' to see what mother would do. I told her mother would do what I would make her do; and to that she replied that she would like to see me make her first. I said I would arrange that everything should be all right, and she said she really preferred to arrange it herself. It was a flat refusal to trust me in the smallest degree. Why then had she pretended so tremendously to care for me? And of course, at present," said Owen, "she trusts me, if possible, still less."

124

Fleda paid this statement the homage of a minute's muteness. "As to that, naturally, she has reason."

"Why on earth has she reason?" Then, as his companion, moving away, simply threw up her hands, "I never looked at you—not to call looking—till she had regularly driven me to it," he went on. "I know what I'm about. I do assure you I'm all right!"

"You're not all right—you're all wrong!" Fleda cried in despair. "You mustn't stay here, you mustn't!" she repeated with clear decision. "You make me say dreadful things, and I feel as if I made *you* say them." But before he could reply she took it up in another tone. "Why in the world, if everything had changed, didn't you break off?"

"I?—" The inquiry seemed to have moved him to stupefaction. "Can you ask me that question when I only wanted to please you? Didn't you seem to show me, in your wonderful way, that that was exactly how? I didn't break off just on purpose to leave it to *her*. I didn't break off so that there shouldn't be a thing to be said against me."

The instant after her challenge Fleda had faced him again in self-reproof. "There *isn't* a thing to be said against you, and I don't know what nonsense you make me talk! You *have* pleased me, and you've been right and good, and it's the only comfort, and you must go. Everything must come from Mona, and if it doesn't come we've said entirely too much. You must leave me alone—forever."

"Forever?" Owen gasped.

"I mean unless everything is different."

"Everything *is* different—when I *know*!"

Fleda winced at what he knew; she made a wild gesture which seemed to whirl it out of the room. The mere allusion was like another embrace. "You know nothing— and you must go and wait! You mustn't break down at this point."

He looked about him and took up his hat: it was as if, in spite of frustration, he had got the essence of what he wanted and could afford to agree with her to the extent of keeping up the forms. He covered her with his fine, simple smile, but made no other approach. "Oh, I'm so awfully happy!" he exclaimed.

She hesitated: she would only be impeccable even though she should have to be sententious. "You'll be happy if you're perfect!" she risked.

125

He laughed out at this, and she wondered if, with a new-born acuteness, he saw the absurdity of her speech, and that no one was happy just because no one could be what she so lightly prescribed. "I don't pretend to be perfect, but I shall find a letter to-night!"

"So much the better, if it's the kind of one you desire." That was the most she could say, and having made it sound as dry as possible she lapsed into a silence so pointed as to deprive him of all pretext for not leaving her. Still, nevertheless, he stood there, playing with his hat and filling the long pause with a strained and anxious smile. He wished to obey her thoroughly, to appear not to presume on any advantage he had won from her; but there was clearly something he longed for beside. While he showed this by hanging on she thought of two other things. One of these was that his countenance, after all, failed to bear out his description of his bliss. As for the other, it had no sooner come into her head than she found it seated, in spite of her resolution, on her lips. It took the form of an inconsequent question. "When did you say Mrs. Brigstock was to have gone back?"

Owen stared. "To Waterbath? She was to have spent the night in town, don't you know? But when she left me, after our talk, I said to myself that she would take an evening train. I know I made her want to get home."

"Where did you separate?" Fleda asked.

"At the West Kensington station—she was going to Victoria. I had walked with her there, and our talk was all on the way."

Fleda pondered a moment. "If she did go back that night you would have heard from Waterbath by this time."

"I don't know," said Owen. "I thought I might hear this morning."

"She can't have gone back," Fleda declared. "Mona would have written on the spot."

"Oh yes, she *will* have written bang off!" Owen cheerfully conceded.

Fleda thought again. "Then, even in the event of her mother's not having got home till the morning, you would have had your letter at the latest to-day. You see she has had plenty of time."

Owen hesitated; then, "Oh, she's all right!" he laughed. "I go by Mrs. Brigstock's certain effect on her—the effect of the temper the old lady showed when we parted.

Do you know what she asked me?" he sociably continued. "She asked me in a kind of nasty manner if I supposed you 'really' cared anything about me. Of course I told her I supposed you didn't—not a solitary rap. How could I suppose you *do*, with your extraordinary ways? It doesn't matter; I could see she thought I lied."

"You should have told her, you know, that I had seen you in town only that one time," Fleda observed.

"By Jove, I did—for *you*! It was only for you."

Something in this touched the girl so that for a moment she could not trust herself to speak. "You're an honest man," she said at last. She had gone to the door and opened it. "Good-bye."

Even yet, however, he hung back; and she remembered how, at the end of his hour at Ricks, she had been put to it to get him out of the house. He had in general a sort of cheerful slowness which helped him at such times, though she could now see his strong fist crumple his big, stiff gloves as if they had been paper. "But even if there's no letter—" he began. He began, but there he left it.

"You mean, even if she doesn't let you off? Ah, you ask me too much!" Fleda spoke from the tiny hall, where she had taken refuge between the old barometer and the old mackintosh. "There are things too utterly for yourselves alone. How can I tell? What do I know? Good-bye, good-bye! If she doesn't let you off, it will be because she *is* attached to you."

"She's not, she's not: there's nothing in it! Doesn't a fellow know?—except with *you*!" Owen ruefully added. With this he came out of the room, lowering his voice to secret supplication, pleading with her really to meet him on the ground of the negation of Mona. It was this betrayal of his need of support and sanction that made her retreat—harden herself in the effort to save what might remain of all she had given, given probably for nothing. The very vision of him as he thus morally clung to her was the vision of a weakness somewhere in the core of his bloom, a blessed manly weakness of which, if she had only the valid right, it would be all a sweetness to take care. She faintly sickened, however, with the sense that there was as yet no valid right poor Owen could give. "You can take it from my honor, you know," he whispered, "that she loathes me."

Fleda had stood clutching the knob of Maggie's little painted stair-rail; she took, on the stairs, a step backward. "Why then doesn't she prove it in the only clear way?"

"She *has* proved it. Will you believe it if you see the letter?"

"I don't want to see any letter," said Fleda. "You'll miss your train."

Facing him, waving him away, she had taken another upward step; but he sprang to the side of the stairs and brought his hand, above the banister, down hard on her wrist. "Do you mean to tell me that I must marry a woman I hate?"

From her step she looked down into his raised face. "Ah, you see it's not true that you're free!" She seemed almost to exult. "It's not true—it's not true!"

He only, at this, like a buffeting swimmer, gave a shake of his head and repeated his question. "Do you mean to tell me I must marry such a woman?"

Fleda hesitated; he held her fast. "No. Anything is better than that."

"Then, in God's name, what must I do?"

"You must settle that with her. You mustn't break faith. Anything is better than that. You must at any rate be utterly sure. She *must* love you—how can she help it? *I* wouldn't give you up!" said Fleda. She spoke in broken bits, panting out her words. "The great thing is to keep faith. Where *is* a man if he doesn't? If he doesn't he may be so cruel. So cruel, so cruel, so cruel!" Fleda repeated. "I couldn't have a hand in *that*, you know: that's my position—that's mine. You offered her marriage: it's a tremendous thing for her." Then looking at him another moment, "*I* wouldn't give you up!" she said again. He still had hold of her arm; she took in his blank alarm. With a quick dip of her face she reached his hand with her lips, pressing them to the back of it with a force that doubled the force of her words. "Never, never, never!" she cried; and before he could succeed in seizing her she had turned and, scrambling up the stairs, got away from him even faster than she had got away from him at Ricks.

XVII

Ten days after his visit she received a communication from Mrs. Gereth—a telegram of eight words, exclusive of signature and date. "Come up immediately and stay with me here"—it was characteristically sharp, as Maggie said; but, as Maggie added, it was also characteristically kind. "Here" was an hotel in London, and Maggie had embraced a condition of life which already began to produce in her some yearning for hotels in London. She would have responded in an instant, and she was surprised that her sister seemed to hesitate. Fleda's hesitation, which lasted but an hour, was expressed in that young lady's own mind by the reflection that in obeying her friend's summons she shouldn't know what she should be "in for." Her friend's summons, however, was but another name for her friend's appeal; and Mrs. Gereth's bounty had laid her under obligations more sensible than any reluctance. In the event—that is at the end of her hour—she testified to her gratitude by taking the train and to her mistrust by leaving her luggage. She went as if she had gone up for the day. In the train, however, she had another thoughtful hour, during which it was her mistrust that mainly deepened. She felt as if for ten days she had sat in darkness, looking to the east for a dawn that had not yet glimmered. Her mind had lately been less occupied with Mrs. Gereth; it had been so exceptionally occupied with Mona. If the sequel was to justify Owen's prevision of Mrs. Brigstock's action upon her daughter, this action was at the end of a week as much a mystery as ever. The stillness, all round, had been exactly what Fleda desired, but it gave her for the time a deep sense of failure, the sense of a sudden drop from a height at which she had all things beneath her. She had nothing beneath her now; she herself was at the bottom of the heap. No sign had reached her from Owen—poor Owen, who had clearly no news to give about his precious letter from Waterbath. If Mrs. Brigstock had hurried back to obtain that this letter should be written, Mrs. Brigstock might then have spared herself so great an inconvenience. Owen had been silent for the best of all reasons—the reason that he had had nothing in life to say. If the letter had not been written he would simply have had to introduce some large qualification into his account of his freedom. He had left his young friend under her refusal to listen to him until he should be able, on the contrary, to extend that picture; and his present submission was all in keeping with the rigid honesty that his young friend had prescribed.

It was this that formed the element through which Mona loomed large; Fleda had enough imagination, a fine enough feeling for life, to be impressed with such an image of successful immobility. The massive maiden at Waterbath *was* successful from the moment she could entertain her resentments as if they had been poor relations who needn't put her to expense. She was a magnificent dead weight; there was something positive and portentous in her quietude. "What game are they all playing?" poor Fleda could only ask; for she had an intimate conviction that Owen was now under the roof of his betrothed. That was stupefying if he really hated Mona; and if he didn't really hate her what had brought him to Raphael Road and to Maggie's? Fleda had no real light, but she felt that to account for the absence of any result of their last meeting would take a supposition of the full sacrifice to charity that she had held up before him. If he had gone to Waterbath it had been simply because he had to go. She had as good as told him that he would have to go; that this was an inevitable incident of his keeping perfect faith—faith so literal that the smallest subterfuge would always be a reproach to him. When she tried to remember that it was for herself he was taking his risk, she felt how weak a way that was of expressing Mona's supremacy. There would be no need of keeping him up if there were nothing to keep him up to. Her eyes grew wan as she discerned in the impenetrable air that Mona's thick outline never wavered an inch. She wondered fitfully what Mrs. Gereth had by this time made of it, and reflected with a strange elation that the sand on which the mistress of Ricks had built a momentary triumph was quaking beneath the surface. As The Morning Post still held its peace, she would be, of course, more confident; but the hour was at hand at which Owen would have absolutely to do either one thing or the other. To keep perfect faith was to inform against his mother, and to hear the police at her door would be Mrs. Gereth's awakening. How much she was beguiled Fleda could see from her having been for a whole month quite as deep and dark as Mona. She had let her young friend alone because of the certitude, cultivated at Ricks, that Owen had done the opposite. He had done the opposite indeed, but much good had that brought forth! To have sent for her now, Fleda felt, was from this point of view wholly natural: she had sent for her to show at last how much she had scored. If, however, Owen was really at Waterbath the refutation of that boast was easy.

Fleda found Mrs. Gereth in modest apartments and with an air of fatigue in her distinguished face—a sign, as she privately remarked, of the strain of that effort to be discreet of which she herself had been having the benefit. It was a constant feature of their relation that this lady could make Fleda blench a little, and that the effect proceeded from the intense pressure of her confidence. If the confidence had been heavy even when the girl, in the early flush of devotion, had been able to feel herself most responsive, it drew her heart into her mouth now that she had reserves and conditions, now that she couldn't simplify with the same bold hand as her protectress. In the very brightening of the tired look, and at the moment of their embrace, Fleda felt on her shoulders the return of the load, so that her spirit frankly quailed as she asked herself what she had brought up from her trusted seclusion to support it. Mrs. Gereth's free manner always made a joke of weakness, and there was in such a welcome a richness, a kind of familiar nobleness, that suggested shame to a harried conscience. Something had happened, she could see, and she could also see, in the bravery that seemed to announce it had changed everything, a formidable assumption that what had happened was what a healthy young woman must like. The absence of luggage had made this young woman feel meagre even before her companion, taking in the bareness at a second glance, exclaimed upon it and roundly rebuked her. Of course she had expected her to stay.

Fleda thought best to show bravery too, and to show it from the first. "What you expected, dear Mrs. Gereth, is exactly what I came up to ascertain. It struck me as right to do that first. I mean to ascertain, without making preparations."

"Then you'll be so good as to make them on the spot!" Mrs. Gereth was most emphatic. "You're going abroad with me."

Fleda wondered, but she also smiled. "To-night—to-morrow?"

"In a few days as possible. That's all that's left for me now." Fleda's heart, at this, gave a bound; she wondered to what particular difference in Mrs. Gereth's situation as last known to her it was an allusion. "I've made my plan," her friend continued: "I go for at least a year. We shall go straight to Florence; we can manage there. I of course don't look to you, however," she added, "to stay with me all that time. That will require to be settled. Owen will have to join us as soon as possible; he may not be quite ready to get off with us. But I'm convinced it's quite the right thing to go. It will make a good change; it will put in a decent interval."

Fleda listened; she was deeply mystified. "How kind you are to me!" she presently said. The picture suggested so many questions that she scarcely knew which to ask first. She took one at a venture. "You really have it from Mr. Gereth that he'll give us his company?"

If Mr. Gereth's mother smiled in response to this, Fleda knew that her smile was a tacit criticism of such a form of reference to her son. Fleda habitually spoke of him as Mr. Owen, and it was a part of her present vigilance to appear to have relinquished that right. Mrs. Gereth's manner confirmed a certain impression of her pretending to more than she felt; her very first words had conveyed it, and it reminded Fleda of the conscious courage with which, weeks before, the lady had met her visitor's first startled stare at the clustered spoils of Poynton. It was her practice to take immensely for granted whatever she wished. "Oh, if you'll answer for him, it will do quite as well!" she said. Then she put her hands on the girl's shoulders and held them at arm's length, as if to shake them a little, while in the depths of her shining eyes Fleda discovered something obscure and unquiet. "You bad, false thing, why didn't you tell me?" Her tone softened her harshness, and her visitor had never had such a sense of her indulgence. Mrs. Gereth could show patience; it was a part of the general bribe, but it was also like the handing in of a heavy bill before which Fleda could only fumble in a penniless pocket. "You must perfectly have known at Ricks, and yet you practically denied it. That's why I call you bad and false!" It was apparently also why she again almost roughly kissed her.

"I think that before I answer you I had better know what you're talking about," Fleda said.

Mrs. Gereth looked at her with a slight increase of hardness. "You've done everything you need for modesty, my dear! If he's sick with love of you, you haven't had to wait for me to inform you."

Fleda hesitated. "Has he informed *you*, dear Mrs. Gereth?"

Dear Mrs. Gereth smiled sweetly. "How could he, when our situation is such that he communicates with me only through you, and that you are so tortuous you conceal everything?"

"Didn't he answer the note in which you let him know that I was in town?" Fleda asked.

"He answered it sufficiently by rushing off on the spot to see you."

Mrs. Gereth met that allusion with a prompt firmness that made almost insolently light of any ground of complaint, and Fleda's own sense of responsibility was now so vivid that all resentments turned comparatively pale. She had no heart to produce a grievance; she could only, left as she was with the little mystery on her hands, produce, after a moment, a question. "How then do you come to know that your son has ever thought—"

"That he would give his ears to get you?" Mrs. Gereth broke in. "I had a visit from Mrs. Brigstock."

Fleda opened her eyes. "She went down to Ricks?"

"The day after she had found Owen at your feet. She knows everything."

Fleda shook her head sadly; she was more startled than she cared to show. This odd journey of Mrs. Brigstock's, which, with a simplicity equal for once to Owen's, she had not divined, now struck her as having produced the hush of the last ten days. "There are things she doesn't know!" she presently exclaimed.

"She knows he would do anything to marry you."

"He hasn't told her so," Fleda said.

"No, but he has told you. That's better still!" laughed Mrs. Gereth. "My dear child," she went on with an air that affected the girl as a sort of blind profanity, "don't try to make yourself out better than you are. *I* know what you are. I haven't lived with you so much for nothing. You're not quite a saint in heaven yet. Lord, what a creature you'd have thought me in my good time! But you do like it, fortunately, you idiot. You're pale with your passion, you sweet thing. That's exactly what I wanted to see. I can't for the life of me think where the shame comes in." Then with a finer significance, a look that seemed to Fleda strange, she added: "It's all right."

"I've seen him but twice," said Fleda.

"But twice?" Mrs. Gereth still smiled.

"On the occasion, at papa's, that Mrs. Brigstock told you of, and one day, since then, down at Maggie's."

"Well, those things are between yourselves, and you seem to me both poor creatures at best." Mrs. Gereth spoke with a rich humor which tipped with light for an instant a real conviction. "I don't know what you've got in your veins: you absurdly exaggerated the difficulties. But enough is as good as a feast, and when once I get you abroad together—!" She checked herself as if from excess of meaning; what might happen when she should get them abroad together was to be gathered only from the way she slowly rubbed her hands.

The gesture, however, made the promise so definite that for a moment her companion was almost beguiled. But there was nothing to account, as yet, for the wealth of Mrs. Gereth's certitude: the visit of the lady of Waterbath appeared but half to explain it. "Is it permitted to be surprised," Fleda deferentially asked, "at Mrs. Brigstock's thinking it would help her to see you?"

"It's never permitted to be surprised at the aberrations of born fools," said Mrs. Gereth. "If a cow should try to calculate, that's the kind of happy thought she'd have. Mrs. Brigstock came down to plead with me."

Fleda mused a moment. "That's what she came to do with *me*," she then honestly returned. "But what did she expect to get of you, with your opposition so marked from the first?"

"She didn't know I want *you*, my dear. It's a wonder, with all my violence—the gross publicity I've given my desires. But she's as stupid as an owl—she doesn't feel your charm."

Fleda felt herself flush slightly, but she tried to smile. "Did you tell her all about it? Did you make her understand you want me?"

"For what do you take me? I wasn't such a donkey."

"So as not to aggravate Mona?" Fleda suggested.

"So as not to aggravate Mona, naturally. We've had a narrow course to steer, but thank God we're at last in the open!"

"What do you call the open, Mrs. Gereth?" Fleda demanded. Then as the other faltered: "Do you know where Mr. Owen is to-day?"

Mrs. Gereth stared. "Do you mean he's at Waterbath? Well, that's your own affair. I can bear it if *you* can."

"Wherever he is, I can bear it," Fleda said. "But I haven't the least idea where he is."

"Then you ought to be ashamed of yourself!" Mrs. Gereth broke out with a change of note that showed how deep a passion underlay everything she had said. The poor woman, catching her companion's hand, however, the next moment, as if to retract something of this harshness, spoke more patiently. "Don't you understand, Fleda, how immensely, how devotedly, I've trusted you?" Her tone was indeed a supplication.

Fleda was infinitely shaken; she was silent a little. "Yes, I understand. Did she go to you to complain of me?"

"She came to see what she could do. She had been tremendously upset, the day before, by what had taken place at your father's, and she had posted down to Ricks on the inspiration of the moment. She hadn't meant it on leaving home; it was the sight of you closeted there with Owen that had suddenly determined her. The whole story, she said, was written in your two faces: she spoke as if she had never seen such an exhibition. Owen was on the brink, but there might still be time to save him, and it was with this idea she had bearded me in my den. 'What won't a mother do, you know?'—that was one of the things she said. What wouldn't a mother do indeed? I thought I had sufficiently shown her what! She tried to break me down by an appeal to my good nature, as she called it, and from the moment she opened on *you*, from the moment she denounced Owen's falsity, I was as good-natured as she could wish. I understood that it was a plea for mere mercy, that you and he between you were killing her child. Of course I was delighted that Mona should be killed, but I was studiously kind to Mrs. Brigstock. At the same time I was honest, I didn't pretend to anything I couldn't feel. I asked her why the marriage hadn't taken place months ago, when Owen was perfectly ready; and I showed her how completely that fatuous mistake on Mona's part cleared his responsibility. It was she who had killed *him*—it was she who had destroyed his affection, his illusions. Did she want him now when he was estranged, when he was disgusted, when he had a sore grievance? She reminded me that Mona had a sore grievance too, but she admitted that she hadn't come to me to speak of that. What she had come to me for was not to get the old things back, but simply to get Owen. What she wanted was that I would, in simple pity, see fair play. Owen had been awfully bedeviled—she didn't call it that, she called it 'misled'—but it was simply you who had bedeviled him. He would be all right still if I would see that you were out of the way. She asked me point-blank if it was possible I could want him to marry you."

Fleda had listened in unbearable pain and growing terror, as if her interlocutress, stone by stone, were piling some fatal mass upon her breast. She had the sense of being buried alive, smothered in the mere expansion of another will; and now there was but one gap left to the air. A single word, she felt, might close it, and with the question that came to her lips as Mrs. Gereth paused she seemed to herself to ask, in cold dread, for her doom. "What did you say to that?" she inquired.

"I was embarrassed, for I saw my danger—the danger of her going home and saying to Mona that I was backing you up. It had been a bliss to learn that Owen had really turned to you, but my joy didn't put me off my guard. I reflected intensely for a few seconds; then I saw my issue."

"Your issue?" Fleda murmured.

"I remembered how you had tied my hands about saying a word to Owen."

Fleda wondered. "And did you remember the little letter that, with your hands tied, you still succeeded in writing to him?"

"Perfectly; my little letter was a model of reticence. What I remembered was all that in those few words I forbade myself to say. I had been an angel of delicacy—I had effaced myself like a saint. It was not for me to have done all that and then figure to such a woman as having done the opposite. Besides, it was none of her business."

"Is that what you said to her?" Fleda asked.

"I said to her that her question revealed a total misconception of the nature of my present relations with my son. I said to her that I had no relations with him at all, and that nothing had passed between us for months. I said to her that my hands were spotlessly clean of any attempt to make him make up to you. I said to her that I had taken from Poynton what I had a right to take, but had done nothing else in the world. I was determined that if I had bit my tongue off to oblige you I would at least have the righteousness that my sacrifice gave me."

"And was Mrs. Brigstock satisfied with your answer?"

"She was visibly relieved."

"It was fortunate for you," said Fleda, "that she's apparently not aware of the manner in which, almost under her nose, you advertised me to him at Poynton."

Mrs. Gereth appeared to recall that scene; she smiled with a serenity remarkably effective as showing how cheerfully used she had grown to invidious allusions to it. "How should she be aware of it?"

"She would if Owen had described your outbreak to Mona."

"Yes, but he didn't describe it. All his instinct was to conceal it from Mona. He wasn't conscious, but he was already in love with you!" Mrs. Gereth declared.

Fleda shook her head wearily. "No—I was only in love with him!"

Here was a faint illumination with which Mrs. Gereth instantly mingled her fire. "You dear old wretch!" she exclaimed; and she again, with ferocity, embraced her young friend.

Fleda submitted like a sick animal: she would submit to everything now. "Then what further passed?"

"Only that she left me thinking she had got something."

"And what had she got?"

"Nothing but her luncheon. But *I* got everything!"

"Everything?" Fleda quavered.

Mrs. Gereth, struck apparently by something in her tone, looked at her from a tremendous height. "Don't fail me now!"

It sounded so like a menace that, with a full divination at last, the poor girl fell weakly into a chair. "What on earth have you done?"

Mrs. Gereth stood there in all the glory of a great stroke. "I've settled you." She filled the room, to Fleda's scared vision, with the glare of her magnificence. "I've sent everything back."

"Everything?" Fleda gasped.

"To the smallest snuff-box. The last load went yesterday. The same people did it. Poor little Ricks is empty." Then as if, for a crowning splendor, to check all deprecation, "They're yours, you goose!" Mrs. Gereth concluded, holding up her handsome head and rubbing her white hands. Fleda saw that there were tears in her deep eyes.

XVIII

She was slow to take in the announcement, but when she had done so she felt it to be more than her cup of bitterness would hold. Her bitterness was her anxiety, the taste of which suddenly sickened her. What had she become, on the spot, but a traitress to her friend? The treachery increased with the view of the friend's motive, a motive magnificent as a tribute to her value. Mrs. Gereth had wished to make sure of her and had reasoned that there would be no such way as by a large appeal to her honor. If it be true, as men have declared, that the sense of honor is weak in women, some of the bearings of this stroke might have thrown a light on the question. What was now, at all events, put before Fleda was that she had been made sure of, for the greatness of the surrender imposed an obligation as great. There was an expression she had heard used by young men with whom she danced: the only word to fit Mrs. Gereth's intention was that Mrs. Gereth had designed to "fetch" her. It was a calculated, it was a crushing bribe; it looked her in the eyes and said simply: "That's what I do for you!" What Fleda was to do in return required no pointing out. The sense, at present, of how little she had done made her almost cry aloud with pain; but her first endeavor, in the face of the fact, was to keep such a cry from reaching her companion. How little she had done Mrs. Gereth didn't yet know, and possibly there would be still some way of turning round before the discovery. On her own side too Fleda had almost made one: she had known she was wanted, but she had not after all conceived how magnificently much. She had been treated by her friend's act as a conscious prize, but what made her a conscious prize was only the power the act itself imputed to her. As high, bold diplomacy it dazzled and carried her off her feet. She admired the noble risk of it, a risk Mrs. Gereth had faced for the utterly poor creature that the girl now felt herself. The change it instantly wrought in her was, moreover, extraordinary: it transformed at a touch her emotion on the subject of concessions. A few weeks earlier she had jumped at the duty of pleading for them, practically quarreling with the lady of Ricks for her refusal to restore what she had taken. She had been sore with the wrong to Owen, she had bled with the wounds of Poynton; now however, as she heard of the replenishment of the void that had so haunted her, she came as near sounding an alarm as if from the deck of a ship she had seen a person she loved jump into the sea. Mrs. Gereth had become in a flash the victim; poor little Ricks had been laid bare in a night. If Fleda's feeling about the old things had taken precipitate form the form would have been a frantic command. It was indeed for mere want of breath that she didn't shout: "Oh, stop them—it's no use; bring them back—it's too late!" And what most kept her breathless was her companion's very grandeur. Fleda distinguished as never before the purity of such a passion; it made Mrs. Gereth august and almost sublime. It was absolutely unselfish—she cared nothing for mere possession. She thought solely and incorruptibly of what was best for the things; she had surrendered them to the presumptive care of the one person of her acquaintance who felt about them as she felt herself, and whose long lease of the future would be the nearest approach that could be compassed to committing them to a museum. Now it was indeed that Fleda knew what rested on her; now it was also that she measured as if for the first time Mrs. Gereth's view of the natural influence of a fine acquisition. She had adopted the idea of blowing away the last doubt of what her young friend would gain, of making good still more than she was obliged to make it the promise of weeks before. It was one thing for the girl to have heard that in a certain event restitution would be made; it was another for her to see the condition, with a noble trust, treated in advance as performed, and to be able to feel that she should have only to open a door to find every old piece in every old corner. To have played such a card was therefore, practically, for Mrs. Gereth, to have won the game. Fleda had certainly to recognize that, so far as the theory of the matter went, the game had been won. Oh, she had been made sure of!

She couldn't, however, succeed for so very many minutes in deferring her exposure. "Why didn't you wait, dearest? Ah, why didn't you wait?"—if that inconsequent appeal kept rising to her lips to be cut short before it was spoken, this was only because at first the humility of gratitude helped her to gain time, enabled her to present herself very honestly as too overcome to be clear. She kissed her companion's hands, she did homage at her feet, she murmured soft snatches of praise, and yet in the midst of it all was conscious that what she really showed most was the wan despair at her heart. She saw Mrs. Gereth's glimpse of this despair suddenly widen, heard the quick chill of her voice pierce through the false courage of endearments. "Do you mean to tell me at such an hour as this that you've really lost him?"

The tone of the question made the idea a possibility for which Fleda had nothing from this moment but terror. "I don't know, Mrs. Gereth; how can I say?" she asked. "I've not seen him for so long; as I told you just now, I don't even know where he is. That's by no fault of his," she hurried on: "he would have been with me every day if I had consented. But I made him understand, the last time, that I'll receive him again only when he's able to show me that his release has been complete and definite. Oh, he can't yet, don't you see, and that's why he hasn't been back. It's far better than his coming only that we should both be miserable. When he does come he'll be in a better position. He'll be tremendously moved by the splendid thing you've done. I know you wish me to feel that you've done it as much for me as for Owen, but your having done it for me is just what will delight him most! When he hears of it," said Fleda, in desperate optimism, "when he hears of it—" There indeed, regretting her advance, she quite broke down. She was wholly powerless to say what Owen would do when he heard of it. "I don't know what he won't make of you and how he won't hug you!" she had to content herself with lamely declaring. She had drawn Mrs. Gereth to a sofa with a vague instinct of pacifying her and still, after all, gaining time; but it was a position in which her great duped benefactress, portentously patient again during this demonstration, looked far from inviting a "hug." Fleda found herself tricking out the situation with artificial flowers, trying to talk even herself into the fancy that Owen, whose name she now made simple and sweet, might come in upon them at any moment. She felt an immense need to be understood and justified; she averted her face in dread from all that she might have to be forgiven. She pressed on her companion's arm as if to keep her quiet till she should really know, and then, after a minute, she poured out the clear essence of what in happier days had been her "secret." "You mustn't think I don't adore him when I've told him so to his face. I love him so that I'd die for him—I love him so that it's horrible. Don't look at me therefore as if I had not been kind, as if I had not been as tender as if he were dying and my tenderness were what would save him. Look at me as if you believe me, as if you feel what I've been through. Darling Mrs. Gereth, I could kiss the ground he walks on. I haven't a rag of pride; I used to have, but it's gone. I used to have a secret, but every one knows it now, and any one who looks at me can say, I think, what's the matter with me. It's not so very fine, my secret, and the less one really says about it the better; but I want you to have it from me because I was stiff before. I want you to see for yourself that I've been brought as low as a girl can very well be. It serves me right," Fleda laughed, "if I was ever proud and horrid to you! I don't know what you wanted me, in those days at Ricks, to do, but I don't think you can have wanted much more than what I've done. The other day at Maggie's I did things that made me, afterwards, think of you! I don't know what girls may do; but if he doesn't know that there isn't an inch of me that isn't his—!" Fleda sighed as if she couldn't express it; she piled it up, as she would have said; holding Mrs. Gereth with dilated eyes, she seemed to sound her for the effect of these words. "It's idiotic," she wearily smiled; "it's so strange that I'm almost angry for it, and the strangest part of all is that it isn't even happiness. It's anguish—it was from the first; from the first there was a bitterness and a kind of dread. But I owe you every word of the truth. You don't do him justice, either: he's a dear, I assure you he's a dear. I'd trust him to the last breath; I don't think you really know him. He's ever so much cleverer than he makes a show of; he's remarkable in his own shy way. You told me at Ricks that you wanted me to let myself go, and I've 'gone' quite far enough to discover as much as that, as well as all sorts of other delightful things about him. You'll tell me I make myself out worse than I am," said the girl, feeling more and more in her companion's attitude a quality that treated her speech as a desperate rigmarole and even perhaps as a piece of cold immodesty. She wanted to make herself out "bad"—it was a part of her justification; but it suddenly occurred to her that such a picture of her extravagance imputed a want of gallantry to the young man. "I don't care for anything you think," she declared, "because Owen, don't you know, sees me as I am. He's so kind that it makes up for everything!"

This attempt at gayety was futile; the silence with which, for a minute, her adversary greeted her troubled plea brought home to her afresh that she was on the bare defensive. "Is it a part of his kindness never to come near you?" Mrs. Gereth inquired at last. "Is it a part of his kindness to leave you without an inkling of where he is?" She rose again from where Fleda had kept her down; she seemed to tower there in the majesty of her gathered wrong. "Is it a part of his kindness that, after I've toiled as I've done for six days, and with my own weak hands, which I haven't spared, to denude myself, in your interest, to that point that I've nothing left, as I may say, but what I have on my back—is it a part of his kindness that you're not even able to produce him for me?"

There was a high contempt in this which was for Owen quite as much, and in the light of which Fleda felt that her effort at plausibility had been mere groveling. She rose from the sofa with an humiliated sense of rising from ineffectual knees. That discomfort, however, lived but an instant: it was swept away in a rush of loyalty to the absent. She herself could bear his mother's scorn; but to avert it from his sweet innocence she broke out with a quickness that was like the raising of an arm. "Don't blame him—don't blame him: he'd do anything on earth for me! It was I," said Fleda, eagerly, "who sent him back to her; I made him go; I pushed him out of the house; I declined to have anything to say to him except on another footing."

Mrs. Gereth stared as at some gross material ravage. "Another footing? What other footing?"

"The one I've already made so clear to you: my having it in black and white, as you may say, from her that she freely gives him up."

141

"Then you think he lies when he tells you that he has recovered his liberty?"

Fleda hesitated a moment; after which she exclaimed with a certain hard pride: "He's enough in love with me for anything!"

"For anything, apparently, except to act like a man and impose his reason and his will on your incredible folly. For anything except to put an end, as any man worthy of the name would have put it, to your systematic, to your idiotic perversity. What are you, after all, my dear, I should like to know, that a gentleman who offers you what Owen offers should have to meet such wonderful exactions, to take such extraordinary precautions about your sweet little scruples?" Her resentment rose to a strange insolence which Fleda took full in the face and which, for the moment at least, had the horrible force to present to her vengefully a showy side of the truth. It gave her a blinding glimpse of lost alternatives. "I don't know what to think of him," Mrs. Gereth went on; "I don't know what to call him: I'm so ashamed of him that I can scarcely speak of him even to *you*. But indeed I'm so ashamed of you both together that I scarcely know in common decency where to look." She paused to give Fleda the full benefit of this remarkable statement; then she exclaimed: "Any one but a jackass would have tucked you under his arm and marched you off to the Registrar!"

Fleda wondered; with her free imagination she could wonder even while her cheek stung from a slap. "To the Registrar?"

"That would have been the sane, sound, immediate course to adopt. With a grain of gumption you'd both instantly have felt it. *I* should have found a way to take you, you know, if I'd been what Owen's supposed to be. *I* should have got the business over first; the rest could come when you liked! Good God, girl, your place was to stand before me as a woman honestly married. One doesn't know what one has hold of in touching you, and you must excuse my saying that you're literally unpleasant to me to meet as you are. Then at least we could have talked, and Owen, if he had the ghost of a sense of humor, could have snapped his fingers at your refinements."

This stirring speech affected our young lady as if it had been the shake of a tambourine borne towards her from a gypsy dance: her head seemed to go round and she felt a sudden passion in her feet. The emotion, however, was but meagrely expressed in the flatness with which she heard herself presently say: "I'll go to the Registrar now."

"Now?" Magnificent was the sound Mrs. Gereth threw into this monosyllable. "And pray who's to take you?" Fleda gave a colorless smile, and her companion continued: "Do you literally mean that you can't put your hand upon him?" Fleda's wan grimace appeared to irritate her; she made a short, imperious gesture. "Find him for me, you fool—*find* him for me!"

"What do you want of him," Fleda sadly asked, "feeling as you do to both of us?"

"Never mind how I feel, and never mind what I say when I'm furious!" Mrs. Gereth still more incisively added. "Of course I cling to you, you wretches, or I shouldn't suffer as I do. What I want of him is to see that he takes you; what I want of him is to go with you myself to the place." She looked round the room as if, in feverish haste, for a mantle to catch up; she bustled to the window as if to spy out a cab: she would allow half an hour for the job. Already in her bonnet, she had snatched from the sofa a garment for the street: she jerked it on as she came back. "Find him, find him," she repeated; "come straight out with me, to try, at least, to get at him!"

"How can I get at him? He'll come when he's ready," Fleda replied.

Mrs. Gereth turned on her sharply. "Ready for what? Ready to see me ruined without a reason or a reward?"

Fleda was silent; the worst of it all was that there was something unspoken between them. Neither of them dared to utter it, but the influence of it was in the girl's tone when she returned at last, with great gentleness: "Don't be harsh to me—I'm very unhappy." The words produced a visible impression on Mrs. Gereth, who held her face averted and sent off through the window a gaze that kept pace with the long caravan of her treasures. Fleda knew she was watching it wind up the avenue of Poynton—Fleda participated indeed fully in the vision; so that after a little the most consoling thing seemed to her to add: "I don't see why in the world you take so for granted that he's, as you say, 'lost.'"

Mrs. Gereth continued to stare out of the window, and her stillness denoted some success in controlling herself. "If he's not lost, why are you unhappy?"

"I'm unhappy because I torment you, and you don't understand me."

"No, Fleda, I don't understand you," said Mrs. Gereth, finally facing her again. "I don't understand you at all, and it's as if you and Owen were of quite another race and another flesh. You make me feel very old-fashioned and simple and bad. But you must take me as I am, since you take so much else *with* me!" She spoke now with the drop of her resentment, with a dry and weary calm. "It would have been better for me if I had never known you," she pursued, "and certainly better if I hadn't taken such an extraordinary fancy to you. But that too was inevitable: everything, I suppose, is inevitable. It was all my own doing—you didn't run after me: I pounced on you and caught you up. You're a stiff little beggar, in spite of your pretty manners: yes, you're hideously misleading. I hope you feel how handsome it is of me to recognize the independence of your character. It was your clever sympathy that did it—your extraordinary feeling for those accursed vanities. You were sharper about them than any one I had ever known, and that was a thing I simply couldn't resist. Well," the poor lady concluded after a pause, "you see where it has landed us!"

"If you'll go for him yourself, I'll wait here," said Fleda.

Mrs. Gereth, holding her mantle together, appeared for a while to consider.

"To his club, do you mean?"

"Isn't it there, when he's in town, that he has a room? He has at present no other London address," Fleda said: "it's there one writes to him."

"How do *I* know, with my wretched relations with him?" Mrs. Gereth asked.

"Mine have not been quite so bad as that," Fleda desperately smiled. Then she added: "His silence, *her* silence, our hearing nothing at all—what are these but the very things on which, at Poynton and at Ricks, you rested your assurance that everything is at an end between them?"

Mrs. Gereth looked dark and void. "Yes, but I hadn't heard from you then that you could invent nothing better than, as you call it, to send him back to her."

"Ah, but, on the other hand, you've learned from them what you didn't know—you've learned by Mrs. Brigstock's visit that he cares for me." Fleda found herself in the position of availing herself of optimistic arguments that she formerly had repudiated; her refutation of her companion had completely changed its ground.

She was in a fever of ingenuity and painfully conscious, on behalf of her success, that her fever was visible. She could herself see the reflection of it glitter in Mrs. Gereth's sombre eyes.

"You plunge me in stupefaction," that lady answered, "and at the same time you terrify me. Your account of Owen is inconceivable, and yet I don't know what to hold on by. He cares for you, it does appear, and yet in the same breath you inform me that nothing is more possible than that he's spending these days at Waterbath. Excuse me if I'm so dull as not to see my way in such darkness. If he's at Waterbath he doesn't care for you. If he cares for you he's not at Waterbath."

"Then where is he?" poor Fleda helplessly wailed. She caught herself up, however; she did her best to be brave and clear. Before Mrs. Gereth could reply, with due obviousness, that this was a question for her not to ask, but to answer, she found an air of assurance to say: "You simplify far too much. You always did and you always will. The tangle of life is much more intricate than you've ever, I think, felt it to be. You slash into it," cried Fleda finely, "with a great pair of shears, you nip at it as if you were one of the Fates! If Owen's at Waterbath he's there to wind everything up."

Mrs. Gereth shook her head with slow austerity. "You don't believe a word you're saying. I've frightened you, as you've frightened me: you're whistling in the dark to keep up our courage. I do simplify, doubtless, if to simplify is to fail to comprehend the insanity of a passion that bewilders a young blockhead with bugaboo barriers, with hideous and monstrous sacrifices. I can only repeat that you're beyond me. Your perversity's a thing to howl over. However," the poor woman continued with a break in her voice, a long hesitation and then the dry triumph of her will, "I'll never mention it to you again! Owen I can just make out; for Owen *is* a blockhead. Owen's a blockhead," she repeated with a quiet, tragic finality, looking straight into Fleda's eyes. "I don't know why you dress up so the fact that he's disgustingly weak."

Fleda hesitated; at last, before her companion's, she lowered her look. "Because I love him. It's because he's weak that he needs me," she added.

"That was why his father, whom he exactly resembles, needed *me*. And I didn't fail his father," said Mrs. Gereth. She gave Fleda a moment to appreciate the remark; after which she pursued: "Mona Brigstock isn't weak; she's stronger than you!"

"I never thought she was weak," Fleda answered. She looked vaguely round the room with a new purpose: she had lost sight of her umbrella.

"I did tell you to let yourself go, but it's clear enough that you really haven't," Mrs. Gereth declared. "If Mona has got him—"

Fleda had accomplished her search; her interlocutress paused. "If Mona has got him?" the girl inquired, tightening the umbrella.

"Well," said Mrs. Gereth profoundly, "it will be clear enough that Mona *has*."

"Has let herself go?"

"Has let herself go." Mrs. Gereth spoke as if she saw it in every detail.

Fleda felt the tone and finished her preparation; then she went and opened the door. "We'll look for him together," she said to her friend, who stood a moment taking in her face. "They may know something about him at the Colonel's."

"We'll go there." Mrs. Gereth had picked up her gloves and her purse. "But the first thing," she went on, "will be to wire to Poynton."

"Why not to Waterbath at once?" Fleda asked.

Her companion hesitated. "In *your* name?"

"In my name. I noticed a place at the corner."

While Fleda held the door open Mrs. Gereth drew on her gloves. "Forgive me," she presently said. "Kiss me," she added.

Fleda, on the threshold, kissed her; then they went out.

XIX

In the place at the corner, on the chance of its saving time, Fleda wrote her telegram—wrote it in silence under Mrs. Gereth's eye and then in silence handed it to her. "I send this to Waterbath, on the possibility of your being there, to ask you to come to me." Mrs. Gereth held it a moment, read it more than once; then keeping it, and with her eyes on her companion, seemed to consider. There was the dawn of a kindness in her look; Fleda perceived in it, as if as the reward of complete submission, a slight relaxation of her rigor.

"Wouldn't it perhaps after all be better," she asked, "before doing this, to see if we can make his whereabouts certain?"

"Why so? It will be always so much done," said Fleda. "Though I'm poor," she added with a smile, "I don't mind the shilling."

"The shilling's *my* shilling," said Mrs. Gereth.

Fleda stayed her hand. "No, no—I'm superstitious."

"Superstitious?"

"To succeed, it must be all me!"

"Well, if that will make it succeed!" Mrs. Gereth took back her shilling, but she still kept the telegram. "As he's most probably not there—"

"If he shouldn't be there," Fleda interrupted, "there will be no harm done."

"If he 'shouldn't be' there!" Mrs. Gereth ejaculated. "Heaven help us, how you assume it!"

"I'm only prepared for the worst. The Brigstocks will simply send any telegram on."

"Where will they send it?"

"Presumably to Poynton."

"They'll read it first," said Mrs. Gereth.

"Read it?"

"Yes, Mona will. She'll open it under the pretext of having it repeated; and then she'll probably do nothing. She'll keep it as a proof of your immodesty."

"What of that?" asked Fleda.

"You don't mind her seeing it?"

Rather musingly and absently Fleda shook her head. "I don't mind anything."

"Well, then, that's all right," said Mrs. Gereth as if she had only wanted to feel that she had been irreproachably considerate. After this she was gentler still, but she had another point to clear up. "Why have you given, for a reply, your sister's address?"

"Because if he *does* come to me he must come to me there. If that telegram goes," said Fleda, "I return to Maggie's to-night."

Mrs. Gereth seemed to wonder at this. "You won't receive him here with me?"

"No, I won't receive him here with you. Only where I received him last—only there again." She showed her companion that as to that she was firm.

But Mrs. Gereth had obviously now had some practice in following queer movements prompted by queer feelings. She resigned herself, though she fingered the paper a moment longer. She appeared to hesitate; then she brought out: "You couldn't then, if I release you, make your message a little stronger?"

Fleda gave her a faint smile. "He'll come if he can."

Mrs. Gereth met fully what this conveyed; with decision she pushed in the telegram. But she laid her hand quickly upon another form and with still greater decision wrote another message. "From *me*, this," she said to Fleda when she had finished: "to catch him possibly at Poynton. Will you read it?"

Fleda turned away. "Thank you."

"It's stronger than yours."

"I don't care," said Fleda, moving to the door. Mrs. Gereth, having paid for the second missive, rejoined her, and they drove together to Owen's club, where the elder lady alone got out. Fleda, from the hansom, watched through the glass doors her brief conversation with the hall-porter and then met in silence her return with the news that he had not seen Owen for a fortnight and was keeping his letters till called for. These had been the last orders; there were a dozen letters lying there. He had no more information to give, but they would see what they could find at Colonel Gereth's. To any connection with this inquiry, however, Fleda now roused herself to object, and her friend had indeed to recognize that on second thoughts it couldn't be quite to the taste of either of them to advertise in the remoter reaches of the family that they had forfeited the confidence of the master of Poynton. The letters lying at the club proved effectively that he was not in London, and this was the question that immediately concerned them. Nothing could concern them further till the answers to their telegrams should have had time to arrive. Mrs. Gereth had got back into the cab, and, still at the door of the club, they sat staring at their need of patience. Fleda's eyes rested, in the great hard street, on passing figures that struck her as puppets pulled by strings. After a little the driver challenged them through the hole in the top. "Anywhere in particular, ladies?"

Fleda decided. "Drive to Euston, please."

"You won't wait for what we may hear?" Mrs. Gereth asked.

"Whatever we hear, I must go." As the cab went on she added: "But I needn't drag *you* to the station."

Mrs. Gereth was silent a moment; then "Nonsense!" she sharply replied.

In spite of this sharpness they were now almost equally and almost tremulously mild; though their mildness took mainly the form of an inevitable sense of nothing left to say. It was the unsaid that occupied them—the thing that for more than an hour they had been going round and round without naming it. Much too early for Fleda's train, they encountered at the station a long half-hour to wait. Fleda made no further allusion to Mrs. Gereth's leaving her; their dumbness, with the elapsing minutes, grew to be in itself a reconstituted bond. They slowly paced the great gray platform, and presently Mrs. Gereth took the girl's arm and leaned on it with a hard demand for support. It seemed to Fleda not difficult for each to know of what the other was thinking—to know indeed that they had in common two alternating visions, one of which, at moments, brought them as by a common impulse to a pause. This was the one that was fixed; the other filled at times the whole space and then was shouldered away. Owen and Mona glared together out of the gloom and disappeared, but the replenishment of Poynton made a shining, steady light. The old splendor was there again, the old things were in their places. Our friends looked at them with an equal yearning; face to face, on the platform, they counted them in each other's eyes. Fleda had come back to them by a road as strange as the road they themselves had followed.

The wonder of their great journeys, the prodigy of this second one, was the question that made her occasionally stop. Several times she uttered it, asked how this and that difficulty had been met. Mrs. Gereth replied with pale lucidity—was naturally the person most familiar with the truth that what she undertook was always somehow achieved. To do it was to do it—she had more than one kind of magnificence. She confessed there, audaciously enough, to a sort of arrogance of energy, and Fleda, going on again, her inquiry more than answered and her arm rendering service, flushed, in her diminished identity, with the sense that such a woman was great.

"You do mean literally everything, to the last little miniature on the last little screen?"

"I mean literally everything. Go over them with the catalogue!"

Fleda went over them while they walked again; she had no need of the catalogue. At last she spoke once more: "Even the Maltese cross?"

"Even the Maltese cross. Why not that as well as everything else?—especially as I remembered how you like it."

Finally, after an interval, the girl exclaimed: "But the mere fatigue of it, the exhaustion of such a feat! I drag you to and fro here while you must be ready to drop."

"I'm very, very tired." Mrs. Gereth's slow head-shake was tragic. "I couldn't do it again."

"I doubt if they'd bear it again!"

"That's another matter: they'd bear it if I could. There won't have been, this time either, a shake or a scratch. But I'm too tired—I very nearly don't care."

"You must sit down, then, till I go," said Fleda. "We must find a bench."

"No. I'm tired of *them*: I'm not tired of you. This is the way for you to feel most how much I rest on you." Fleda had a compunction, wondering as they continued to stroll whether it was right after all to leave her. She believed, however, that if the flame might for the moment burn low, it was far from dying out; an impression presently confirmed by the way Mrs. Gereth went on: "But one's fatigue is nothing. The idea under which one worked kept one up. For you I *could*—I can still. Nothing will have mattered if *she's* not there."

There was a question that this imposed, but Fleda at first found no voice to utter it: it was the thing that, between them, since her arrival, had been so consciously and vividly unsaid. Finally she was able to breathe: "And if she *is* there—if she's there already?"

Mrs. Gereth's rejoinder too hung back; then when it came—from sad eyes as well as from lips barely moved—it was unexpectedly merciful. "It will be very hard." That was all, now; and it was poignantly simple. The train Fleda was to take had drawn up; the girl kissed her as if in farewell. Mrs. Gereth submitted, then after a little brought out: "If we *have* lost—"

"If we have lost?" Fleda repeated as she paused again.

"You'll all the same come abroad with me?"

"It will seem very strange to me if you want me. But whatever you ask, whatever you need, that I will always do."

"I shall need your company," said Mrs. Gereth. Fleda wondered an instant if this were not practically a demand for penal submission—for a surrender that, in its complete humility, would be a long expiation. But there was none of the latent chill of the vindictive in the way Mrs. Gereth pursued: "We can always, as time goes on, talk of them together."

"Of the old things?" Fleda had selected a third-class compartment: she stood a moment looking into it and at a fat woman with a basket who had already taken possession. "Always?" she said, turning again to her companion. "Never!" she exclaimed. She got into the carriage, and two men with bags and boxes immediately followed, blocking up door and window so long that when she was able to look out again Mrs. Gereth had gone.

XX

There came to her at her sister's no telegram in answer to her own: the rest of that day and the whole of the next elapsed without a word either from Owen or from his mother. She was free, however, to her infinite relief, from any direct dealing with suspense, and conscious, to her surprise, of nothing that could show her, or could show Maggie and her brother-in-law, that she was excited. Her excitement was composed of pulses as swift and fine as the revolutions of a spinning top: she supposed she was going round, but she went round so fast that she couldn't even feel herself move. Her emotion occupied some quarter of her soul that had closed its doors for the day and shut out even her own sense of it; she might perhaps have heard something if she had pressed her ear to a partition. Instead of that she sat with her patience in a cold, still chamber from which she could look out in quite another direction. This was to have achieved an equilibrium to which she couldn't have given a name: indifference, resignation, despair were the terms of a forgotten tongue. The time even seemed not long, for the stages of the journey were the items of Mrs. Gereth's surrender. The detail of that performance, which filled the scene, was what Fleda had now before her eyes. The part of her loss that she could think of was the reconstituted splendor of Poynton. It was the beauty she was most touched by that, in tons, she had lost—the beauty that, charged upon big wagons, had safely crept back to its home. But the loss was a gain to memory and love; it was to her too, at last, that, in condonation of her treachery, the old things had crept back. She greeted them with open arms; she thought of them hour after hour; they made a company with which solitude was warm and a picture that, at this crisis, overlaid poor Maggie's scant mahogany. It was really her obliterated passion that had revived, and with it an immense assent to Mrs. Gereth's early judgment of her. She too, she felt, was of the religion, and like any other of the passionately pious she could worship now even in the desert. Yes, it was all for her; far round as she had gone she had been strong enough: her love had gathered in the spoils. She wanted indeed no catalogue to count them over; the array of them, miles away, was complete; each piece, in its turn, was perfect to her; she could have drawn up a catalogue from memory. Thus again she lived with them, and she thought of them without a question of any personal right. That they might have been, that they might still be hers, that they were perhaps already another's, were ideas that had too little to say to her. They were nobody's at all—too proud, unlike base animals and humans, to be reducible to anything so narrow. It was Poynton that was theirs; they had simply recovered their own. The joy of that for them was the source of the strange peace in which the girl found herself floating.

It was broken on the third day by a telegram from Mrs. Gereth. "Shall be with you at 11.30—don't meet me at station." Fleda turned this over, but was sufficiently expert not to disobey the injunction. She had only an hour to take in its meaning, but that hour was longer than all the previous time. If Maggie had studied her convenience the day Owen came, Maggie was also at the present juncture a miracle of refinement. Increasingly and resentfully mystified, in spite of all reassurance, by the impression that Fleda suffered more than she gained from the grandeur of the Gereths, she had it at heart to exemplify the perhaps truer distinction of nature that characterized the house of Vetch. She was not, like poor Fleda, at every one's beck, and the visitor was to see no more of her than what the arrangement of luncheon might tantalizingly show. Maggie described herself to her sister as intending for a just provocation even the understanding she had had with her husband that he also should remain invisible. Fleda accordingly awaited alone the subject of so many manœuvres—a period that was slightly prolonged even after the drawing-room door, at 11.30, was thrown open. Mrs. Gereth stood there with a face that spoke plain, but no sound fell from her till the withdrawal of the maid, whose attention had immediately attached itself to the rearrangement of a window-blind and who seemed, while she bustled at it, to contribute to the pregnant silence; before the duration of which, however, she retreated with a sudden stare.

"He has done it," said Mrs. Gereth, turning her eyes avoidingly but not unperceivingly about her and in spite of herself dropping an opinion upon the few objects in the room. Fleda, on her side, in her silence, observed how characteristically she looked at Maggie's possessions before looking at Maggie's sister. The girl understood and at first had nothing to say; she was still dumb while Mrs. Gereth selected, with hesitation, a seat less distasteful than the one that happened to be nearest. On the sofa near the window the poor woman finally showed what the two past days had done for the age of her face. Her eyes at last met Fleda's. "It's the end."

"They're married?"

"They're married."

Fleda came to the sofa in obedience to the impulse to sit down by her; then paused before her while Mrs. Gereth turned up a dead gray mask. A tired old woman sat there with empty hands in her lap. "I've heard nothing," said Fleda. "No answer came."

"That's the only answer. It's the answer to everything." So Fleda saw; for a minute she looked over her companion's head and far away. "He wasn't at Waterbath; Mrs. Brigstock must have read your telegram and kept it. But mine, the one to Poynton, brought something. 'We are here—what do you want?'" Mrs. Gereth stopped as if with a failure of voice; on which Fleda sank upon the sofa and made a movement to take her hand. It met no response; there could be no attenuation. Fleda waited; they sat facing each other like strangers. "I wanted to go down," Mrs. Gereth presently continued. "Well, I went."

All the girl's effort tended for the time to a single aim—that of taking the thing with outward detachment, speaking of it as having happened to Owen and to his mother and not in any degree to herself. Something at least of this was in the encouraging way she said: "Yesterday morning?"

"Yesterday morning. I saw him."

Fleda hesitated. "Did you see *her*?"

"Thank God, no!"

Fleda laid on her arm a hand of vague comfort, of which Mrs. Gereth took no notice. "You've been capable, just to tell me, of this wretched journey, of this consideration that I don't deserve?"

"We're together, we're together," said Mrs. Gereth. She looked helpless as she sat there, her eyes, unseeingly enough, on a tall Dutch clock, old but rather poor, that Maggie had had as a wedding-gift and that eked out the bareness of the room.

To Fleda, in the face of the event, it appeared that this was exactly what they were not: the last inch of common ground, the ground of their past intercourse, had fallen from under them. Yet what was still there was the grand style of her companion's treatment of her. Mrs. Gereth couldn't stand upon small questions, couldn't, in conduct, make small differences. "You're magnificent!" her young friend exclaimed. "There's a rare greatness in your generosity."

"We're together, we're together," Mrs. Gereth lifelessly repeated. "That's all we *are* now; it's all we have." The words brought to Fleda a sudden vision of the empty little house at Ricks; such a vision might also have been what her companion found in the face of the stopped Dutch clock. Yet with this it was clear that she would now show no bitterness: she had done with that, had given the last drop to those horrible hours in London. No passion even was left to her, and her forbearance only added to the force with which she represented the final vanity of everything.

Fleda was so far from a wish to triumph that she was absolutely ashamed of having anything to say for herself; but there was one thing, all the same, that not to say was impossible. "That he has done it, that he couldn't *not* do it, shows how right I was." It settled forever her attitude, and she spoke as if for her own mind; then after a little she added very gently, for Mrs. Gereth's: "That's to say, it shows that he was bound to her by an obligation that, however much he may have wanted to, he couldn't in any sort of honor break."

Blanched and bleak, Mrs. Gereth looked at her. "What sort of an obligation do you call that? No such obligation exists for an hour between any man and any woman who have hatred on one side. He had ended by hating her, and now he hates her more than ever."

"Did he tell you so?" Fleda asked.

"No. He told me nothing but the great gawk of a fact. I saw him but for three minutes." She was silent again, and Fleda, as before some lurid image of this interview, sat without speaking. "Do you wish to appear as if you don't care?" Mrs. Gereth presently demanded.

"I'm trying not to think of myself."

"Then if you're thinking of Owen, how can you *bear* to think?"

Sadly and submissively Fleda shook her head; the slow tears had come into her eyes. "I can't. I don't understand—I don't understand!" she broke out.

"*I* do, then." Mrs. Gereth looked hard at the floor. "There was no obligation at the time you saw him last—when you sent him, hating her as he did, back to her."

"If he went," Fleda asked, "doesn't that exactly prove that he recognized one?"

"He recognized rot! You know what *I* think of him." Fleda knew; she had no wish to challenge a fresh statement. Mrs. Gereth made one—it was her sole, faint flicker of passion—to the extent of declaring that he was too abjectly weak to deserve the name of a man. For all Fleda cared!—it was his weakness she loved in him. "He took strange ways of pleasing you!" her friend went on. "There was no obligation till suddenly, the other day, the situation changed."

Fleda wondered. "The other day?"

"It came to Mona's knowledge—I can't tell you how, but it came—that the things I was sending back had begun to arrive at Poynton. I had sent them for you, but it was *her* I touched." Mrs. Gereth paused; Fleda was too absorbed in her explanation to do anything but take blankly the full, cold breath of this. "They were there, and that determined her."

"Determined her to what?"

"To act, to take means."

"To take means?" Fleda repeated.

"I can't tell you what they were, but they were powerful. She knew how," said Mrs. Gereth.

Fleda received with the same stoicism the quiet immensity of this allusion to the person who had not known how. But it made her think a little, and the thought found utterance, with unconscious irony, in the simple interrogation: "Mona?"

"Why not? She's a brute."

"But if he knew that so well, what chance was there in it for her?"

"How can I tell you? How can I talk of such horrors? I can only give you, of the situation, what I see. He knew it, yes. But as she couldn't make him forget it, she tried to make him like it. She tried and she succeeded: that's what she did. She's after all so much less of a fool than he. And what *else* had he originally liked?" Mrs. Gereth shrugged her shoulders. "She did what you wouldn't!" Fleda's face had grown dark with her wonder, but her friend's empty hands offered no balm to the pain in it. "It was that if it was anything. Nothing else meets the misery of it. Then there was quick work. Before he could turn round he was married."

Fleda, as if she had been holding her breath, gave the sigh of a listening child. "At that place you spoke of in town?"

"At the Registrar's, like a pair of low atheists."

The girl hesitated. "What do people say of that? I mean the 'world.'"

"Nothing, because nobody knows. They're to be married on the 17th, at Waterbath church. If anything else comes out, everybody is a little prepared. It will pass for some stroke of diplomacy, some move in the game, some outwitting of *me*. It's known there has been a row with me."

Fleda was mystified. "People surely knew at Poynton," she objected, "if, as you say, she's there."

"She was there, day before yesterday, only for a few hours. She met him in London and went down to see the things."

Fleda remembered that she had seen them only once. "Did *you* see them?" she then ventured to ask.

"Everything."

"Are they right?"

"Quite right. There's nothing like them," said Mrs. Gereth. At this her companion took up one of her hands again and kissed it as she had done in London. "Mona went back that night; she was not there yesterday. Owen stayed on," she added.

Fleda stared. "Then she's not to live there?"

"Rather! But not till after the public marriage." Mrs. Gereth seemed to muse; then she brought out: "She'll live there alone."

"Alone?"

"She'll have it to herself."

"He won't live with her?"

"Never! But she's none the less his wife, and you're not," said Mrs. Gereth, getting up. "Our only chance is the chance she may die."

Fleda appeared to consider: she appreciated her visitor's magnanimous use of the plural. "Mona won't die," she replied.

"Well, *I* shall, thank God! Till then"—and with this, for the first time, Mrs. Gereth put out her hand—"don't desert me."

Fleda took her hand, and her clasp of it was a reiteration of a promise already given. She said nothing, but her silence was an acceptance as responsible as the vow of a nun. The next moment something occurred to her. "I mustn't put myself in your son's way."

Mrs. Gereth gave a dry, flat laugh. "You're prodigious! But how shall you possibly be more out of it? Owen and I—" She didn't finish her sentence.

"That's your great feeling about *him*," Fleda said; "but how, after what has happened, can it be his about you?"

Mrs. Gereth hesitated. "How do you know what has happened? You don't know what I said to him."

"Yesterday?"

"Yesterday."

They looked at each other with a long, deep gaze. Then, as Mrs. Gereth seemed again about to speak, the girl, closing her eyes, made a gesture of strong prohibition. "Don't tell me!"

"Merciful powers, how you worship him!" Mrs. Gereth wonderingly moaned. It was, for Fleda, the shake that made the cup overflow. She had a pause, that of the child who takes time to know that he responds to an accident with pain; then, dropping again on the sofa, she broke into tears. They were beyond control, they came in long sobs, which for a moment Mrs. Gereth, almost with an air of indifference, stood hearing and watching. At last Mrs. Gereth too sank down again. Mrs. Gereth soundlessly, wearily wept.

<u>XXI</u>

"It looks just like Waterbath; but, after all, we bore *that* together:" these words formed part of a letter in which, before the 17th, Mrs. Gereth, writing from disfigured Ricks, named to Fleda the day on which she would be expected to arrive there on a second visit. "I sha'n't, for a long time to come," the missive continued, "be able to receive any one who may *like* it, who would try to smooth it down, and me with it; but there are always things you and I can comfortably hate together, for you're the only person who comfortably understands. You don't understand quite everything, but of all my acquaintance you're far away the least stupid. For action you're no good at all; but action is over, for me, forever, and you will have the great merit of knowing, when I'm brutally silent, what I shall be thinking about. Without setting myself up for your equal, I dare say I shall also know what are your own thoughts. Moreover, with nothing else but my four walls, you'll at any rate be a bit of furniture. For that, you know, a little, I've always taken you—quite one of my best finds. So come, if possible, on the 15th."

The position of a bit of furniture was one that Fleda could conscientiously accept, and she by no means insisted on so high a place in the list. This communication made her easier, if only by its acknowledgment that her friend had some thing left: it still implied recognition of the principle of property. Something to hate, and to hate "comfortably," was at least not the utter destitution to which, after their last interview, she had helplessly seemed to see Mrs. Gereth go forth. She remembered indeed that, in the state in which they first saw it, she herself had "liked" the blessed refuge of Ricks; and she now wondered if the tact for which she was commended had then operated to make her keep her kindness out of sight. She was at present ashamed of such obliquity, and made up her mind that if this happy impression, quenched in the spoils of Poynton, should revive on the spot, she would utter it to her companion without reserve. Yes, she was capable of as much "action" as that: all the more that the spirit of her hostess seemed, for the time at least, wholly to have failed. Mrs. Gereth's three minutes with Owen had been a blow to all talk of travel, and after her woeful hour at Maggie's she had, like some great moaning, wounded bird, made her way, with wings of anguish, back to the nest she knew she should find empty. Fleda, on that dire day, could neither keep her nor give her up; she had pressingly offered to return with her, but Mrs. Gereth, in spite of the theory that their common grief was a bond, had even declined all escort to the station, conscious apparently of something abject in her collapse and almost fiercely eager, as with a personal shame, to be unwatched. All she had said to Fleda was that she would go back to Ricks that night, and the girl had lived for days after with a dreadful image of her position and her misery there. She had had a vision of her now lying prone on some unmade bed, now pacing a bare floor like a lioness deprived of her cubs. There had been moments when her mind's ear was strained to listen for some sound of grief wild enough to be wafted from afar. But the first sound, at the end of a week, had been a note announcing, without reflections, that the plan of going abroad had been abandoned. "It has come to me indirectly, but with much appearance of truth, that *they* are going—for an indefinite time. That quite settles it; I shall stay where I am, and as soon as I've turned round again I shall look for you." The second letter had come a week later, and on the 15th Fleda was on her way to Ricks.

Her arrival took the form of a surprise very nearly as violent as that of the other time. The elements were different, but the effect, like the other, arrested her on the threshold: she stood there stupefied and delighted at the magic of a passion of which such a picture represented the low-water mark. Wound up but sincere, and passing quickly from room to room, Fleda broke out before she even sat down. "If you turn me out of the house for it, my dear, there isn't a woman in England for whom it wouldn't be a privilege to live here." Mrs. Gereth was as honestly bewildered as she had of old been falsely calm. She looked about at the few sticks that, as she afterwards phrased it, she had gathered in, and then hard at her guest, as if to protect herself against a joke sufficiently cruel. The girl's heart gave a leap, for this stare was the sign of an opportunity. Mrs. Gereth was all unwitting; she didn't in the least know what she had done, and as Fleda could tell her Fleda suddenly became the one who knew most. That counted for the moment as a magnificent position; it almost made all the difference. Yet what contradicted it was the vivid presence of the artist's idea. "Where on earth did you put your hand on such beautiful things?"

"Beautiful things?" Mrs. Gereth turned again to the little worn, bleached stuffs and the sweet spindle-legs. "They're the wretched things that were here—that stupid, starved old woman's."

"The maiden aunt's, the nicest, the dearest old woman that ever lived? I thought you had got rid of the maiden aunt."

"She was stored in an empty barn—stuck away for a sale; a matter that, fortunately, I've had neither time nor freedom of mind to arrange. I've simply, in my extremity, fished her out again."

"You've simply, in your extremity, made a delight of her." Fleda took the highest line and the upper hand, and as Mrs. Gereth, challenging her cheerfulness, turned again a lustreless eye over the contents of the place, she broke into a rapture that was unforced, but that she was conscious of an advantage in being able to feel. She moved, as she had done on the previous occasion, from one piece to another, with looks of recognition and hands that lightly lingered, but she was as feverishly jubilant now as she had formerly been anxious and mute. "Ah, the little melancholy, tender, tell-tale things: how can they *not* speak to you and find a way to your heart? It's not the great chorus of Poynton; but you're not, I'm sure, either so proud or so broken as to be reached by nothing but that. This is a voice so gentle, so human, so feminine—a faint, far-away voice with the little quaver of a heart-break. You've listened to it unawares; for the arrangement and effect of everything—when I compare them with what we found the first day we came down—shows, even if mechanically and disdainfully exercised, your admirable, infallible hand. It's your extraordinary genius; you make things 'compose' in spite of yourself. You've only to be a day or two in a place with four sticks for something to come of it!"

"Then if anything has come of it here, it has come precisely of just four. That's literally, by the inventory, all there are!" said Mrs. Gereth.

"If there were more there would be too many to convey the impression in which half the beauty resides—the impression, somehow, of something dreamed and missed, something reduced, relinquished, resigned: the poetry, as it were, of something sensibly *gone*." Fleda ingeniously and triumphantly worked it out. "Ah, there's something here that will never be in the inventory!"

"Does it happen to be in your power to give it a name?" Mrs. Gereth's face showed the dim dawn of an amusement at finding herself seated at the feet of her pupil.

"I can give it a dozen. It's a kind of fourth dimension. It's a presence, a perfume, a touch. It's a soul, a story, a life. There's ever so much more here than you and I. We're in fact just three!"

"Oh, if you count the ghosts!"

"Of course I count the ghosts. It seems to me ghosts count double—for what they were and for what they are. Somehow there were no ghosts at Poynton," Fleda went on. "That was the only fault."

Mrs. Gereth, considering, appeared to fall in with the girl's fine humor. "Poynton was too splendidly happy."

"Poynton was too splendidly happy," Fleda promptly echoed.

"But it's cured of that now," her companion added.

"Yes, henceforth there'll be a ghost or two."

Mrs. Gereth thought again: she found her young friend suggestive. "Only *she* won't see them."

"No, 'she' won't see them." Then Fleda said, "What I mean is, for this dear one of ours, that if she had (as I *know* she did; it's in the very taste of the air!) a great accepted pain—"

She had paused an instant, and Mrs. Gereth took her up. "Well, if she had?"

Fleda still hesitated. "Why, it was worse than yours."

Mrs. Gereth reflected. "Very likely." Then she too hesitated. "The question is if it was worse than yours."

"Mine?" Fleda looked vague.

"Precisely. Yours."

At this our young lady smiled. "Yes, because it was a disappointment. She had been so sure."

"I see. And you were never sure."

"Never. Besides, I'm happy," said Fleda.

Mrs. Gereth met her eyes awhile. "Goose!" she quietly remarked as she turned away. There was a curtness in it; nevertheless it represented a considerable part of the basis of their new life.

On the 18th The Morning Post had at last its clear message, a brief account of the marriage, from the residence of the bride's mother, of Mr. Owen Gereth of Poynton Park to Miss Mona Brigstock of Waterbath. There were two ecclesiastics and six bridesmaids and, as Mrs. Gereth subsequently said, a hundred frumps, as well as a special train from town: the scale of the affair sufficiently showed that the preparations had been complete for weeks. The happy pair were described as having taken their departure for Mr. Gereth's own seat, famous for its unique collection of artistic curiosities. The newspapers and letters, the fruits of the first London post, had been brought to the mistress of Ricks in the garden; and she lingered there alone a long time after receiving them. Fleda kept at a distance; she knew what must have happened, for from one of the windows she saw her rigid in a chair, her eyes strange and fixed, the newspaper open on the ground and the letters untouched in her lap. Before the morning's end she had disappeared, and the rest of that day she remained in her room: it recalled to Fleda, who had picked up the newspaper, the day, months before, on which Owen had come down to Poynton to make his engagement known. The hush of the house was at least the same, and the girl's own waiting, her soft wandering, through the hours: there was a difference indeed sufficiently great, of which her companion's absence might in some degree have represented a considerate recognition. That was at any rate the meaning Fleda, devoutly glad to be alone, attached to her opportunity. Mrs. Gereth's sole allusion, the next day, to the subject of their thoughts, has already been mentioned: it was a dazzled glance at the fact that Mona's quiet pace had really never slackened.

Fleda fully assented. "I said of our disembodied friend here that she had suffered in proportion as she had been sure. But that's not always a source of suffering. It's Mona who must have been sure!"

"She was sure of *you!*" Mrs. Gereth returned. But this didn't diminish the satisfaction taken by Fleda in showing how serenely and lucidly she could talk.

Her relation with her wonderful friend had, however, in becoming a new one, begun to shape itself almost wholly on breaches and omissions. Something had dropped out altogether, and the question between them, which time would answer, was whether the change had made them strangers or yokefellows. It was as if at last, for better or worse, they were, in a clearer, cruder air, really to know each other. Fleda wondered how Mrs. Gereth had escaped hating her: there were hours when it seemed that such a feat might leave after all a scant margin for future accidents. The thing indeed that now came out in its simplicity was that even in her shrunken state the lady of Ricks was larger than her wrongs. As for the girl herself, she had made up her mind that her feelings had no connection with the case. It was her pretension that they had never yet emerged from the seclusion into which, after her friend's visit to her at her sister's, we saw them precipitately retire: if she should suddenly meet them in straggling procession on the road it would be time enough to deal with them. They were all bundled there together, likes with dislikes and memories with fears; and she had for not thinking of them the excellent reason that she was too occupied with the actual. The actual was not that Owen Gereth had seen his necessity where she had pointed it out; it was that his mother's bare spaces demanded all the tapestry that the recipient of her bounty could furnish. There were moments during the month that followed when Mrs. Gereth struck her as still older and feebler, and as likely to become quite easily amused.

At the end of it, one day, the London paper had another piece of news: "Mr. and Mrs. Owen Gereth, who arrived in town last week, proceed this morning to Paris." They exchanged no word about it till the evening, and none indeed would then have been uttered had not Mrs. Gereth irrelevantly broken out: "I dare say you wonder why I declared the other day with such assurance that he wouldn't live with her. He apparently *is* living with her."

"Surely it's the only proper thing for him to do."

"They're beyond me—I give it up," said Mrs. Gereth.

"I don't give it up—I never did," Fleda returned.

"Then what do you make of his aversion to her?"

"Oh, she has dispelled it."

Mrs. Gereth said nothing for a minute. "You're prodigious in your choice of terms!" she then simply ejaculated.

But Fleda went luminously on; she once more enjoyed her great command of her subject: "I think that when you came to see me at Maggie's you saw too many things, you had too many ideas."

"You had none," said Mrs. Gereth: "you were completely bewildered."

"Yes, I didn't quite understand—but I think I understand now. The case is simple and logical enough. She's a person who's upset by failure and who blooms and expands with success. There was something she had set her heart upon, set her teeth about—the house exactly as she had seen it."

"She never saw it at all, she never looked at it!" cried Mrs. Gereth.

"She doesn't look with her eyes; she looks with her ears. In her own way she had taken it in; she knew, she felt when it had been touched. That probably made her take an attitude that was extremely disagreeable. But the attitude lasted only while the reason for it lasted."

"Go on—I can bear it now," said Mrs. Gereth. Her companion had just perceptibly paused.

"I know you can, or I shouldn't dream of speaking. When the pressure was removed she came up again. From the moment the house was once more what it had to be, her natural charm reasserted itself."

"Her natural charm!" Mrs. Gereth could barely articulate.

"It's very great; everybody thinks so; there must be something in it. It operated as it had operated before. There's no need of imagining anything very monstrous. Her restored good humor, her splendid beauty, and Mr. Owen's impressibility and generosity sufficiently cover the ground. His great bright sun came out!"

"And his great bright passion for another person went in. Your explanation would doubtless be perfection if he didn't love you."

Fleda was silent a little. "What do you know about his 'loving' me?"

"I know what Mrs. Brigstock herself told me."

165

"You never in your life took her word for any other matter."

"Then won't yours do?" Mrs. Gereth demanded. "Haven't I had it from your own mouth that he cares for you?"

Fleda turned pale, but she faced her companion and smiled. "You confound, Mrs. Gereth, you mix things up. You've only had it from my own mouth that I care for *him*!"

It was doubtless in contradictious allusion to this (which at the time had made her simply drop her head as in a strange, vain reverie) that Mrs. Gereth, a day or two later, said to Fleda: "Don't think I shall be a bit affected if I'm here to see it when he comes again to make up to you."

"He won't do that," the girl replied. Then she added, smiling: "But if he should be guilty of such bad taste, it wouldn't be nice of you not to be disgusted."

"I'm not talking of disgust; I'm talking of its opposite," said Mrs. Gereth.

"Of its opposite?"

"Why, of any reviving pleasure that one might feel in such an exhibition. I shall feel none at all. You may personally take it as you like; but what conceivable good will it do?"

Fleda wondered. "To me, do you mean?"

"Deuce take you, no! To what we don't, you know, by your wish, ever talk about."

"The old things?" Fleda considered again. "It will do no good of any sort to anything or any one. That's another question I would rather we shouldn't discuss, please," she gently added.

Mrs. Gereth shrugged her shoulders.

"It certainly isn't worth it!"

Something in her manner prompted her companion, with a certain inconsequence, to speak again. "That was partly why I came back to you, you know—that there should be the less possibility of anything painful."

"Painful?" Mrs. Gereth stared. "What pain can I ever feel again?"

"I meant painful to myself," Fleda, with a slight impatience, explained.

"Oh, I see." Her friend was silent a minute. "You use sometimes such odd expressions. Well, I shall last a little, but I sha'n't last forever."

"You'll last quite as long—" Here Fleda suddenly hesitated.

Mrs. Gereth took her up with a cold smile that seemed the warning of experience against hyperbole. "As long as what, please?"

The girl thought an instant; then met the difficulty by adopting, as an amendment, the same tone. "As any danger of the ridiculous."

That did for the time, and she had moreover, as the months went on, the protection of suspended allusions. This protection was marked when, in the following November, she received a letter directed in a hand at which a quick glance sufficed to make her hesitate to open it. She said nothing, then or afterwards; but she opened it, for reasons that had come to her, on the morrow. It consisted of a page and a half from Owen Gereth, dated from Florence, but with no other preliminary. She knew that during the summer he had returned to England with his wife, and that after a couple of months they had again gone abroad. She also knew, without communication, that Mrs. Gereth, round whom Ricks had grown submissively and indescribably sweet, had her own interpretation of her daughter-in-law's share in this second migration. It was a piece of calculated insolence—a stroke odiously directed at showing whom it might concern that now she had Poynton fast she was perfectly indifferent to living there. The Morning Post, at Ricks, had again been a resource: it was stated in that journal that Mr. and Mrs. Owen Gereth proposed to spend the winter in India. There was a person to whom it was clear that she led her wretched husband by the nose. Such was the light in which contemporary history was offered to Fleda until, in her own room, late at night, she broke the seal of her letter.

"I want you, inexpressibly, to have, as a remembrance, something of mine—something of real value. Something from Poynton is what I mean and what I should prefer. You know everything there, and far better than I what's best and what isn't. There are a lot of differences, but aren't some of the smaller things the most remarkable? I mean for judges, and for what they'd bring. What I want you to take from me, and to choose for yourself, is the thing in the whole house that's most beautiful and precious. I mean the 'gem of the collection,' don't you know? If it happens to be of such a sort that you can take immediate possession of it—carry it right away with you—so much the better. You're to have it on the spot, whatever it is. I humbly beg of you to go down there and see. The people have complete instructions: they'll act for you in every possible way and put the whole place at your service. There's a thing mamma used to call the Maltese cross and that I think I've heard her say is very wonderful. Is *that* the gem of the collection? Perhaps you would take it, or anything equally convenient. Only I do want you awfully to let it be the very pick of the place. Let me feel that I can trust you for this. You won't refuse if you will think a little what it must be that makes me ask."

Fleda read that last sentence over more times even than the rest; she was baffled—she couldn't think at all of what it might be. This was indeed because it might be one of so many things. She made for the present no answer; she merely, little by little, fashioned for herself the form that her answer should eventually wear. There was only one form that was possible—the form of doing, at her time, what he wished. She would go down to Poynton as a pilgrim might go to a shrine, and as to this she must look out for her chance. She lived with her letter, before any chance came, a month, and even after a month it had mysteries for her that she couldn't meet. What did it mean, what did it represent, to what did it correspond in his imagination or his soul? What was behind it, what was beyond it, what was, in the deepest depth, within it? She said to herself that with these questions she was under no obligation to deal. There was an explanation of them that, for practical purposes, would do as well as another: he had found in his marriage a happiness so much greater than, in the distress of his dilemma, he had been able to take heart to believe, that he now felt he owed her a token of gratitude for having kept him in the straight path. That explanation, I say, she could throw off; but no explanation in the least mattered: what determined her was the simple strength of her impulse to respond. The passion for which what had happened had made no difference, the passion that had taken this into account before as well as after, found here an issue that there was nothing whatever to choke. It found even a relief to which her imagination immensely contributed. Would she act upon his offer? She would act with secret rapture. To have as her own something splendid that he had given her, of which the gift had been his signed desire, would be a greater joy than the greatest she had supposed to be left to her, and she felt that till the sense of this came home she had even herself not known what burned in her successful stillness. It was an hour to dream of and watch for; to be patient was to draw out the sweetness. She was capable of feeling it as an hour of triumph, the triumph of everything in her recent life that had not held up its head. She moved there in thought—in the great rooms she knew; she should be able to say to herself that, for once at least, her possession was as complete as that of either of the others whom it had filled only with bitterness. And a thousand times yes—her choice should know no scruple: the thing she should go down to take would be up to the height of her privilege. The whole place was in her eyes, and she spent for weeks her private hours in a luxury of comparison and debate. It should be one of the smallest things because it should be one she could have close to her; and it should be one of the finest because it was in the finest he saw his symbol. She said to herself that of what it would symbolize she was content to know nothing more than just what her having it would tell her. At bottom she inclined to the Maltese cross—with the added reason that he had named it. But she would look again and judge afresh; she would on the spot so handle and ponder that there shouldn't be the shade of a mistake.

Before Christmas she had a natural opportunity to go to London; there was her periodical call upon her father to pay as well as a promise to Maggie to redeem. She spent her first night in West Kensington, with the idea of carrying out on the morrow the purpose that had most of a motive. Her father's affection was not inquisitive, but when she mentioned to him that she had business in the country that would oblige her to catch an early train, he deprecated her excursion in view of the menace of the weather. It was spoiling for a storm; all the signs of a winter gale were in the air. She replied that she would see what the morning might bring; and it brought, in fact, what seemed in London an amendment. She was to go to Maggie the next day, and now that she had started her eagerness had become suddenly a pain. She pictured her return that evening with her trophy under her cloak; so that after looking, from the doorstep, up and down the dark street, she decided, with a new nervousness, and sallied forth to the nearest place of access to the "Underground." The December dawn was dolorous, but there was neither rain nor snow; it was not even cold, and the atmosphere of West Kensington, purified by the wind, was like a dirty old coat that had been bettered by a dirty brush. At the end of almost an hour, in the larger station, she had taken her place in a third-class compartment; the prospect before her was the run of eighty minutes to Poynton. The train was a fast one, and she was familiar with the moderate measure of the walk to the park from the spot at which it would drop her.

Once in the country, indeed, she saw that her father was right: the breath of December was abroad with a force from which the London labyrinth had protected her. The green fields were black, the sky was all alive with the wind; she had, in her anxious sense of the elements, her wonder at what might happen, a reminder of the surmises, in the old days of going to the Continent, that used to worry her on the way, at night, to the horrid cheap crossings by long sea. Something, in a dire degree, at this last hour, had begun to press on her heart: it was the sudden imagination of a disaster, or at least of a check, before her errand was achieved. When she said to herself that something might happen she wanted to go faster than the train. But nothing could happen save a dismayed discovery that, by some altogether unlikely chance, the master and mistress of the house had already come back. In that case she must have had a warning, and the fear was but the excess of her hope. It was every one's being exactly where every one was that lent the quality to her visit. Beyond lands and seas and alienated forever, they in their different ways gave her the impression to take as she had never taken it. At last it was already there, though the darkness of the day had deepened; they had whizzed past Chater—Chater, which was the station before the right one. Off in that quarter was an air of wild rain, but there shimmered straight across it a brightness that was the color of the great interior she had been haunting. That vision settled before her—in the house the house was all; and as the train drew up she rose, in her mean compartment, quite proudly erect with the thought that all for Fleda Vetch then the house was standing there.

But with the opening of the door she encountered a shock, though for an instant she couldn't have named it; the next moment she saw it was given her by the face of the man advancing to let her out, an old lame porter of the station, who had been there in Mrs. Gereth's time and who now recognized her. He looked up at her so hard that she took an alarm and before alighting broke out to him: "They've come back?" She had a confused, absurd sense that even he would know that in this case she mustn't be there. He hesitated, and in the few seconds her alarm had completely changed its ground: it seemed to leap, with her quick jump from the carriage, to the ground that was that of his stare at her. "Smoke?" She was on the platform with her frightened sniff: it had taken her a minute to become aware of an extraordinary smell. The air was full of it, and there were already heads at the window of the train, looking out at something she couldn't see. Some one, the only other passenger, had got out of another carriage, and the old porter hobbled off to close his door. The smoke was in her eyes, but she saw the station-master, from the end of the platform, recognize her too and come straight to her. He brought her a finer shade of surprise than the porter, and while he was coming she heard a voice at a window of the train say that something was "a good bit off—a mile from the town." That was just what Poynton was. Then her heart stood still at the white wonder in the station-master's face.

"You've come down to it, miss, already?"

At this she knew. "Poynton's on fire?"

"Gone, miss—with this awful gale. You weren't wired? Look out!" he cried in the next breath, seizing her; the train was going on, and she had given a lurch that almost made it catch her as it passed. When it had drawn away she became more conscious of the pervading smoke, which the wind seemed to hurl in her face.

"*Gone?*" She was in the man's hands; she clung to him.

"Burning still, miss. Ain't it quite too dreadful? Took early this morning—the whole place is up there."

In her bewildered horror she tried to think. "Have they come back?"

"Back? They'll be there all day!"

"Not Mr. Gereth, I mean—nor his wife?"

"Nor his mother, miss—not a soul of *them* back. A pack o' servants in charge—not the old lady's lot, eh? A nice job for care-takers! Some rotten chimley or one of them portable lamps set down in the wrong place. What has done it is this cruel, cruel night." Then as a great wave of smoke half choked them, he drew her with force to the little waiting room. "Awkward for you, miss—I see!"

She felt sick; she sank upon a seat, staring up at him. "Do you mean that great house is *lost?*"

"It was near it, I was told, an hour ago—the fury of the flames had got such a start. I was there myself at six, the very first I heard of it. They were fighting it then, but you couldn't quite say they had got it down."

Fleda jerked herself up. "Were they saving the things?"

"That's just where it was, miss—to get *at* the blessed things. And the want of right help—it maddened me to stand and see 'em muff it. This ain't a place, like, for anything organized. They don't come up to a *reel* emergency."

She passed out of the door that opened toward the village and met a great acrid gust. She heard a far-off windy roar which, in her dismay, she took for that of flames a mile away, and which, the first instant, acted upon her as a wild solicitation. "I must go there." She had scarcely spoken before the same omen had changed into an appalling check.

Her vivid friend, moreover, had got before her; he clearly suffered from the nature of the control he had to exercise. "Don't do that, miss—you won't care for it at all." Then as she waveringly stood her ground, "It's not a place for a young lady, nor, if you'll believe me, a sight for them as are in any way affected."

171

Fleda by this time knew in what way she was affected: she became limp and weak again; she felt herself give everything up. Mixed with the horror, with the kindness of the station-master, with the smell of cinders and the riot of sound, was the raw bitterness of a hope that she might never again in life have to give up so much at such short notice. She heard herself repeat mechanically, yet as if asking it for the first time: "Poynton's *gone?*"

The man hesitated. "What can you call it, miss, if it ain't really saved?"

A minute later she had returned with him to the waiting-room, where, in the thick swim of things, she saw something like the disk of a clock. "Is there an up-train?" she asked.

"In seven minutes."

She came out on the platform: everywhere she met the smoke. She covered her face with her hands. "I'll go back."

VIEWS AND REVIEWS

INTRODUCTION

Those whose palates are accustomed to the subtle flavours of the wines of the Rhine and Moselle can smack their lips and name the vintage at the first taste. Likewise any one fairly familiar with the work of Mr. James during his forty years of literary activity can, after the reading of a single page taken at random, judge with a remarkable accuracy the date of its composition. Yet the transition has not been abrupt and the styles of writing which the author has adopted, early, middle and late, have blended in such a way that he has been bringing many of his earlier readers, though some have fallen by the wayside, along with him to a genuine appreciation of his present work.

It is not unnatural but disappointing that those of the present generation who chance to meet Mr. James in one of the later novels are not as likely to seek a second volume as those who read Daisy Miller *some thirty years ago when that study first appeared, so fresh in its note of charm and pathos, in the now almost unfindable brown wrappers of Harper's Half Hour Series, for they may forever miss a rare enjoyment.*

In the critical papers which make up the contents of this book, the characteristics of the author's later style are wholly absent. Without the date of the original appearance of these essays in periodical form being indicated, the chronological setting of this work is apparent. No sentences with marvelously intricate complications of construction and with expressions involved are in the author's method at this time, while for clearness and charm these views and reviews are admirable specimens, showing qualities which brought Mr. James his early readers and first made his name an essential feature of the announcements of publishers of the more discriminating periodicals forty years ago.

The earliest authenticated magazine article by Mr. James—printed when he was twenty-one—is a critical notice of Nassau W. Senior's Essays on Fiction *in* The North American Review *for October, 1864. From this time until the appearance of his first volume—*A Passionate Pilgrim and Other Tales, *Boston: 1875—as many as one hundred and twenty-five serious literary notices contributed to periodicals can be traced to him.*

During this period it must also be remembered that Mr. James was equally employed in writing short stories, art criticism and notes of travel, both at home and abroad, and that these were also distinctive features of the widely scattered journals in which they appeared.

In The North American Review, The Atlantic Monthly, The Galaxy, Lippincott's Magazine, The New York Tribune, The Independent *and some other periodicals, the authorship of such work was attributed to Mr. James on the publication of the articles or in regularly issued indexes.*

The articles in The Nation *are seldom signed, and there is no published index showing the contributors to its files. In preparing a recent*[*] *Bibliography of the writings of Henry James I had access to a record which the late Wendell Phillips Garrison, who was Mr. Godkin's associate from the founding of the paper and after 1881 editor in charge until June 28, 1906, had carefully kept of every author's work which his paper had published since its first issue. The amount of matter which Mr. James had provided, and the variety of interests concerning which he wrote, made an amazing array of notes. It is from the early issues of* The Nation *that much of the contents of this volume is reprinted. Of Mr. James's contributions to periodicals those to this paper were perhaps the most notable as well as the most frequent. He was represented in its first number—July 6, 1865—by some critical notes on Henry W. Kingsley's novel,* "The Hillyars and the Bartons: A Story of Two Families," *under the title,* "The Noble School of Fiction," *and the name* "Henry James" *appears in the publisher's announced list of contributors to the early volumes. Many of these papers which first appeared in* The Nation *have been reprinted, but few readers at this distance can realize how much the esteem in which that journal was immediately held under the editorial supervision of Mr. Godkin was due to perhaps its youngest regular contributor.*

[*] *A Bibliography of the Writings of Henry James. Boston and New York: Houghton, Mifflin and Company, 1906.*

Volumes of the collected critical papers have already appeared,—French Poets and Novelists, London: *1878, and* Partial Portraits, *London: 1888, are the more notable,— but by far the greater part of these contemporary Essays on the literature of the late sixties and the seventies are now almost lost in the files of old or extinct periodicals.*

We are accustomed these later years to think of Mr. James as novelist rather than literary essayist and he has been cited by a recent writer as an author of fiction who becomes a critic on occasion and, he also adds, that his analytical system of novel writing excellently fits him for the office of critic; but, on the contrary, the papers in this volume seem to show that his early self-training as a critic has been the preparation for the creation of his characters in fiction.

The true lover of Mr. James's work feels the same delightful sense of intimate discovery in touching these early papers that an artist does in finding a portfolio of early sketches by a beloved master whose developed power and strength is known to him. There is the recognition of the characteristic touch even here—the insight, the thought within a thought, (more lately the despair of privileged psychologic athletes), the mystery of seeing—not what is apparent to the outward eye but what we fancied we concealed successfully within our inmost selves. There is the extraordinary sense of his having put on paper what we really thought—what we now think—that gives us more faith than ever in our artist who is expression for us who feel, but who are yet dumb.

LE ROY PHILLIPS.

Boston, April 10, 1908.

THE NOVELS OF GEORGE ELIOT

THE critic's first duty in the presence of an author's collective works is to seek out some key to his method, some utterance of his literary convictions, some indication of his ruling theory. The amount of labour involved in an inquiry of this kind will depend very much upon the author. In some cases the critic will find express declarations; in other cases he will have to content himself with conscientious inductions. In a writer so fond of digressions as George Eliot, he has reason to expect that broad evidences of artistic faith will not be wanting. He finds in *Adam Bede* the following passage:—

"Paint us an angel if you can, with a floating violet robe and a face paled by the celestial light; paint us yet oftener a Madonna, turning her mild face upward, and opening her arms to welcome the divine glory; but do not impose on us any æsthetic rules which shall banish from the region of art those old women scraping carrots with their work-worn hands,—those heavy clowns taking holiday in a dingy pot-house,— those rounded backs and stupid weather-beaten faces that have bent over the spade and done the rough work of the world,—those homes with their tin cans, their brown pitchers, their rough curs, and their clusters of onions. In this world there are so many of these common, coarse people, who have no picturesque, sentimental wretchedness. It is so needful we should remember their existence, else we may happen to leave them quite out of our religion and philosophy, and frame lofty theories which only fit a world of extremes...

"There are few prophets in the world,—few sublimely beautiful women,—few heroes. I can't afford to give all my love and reverence to such rarities; I want a great deal of those feelings for my every-day fellowmen, especially for the few in the foreground of the great multitude, whose faces I know, whose hands I touch, for whom I have to make way with kindly courtesy....

"I herewith discharge my conscience," our author continues, "and declare that I have had quite enthusiastic movements of admiration toward old gentlemen who spoke the worst English, who were occasionally fretful in their temper, and who had never moved in a higher sphere of influence than that of parish overseer; and that the way in which I have come to the conclusion that human nature is loveable—the way I have learnt something of its deep pathos, its sublime mysteries—has been by living a great deal among people more or less commonplace and vulgar, of whom you would perhaps hear nothing very surprising if you were to inquire about them in the neighbourhoods where they dwelt."

But even in the absence of any such avowed predilections as these, a brief glance over the principal figures of her different works would assure us that our author's sympathies are with common people. Silas Marner is a linen-weaver, Adam Bede is a carpenter, Maggie Tulliver is a miller's daughter, Felix Holt is a watchmaker, Dinah Morris works in a factory, and Hetty Sorrel is a dairy-maid. Esther Lyon, indeed, is a daily governess; but Tito Melema alone is a scholar. In the *Scenes of Clerical Life*, the author is constantly slipping down from the clergymen, her heroes, to the most ignorant and obscure of their parishioners. Even in *Romola* she consecrates page after page to the conversation of the Florentine populace. She is as unmistakably a painter of *bourgeois* life as Thackeray was a painter of the life of drawing-rooms.

Her opportunities for the study of the manners of the solid lower classes have evidently been very great. We have her word for it that she has lived much among the farmers, mechanics, and small traders of that central region of England which she has made known to us under the name of Loamshire. The conditions of the popular life in this district in that already distant period to which she refers the action of most of her stories—the end of the last century and the beginning of the present—were so different from any that have been seen in America, that an American, in treating of her books, must be satisfied not to touch upon the question of their accuracy and fidelity as pictures of manners and customs. He can only say that they bear strong internal evidence of truthfulness.

If he is a great admirer of George Eliot, he will indeed be tempted to affirm that they must be true. They offer a completeness, a rich density of detail, which could be the fruit only of a long term of conscious contact,—such as would make it much more difficult for the author to fall into the perversion and suppression of facts, than to set them down literally. It is very probable that her colours are a little too bright, and her shadows of too mild a gray, that the sky of her landscapes is too sunny, and their atmosphere too redolent of peace and abundance. Local affection may be accountable for half of this excess of brilliancy; the author's native optimism is accountable for the other half.

I do not remember, in all her novels, an instance of gross misery of any kind not directly caused by the folly of the sufferer. There are no pictures of vice or poverty or squalor. There are no rags, no gin, no brutal passions. That average humanity which she favours is very *borné* in intellect, but very genial in heart, as a glance at its representatives in her pages will convince us. In *Adam Bede*, there is Mr. Irwine, the vicar, with avowedly no qualification for his profession, placidly playing chess with his mother, stroking his dogs, and dipping into Greek tragedies; there is the excellent Martin Poyser at the Farm, good-natured and rubicund; there is his wife, somewhat too sharply voluble, but only in behalf of cleanliness and honesty and order; there is Captain Donnithorne at the Hall, who does a poor girl a mortal wrong, but who is, after all, such a nice, good-looking fellow; there are Adam and Seth Bede, the carpenter's sons, the strongest, purest, most discreet of young rustics. The same broad felicity prevails in *The Mill on the Floss*. Mr. Tulliver, indeed, fails in business; but his failure only serves as an offset to the general integrity and prosperity. His son is obstinate and wilful; but it is all on the side of virtue. His daughter is somewhat sentimental and erratic; but she is more conscientious yet.

Conscience, in the classes from which George Eliot recruits her figures, is a universal gift. Decency and plenty and good-humour follow contentedly in its train. The word which sums up the common traits of our author's various groups is the word *respectable*. Adam Bede is pre-eminently a respectable young man; so is Arthur Donnithorne; so, although he will persist in going without a cravat, is Felix Holt. So, with perhaps the exception of Maggie Tulliver and Stephen Guest, is every important character to be found in our author's writings. They all share this fundamental trait,— that in each of them passion proves itself feebler than conscience.

The first work which made the name of George Eliot generally known, contains, to my perception, only a small number of the germs of her future power. From the *Scenes of Clerical Life* to *Adam Bede* she made not so much a step as a leap. Of the three tales contained in the former work, I think the first is much the best. It is short, broadly descriptive, humourous, and exceedingly pathetic. "The Sad Fortunes of the Reverend Amos Barton" are fortunes which clever story-tellers with a turn for pathos, from Oliver Goldsmith downward, have found of very good account,—the fortunes of a hapless clergyman of the Church of England in daily contention with the problem how upon eighty pounds a year to support a wife and six children in all due ecclesiastical gentility.

"Mr. Gilfil's Love-Story," the second of the tales in question, I cannot hesitate to pronounce a failure. George Eliot's pictures of drawing-room life are only interesting when they are linked or related to scenes in the tavern parlour, the dairy, and the cottage. Mr. Gilfil's love-story is enacted entirely in the drawing-room, and in consequence it is singularly deficient in force and reality. Not that it is vulgar,—for our author's good taste never forsakes her,—but it is thin, flat, and trivial. But for a certain family likeness in the use of language and the rhythm of the style, it would be hard to believe that these pages are by the same hand as *Silas Marner*.

In "Janet's Repentance," the last and longest of the three clerical stories, we return to middle life,—the life represented by the Dodsons in *The Mill on the Floss*. The subject of this tale might almost be qualified by the French epithet *scabreux*. It would be difficult for what is called *realism* to go further than in the adoption of a heroine stained with the vice of intemperance. The theme is unpleasant; the author chose it at her peril. It must be added, however, that Janet Dempster has many provocations. Married to a brutal drunkard, she takes refuge in drink against his ill-usage; and the story deals less with her lapse into disgrace than with her redemption, through the kind offices of the Reverend Edgar Tryan,—by virtue of which, indeed, it takes its place in the clerical series. I cannot help thinking that the stern and tragical character of the subject has been enfeebled by the over-diffuseness of the narrative and the excess of local touches. The abundance of the author's recollections and observations of village life clogs the dramatic movement, over which she has as yet a comparatively slight control. In her subsequent works the stouter fabric of the story is better able to support this heavy drapery of humour and digression.

To a certain extent, I think *Silas Marner* holds a higher place than any of the author's works. It is more nearly a masterpiece; it has more of that simple, rounded, consummate aspect, that absence of loose ends and gaping issues, which marks a classical work. What was attempted in it, indeed, was within more immediate reach than the heart-trials of Adam Bede and Maggie Tulliver. A poor, dull-witted, disappointed Methodist cloth-weaver; a little golden-haired foundling child; a well-meaning, irresolute country squire, and his patient, childless wife;—these, with a chorus of simple, beer-loving villagers, make up the *dramatis personae*. More than any of its brother-works, *Silas Marner*, I think, leaves upon the mind a deep impression of the grossly material life of agricultural England in the last days of the old *régime*,— the days of full-orbed Toryism, of Trafalgar and of Waterloo, when the invasive spirit of French domination threw England back upon a sense of her own insular solidity, and made her for the time doubly, brutally, morbidly English. Perhaps the best pages in the work are the first thirty, telling the story of poor Marner's disappointments in friendship and in love, his unmerited disgrace, and his long, lonely twilight-life at Raveloe, with the sole companionship of his loom, in which his muscles moved "with such even repetition, that their pause seemed almost as much a constraint as the holding of his breath."

Here, as in all George Eliot's books, there is a middle life and a low life; and here, as usual, I prefer the low life. In *Silas Marner*, in my opinion, she has come nearest the mildly rich tints of brown and gray, the mellow lights and the undreadful corner-shadows of the Dutch masters whom she emulates. One of the chapters contains a scene in a pot-house, which frequent reference has made famous. Never was a group of honest, garrulous village simpletons more kindly and humanely handled. After a long and somewhat chilling silence, amid the pipes and beer, the landlord opens the conversation "by saying in a doubtful tone to his cousin the butcher:—

"'Some folks 'ud say that was a fine beast you druv in yesterday, Bob?'

"The butcher, a jolly, smiling, red-haired man, was not disposed to answer rashly. He gave a few puffs before he spat, and replied, 'And they wouldn't be fur wrong, John.'

"After this feeble, delusive thaw, silence set in as severely as before.

"'Was it a red Durham?' said the farrier, taking up the thread of discourse after the lapse of a few minutes.

"The farrier looked at the landlord, and the landlord looked at the butcher, as the person who must take the responsibility of answering.

"'Red it was,' said the butcher, in his good-humoured husky treble,—'and a Durham it was.'

"'Then you needn't tell me who you bought it of,' said the farrier, looking round with some triumph; 'I know who it is has got the red Durhams o' this country-side. And she'd a white star on her brow, I'll bet a penny?'

"'Well; yes—she might,' said the butcher, slowly, considering that he was giving a decided affirmation. 'I don't say contrairy.'

"'I knew that very well,' said the farrier, throwing himself back defiantly; 'if I don't know Mr. Lammeter's cows, I should like to know who does,—that's all. And as for the cow you bought, bargain or no bargain, I've been at the drenching of her,—contradick me who will.'

"The farrier looked fierce, and the mild butcher's conversational spirit was roused a little.

"'I'm not for contradicking no man,' he said; 'I'm for peace and quietness. Some are for cutting long ribs. I'm for cutting 'em short myself; but *I* don't quarrel with 'em. All I say is, it's a lovely carkiss,—and anybody as was reasonable, it'ud bring tears into their eyes to look at it.'

"'Well, it's the cow as I drenched, whatever it is,' pursued the farrier, angrily; 'and it was Mr. Lammeter's cow, else you told a lie when you said it was a red Durham.'

"'I tell no lies,' said the butcher, with the same mild huskiness as before; 'and I contradick none,—not if a man was to swear himself black; he's no meat of mine, nor none of my bargains. All I say is, it's a lovely carkiss. And what I say I'll stick to; but I'll quarrel wi' no man.'

"'No,' said the farrier, with bitter sarcasm, looking at the company generally; 'and p'rhaps you didn't say the cow was a red Durham; and p'rhaps you didn't say she'd got a star on her brow,—stick to that, now you are at it.'"

Matters having come to this point, the landlord interferes *ex officio* to preserve order. The Lammeter family having come up, he discreetly invites Mr. Macey, the parish clerk and tailor, to favour the company with his recollections on the subject. Mr. Macey, however, "smiled pityingly in answer to the landlord's appeal, and said: 'Ay, ay; I know, I know: but I let other folks talk. I've laid by now, and gev up to the young uns. Ask them as have been to school at Tarley: they've learn't pernouncing; that's came up since my day.'"

Mr. Macey is nevertheless persuaded to dribble out his narrative; proceeding by instalments, and questioned from point to point, in a kind of Socratic manner, by the landlord. He at last arrives at Mr. Lammeter's marriage, and how the clergyman, when he came to put the questions, inadvertently transposed the position of the two essential names, and asked, "Wilt thou have this man to be thy wedded wife?" etc.

"'But the partic'larest thing of all,' pursues Mr. Macey, 'is, as nobody took any notice on it but me, and they answered straight off "Yes," like as if it had been me saying "Amen" i' the right place, without listening to what went before.'

"'But *you* knew what was going on well enough, didn't you, Mr. Macey? You were live enough, eh?' said the butcher.

"'Yes, bless you!' said Mr. Macey, pausing, and smiling in pity at the impatience of his hearer's imagination,—'why, I was all of a tremble; it was as if I'd been a coat pulled by two tails, like; for I couldn't stop the parson, I couldn't take upon me to do that; and yet I said to myself, I says, "Suppose they shouldn't be fast married," 'cause the words are contrairy, and my head went working like a mill, for I was always uncommon for turning things over and seeing all round 'em; and I says to myself, "Is't the meaning or the words as makes folks fast i' wedlock?" For the parson meant right, and the bride and bride-groom meant right. But then, when I came to think on it, meaning goes but a little way i' most things, for you may mean to stick things together and your glue may be bad, and then where are you?'"

Mr. Macey's doubts, however, are set at rest by the parson after the service, who assures him that what does the business is neither the meaning nor the words, but the register. Mr. Macey then arrives at the chapter—or rather is gently inducted thereunto by his hearers—of the ghosts who frequent certain of the Lammeter stables. But ghosts threatening to prove as pregnant a theme of contention as Durham cows, the landlord again meditates: "'There's folks i' my opinion, they can't see ghos'es, not if they stood as plain as a pikestaff before 'em. And there's reason i' that. For there's my wife, now, can't smell, not if she'd the strongest o' cheese under her nose. I never seed a ghost myself, but then I says to myself, "Very like I haven't the smell for 'em." I mean, putting a ghost for a smell or else contrairiways. And so I'm for holding with both sides.... For the smell's what I go by.'"

The best drawn of the village worthies in *Silas Marner* are Mr. Macey, of the scene just quoted, and good Dolly Winthrop, Marner's kindly patroness. I have room for only one more specimen of Mr. Macey. He is looking on at a New Year's dance at Squire Cass's, beside Ben Winthrop, Dolly's husband.

"'The Squire's pretty springy, considering his weight,' said Mr. Macey, 'and he stamps uncommon well. But Mr. Lammeter beats 'em all for shapes; you see he holds his head like a sodger, and he isn't so cushiony as most o' the oldish gentlefolks,—they run fat in gineral;—and he's got a fine leg. The parson's nimble enough, but he hasn't got much of a leg: it is a bit too thick downward, and his knees might be a bit nearer without damage; but he might do worse, he might do worse. Though he hasn't that grand way o' waving his hand as the Squire has.'

"'Talk o' nimbleness, look at Mrs. Osgood,' said Ben Winthrop.... 'She's the finest made woman as is, let the next be where she will.'

"'I don't heed how the women are made,' said Mr. Macey, with some contempt. 'They wear nayther coat nor breeches; you can't make much out o' their shapes!'"

Mrs. Winthrop, the wheelwright's wife who, out of the fullness of her charity, comes to comfort Silas in the season of his distress, is in her way one of the most truthfully sketched of the author's figures. "She was in all respects a woman of scrupulous conscience, so eager for duties that life seemed to offer them too scantily unless she rose at half past four, though this threw a scarcity of work over the more advanced hours of the morning, which it was a constant problem for her to remove.... She was a very mild, patient woman, whose nature it was to seek out all the sadder and more serious elements of life and pasture her mind upon them." She stamps I. H. S. on her cakes and loaves without knowing what the letters mean, or indeed without knowing that they are letters, being very much surprised that Marner can "read 'em off,"—chiefly because they are on the pulpit cloth at church. She touches upon religions themes in a manner to make the superficial reader apprehend that she cultivates some polytheistic form of faith,—extremes meet. She urges Marner to go to church, and describes the satisfaction which she herself derives from the performance of her religious duties.

"If you've niver had no church, there 's no telling what good it'll do you. For I feel as set up and comfortable as niver was, when I've been and heard the prayers and the singing to the praise and glory o' God, as Mr. Macey gives out,—and Mr. Crackenthorp saying good words and more partic'lar on Sacramen' day; and if a bit o' trouble comes, I feel as I can put up wi' it, for I've looked for help i' the right quarter, and giv myself up to Them as we must all give ourselves up to at the last: and if we've done our part, it isn't to be believed as Them as are above us 'ud be worse nor we are, and come short o' Theirn."

"The plural pronoun," says the author, "was no heresy of Dolly's, but only her way of avoiding a presumptuous familiarity." I imagine that there is in no other English novel a figure so simple in its elements as this of Dolly Winthrop, which is so real without being contemptible, and so quaint without being ridiculous.

In all those of our author's books which have borne the name of the hero or heroine,—*Adam Bede, Silas Marner, Romola,* and *Felix Holt,*—the person so put forward has really played a subordinate part. The author may have set out with the intention of maintaining him supreme; but her material has become rebellious in her hands, and the technical hero has been eclipsed by the real one. Tito is the leading figure in *Romola.* The story deals predominantly, not with Romola as affected by Tito's faults, but with Tito's faults as affecting first himself, and incidentally his wife. Godfrey Cass, with his lifelong secret, is by right the hero of *Silas Marner.* Felix Holt, in the work which bears his name, is little more than an occasional apparition; and indeed the novel has no hero, but only a heroine.

The same remark applies to *Adam Bede,* as the work stands. The central figure of the book, by virtue of her great misfortune, is Hetty Sorrel. In the presence of that misfortune no one else, assuredly, has a right to claim dramatic pre-eminence. The one person for whom an approach to equality may be claimed is, not Adam Bede, but Arthur Donnithorne. If the story had ended, as I should have infinitely preferred to see it end, with Hetty's execution, or even with her reprieve, and if Adam had been left to his grief, and Dinah Morris to the enjoyment of that distinguished celibacy for which she was so well suited, then I think Adam might have shared the honours of pre-eminence with his hapless sweetheart. But as it is, the continuance of the book in his interest is fatal to him. His sorrow at Hetty's misfortune is not a *sufficient* sorrow for the situation. That his marriage at some future time was quite possible, and even natural, I readily admit; but that was matter for a new story.

This point illustrates, I think, the great advantage of the much-censured method, introduced by Balzac, of continuing his heroes' adventures from tale to tale. Or, admitting that the author was indisposed to undertake, or even to conceive, in its completeness, a new tale, in which Adam, healed of his wound by time, should address himself to another woman, I yet hold that it would be possible tacitly to foreshadow some such event at the close of the tale which we are supposing to end with Hetty's death,—to make it the logical consequence of Adam's final state of mind. Of course circumstances would have much to do with bringing it to pass, and these circumstances could not be foreshadowed; but apart from the action of circumstances would stand the fact that, to begin with, the event was *possible*.

The assurance of this possibility is what I should have desired the author to place the sympathetic reader at a stand-point to deduce for himself. In every novel the work is divided between the writer and the reader; but the writer makes the reader very much as he makes his characters. When he makes him ill, that is, makes him different, he does no work; the writer does all. When he makes him well, that is, makes him interested, then the reader does quite half the labour. In making such a deduction as I have just indicated, the reader would be doing but his share of the task; the grand point is to get him to make it. I hold that there is a way. It is perhaps a secret; but until it is found out, I think that the art of story-telling cannot be said to have approached perfection.

When you re-read coldly and critically a book which in former years you have read warmly and carelessly, you are surprised to see how it changes its proportions. It falls away in those parts which have been pre-eminent in your memory, and it increases in the small portions. Until I lately read *Adam Bede* for a second time, Mrs. Poyser was in my mind its representative figure; for I remembered a number of her epigrammatic sallies. But now, after a second reading, Mrs. Poyser is the last figure

I think of, and a fresh perusal of her witticisms has considerably diminished their classical flavour. And if I must tell the truth, Adam himself is next to the last, and sweet Dinah Morris third from the last. The person immediately evoked by the title of the work is poor Hetty Sorrel.

Mrs. Poyser is *too* epigrammatic; her wisdom smells of the lamp. I do not mean to say that she is not natural, and that women of her class are not often gifted with her homely fluency, her penetration, and her turn for forcible analogies. But she is too sustained; her morality is too shrill,—too much in *staccato*; she too seldom subsides into the commonplace. Yet it cannot be denied that she puts things very happily. Remonstrating with Dinah Morris on the undue disinterestedness of her religious notions, "But for the matter o' that," she cries, "if everybody was to do like you, the world must come to a stand-still; for if everybody tried to do without house and home and eating and drinking, and was always talking as we must despise the things o' the world, as you say, I should like to know where the pick of the stock, and the corn, and the best new milk-cheeses 'ud have to go? *Everybody 'ud be wanting to make bread o' tail ends*, and everybody 'ud be running after everybody else to preach to 'em, i'stead o' bringing up their families and laying by against a bad harvest." And when Hetty comes home late from the Chase, and alleges in excuse that the clock at home is so much earlier than the clock at the great house: "What, you'd be wanting the clock set by gentlefolks' time, would you? an' sit up burning candle, and lie a-bed wi' the sun a-bakin' you, like a cowcumber i' the frame?" Mrs. Poyser has something almost of Yankee shrewdness and angularity; but the figure of a New England rural housewife would lack a whole range of Mrs. Poyser's feelings, which, whatever may be its effect in real life, gives its subject in a novel at least a very picturesque richness of colour; the constant sense, namely, of a superincumbent layer of "gentlefolks," whom she and her companions can never raise their heads unduly without hitting.

My chief complaint with Adam Bede himself is that he is too good. He is meant, I conceive, to be every inch a man; but, to my mind, there are several inches wanting. He lacks spontaneity and sensibility, he is too stiff-backed. He lacks that supreme quality without which a man can never be interesting to men,—the capacity to be tempted. His nature is without richness or responsiveness. I doubt not that such men as he exist, especially in the author's thrice-English Loamshire; she has partially described them as a class, with a felicity which carries conviction. She claims for her hero that, although a plain man, he was as little an ordinary man as he was a genius.

"He was not an average man. Yet such men as he are reared here and there in every generation of our peasant artisans, with an inheritance of affections nurtured by a simple family life of common need and common industry, and an inheritance of faculties trained in skillful, courageous labour; they make their way upward, rarely as geniuses, most commonly as painstaking, honest men, with the skill and conscience to do well the tasks that lie before them. Their lives have no discernible echo beyond the neighbourhood where they dwelt; but you are almost sure to find there some good piece of road, some building, some application of mineral produce, some improvement in farming practice, some reform of parish abuses, with which their names are associated by one or two generations after them. Their employers were the richer for them; the work of their hands has worn well, and the work of their brains has guided well the hands of other men."

One cannot help feeling thankful to the kindly writer who attempts to perpetuate their memories beyond the generations which profit immediately by their toil. If she is not a great dramatist, she is at least an exquisite describer. But one can as little help feeling that it is no more than a strictly logical retribution, that in her hour of need (dramatically speaking) she should find them indifferent to their duties as heroes. I profoundly doubt whether the central object of a novel may successfully be a passionless creature. The ultimate eclipse, both of Adam Bede and of Felix Holt would seem to justify my question. Tom Tulliver is passionless, and Tom Tulliver lives gratefully in the memory; but this, I take it, is because he is strictly a subordinate figure, and awakens no reaction of feeling on the reader's part by usurping a position which he is not the man to fill.

Dinah Morris is apparently a study from life; and it is warm praise to say, that, in spite of the high key in which she is conceived, morally, she retains many of the warm colours of life. But I confess that it is hard to conceive of a woman so exalted by religious fervour remaining so cool-headed and so temperate. There is in Dinah Morris too close an agreement between her distinguished natural disposition and the action of her religious faith. If by nature she had been passionate, rebellious, selfish, I could better understand her actual self-abnegation. I would look upon it as the logical fruit of a profound religious experience. But as she stands, heart and soul go easily hand in hand. I believe it to be very uncommon for what is called a religious conversion merely to intensify and consecrate pre-existing inclinations. It is usually a change, a wrench; and the new life is apt to be the more sincere as the old one had less in common with it. But, as I have said, Dinah Morris bears so many indications of being a reflection of facts well known to the author,—and the phenomena of Methodism, from the frequency with which their existence is referred to in her pages, appear to be so familiar to her,—that I hesitate to do anything but thankfully accept her portrait.

About Hetty Sorrel I shall have no hesitation whatever: I accept her with all my heart. Of all George Eliot's female figures she is the least ambitious, and on the whole, I think, the most successful. The part of the story which concerns her is much the most forcible; and there is something infinitely tragic in the reader's sense of the contrast between the sternly prosaic life of the good people about her, their wholesome decency and their noon-day probity, and the dusky sylvan path along which poor Hetty is tripping, light-footed, to her ruin. Hetty's conduct throughout seems to me to be thoroughly consistent. The author has escaped the easy error of representing her as in any degree made serious by suffering. She is vain and superficial by nature; and she remains so to the end.

As for Arthur Donnithorne, I would rather have had him either better or worse. I would rather have had a little more premeditation before his fault, or a little more repentance after it; that is, while repentance could still be of use. Not that, all things considered, he is not a very fair image of a frank-hearted, well-meaning, careless, self-indulgent young gentleman; but the author has in his case committed the error which in Hetty's she avoided,—the error of showing him as redeemed by suffering. I cannot but think that he was as weak as she. A weak woman, indeed, is weaker than a weak man; but Arthur Donnithorne was a superficial fellow, a person emphatically not to be moved by a shock of conscience into a really interesting and dignified attitude, such as he is made to assume at the close of the book. Why not see things in their nakedness? the impatient reader is tempted to ask. Why not let passions and foibles play themselves out?

It is as a picture, or rather as a series of pictures, that I find *Adam Bede* most valuable. The author succeeds better in drawing attitudes of feeling than in drawing movements of feeling. Indeed, the only attempt at development of character or of purpose in the book occurs in the case of Arthur Donnithorne, where the materials are of the simplest kind. Hetty's lapse into disgrace is not gradual, it is immediate: it is without struggle and without passion. Adam himself has arrived at perfect righteousness when the book opens; and it is impossible to go beyond that. In his case too, therefore, there is no dramatic progression. The same remark applies to Dinah Morris.

It is not in her conceptions nor her composition that George Eliot is strongest: it is in her *touches*. In these she is quite original. She is a good deal of a humourist, and something of a satirist; but she is neither Dickens nor Thackeray. She has over them the great advantage that she is also a good deal of a philosopher; and it is to this union of the keenest observation with the ripest reflection, that her style owes its essential force. She is a thinker,—not, perhaps, a passionate thinker, but at least a serious one; and the term can be applied with either adjective neither to Dickens nor Thackeray. The constant play of lively and vigourous thought about the objects furnished by her observation animates these latter with a surprising richness of colour and a truly human interest. It gives to the author's style, moreover, that lingering, affectionate, comprehensive quality which is its chief distinction; and perhaps occasionally it makes her tedious. George Eliot is so little tedious, however, because, if, on the one hand, her reflection never flags, so, on the other, her observation never ceases to supply it with material. Her observation, I think, is decidedly of the feminine kind: it deals, in preference, with small things. This fact may be held to explain the excellence of what I have called her pictures, and the comparative feebleness of her dramatic movement.

The contrast here indicated, strong in *Adam Bede*, is most striking in *Felix Holt, the Radical*. The latter work is an admirable tissue of details; but it seems to me quite without character as a composition. It leaves upon the mind no single impression. Felix Holt's radicalism, the pretended motive of the story, is utterly choked amidst a mass of subordinate interests. No representation is attempted of the growth of his opinions, or of their action upon his character; he is marked by the same singular rigidity of outline and fixedness of posture which characterized Adam Bede,—except, perhaps, that there is a certain inclination towards poetry in Holt's attitude. But if the general outline is timid and undecided in *Felix Holt*, the different parts are even richer than in former works. There is no person in the book who attains to triumphant vitality; but there is not a single figure, of however little importance, that has not caught from without a certain reflection of life. There is a little old waiting-woman to a great lady,—Mrs. Denner by name,—who does not occupy five pages in the story, but who leaves upon the mind a most vivid impression of decent, contented, intelligent, half-stoical servility.

"There were different orders of beings,—so ran Denner's creed,—and she belonged to another order than that to which her mistress belonged. She had a mind as sharp as a needle, and would have seen through and through the ridiculous pretensions of a born servant who did not submissively accept the rigid fate which had given her born superiors. She would have called such pretensions the wrigglings of a worm that tried to walk on its tail.... She was a hard-headed, godless little woman, but with a character to be reckoned on as you reckon on the qualities of iron."

"I'm afraid of ever expecting anything good again," her mistress says to her in a moment of depression.

"'That's weakness, madam. Things don't happen because they are bad or good, else all eggs would be addled or none at all, and at the most it is but six to the dozen. There's good chances and bad chances, and nobody's luck is pulled only by one string.... There's a good deal of pleasure in life for you yet.'

"'Nonsense! There's no pleasure for old women.... What are your pleasures, Denner, besides being a slave to me?'

"O, there's pleasure in knowing one is not a fool, like half the people one sees about. And managing one's husband is some pleasure, and doing one's business well. Why, if I've only got some orange-flowers to candy, I shouldn't like to die till I see them all right. Then there's the sunshine now and then; I like that, as the cats do. I look upon it life is like our game at whist, when Banks and his wife come to the still-room of an evening. I don't enjoy the game much, but I like to play my cards well, and see what will be the end of it; and I want to see you make the best of your hand, madam, for your luck has been mine these forty years now."

And, on another occasion, when her mistress exclaims, in a fit of distress, that "God was cruel when he made women," the author says:—

"The waiting-woman had none of that awe which could be turned into defiance; the sacred grove was a common thicket to her.

"'It mayn't be good luck to be a woman,' she said. 'But one begins with it from a baby; one gets used to it. And I shouldn't like to be a man,—to cough so loud, and stand straddling about on a wet day, and be so wasteful with meat and drink. *They're a coarse lot, I think.*'"

I should think they were, beside Mrs. Denner.

This glimpse of her is made up of what I have called the author's *touches*. She excels in the portrayal of homely stationary figures for which her well-stored memory furnishes her with types. Here is another touch, in which satire predominates. Harold Transome makes a speech to the electors at Treby.

"Harold's only interruption came from his own party. The oratorical clerk at the Factory, acting as the tribune of the dissenting interest, and feeling bound to put questions, might have been troublesome; *but his voice being unpleasantly sharp, while Harold's was full and penetrating, the questioning was cried down.*"

Of the four English stories, *The Mill on the Floss* seems to me to have most dramatic continuity, in distinction from that descriptive, discursive method of narration which I have attempted to indicate. After Hetty Sorrel, I think Maggie Tulliver the most successful of the author's young women, and after Tito Melema, Tom Tulliver the best of her young men. English novels abound in pictures of childhood; but I know of none more truthful and touching than the early pages of this work. Poor erratic Maggie is worth a hundred of her positive brother, and yet on the very threshold of life she is compelled to accept him as her master. He falls naturally into the man's privilege of always being in the right. The following scene is more than a reminiscence; it is a real retrospect. Tom and Maggie are sitting upon the bough of an elder-tree, eating jam-puffs. At last only one remains, and Tom undertakes to divide it.

"The knife descended on the puff, and it was in two; but the result was not satisfactory to Tom, for he still eyed the halves doubtfully. At last he said, 'Shut your eyes, Maggie.'

"'What for?'

"'You never mind what for,—shut 'em when I tell you.'

"Maggie obeyed.

"'Now, which'll you have, Maggie, right hand or left?'

"'I'll have that one with the jam run out,' said Maggie, keeping her eyes shut to please Tom.

"'Why, you don't like that, you silly. You may have it if it comes to you fair, but I sha'n't give it to you without. Right or left,—you choose now. Ha-a-a!' said Tom, in a tone of exasperation, as Maggie peeped. 'You keep your eyes shut now, else you sha'n't have any.'

"Maggie's power of sacrifice did not extend so far; indeed, I fear she cared less that Tom should enjoy the utmost possible amount of puff, than that he should be pleased with her for giving him the best bit. So she shut her eyes quite close until Tom told her to 'say which,' and then she said, 'Left hand.'

"'You've got it,' said Tom, in rather a bitter tone.

"'What! the bit with the jam run out?'

"'No; here, take it,' said Tom, firmly, handing decidedly the best piece to Maggie.

"'O, please, Tom, have it; I don't mind,—I like the other; please take this.'

"'No, I sha'n't,' said Tom, almost crossly, beginning on his own inferior piece.

"Maggie, thinking it was of no use to contend further, began too, and ate up her half puff with considerable relish as well as rapidity. But Tom had finished first, and had to look on while Maggie ate her last morsel or two, feeling in himself a capacity for more. *Maggie didn't know Tom was looking at her: she was see-sawing on the elder-bough, lost to everything but a vague sense of jam and idleness.*

"'O, you greedy thing!' said Tom, when she had swallowed the last morsel."

The portions of the story which bear upon the Dodson family are in their way not unworthy of Balzac; only that, while our author has treated its peculiarities humourously, Balzac would have treated them seriously, almost solemnly. We are reminded of him by the attempt to classify the Dodsons socially in a scientific manner, and to accumulate small examples of their idiosyncrasies, I do not mean to say that the resemblance is very deep.

The chief defect—indeed, the only serious one—in *The Mill on the Floss* is its conclusion. Such a conclusion is in itself assuredly not illegitimate, and there is nothing in the fact of the flood, to my knowledge, essentially unnatural: what I object to is its relation to the preceding part of the story. The story is told as if it were destined to have, if not a strictly happy termination, at least one within ordinary probabilities. As it stands, the *dénouement* shocks the reader most painfully. Nothing has prepared him for it; the story does not move towards it; it casts no shadow before it. Did such a *dénouement* lie within the author's intentions from the first, or was it a tardy expedient for the solution of Maggie's difficulties? This question the reader asks himself, but of course he asks it in vain.

For my part, although, as long as humanity is subject to floods and earthquakes, I have no objection to see them made use of in novels, I would in this particular case have infinitely preferred that Maggie should have been left to her own devices. I understand the author's scruples, and to a certain degree I respect them. A lonely spinsterhood seemed but a dismal consummation of her generous life; and yet, as the author conceives, it was unlikely that she would return to Stephen Guest. I respect Maggie profoundly; but nevertheless I ask, Was this after all so unlikely? I will not try to answer the question. I have shown enough courage in asking it. But one thing is certain: a *dénouement* by which Maggie should have called Stephen back would have been extremely interesting, and would have had far more in its favour than can be put to confusion by a mere exclamation of horror.

I have come to the end of my space without speaking of *Romola*, which, as the most important of George Eliot's works, I had kept in reserve. I have only room to say that on the whole I think it *is* decidedly the most important,—not the most entertaining nor the most readable, but the one in which the largest things are attempted and grasped. The figure of Savonarola, subordinate though it is, is a figure on a larger scale than any which George Eliot has elsewhere undertaken; and in the career of Tito Melema there is a fuller representation of the development of a character.

Considerable as are our author's qualities as an artist, and largely as they are displayed in "Romola," the book strikes me less as a work of art than as a work of morals. Like all of George Eliot's works, its dramatic construction is feeble; the story drags and halts,—the setting is too large for the picture; but I remember that, the first time I read it, I declared to myself that much should be forgiven it for the sake of its generous feeling and its elevated morality. I still recognize this latter fact, but I think I find it more on a level than I at first found it with the artistic conditions of the book.

"Our deeds determine us," George Eliot says somewhere in *Adam Bede*, "as much as we determine our deeds." This is the moral lesson of *Romola*. A man has no associate so intimate as his own character, his own career,—his present and his past; and if he builds up his career of timid and base actions, they cling to him like evil companions, to sophisticate, to corrupt, and to damn him. As in Maggie Tulliver we had a picture of the elevation of the moral tone by honesty and generosity, so that when the mind found itself face to face with the need for a strong muscular effort, it was competent to perform it; so in Tito we have a picture of that depression of the moral tone by falsity and self-indulgence, which gradually evokes on every side of the subject some implacable claim, to be avoided or propitiated. At last all his unpaid debts join issue before him, and he finds the path of life a hideous blind alley.

Can any argument be more plain? Can any lesson be more salutary? "Under every guilty secret," writes the author, with her usual felicity, "there is a hidden brood of guilty wishes, whose unwholesome, infecting life is cherished by the darkness. The contaminating effect of deeds often lies less in the commission than in the consequent adjustment of our desires,—the enlistment of self-interest on the side of falsity; as, on the other hand, the purifying influence of public confession springs from the fact, that by it the hope in lies is forever swept away, *and the soul recovers the noble attitude of simplicity*." And again: "Tito was experiencing that inexorable law of human souls, that we prepare ourselves for sudden deeds by the reiterated choice of good or evil that gradually determines character." Somewhere else I think she says, in purport, that our deeds are like our children; we beget them, and rear them and cherish them, and they grow up and turn against us and misuse us.

The fact that has led me to a belief in the fundamental equality between the worth of *Romola* as a moral argument and its value as a work of art, is the fact that in each character it seems to me essentially prosaic. The excellence both of the spirit and of the execution of the book is emphatically an obvious excellence. They make no demand upon the imagination of the reader. It is true of both of them that he who runs may read them. It may excite surprise that I should intimate that George Eliot is deficient in imagination; but I believe that I am right in so doing. Very readable novels have been written without imagination; and as compared with writers who, like Mr. Trollope, are totally destitute of the faculty, George Eliot may be said to be richly endowed with it. But as compared with writers whom we are tempted to call decidedly imaginative, she must, in my opinion, content herself with the very solid distinction of being exclusively an observer. In confirmation of this I would suggest a comparison of those chapters in *Adam Bede* which treat of Hetty's flight and wanderings, and those of Miss Brontë's *Jane Eyre* which describe the heroine's escape from Rochester's house and subsequent perambulations. The former are throughout admirable prose; the latter are in portions very good poetry.

One word more. Of all the impressions—and they are numerous—which a reperusal of George Eliot's writings has given me, I find the strongest to be this: that (with all deference to *Felix Holt, the Radical*) the author is in morals and æsthetics essentially a conservative. In morals her problems are still the old, passive problems. I use the word "old" with all respect. What moves her most is the idea of a conscience harassed by the memory of slighted obligations. Unless in the case of Savonarola, she has made no attempt to depict a conscience taking upon itself great and novel responsibilities. In her last work, assuredly such an attempt was—considering the title—conspicuous by its absence.

Of a corresponding tendency in the second department of her literary character,—or perhaps I should say in a certain middle field where morals and æsthetics move in concert,—it is very difficult to give an example. A tolerably good one is furnished by her inclination to compromise with the old tradition—and here I use the word "old" *without* respect—which exacts that a serious story of manners shall close with the factitious happiness of a fairy-tale. I know few things more irritating in a literary way than each of her final chapters,—for even in *The Mill on the Floss* there is a fatal

"Conclusion." Both as an artist and a thinker, in other words, our author is an optimist; and although a conservative is not necessarily an optimist, I think an optimist is pretty likely to be a conservative.

ON A DRAMA OF MR. BROWNING

THIS is a decidedly irritating and displeasing performance. It is growing more difficult every year for Mr. Browning's old friends to fight his battles for him, and many of them will feel that on this occasion the cause is really too hopeless, and the great poet must himself be answerable for his indiscretions.

Nothing that Mr. Browning writes, of course, can be vapid; if this were possible, it would be a much simpler affair. If it were a case of a writer "running thin," as the phrase is, there would be no need for criticism; there would be nothing in the way of matter to criticise, and old readers would have no heart to reproach. But it may be said of Mr. Browning that he runs thick rather than thin, and he need claim none of the tenderness granted to those who have used themselves up in the service of their admirers. He is robust and vigorous; more so now, even, than heretofore, and he is more prolific than in the earlier part of his career. But his wantonness, his wilfulness, his crudity, his inexplicable want of secondary thought, as we may call it, of the stage of reflection that follows upon the first outburst of the idea, and smooths, shapes, and adjusts it—all this alloy of his great genius is more sensible now than ever.

The Inn Album reads like a series of rough notes for a poem—of hasty hieroglyphics and symbols, decipherable only to the author himself. A great poem might perhaps have been made of it, but assuredly it is not a great poem, nor any poem whatsoever. It is hard to say very coherently what it is. Up to a certain point, like everything of Mr. Browning's, it is highly dramatic and vivid and beyond that point, like all its companions, it is as little dramatic as possible. It is not narrative, for there is not a line of comprehensible, consecutive statement in the two hundred and eleven pages of the volume. It is not lyrical, for there is not a phrase which in any degree does the office of the poetry that comes lawfully into the world—chants itself, images itself, or lingers in the memory.

"That bard's a Browning; he neglects the form!" one of the characters exclaims with irresponsible frankness. That Mr. Browning knows he "neglects the form," and does not particularly care, does not very much help matters; it only deepens the reader's sense of the graceless and thankless and altogether unavailable character of the poem. And when we say unavailable, we make the only reproach which is worth addressing to a writer of Mr. Browning's intellectual power. A poem with so many presumptions in its favour as such an authorship carries with it is a thing to make some intellectual use of, to care for, to remember, to return to, to linger over, to become intimate with. But we can as little imagine a reader (who has not the misfortune to be a reviewer) addressing himself more than once to the perusal of *The Inn Album*, as we fancy cultivating for conversational purposes the society of a person afflicted with a grievous impediment of speech.

Two gentlemen have been playing cards all night in an inn-parlour, and the peep of day finds one of them ten thousand pounds in debt to the other. The tables have been turned, and the victim is the actual victor. The elder man is a dissolute and penniless nobleman, who has undertaken the social education of the aspiring young heir of a great commercial fortune, and has taught him so well that the once ingenuous lad knows more than his clever master. The young man has come down into the country to see his cousin, who lives, hard by at the Hall, with her aunt, and with whom his aristocratic preceptor recommends him, for good worldly reasons, to make a match.

Infinite discourse, of that formidable full-charged sort that issues from the lips of all Mr. Browning's characters, follows the play, and as the morning advances the two gentlemen leave the inn and go for a walk. Lord K. has meanwhile related to his young companion the history of one of his own earlier loves—how he had seduced a magnificent young woman, and she had fairly frightened him into offering her marriage. On learning that he had meant to go free if he could, her scorn for him becomes such that she rejects his offer of reparation (a very fine stroke) and enters into wedlock with a "smug, crop-haired, smooth-chinned sort of curate-creature." The young man replies that he himself was once in love with a person that quite answers to this description, and then the companions separate—the pupil to call at the Hall, and the preceptor to catch the train for London.

The reader is then carried back to the inn-parlour, into which, on the departure of the gentlemen, two ladies have been ushered. One of them is the young man's cousin, who is playing at cross-purposes with her suitor; the other is her intimate friend, arrived on a flying visit. The intimate friend is of course the ex-victim of Lord K. The ladies have much conversation—all of it rather more ingeniously inscrutable than that of their predecessors; it terminates in the exit of the cousin and the entrance of the young man. He recognizes the curate's wife as the object of his own stifled affection, and the two have, as the French say, an *intime* conversation.

At last Lord K. comes back, having missed his train, and finds himself confronted with his stormy mistress. Very stormy she proves to be, and her outburst of renewed indignation and irony contains perhaps the most successful writing in the poem. Touched by the lady's eloquence, the younger man, who has hitherto professed an almost passionate admiration for his companion, begins to see him in a less interesting light, and in fact promptly turns and reviles him. The situation is here extremely dramatic. Lord K. is a cynic of a sneaking pattern, but he is at any rate a man of ideas. He holds the destiny of his adversaries in his hands, and, snatching up the inn album (which has been knocking about the table during the foregoing portions of the narrative), he scrawls upon it his ultimatum. Let the lady now bestow her affection on his companion, and let the latter accept this boon as a vicarious payment of the gambling debt, otherwise Lord K. will enlighten the lady's husband as to the extent of her acquaintance with himself.

He presents the open page to the heroine, who reads it aloud, and for an answer her younger and more disinterested lover, "with a tiger-flash yell, spring, and scream," throws himself on the insulter, half an hour since, his guide, philosopher, and friend, and, by some means undescribed by Mr. Browning puts an end to his life. This incident is related in two pregnant lines, which, judged by the general standard of style of the *Inn Album*, must be considered fine:

"A tiger-flash, yell, spring and scream: halloo!

Death's out and on him, has and holds him—ugh!"

The effect is of course augmented if the reader is careful to make the "ugh!" rhyme correctly with the "halloo!" The lady takes poison, which she carries on her person and which operates instantaneously, and the young man's cousin, re-entering the room, has a sufficiently tremendous surprise.

The whole picture indefinably appeals to the imagination. There is something very curious about it and even rather arbitrary, and the reader wonders how it came, in the poet's mind, to take exactly that shape. It is very much as if he had worked backwards, had seen his dénouement first, as a mere picture—the two corpses in the inn-parlour, and the young man and his cousin confronted above them—and then had traced back the possible motives and sources. In looking for these Mr. Browning has of course encountered a vast number of deep discriminations and powerful touches of portraitures. He deals with human character as a chemist with his acids and alkalies, and while he mixes his coloured fluids in a way that surprises the profane, knows perfectly well what he is about. But there is too apt to be in his style that hiss and sputter and evil aroma which characterise the proceedings of the laboratory. The idea, with Mr. Browning, always tumbles out into the world in some grotesque hind-foremost manner; it is like an unruly horse backing out of his stall, and stamping and plunging as he comes. His thought knows no simple stage—at the very moment of its birth it is a terribly complicated affair.

We frankly confess, at the risk of being accused of deplorable levity of mind, that we have found this want of clearness of explanation, of continuity, of at least superficial verisimilitude, of the smooth, the easy, the agreeable, quite fatal to our enjoyment of *The Inn Album*. It is all too argumentative, too curious and recondite. The people talk too much in long set speeches, at a moment's notice, and the anomaly so common in Browning, that the talk of the women is even more rugged and insoluble than that of the men, is here greatly exaggerated. We are reading neither prose nor poetry; it is too real for the ideal, and too ideal for the real. The author of *The Inn Album* is not a writer to whom we care to pay trivial compliments, and, it is not a trivial complaint to say that his book is only barely comprehensible. Of a successful dramatic poem one ought to be able to say more.

SWINBURNE'S ESSAYS

MR. SWINBURNE has by this time impressed upon the general public a tolerably vivid image of his literary personality. His line is a definite one; his note is familiar, and we know what to expect from him. He was at pains, indeed, a year ago to quicken the apprehension of American readers by an effusion directed more or less explicitly to themselves. This piece of literature was brief, but it was very remarkable. Mr. Emerson had had occasion to speak of Mr. Swinburne with qualified admiration and this circumstance, coming to Mr. Swinburne's ears, had prompted him to uncork on the spot the vials of his wrath. He addressed to a newspaper a letter of which it is but a colourless account to say that it embodied the very hysterics of gross vituperation.

Mr. Swinburne has some extremely just remarks about Byron's unamenableness to quotation, his having to be taken in the gross. This is almost equally true of our author himself; he must be judged by all he has done, and we must allow, in our judgment, the weight he would obviously claim for it to his elaborate tribute to the genius of Mr. Emerson. His tone has two distinct notes—the note of measureless praise and the note of furious denunciation. Each is in need of a correction, but we confess that, with all its faults, we prefer the former. That Mr. Swinburne has a kindness for his more restrictive strain is, however, very obvious. He is over-ready to sound it, and he is not particular about his pretext.

Some people, he says, for instance, affirm that a writer may have a very effective style, yet have nothing of value to express with it. Mr. Swinburne demands that they prove their assertion. "This flattering unction the very foolishest of malignants will hardly, in this case (that of Mr. D. G. Rossetti), be able to lay upon the corrosive sore which he calls his soul; the ulcer of ill-will must rot unrelieved by the rancid ointment of such fiction." In Mr. W. M. Rossetti's edition of *Shelley* there is in a certain line, an interpolation of the word "autumn." "For the conception of this atrocity the editor is not responsible; for its adoption he is. A thousand years of purgatorial fire would be insufficient expiation for the criminal on whose deaf and desperate head must rest the original guilt of defacing the text of Shelley with this most damnable corruption."

The essays before us are upon Victor Hugo, D. G. Rossetti, William Morris, Matthew Arnold as a poet, Shelley, Byron, Coleridge, and John Ford. To these are added two papers upon pictures—the drawings of the old masters at Florence and the Royal Academy Exhibition of 1868. Mr. Swinburne, in writing of poets, cannot fail to say a great many felicitous things. His own insight into the poetic mystery is so deep, his perception in matters of language so refined, his power of appreciation so large and active, his imagination, especially, so sympathetic and flexible, that we constantly feel him to be one who has a valid right to judge and pass sentence. The variety of his sympathies in poetry is especially remarkable, and is in itself a pledge of criticism of a liberal kind. Victor Hugo is his divinity—a divinity whom indeed, to our sense, he effectually conceals and obliterates in the suffocating fumes of his rhetoric. On the other hand, one of the best papers in the volume is a disquisition on the poetry of Mr. Matthew Arnold, of which his relish seems hardly less intense and for whom he states the case with no less prodigious a redundancy of phrase.

Matthew Arnold's canons of style, we should have said, are a positive negation of those of Mr. Swinburne's, and it is to the credit of the latter's breadth of taste that he should have entered into an intellectual temperament which is so little his own. The other articles contain similar examples of his vivacity and energy of perception, and offer a number of happy judgments and suggestive observations. His estimate of Byron as a poet (not in the least as a man—on this point his utterances are consummately futile) is singularly discriminating; his measurement of Shelley's lyric force is eloquently adequate; his closing words upon John Ford are worth quoting as a specimen of strong apprehension and solid statement. Mr. Swinburne is by no means always solid, and this passage represents him at his best:—

"No poet is less forgettable than Ford; none fastens (as it were) the fangs of his genius and his will more deeply in your memory. You cannot shake hands with him and pass him by; you cannot fall in with him and out again at pleasure; if he touch you once he takes you, and what he takes he keeps his hold of; his work becomes a part of your thought and parcel of your spiritual furniture for ever; he signs himself upon you as with a seal of deliberate and decisive power. His force is never the force of accident; the casual divinity of beauty which falls, as though direct from heaven, upon stray lines and phrases of some poets, fails never by any such heavenly chance on his; his strength of impulse is matched by his strength of will; he never works more by instinct than by resolution; he knows what he would have and what he will do, and gains his end and does his work with full conscience of purpose and insistence of design. By the might of a great will seconded by the force of a great hand he won the place he holds against all odds of rivalry in a race of rival giants."

On the other hand, Mr. Swinburne is constantly liable on this same line to lapse into flagrant levity and perversity of taste; as in saying that he cannot consider

Wordsworth "as mere poet" equal to Coleridge as mere poet; in speaking of Alfred de Musset as "the female page or attendant dwarf" of Byron, and his poems as "decoctions of watered Byronism"; or in alluding jauntily and *en passant* to Gautier's *Mademoiselle de Maupin* as "the most perfect and exquisite book of modern times."

To note, however, the points at which Mr. Swinburne's judgment hits the mark, or the points at which it misses it, is comparatively superfluous, inasmuch as both of these cases seem to us essentially accidental. His book is not at all a book of judgment; it is a book of pure imagination. His genius is for style simply, and not in the least for thought nor for real analysis; he goes through the motions of criticism, and makes a considerable show of logic and philosophy, but with deep appreciation his writing seems to us to have very little to do.

He is an imaginative commentator, often of a very splendid kind, but he is never a real interpreter and rarely a trustworthy guide. He is a writer, and a writer in constant quest of a theme. He has an inordinate sense of the picturesque, and he finds his theme in those subjects and those writers which gratify it. When they gratify it highly, he conceives a boundless relish for them; they give him his chance, and he turns-on the deluge of his exorbitant homage. His imagination kindles, he abounds in their own sense, when they give him an inch he takes an ell, and quite loses sight of the subject in the entertainment he finds in his own word-spinning. In this respect he is extraordinarily accomplished: he very narrowly misses having a magnificent style. On the imaginative side, his style is almost complete, and seems capable of doing everything that picturesqueness demands. There are few writers of our day who could have produced this description of a thunderstorm at sea. Mr. Swinburne gives it to us as the likeness of Victor Hugo's genius:—

"About midnight, the thundercloud was full overhead, full of incessant sound and fire, lightening and darkening so rapidly that it seemed to have life, and a delight in its life. At the same hour, the sky was clear to the west, and all along the sea-line there sprang and sank as to music a restless dance or chase of summer lightnings across the lower sky: a race and riot of lights, beautiful and rapid as a course of shining Oceanides along the tremulous floor of the sea. Eastward, at the same moment, the space of clear sky was higher and wider, a splendid semicircle of too intense purity to be called blue; it was of no colour nameable by man; and midway in it, between the stars and the sea, hung the motionless full moon; Artemis watching with serene splendour of scorn the battle of Titans and the revel of nymphs from her stainless and Olympian summit of divine indifferent light. Underneath and about us, the sea was paved with flame; the whole water trembled and hissed with phosphoric fire; even through the wind and thunder I could hear the crackling and sputtering of the water-sparks. In the same heaven and in the same hour there shone at once the three contrasted glories, golden and fiery and white, of moonlight, and of the double lightning, forked and sheet; and under all this miraculous heaven lay a flaming floor of water."

But with this extravagant development of the imagination there is no commensurate development either of the reason or of the moral sense. One of these defects is, to our mind, fatal to Mr. Swinburne's style; the other is fatal to his tone, to his temper, to his critical pretensions. His style is without measure, without discretion, without sense of what to take and what to leave; after a few pages, it becomes intolerably fatiguing. It is always listening to itself—always turning its head over its shoulders to see its train flowing behind it. The train shimmers and tumbles in a very gorgeous fashion, but the rustle of its embroidery is fatally importunate.

Mr. Swinburne is a dozen times too verbose; at least one-half of his phrases are what the French call phrases in the air. One-half of his sentence is always a repetition, for mere fancy's sake and nothing more, of the meaning of the other half—a play upon its words, an echo, a reflection, a duplication. This trick, of course, makes a writer formidably prolix. What we have called the absence of the moral sense of the writer of these essays is, however, their most disagreeable feature. By this we do not mean that Mr. Swinburne is not didactic, nor edifying, nor devoted to pleading the cause of virtue. We mean simply that his moral plummet does not sink at all, and that when he pretends to drop it he is simply dabbling in the relatively very shallow pool of the picturesque.

A sense of the picturesque so refined as Mr. Swinburne's will take one a great way, but it will by no means, in dealing with things whose great value is in what they tell us of human character, take one all the way. One breaks down with it (if one treats it as one's sole support) sooner or later in æsthetics; one breaks down with it very soon indeed in psychology.

We do not remember in this whole volume a single instance of delicate moral discrimination—a single case in which the moral note has been struck, in which the idea betrays the smallest acquaintance with the conscience. The moral realm for Mr. Swinburne is simply a brilliant chiaroscuro of costume and posture. This makes all Mr. Swinburne's magnificent talk about Victor Hugo's great criminals and monstrosities, about Shelley's Count Cenci, and Browning's Guido Franchesini, and about dramatic figures generally, quite worthless as anything but amusing fantasy. As psychology it is, to our sense, extremely puerile; for we do not mean simply to say that the author does not understand morality—a charge to which he would be probably quite indifferent; but that he does not at all understand immorality. Such a passage as his rhapsody upon Victor Hugo's Josiane ("such a pantheress may be such a poetess," etc.) means absolutely nothing. It is entertaining as pictorial writing—though even in this respect as we have said, thanks to excess and redundancy, it is the picturesque spoiled rather than achieved; but as an attempt at serious analysis it seems to us, like many of its companions, simply ghastly—ghastly in its poverty of insight and its pretension to make mere lurid imagery do duty as thought.

THE POETRY OF WILLIAM MORRIS

I. THE LIFE AND DEATH OF JASON

IN this poetical history of the fortunate—the unfortunate—Jason, Mr. Morris has written a book of real value. It is some time since we have met with a work of imagination of so thoroughly satisfactory a character,—a work read with an enjoyment so unalloyed and so untempered by the desire to protest and to criticise. The poetical firmament within these recent years has been all alive with unprophesied comets and meteors, many of them of extraordinary brilliancy, but most of them very rapid in their passage. Mr. Morris gives us the comfort of feeling that he is a fixed star, and that his radiance is not likely to be extinguished in a draught of wind,—after the fashion of Mr. Alexander Smith, Mr. Swinburne and Miss Ingelow.

Mr. Morris's poem is ushered into the world with a very florid birthday speech from the pen of the author of the too famous *Poems and Ballads*,—a circumstance, we apprehend, in no small degree prejudicial to its success. But we hasten to assure all persons whom the knowledge of Mr. Swinburne's enthusiasm may have led to mistrust the character of the work, that it has to our perception nothing in common with this gentleman's own productions, and that his article proves very little more than that his sympathies are wiser than his performance. If Mr. Morris's poem may be said to remind us of the manner of any other writer, it is simply of that of Chaucer; and to resemble Chaucer is a great safeguard against resembling Swinburne.

The Life and Death of Jason, then, is a narrative poem on a Greek subject, written in a genuine English style. With the subject all reading people are familiar, and we have no need to retrace its details. But it is perhaps not amiss to transcribe the few pregnant lines of prose into which, at the outset, Mr. Morris has condensed the argument of his poem:—

"Jason the son of Æson, king of Iolchos, having come to man's estate, demanded of Pelias his father's kingdom, which he held wrongfully. But Pelias answered, that if he would bring from Colchis the golden fleece of the ram that had carried Phryxus thither, he would yield him his right. Whereon Jason sailed to Colchis in the ship Argo, with other heroes, and by means of Medea, the king's daughter, won the fleece; and carried off also Medea; and so, after many troubles, came back to Iolchos again. There, by Medea's wiles, was Pelias slain; but Jason went to Corinth, and lived with Medea happily, till he was taken with the love of Glauce, the king's daughter of Corinth, and must needs wed her; whom also Medea destroyed, and fled to Ægeus at Athens; and not long after Jason died strangely."

The style of this little fragment of prose is not an unapt measure of the author's poetical style,—quaint, but not too quaint, more Anglo-Saxon than Latin, and decidedly laconic. For in spite of the great length of his work, his manner is by no means diffuse. His story is a long one, and he wishes to do it justice; but the movement is rapid and business-like, and the poet is quite guiltless of any wanton lingering along the margin of the subject matter,—after the manner, for instance, of Keats,—to whom, individually, however, we make this tendency no reproach. Mr. Morris's subject is immensely rich,—heavy with its richness,—and in the highest degree romantic and poetical. For the most part, of course, he found not only the great *contours*, but the various incidents and episodes, ready drawn to his hand; but still there was enough wanting to make a most exhaustive drain upon his ingenuity and his imagination. And not only these faculties have been brought into severe exercise, but the strictest good taste and good sense were called into play, together with a certain final gift which we hardly know how to name, and which is by no means common, even among very clever poets,—a comprehensive sense of form, of proportion, and of real completeness, without which the most brilliant efforts of the imagination are a mere agglomeration of ill-reconciled beauties. The legend of Jason is full of strangely constructed marvels and elaborate prodigies and horrors, calculated to task heavily an author's adroitness.

We have so pampered and petted our sense of the ludicrous of late years, that it is quite the spoiled child of the house, and without its leave no guest can be honourably entertained. It is very true that the atmosphere of Grecian mythology is so entirely an artificial one, that we are seldom tempted to refer its weird anomalous denizens to our standard of truth and beauty. Truth, indeed, is at once put out of the question; but one would say beforehand, that many of the creations of Greek fancy were wanting even in beauty, or at least in that ease and simplicity which has been acquired in modern times by force of culture. But habit and tradition have reconciled us to these things in their native forms, and Mr. Morris's skill reconciles us to them in his modern and composite English.

The idea, for instance, of a *flying ram*, seems, to an undisciplined fancy, a not especially happy creation, nor a very promising theme for poetry; but Mr. Morris, without diminishing its native oddity, has given it an ample romantic dignity. So, again, the sowing of the dragon's teeth at Colchis, and the springing up of mutually opposed armed men, seems too complex and recondite a scene to be vividly and gracefully realized; but as it stands, it is one of the finest passages in Mr. Morris's poem. His great stumbling-block, however, we take it, was the necessity of maintaining throughout the dignity and prominence of his hero. From the moment that Medea comes into the poem, Jason falls into the second place, and keeps it to the end. She is the all-wise and all-brave helper and counsellor at Colchis, and the guardian angel of the returning journey. She saves her companions from the Circean enchantments, and she withholds them from the embraces of the Sirens. She effects the death of Pelias, and assures the successful return of the Argonauts. And finally—as a last claim upon her interest— she is slighted and abandoned by the man of her love. Without question, then, she is the central figure of the poem,—a powerful and enchanting figure,—a creature of barbarous arts, and of exquisite human passions. Jason accordingly possesses only that indirect hold upon our attention which belongs to the Virgilian Æneas; although Mr. Morris has avoided Virgil's error of now and then allowing his hero to be contemptible.

A large number, however, of far greater drawbacks than any we are able to mention could not materially diminish the powerful beauty of this fantastic legend. It is as rich in adventure as the Odyssey, and very much simpler. Its prime elements are of the most poetical and delightful kind. What can be more thrilling than the idea of a great boatful of warriors embarking upon dreadful seas, not for pleasure, nor for conquest, nor for any material advantage, but for the simple discovery of a jealously watched, magically guarded relic? There is in the character of the object of their quest something heroically unmarketable, or at least unavailable.

But of course the story owes a vast deal to its episodes, and these have lost nothing in Mr. Morris's hands. One of the most beautiful—the well known adventure of Hylas—occurs at the very outset. The beautiful young man, during a halt of the ship, wanders inland through the forest, and, passing beside a sylvan stream, is espied and incontinently loved by the water nymphs, who forthwith "detach" one of their number to work his seduction. This young lady assumes the disguise and speech of a Northern princess, clad in furs, and in this character sings to her victim "a sweet song, sung not yet to any man." Very sweet and truly lyrical it is like all the songs scattered through Mr. Morris's narrative. We are, indeed, almost in doubt whether the most beautiful passages in the poem do not occur in the series of songs in the fourteenth book.

211

The ship has already touched at the island of Circe, and the sailors, thanks to the earnest warnings of Medea, have abstained from setting foot on the fatal shore; while Medea has, in turn, been warned by the enchantress against the allurements of the Sirens. As soon as the ship draws nigh, these fair beings begin to utter their irresistible notes. All eyes are turned lovingly on the shore, the rowers' charmed muscles relax, and the ship drifts landward. But Medea exhorts and entreats her companions to preserve their course. Jason himself is not untouched, as Mr. Morris delicately tells us,—"a moment Jason gazed." But Orpheus smites his lyre before it is too late, and stirs the languid blood of his comrades. The Sirens strike their harps amain, and a conflict of song arises. The Sirens sing of the cold, the glittering, the idle delights of their submarine homes; while Orpheus tells of the warm and pastoral landscapes of Greece. We have no space for quotation; of course Orpheus carries the day. But the finest and most delicate practical sense is shown in the alternation of the two lyrical arguments,—the soulless sweetness of the one, and the deep human richness of the other.

There is throughout Mr. Morris's poem a great unity and evenness of excellence, which make selection and quotation difficult; but of impressive touches in our reading we noticed a very great number. We content ourselves with mentioning a single one. When Jason has sown his bag of dragon's teeth at Colchis, and the armed fighters have sprung up along the furrows, and under the spell contrived by Medea have torn each other to death:—

> "One man was left alive, but wounded sore,
>
> Who, staring round about and seeing no more
>
> His brothers' spears against him, fixed his eyes
>
> Upon the queller of those mysteries.
>
> Then dreadfully they gleamed, and with no word,
>
> He tottered towards him with uplifted sword.
>
> But scarce he made three paces down the field,
>
> Ere chill death seized his heart, and on his shield
>
> Clattering he fell."

We have not spoken of Mr. Morris's versification nor of his vocabulary. We have only room to say that, to our perception, the first in its facility and harmony, and the second in its abundance and studied simplicity, leave nothing to be desired. There are of course faults and errors in his poem, but there are none that are not trivial and easily pardoned in the light of the fact that he has given us a work of consummate art and of genuine beauty. He has foraged in a treasure-house; he has visited the ancient world, and come back with a massive cup of living Greek wine. His project was no light task, but he has honourably fulfilled it. He has enriched the language with a narrative poem which we are sure that the public will not suffer to fall into the ranks of honoured but uncherished works,—objects of vague and sapient reference,—but will continue to read and to enjoy. In spite of its length, the interest of the story never flags, and as a work of art it never ceases to be pure. To the jaded intellects of the present moment, distracted with the strife of creeds and the conflict of theories, it opens a glimpse into a world where they will be called upon neither to choose, to criticise, nor to believe, but simply to feel, to look, and to listen.

II. THE EARTHLY PARADISE

This new volume of Mr. Morris is, we think, a book for all time; but it is especially a book for these ripening summer days. To sit in the open shade, inhaling the heated air, and, while you read these perfect fairy tales, these rich and pathetic human traditions to glance up from your page at the clouds and the trees, is to do as pleasant a thing as the heart of man can desire. Mr. Morris's book abounds in all the sounds and sights and sensations of nature, in the warmth of the sunshine, the murmur of forests, and the breath of ocean-scented breezes. The fullness of physical existence which belongs to climates where life is spent in the open air, is largely diffused through its pages:

... "Hot July was drawing to an end,

And August came the fainting year to mend

With fruit and grain; so 'neath the trellises,

Nigh blossomless, did they lie well at ease,

213

And watched the poppies burn across the grass,

And o'er the bindweed's bells the brown bee pass,

Still murmuring of his gains: windless and bright

The morn had been, to help their dear delight.

... Then a light wind arose

That shook the light stems of that flowery close,

And made men sigh for pleasure."

This is a random specimen. As you read, the fictitious universe of the poem seems to expand and advance out of its remoteness, to surge musically about your senses, and merge itself utterly in the universe which surrounds you. The summer brightness of the real world goes halfway to meet it; and the beautiful figures which throb with life in Mr. Morris's stories pass lightly to and fro between the realm of poetry and the mild atmosphere of fact. This quality was half the charm of the author's former poem, *The Life and Death of Jason*, published last summer. We seemed really to follow, beneath the changing sky, the fantastic boatload of wanderers in their circuit of the ancient world. For people compelled to stay at home, the perusal of the book in a couple of mornings was very nearly as good as a fortnight's holiday. The poem appeared to reflect so clearly and forcibly the poet's natural sympathies with the external world, and his joy in personal contact with it, that the reader obtained something very like a sense of physical transposition, without either physical or intellectual weariness.

This ample and direct presentment of the joys of action and locomotion seems to us to impart to these two works a truly national and English tone. They taste not perhaps of the English soil, but of those strong English sensibilities which the great insular race carry with them through their wanderings, which they preserve and apply with such energy in every terrestrial clime, and which make them such incomparable travellers. We heartily recommend such persons as have a desire to accommodate their reading to the season—as are vexed with a delicate longing to place themselves intellectually in relation with the genius of the summer—to take this *Earthly Paradise* with them to the country.

The book is a collection of tales in verse—found, without exception, we take it, rather than imagined, and linked together, somewhat loosely, by a narrative prologue.

The following is the "argument" of the prologue—already often enough quoted, but pretty enough, in its ingenious prose, to quote again:—

"Certain gentlemen and mariners of Norway, having considered all that they had heard of the Earthly Paradise, set sail to find it, and, after many troubles and the lapse of many years, came old men to some western land, of which they had never before heard: there they died, when they had dwelt there certain years, much honoured of the strange people."

The adventures of these wanderers, told by one of their number, Rolf the Norseman, born at Byzantium—a happy origin for the teller of a heroic tale, as the author doubtless felt—make, to begin with, a poem of considerable length, and of a beauty superior perhaps to that of the succeeding tales. An admirable romance of adventure has Mr. Morris unfolded in the melodious energy of this half-hurrying, half-lingering narrative—a romance to make old hearts beat again with the boyish longing for transmarine mysteries, and to plunge boys themselves into a delicious agony of unrest.

The story is a tragedy, or very near it—as what story of the search for an Earthly Paradise could fail to be? Fate reserves for the poor storm-tossed adventurers a sort of fantastic compromise between their actual misery and their ideal bliss, whereby a kindly warmth is infused into the autumn of their days, and to the reader, at least, a very tolerable Earthly Paradise is laid open. The elders and civic worthies of the western land which finally sheltered them summon them every month to a feast, where, when all grosser desires have been duly pacified, the company sit at their ease and listen to the recital of stories. Mr. Morris gives in this volume the stories of the six midmonths of the year, two tales being allotted to each month—one from the Greek Mythology, and one, to express it broadly, of a Gothic quality. He announces a second series in which, we infer, he will in the same manner give us the stories rehearsed at the winter fireside.

The Greek stories are the various histories of Atalanta, of Perseus, of Cupid and Psyche, of Alcestis, of Atys, the hapless son of Crœsus, and of Pygmalion. The companion pieces, which always serve excellently well to place in relief the perfect pagan character of their elder mates, deal of course with elements less generally known.

"Atalanta's Race," the first of Mr. Morris's Greek legends, is to our mind almost the best. There is something wonderfully simple and childlike in the story, and the author has given it ample dignity, at the same time that he has preserved this quality.

Most vividly does he present the mild invincibility of his fleet-footed heroine and the half-boyish simplicity of her demeanour—a perfect model of a *belle inhumaine*. But the most beautiful passage in the poem is the description of the vigil of the love-sick Milanion in the lonely sea-side temple of Venus. The author has conveyed with exquisite art the sense of devout stillness and of pagan sanctity which invests this remote and prayerful spot. The yellow torch-light,

"Wherein with fluttering gown and half-bared limb

The temple damsels sung their evening hymn;"

the sound of the shallow flowing sea without, the young man's restless sleep on the pavement, besprinkled with the ocean spray, the apparition of the goddess with the early dawn, bearing the golden apple—all these delicate points are presented in the light of true poetry.

The narrative of the adventures of Danaë and of Perseus and Andromeda is, with the exception of the tale of Cupid and Psyche which follows it, the longest piece in the volume. Of the two, we think we prefer the latter. Unutterably touching is the career of the tender and helpless Psyche, and most impressive the terrible hostility of Venus. The author, we think, throughout manages this lady extremely well. She appears to us in a sort of rosy dimness, through which she looms as formidable as she is beautiful, and gazing with "gentle eyes and unmoved smiles,"

"Such as in Cyprus, the fair blossomed isle,

When on the altar in the summer night

They pile the roses up for her delight,

Men see within their hearts."

"The Love of Alcestis" is the beautiful story of the excellent wife who, when her husband was ill, gave up her life, so that he might recover and live for ever. Half the interest here, however, lies in the servitude of Apollo in disguise, and in the touching picture of the radiant god doing in perfection the homely work of his office, and yet from time to time emitting flashes, as it were, of genius and deity, while the good Admetus observes him half in kindness and half in awe.

The story of the "Son of Crœsus," the poor young man who is slain by his best friend because the gods had foredoomed it, is simple, pathetic, and brief. The finest and sweetest poem in the volume, to our taste, is the tale of "Pygmalion and the Image." The merit of execution is perhaps not appreciably greater here than in the other pieces, but the legend is so unutterably charming that it claims precedence of its companions. As beautiful as anything in all our later poetry, we think, is the description of the growth and dominance in the poor sculptor's heart of his marvellous passion for the stony daughter of his hands. Borne along on the steady, changing flow of his large and limpid verse, the author glides into the situation with an ease and grace and fullness of sympathy worthy of a great master. Here, as elsewhere, there is no sign of effort or of strain. In spite of the studied and *recherché* character of his diction, there is not a symptom of affectation in thought or speech. We seem in this tale of "Pygmalion" truly to inhabit the bright and silent workroom of a great Greek artist, and, standing among shapes and forms of perfect beauty, to breathe the incense-tainted air in which lovely statues were conceived and shining stones chiselled into immortality.

Mr. Morris is indubitably a sensuous poet, to his credit be it said; his senses are constantly proffering their testimony and crying out their delight. But while they take their freedom, they employ it in no degree to their own debasement. Just as there is modesty of temperament we conceive there is modesty of imagination, and Mr. Morris possesses the latter distinction. The total absence of it is, doubtless, the long and short of Mr. Swinburne's various troubles. We may imagine Mr. Swinburne making a very clever poem of this story of "Pygmalion," but we cannot fancy him making it anything less than utterly disagreeable. The thoroughly agreeable way in which Mr. Morris tells it is what especially strikes us. We feel that his imagination is equally fearless and irreproachable, and that while he tells us what we may call a sensuous story in all its breadth, he likewise tells it in all its purity. It has, doubtless, an impure side; but of the two he prefers the other. While Pygmalion is all aglow with his unanswered passion, he one day sits down before his image:

"And at the last drew forth a book of rhymes,

Wherein were writ the tales of many climes,

And read aloud the sweetness hid therein

Of lovers' sorrows and their tangled sin."

He reads aloud to his marble torment: would Mr. Swinburne have touched that note?

We have left ourselves no space to describe in detail the other series of tales—"The Man born to be King," "The Proud King," "The Writing on the Image," "The Lady of the Land," "The Watching of the Falcon," and "Ogier the Dane."

The author in his *Jason* identified himself with the successful treatment of Greek subjects to such a degree as to make it easy to suppose that these matters were the specialty of his genius. But in these romantic modern stories the same easy power is revealed, the same admirable union of natural gifts and cultivated perceptions. Mr. Morris is evidently a poet in the broad sense of the word—a singer of human joys and sorrows, whenever and wherever found. His somewhat artificial diction, which would seem to militate against our claim that his genius is of the general and comprehensive order, is, we imagine, simply an achievement of his own. It is not imposed from without, but developed from within. Whatever may be said of it, it certainly will not be accused of being unpoetical; and except this charge, what serious one can be made?

The author's style—according to our impression—is neither Chaucerian, Spenserian, nor imitative; it is literary, indeed, but it has a freedom and irregularity, an adaptability to the movements of the author's mind, which make it an ample vehicle of poetical utterance. He says in this language of his own the most various and the most truthful things; he moves, melts, and delights. Such at least, is our own experience. Other persons, we know, find it difficult to take him entirely *au sérieux*. But we, taking him—and our critical duties too—in the most serious manner our mind permits of, feel strongly impelled, both by gratitude and by reflection, to pronounce him a noble and delightful poet. To call a man healthy nowadays is almost an insult—invalids learn so many secrets. But the health of the intellect is often promoted by physical disability. We say therefore, finally, that however the faculty may have been promoted—with the minimum of suffering, we certainly hope—Mr. Morris is a supremely healthy writer. This poem is marked by all that is broad and deep in nature, and all that is elevating, profitable, and curious in art.

MATTHEW ARNOLD'S ESSAYS

MR. ARNOLD'S *Essays in Criticism* come to American readers with a reputation already made,—the reputation of a charming style, a great deal of excellent feeling, and an almost equal amount of questionable reasoning. It is for us either to confirm the verdict passed in the author's own country, or to judge his work afresh. It is often the fortune of English writers to find mitigation of sentence in the United States.

The Essays contained in this volume are on purely literary subjects; which is for us, by itself, a strong recommendation. English literature, especially contemporary literature, is, compared with that of France and Germany, very poor in collections of this sort. A great deal of criticism is written, but little of it is kept; little of it is deemed to contain any permanent application. Mr. Arnold will doubtless find in this fact—if indeed he has not already signalized it—but another proof of the inferiority of the English to the Continental school of criticism, and point to it as a baleful effect of the narrow practical spirit which animates, or, as he would probably say, paralyzes, the former. But not only is his book attractive as a whole, from its exclusively literary character; the subject of each essay is moreover particularly interesting. The first paper is on the function of Criticism at the present time; a question, if not more important, perhaps more directly pertinent here than in England. The second, discussing the literary influence of Academies, contains a great deal of valuable observation and reflection in a small compass and under an inadequate title. The other essays are upon the two De Guérins, Heinrich Heine, Pagan and Mediæval Religious Sentiment, Joubert, Spinoza, and Marcus Aurelius. The first two articles are, to our mind, much the best; the next in order of excellence is the paper on Joubert; while the others, with the exception, perhaps, of that on Spinoza, are of about equal merit.

Mr. Arnold's style has been praised at once too much and too little. Its resources are decidedly limited; but if the word had not become so cheap, we should nevertheless call it fascinating. This quality implies no especial force; it rests in this case on the fact that, whether or not you agree with the matter beneath it, the manner inspires you with a personal affection for the author. It expresses great sensibility, and at the same time great good-nature; it indicates a mind both susceptible and healthy. With the former element alone it would savour of affectation; with the latter, it would be coarse. As it stands, it represents a spirit both sensitive and generous. We can best describe it, perhaps, by the word sympathetic. It exhibits frankly, and without detriment to its national character, a decided French influence. Mr. Arnold is too wise to attempt to write French English; he probably knows that a language can only be indirectly enriched; but as nationality is eminently a matter of form, he knows too that he can really violate nothing so long as he adheres to the English letter.

His Preface is a striking example of the intelligent amiability which animates his style. His two leading Essays were, on their first appearance, made the subject of much violent contention, their moral being deemed little else than a wholesale schooling of the English press by the French programme. Nothing could have better proved the justice of Mr. Arnold's remarks upon the "provincial" character of the English critical method than the reception which they provoked. He now acknowledges this reception in a short introduction, which admirably reconciles smoothness of temper with sharpness of wit. The taste of this performance has been questioned; but wherever it may err, it is assuredly not in being provincial; it is essentially civil. Mr. Arnold's amiability is, in our eye, a strong proof of his wisdom. If he were a few degrees more short-sighted, he might have less equanimity at his command. Those who sympathise with him warmly will probably like him best as he is; but with such as are only half his friends, this freedom from party passion, from what is after all but a lawful professional emotion, will argue against his sincerity.

For ourselves, we doubt not that Mr. Arnold possesses thoroughly what the French call the courage of his opinions. When you lay down a proposition which is forthwith controverted, it is of course optional with you to take up the cudgels in its defence. If you are deeply convinced of its truth, you will perhaps be content to leave it to take care of itself; or, at all events, you will not go out of your way to push its fortunes; for you will reflect that in the long run an opinion often borrows credit from the forbearance of its patrons. In the long run, we say; it will meanwhile cost you an occasional pang to see your cherished theory turned into a football by the critics. A football is not, as such, a very respectable object, and the more numerous the players, the more ridiculous it becomes. Unless, therefore, you are very confident of your ability to rescue it from the chaos of kicks, you will best consult its interests by not mingling in the game. Such has been Mr. Arnold's choice. His opponents say that he is too much of a poet to be a critic; he is certainly too much of a poet to be a disputant. In the Preface in question he has abstained from reiterating any of the views put forth in the two offensive Essays; he has simply taken a delicate literary vengeance upon his adversaries.

For Mr. Arnold's critical feeling and observation, used independently of his judgment, we profess a keen relish. He has these qualities, at any rate, of a good critic, whether or not he have the others,—the science and the logic. It is hard to say whether the literary critic is more called upon to understand or to feel. It is certain that he will accomplish little unless he can feel acutely; although it is perhaps equally certain that he will become weak the moment that he begins to "work," as we may say, his natural sensibilities. The best critic is probably he who leaves his feelings out of account, and relies upon reason for success. If he actually possesses delicacy of feeling, his work will be delicate without detriment to its solidity. The complaint of Mr. Arnold's critics is that his arguments are too sentimental. Whether this complaint is well founded, we shall hereafter inquire; let us determine first what sentiment has done for him. It has given him, in our opinion, his greatest charm and his greatest worth. Hundreds of other critics have stronger heads; few, in England at least, have more delicate perceptions. We regret that we have not the space to confirm this assertion by extracts. We must refer the reader to the book itself, where he will find on every page an illustration of our meaning. He will find one, first of all, in the apostrophe to the University of Oxford, at the close of the Preface,—"home of lost causes and forsaken beliefs and unpopular names and impossible loyalties." This is doubtless nothing but sentiment, but it seizes a shade of truth, and conveys it with a directness which is not at the command of logical demonstration. Such a process might readily prove, with the aid of a host of facts, that the University is actually the abode of much retarding conservatism; a fine critical instinct alone, and the measure of audacity which accompanies such an instinct, could succeed in placing her on the side of progress by boldly saluting her as the Queen of Romance: romance being the deadly enemy of the commonplace; the commonplace being the fast ally of Philistinism, and Philistinism the heaviest drag upon the march of civilisation.

Mr. Arnold is very fond of quoting Goethe's eulogy upon Schiller, to the effect that his friend's greatest glory was to have left so far behind him *was uns alle bändigt, das Gemeine*, that bane of mankind, the common. Exactly how much the inscrutable Goethe made of this fact, it is hard at this day to determine; but it will seem to many readers that Mr. Arnold makes too much of it. Perhaps he does, for himself; but for the public in general he decidedly does not. One of the chief duties of criticism is to exalt the importance of the ideal; and Goethe's speech has a long career in prospect before we can say with the vulgar that it is "played out." Its repeated occurrence in Mr. Arnold's pages is but another instance of poetic feeling subserving the ends of criticism.

The famous comment upon the girl Wragg, over which the author's opponents made so merry, we likewise owe—we do not hesitate to declare it—to this same poetic feeling. Why cast discredit upon so valuable an instrument of truth? Why not wait at least until it is used in the service of error? The worst that can be said of the paragraph in question is, that it is a great ado about nothing. All thanks, say we, to the critic who will pick up such nothings as these; for if he neglects them, they are blindly trodden under foot. They may not be especially valuable, but they are for that very reason the critic's particular care. Great truths take care of themselves; great truths are carried aloft by philosophers and poets; the critic deals in contributions to truth.

Another illustration of the nicety of Mr. Arnold's feeling is furnished by his remarks upon the quality of *distinction* as exhibited in Maurice and Eugénie de Guérin, "that quality which at last inexorably corrects the world's blunders and fixes the world's ideals, [which] procures that the popular poet shall not pass for a Pindar, the popular historian for a Tacitus, nor the popular preacher for a Bossuet." Another is offered by his incidental remarks upon Coleridge, in the article on Joubert; another, by the remarkable felicity with which he has translated Maurice de Guérin's *Centaur*; and another, by the whole body of citations with which, in his second Essay, he fortifies his proposition that the establishment in England of an authority answering to the French Academy would have arrested certain evil tendencies of English literature,—for to nothing more offensive than this, as far as we can see, does this argument amount.

In the first and most important of his Essays Mr. Arnold puts forth his views upon the actual duty of criticism. They may be summed up as follows. Criticism has no concern with the practical; its function is simply to get at the best thought which is current,—to see things in themselves as they are,—to be disinterested. Criticism can be disinterested, says Mr. Arnold,

"by keeping from practice; by resolutely following the law of its own nature, which is to be a free play of the mind on all subjects which it touches, by steadily refusing to lend itself to any of those ulterior political, practical considerations about ideas which plenty of people will be sure to attach to them, which perhaps ought often to be attached to them, which in this country, at any rate, are certain to be attached to them, but which criticism has really nothing to do with. Its business is simply to know the best that is known and thought in the world, and, by in its turn making this known, to create a current of true and fresh ideas. Its business is to do this with inflexible honesty, with due ability; but its business is to do no more, and to leave alone all questions of practical consequences and applications,—questions which will never fail to have due prominence given to them."

We used just now a word of which Mr. Arnold is very fond,—a word of which the general reader may require an explanation, but which, when explained, he will be likely to find indispensable; we mean the word *Philistine*. The term is of German origin, and has no English synonym. "At Soli," remarks Mr. Arnold, "I imagined they did not talk of solecisms; and here, at the very head-quarters of Goliath, nobody talks of Philistinism." The word *épicier*, used by Mr. Arnold as a French synonym, is not so good as *bourgeois*, and to those who know that *bourgeois* means a citizen, and who reflect that a citizen is a person seriously interested in the maintenance of order, the German term may now assume a more special significance. An English review briefly defines it by saying that "it applies to the fat-headed respectable public in general." This definition must satisfy us here. The Philistine portion of the English press, by which we mean the considerably larger portion, received Mr. Arnold's novel programme of criticism with the uncompromising disapprobation which was to be expected from a literary body, the principle of whose influence, or indeed of whose being is its subservience, through its various members, to certain political and religious interests.

Mr. Arnold's general theory was offensive enough; but the conclusions drawn by him from the fact that English practice has been so long and so directly at variance with it, were such as to excite the strongest animosity. Chief among these was the conclusion that this fact has retarded the development and vulgarised the character of the English mind, as compared with the French and the German mind. This rational inference may be nothing but a poet's flight; but for ourselves, we assent to it. It reaches us too. The facts collected by Mr. Arnold on this point have long wanted a voice. It has long seemed to us that, as a nation, the English are singularly incapable of large, of high, of general views. They are indifferent to pure truth, to *la verité vraie*. Their views are almost exclusively practical, and it is in the nature of practical views to be narrow. They seldom indeed admit a fact but on compulsion; they demand of an idea some better recommendation, some longer pedigree, than that it is true. That this lack of spontaneity in the English intellect is caused by the tendency of English criticism, or that it is to be corrected by a diversion, or even by a complete reversion, of this tendency, neither Mr. Arnold nor ourselves suppose, nor do we look upon such a result as desirable. The part which Mr. Arnold assigns to his reformed method of criticism is a purely tributary part. Its indirect result will be to quicken the naturally irrational action of the English mind; its direct result will be to furnish that mind with a larger stock of ideas than it has enjoyed under the time-honoured *régime* of Whig and Tory, High-Church and Low-Church organs.

We may here remark, that Mr. Arnold's statement of his principles is open to some misinterpretation,—an accident against which he has, perhaps, not sufficiently guarded it. For many persons the word *practical* is almost identical with the word *useful*, against which, on the other hand, they erect the word *ornamental*. Persons who are fond of regarding these two terms as irreconcilable, will have little patience with Mr. Arnold's scheme of criticism. They will look upon it as an organised preference of unprofitable speculation to common sense. But the great beauty of the critical movement advocated by Mr. Arnold is that in either direction its range of action is unlimited. It deals with plain facts as well as with the most exalted fancies; but it deals with them only for the sake of the truth which is in them, and not for *your* sake, reader, and that of your party. It takes *high ground*, which is the ground of theory. It does not busy itself with consequences, which are all in all to you. Do not suppose that it for this reason pretends to ignore or to undervalue consequences; on the contrary, it is because it knows that consequences are inevitable that it leaves them alone. It cannot do two things at once; it cannot serve two masters. Its business is to make truth generally accessible, and not to apply it. It is only on condition of having its hands free, that it can make truth generally accessible. We said just now that its duty was, among other things, to exalt, if possible, the importance of the ideal. We should perhaps have said the intellectual; that is, of the principle of understanding things. Its business is to urge the claims of all things to be understood. If this is its function in England, as Mr. Arnold represents, it seems to us that it is doubly its function in this country. Here is no lack of votaries of the practical, of experimentalists, of empirics. The tendencies of our civilisation are certainly not such as foster a preponderance of morbid speculation. Our national genius inclines yearly more and more to resolve itself into a vast machine for sifting, in all things, the wheat from the chaff. American society is so shrewd, that we may safely allow it to make application of the truths of the study. Only let us keep it supplied with the truths of the study, and not with the half-truths of the forum. Let criticism take the stream of truth at its source, and then practice can take it half-way down. When criticism takes it half-way down, practice will come poorly off.

If we have not touched upon the faults of Mr. Arnold's volume, it is because they are faults of detail, and because, when, as a whole, a book commands our assent, we do not incline to quarrel with its parts. Some of the parts in these Essays are weak, others are strong; but the impression which they all combine to leave is one of such beauty as to make us forget, not only their particular faults, but their particular merits. If we were asked what is the particular merit of a given essay, we should reply that it is a merit much less common at the present day than is generally supposed,—the merit which pre-eminently characterises Mr. Arnold's poems, the merit, namely, of having a *subject*. Each essay is *about* something. If a literary work now-a-days start with a certain topic, that is all that is required of it; and yet it is a work of art only on condition of ending with that topic, on condition of being written, not from it, but to it. If the average modern essay or poem were to wear its title at the close, and not at the beginning, we wonder in how many cases the reader would fail to be surprised by it. A book or an article is looked upon as a kind of Staubbach waterfall, discharging itself into infinite space.

If we were questioned as to the merit of Mr. Arnold's book as a whole, we should say that it lay in the fact that the author takes high ground. The manner of his Essays is a model of what criticisms should be. The foremost English critical journal, the Saturday Review, recently disposed of a famous writer by saying, in a parenthesis, that he had done nothing but write nonsense all his life. Mr. Arnold does not pass judgment in parenthesis. He is too much of an artist to use leading propositions for merely literary purposes. The consequence is, that he says a few things in such a way as that almost in spite of ourselves we remember them, instead of a number of things which we cannot for the life of us remember. There are many things which we wish he had said better. It is to be regretted, for instance, that, when Heine is for once in a way seriously spoken of, he should not be spoken of more as the great poet which he is, and which even in New England he will one day be admitted to be, than with reference to the great moralist which he is not, and which he never claimed to be. But here, as in other places, Mr. Arnold's excellent spirit reconciles us with his shortcomings. If he has not spoken of Heine exhaustively, he has at all events spoken of him seriously, which for an Englishman is a good deal.

Mr. Arnold's supreme virtue is that he speaks of all things seriously, or, in other words, that he is not offensively clever. The writers who are willing to resign themselves to this obscure distinction are in our opinion the only writers who understand their time. That Mr. Arnold thoroughly understands his time we do not mean to say, for this is the privilege of a very select few; but he is, at any rate, profoundly conscious of his time. This fact was clearly apparent in his poems, and it is even more apparent in these Essays. It gives them a peculiar character of melancholy,—that melancholy which arises from the spectacle of the old-fashioned instinct of enthusiasm in conflict (or at all events in contact) with the modern desire to be fair,—the melancholy of an age which not only has lost its *naïveté*, but which knows it has lost it.

MR. WALT WHITMAN

IT has been a melancholy task to read this book; and it is a still more melancholy one to write about it. Perhaps since the day of Mr. Tupper's *Philosophy* there has been no more difficult reading of the poetic sort. It exhibits the effort of an essentially prosaic mind to lift itself, by a prolonged muscular strain, into poetry. Like hundreds of other good patriots, during the last four years, Mr. Walt Whitman has imagined that a certain amount of violent sympathy with the great deeds and sufferings of our soldiers, and of admiration for our national energy, together with a ready command of picturesque language, are sufficient inspiration for a poet. If this were the case, we had been a nation of poets. The constant developments of the war moved us continually to strong feeling and to strong expression of it. But in those cases in which these expressions were written out and printed with all due regard to prosody, they failed to make poetry, as any one may see by consulting now in cold blood the back volumes of the *Rebellion Record*.

Of course the city of Manhattan, as Mr. Whitman delights to call it, when regiments poured through it in the first months of the war, and its own sole god, to borrow the words of a real poet, ceased for a while to be the millionaire, was a noble spectacle, and a poetical statement to this effect is possible. *Of course* the tumult of a battle is grand, the results of a battle tragic, and the untimely deaths of young men a theme for elegies. But he is not a poet who merely reiterates these plain facts *ore rotundo*. He only sings them worthily who views them from a height. Every tragic event collects about it a number of persons who delight to dwell upon its superficial points—of minds which are bullied by the *accidents* of the affair. The temper of such minds seems to us to be the reverse of the poetic temper; for the poet, although he incidentally masters, grasps, and uses the superficial traits of his theme, is really a poet only in so far as he extracts its latent meaning and holds it up to common eyes. And yet from such minds most of our war-verses have come, and Mr. Whitman's utterances, much as the assertion may surprise his friends, are in this respect no exception to general fashion. They are an exception, however, in that they openly pretend to be something better; and this it is that makes them melancholy reading.

Mr. Whitman is very fond of blowing his own trumpet, and he has made very explicit claims for his books. "Shut not your doors," he exclaims at the outset—

"Shut not your doors to me, proud libraries,

For that which was lacking among you all, yet needed most, I bring;

A book I have made for your dear sake, O soldiers,

And for you, O soul of man, and you, love of comrades;

The words of my book nothing, the life of it everything;

A book separate, not link'd with the rest, nor felt by the intellect;

But you will feel every word, O Libertad! arm'd Libertad!

It shall pass by the intellect to swim the sea, the air,

    With joy with you, O soul of man."

These are great pretensions, but it seems to us that the following are even greater:

"From Paumanok starting, I fly like a bird,

Around and around to soar, to sing the idea of all;

To the north betaking myself, to sing there arctic songs,

To Kanada, 'till I absorb Kanada in myself—to Michigan then,

To Wisconsin, Iowa, Minnesota, to sing their songs (they are inimitable);

Then to Ohio and Indiana, to sing theirs—to Missouri and Kansas and Arkansas to sing theirs,

To Tennessee and Kentucky—to the Carolinas and Georgia, to sing theirs,

To Texas, and so along up toward California, to roam accepted everywhere;

To sing first (to the tap of the war-drum, if need be)

The idea of all—of the western world, one and inseparable,

And then the song of each member of these States."

Mr. Whitman's primary purpose is to celebrate the greatness of our armies; his secondary purpose is to celebrate the greatness of the city of New York. He pursues these objects through a hundred pages of matter which remind us irresistibly of the story of the college professor who, on a venturesome youth bringing him a theme done in blank verse, reminded him that it was not customary in writing prose to begin each line with a capital. The frequent capitals are the only marks of verse in Mr. Whitman's writings. There is, fortunately, but one attempt at rhyme. We say fortunately, for if the inequality of Mr. Whitman's lines were self-registering, as it would be in the case of an anticipated syllable at their close, the effect would be painful in the extreme. As the case stands, each line stands off by itself, in resolute independence of its companions, without a visible goal.

But if Mr. Whitman does not write verse, he does not write ordinary prose. The reader has seen that liberty is "libertad." In like manner, comrade is "camerado"; Americans are "Americanos"; a pavement is a "trottoir," and Mr. Whitman himself is a "chansonnier." If there is one thing that Mr. Whitman is not, it is this, for Béranger was a *chansonnier*. To appreciate the force of our conjunction, the reader should compare his military lyrics with Mr. Whitman's declamations. Our author's novelty, however, is not in his words, but in the form of his writing. As we have said, it begins for all the world like verse and turns out to be arrant prose. It is more like Mr. Tupper's proverbs than anything we have met.

But what if, in form, it *is* prose? it may be asked. Very good poetry has come out of prose before this. To this we would reply that it must first have gone into it. Prose, in order to be good poetry, must first be good prose. As a general principle, we know of no circumstance more likely to impugn a writer's earnestness than the adoption of an anomalous style. He must have something very original to say if none of the old vehicles will carry his thoughts. Of course he *may* be surprisingly original. Still, presumption is against him. If on examination the matter of his discourse proves very valuable, it justifies, or at any rate excuses, his literary innovation.

But if, on the other hand, it is of a common quality, with nothing new about it but its manners, the public will judge the writer harshly. The most that can be said of Mr. Whitman's vaticinations is, that, cast in a fluent and familiar manner, the average substance of them might escape unchallenged. But we have seen that Mr. Whitman prides himself especially on the substance—the life—of his poetry. It may be rough, it may be grim, it may be clumsy—such we take to be the author's argument—but it is sincere, it is sublime, it appeals to the soul of man, it is the voice of a people. He tells us, in the lines quoted, that the words of his book are nothing. To our perception they are everything, and very little at that.

A great deal of verse that is nothing but words has, during the war, been sympathetically sighed over and cut out of newspaper corners, because it has possessed a certain simple melody. But Mr. Whitman's verse, we are confident, would have failed even of this triumph, for the simple reason that no triumph, however small, is won but through the exercise of art, and that this volume is an offence against art. It is not enough to be grim and rough and careless; common sense is also necessary, for it is by common sense that we are judged. There exists in even the commonest minds, in literary matters, a certain precise instinct of conservatism, which is very shrewd in detecting wanton eccentricities.

To this instinct Mr. Whitman's attitude seems monstrous. It is monstrous because it pretends to persuade the soul while it slights the intellect; because it pretends to gratify the feelings while it outrages the taste. The point is that it does this *on theory*, wilfully, consciously, arrogantly. It is the little nursery game of "open your mouth and shut your eyes." Our hearts are often touched through a compromise with the artistic sense, but never in direct violation of it. Mr. Whitman sits down at the outset and counts out the intelligence. This were indeed a wise precaution on his part if the intelligence were only submissive! But when she is deliberately insulted, she takes her revenge by simply standing erect and open-eyed. This is assuredly the best she can do. And if she could find a voice she would probably address Mr. Whitman as follows:—

"You came to woo my sister, the human soul. Instead of giving me a kick as you approach, you should either greet me courteously, or, at least, steal in unobserved. But now you have me on your hands. Your chances are poor. What the human heart desires above all is sincerity, and you do not appear to me sincere. For a lover you talk entirely too much about yourself. In one place you threaten to absorb Kanada. In another you call upon the city of New York to incarnate you, as you have incarnated it. In another you inform us that neither youth pertains to you nor 'delicatesse,' that you are awkward in the parlour, that you do not dance, and that you have neither bearing, beauty, knowledge, nor fortune. In another place, by an allusion to your 'little songs,' you seem to identify yourself with the third person of the Trinity.

"For a poet who claims to sing 'the idea of all,' this is tolerably egotistical. We look in vain, however, through your book for a single idea. We find nothing but flashy imitations of ideas. We find a medley of extravagances and commonplaces. We find art, measure, grace, sense sneered at on every page, and nothing positive given us in their stead. To be positive one must have something to say; to be positive requires reason, labour, and art; and art requires, above all things, a suppression of one's self, a subordination of one's self to an idea. This will never do for you, whose plan is to adapt the scheme of the universe to your own limitations. You cannot entertain and exhibit ideas; but, as we have seen, you are prepared to incarnate them. It is for this reason, doubtless, that when once you have planted yourself squarely before the public, and in view of the great service you have done to the ideal, have become, as you say, 'accepted everywhere,' you can afford to deal exclusively in words. What would be bald nonsense and dreary platitudes in any one else becomes sublimity in you.

"But all this is a mistake. To become adopted as a national poet, it is not enough to discard everything in particular and to accept everything in general, to amass crudity upon crudity, to discharge the undigested contents of your blotting-book into the lap of the public. You must respect the public which you address; for it has taste, if you have not. It delights in the grand, the heroic, and the masculine; but it delights to see these conceptions cast into worthy form. It is indifferent to brute sublimity. It will never do for you to thrust your hands into your pockets and cry out that, as the research of form is an intolerable bore, the shortest and most economical way for the public to embrace its idols—for the nation to realise its genius—is in your own person.

"This democratic, liberty-loving, American populace, this stern and war-tried people, is a great civiliser. It is devoted to refinement. If it has sustained a monstrous war, and practised human nature's best in so many ways for the last five years, it is not to put up with spurious poetry afterwards. To sing aright our battles and our glories it is not enough to have served in a hospital (however praiseworthy the task in itself), to be aggressively careless, inelegant, and ignorant, and to be constantly preoccupied with yourself. It is not enough to be rude, lugubrious, and grim. You must also be serious. You must forget yourself in your ideas. Your personal qualities—the vigour of your temperament, the manly independence of your nature, the tenderness of your heart—these facts are impertinent. You must be *possessed*, and you must thrive to possess your possession. If in your striving you break into divine eloquence, then you are a poet. If the idea which possesses you is the idea of your country's greatness, then you are a national poet; and not otherwise."

THE POETRY OF GEORGE ELIOT

I. THE SPANISH GYPSY

IKNOW not whether George Eliot has any enemies, nor why she should have any; but if perchance she has, I can imagine them to have hailed the announcement of a poem from her pen as a piece of particularly good news. "Now, finally," I fancy them saying, "this sadly over-rated author will exhibit all the weakness that is in her; now she will prove herself what we have all along affirmed her to be—not a serene, self-directing genius of the first order, knowing her powers and respecting them, and content to leave well enough alone, but a mere showy rhetorician, possessed and prompted, not by the humble spirit of truth, but by an insatiable longing for applause." Suppose Mr. Tennyson were to come out with a novel, or Madame George Sand were to produce a tragedy in French alexandrines. The reader will agree with me, that these are hard suppositions; yet the world has seen stranger things, and been reconciled to them. Nevertheless, with the best possible will toward our illustrious novelist, it is easy to put ourselves in the shoes of these hypothetical detractors. No one, assuredly, but George Eliot could mar George Eliot's reputation; but there was room for the fear that she might do it. This reputation was essentially prose-built, and in the attempt to insert a figment of verse of the magnitude of *The Spanish Gypsy*, it was quite possible that she might injure its fair proportions.

In consulting her past works, for approval of their hopes and their fears, I think both her friends and her foes would have found sufficient ground for their arguments. Of all our English prose-writers of the present day, I think I may say, that, as a writer simply, a mistress of style, I have been very near preferring the author of *Silas Marner* and of *Romola*,—the author, too, of *Felix Holt*. The motive of my great regard for her style I take to have been that I fancied it such perfect solid prose. Brilliant and lax as it was in tissue, it seemed to contain very few of the silken threads of poetry; it lay on the ground like a carpet, instead of floating in the air like a banner. If my impression was correct, *The Spanish Gypsy* is not a genuine poem. And yet, looking over the author's novels in memory, looking them over in the light of her unexpected assumption of the poetical function, I find it hard at times not to mistrust my impression. I like George Eliot well enough, in fact, to admit, for the time, that I might have been in the wrong. If I had liked her less, if I had rated lower the quality of her prose, I should have estimated coldly the possibilities of her verse. Of course, therefore, if, as I am told many persons do in England, who consider carpenters and weavers and millers' daughters no legitimate subject for reputable fiction, I had denied her novels any qualities at all, I should have made haste, on reading the announcement of her poem, to speak of her as the world speaks of a lady, who, having reached a comfortable middle age, with her shoulders decently covered, "for reasons deep below the reach of thought," (to quote our author), begins to go out to dinner in a low-necked dress "of the period," and say in fine, in three words, that she was going to make a fool of herself.

But here, meanwhile, is the book before me, to arrest all this *a priori* argumentation. Time enough has elapsed since its appearance for most readers to have uttered their opinions, and for the general verdict of criticism to have been formed. In looking over several of the published reviews, I am struck with the fact that those immediately issued are full of the warmest delight and approval, and that, as the work ceases to be a novelty, objections, exceptions, and protests multiply. This is quite logical. Not only does it take a much longer time than the reviewer on a weekly journal has at his command to properly appreciate a work of the importance of *The Spanish Gypsy*, but the poem was actually much more of a poem than was to be expected. The foremost feeling of many readers must have been—it was certainly my own—that we had hitherto only half known George Eliot. Adding this dazzling new half to the old one, readers constructed for the moment a really splendid literary figure. But gradually the old half began to absorb the new, and to assimilate its virtues and failings, and critics finally remembered that the cleverest writer in the world is after all nothing and no one but himself.

The most striking quality in *The Spanish Gypsy*, on a first reading, I think, is its extraordinary rhetorical energy and elegance. The richness of the author's style in her novels gives but an inadequate idea of the splendid generosity of diction displayed in the poem. She is so much of a thinker and an observer that she draws very heavily on her powers of expression, and one may certainly say that they not only never fail her, but that verbal utterance almost always bestows upon her ideas a peculiar beauty and fullness, apart from their significance. The result produced in this manner, the reader will see, may come very near being poetry; it is assuredly eloquence. The faults in the present work are very seldom faults of weakness, except in so far as it is weak to lack an absolute mastery of one's powers; they arise rather from an excess of rhetorical energy, from a desire to attain to perfect fullness and roundness of utterance; they are faults of overstatement. It is by no means uncommon to find a really fine passage injured by the addition of a clause which dilutes the idea under pretence of completing it. The poem opens, for instance, with a description of

> "Broad-breasted Spain, leaning with equal love
>
>   (A calm earth-goddess crowned with corn and vines)
>
> On the Mid Sea that moans with memories,
>
> And on the untravelled Ocean, whose vast tides
>
> Pant dumbly passionate with dreams of youth."

The second half of the fourth line and the fifth, here, seem to me as poor as the others are good. So in the midst of the admirable description of Don Silva, which precedes the first scene in the castle:—

> "A spirit framed
>
> Too proudly special for obedience,
>
> Too subtly pondering for mastery:
>
> Born of a goddess with a mortal sire,
>
> Heir of flesh-fettered, weak divinity,
>
> *Doom-gifted with long resonant consciousness*
>
> *And perilous heightening of the sentient soul.*"

The transition to the lines in Italic is like the passage from a well-ventilated room into a vacuum. On reflection, we see "long resonant consciousness" to be a very good term; but, as it stands, it certainly lacks breathing-space. On the other hand, there are more than enough passages of the character of the following to support what I have said of the genuine splendour of the style:—

"I was right!

These gems have life in them: their colours speak,

Say what words fail of. So do many things,—

The scent of jasmine and the fountain's plash,

The moving shadows on the far-off hills,

The slanting moonlight and our clasping hands.

O Silva, there's an ocean round our words,

That overflows and drowns them. Do you know.

Sometimes when we sit silent, and the air

Breathes gently on us from the orange-trees,

It seems that with the whisper of a word

Our souls must shrink, get poorer, more apart?

Is it not true?

DON SILVA.

Yes, dearest, it is true.

Speech is but broken light upon the depth

Of the unspoken: even your loved words

Float in the larger meaning of your voice

As something dimmer."

I may say in general, that the author's admirers must have found in *The Spanish Gypsy* a presentment of her various special gifts stronger and fuller, on the whole, than any to be found in her novels. Those who valued her chiefly for her humour—the gentle humour which provokes a smile, but deprecates a laugh—will recognise that delightful gift in Blasco, and Lorenzo, and Roldan, and Juan,—slighter in quantity than in her prose-writings, but quite equal, I think, in quality. Those who prize most her descriptive powers will see them wondrously well embodied in these pages. As for those who have felt compelled to declare that she possesses the Shakespearian touch, they must consent, with what grace they may, to be disappointed. I have never thought our author a great dramatist, nor even a particularly dramatic writer. A real dramatist, I imagine, could never have reconciled himself to the odd mixture of the narrative and dramatic forms by which the present work is distinguished; and that George Eliot's genius should have needed to work under these conditions seems to me strong evidence of the partial and incomplete character of her dramatic instincts. An English critic lately described her, with much correctness, as a critic rather than a creator of characters. She puts her figures into action very successfully, but on the whole she thinks for them more than they think for themselves. She thinks, however, to wonderfully good purpose. In none of her works are there two more distinctly human representations than the characters of Silva and Juan. The latter, indeed, if I am not mistaken, ranks with Tito Melema and Hetty Sorrel, as one of her very best conceptions.

What is commonly called George Eliot's humour consists largely, I think, in a certain tendency to epigram and compactness of utterance,—not the short-clipped, biting, ironical epigram, but a form of statement in which a liberal dose of truth is embraced in terms none the less comprehensive for being very firm and vivid. Juan says of Zarca that

> He is one of those
>
> Who steal the keys from snoring Destiny,
>
> And make the prophets lie."

Zarca himself, speaking of "the steadfast mind, the undivided will to seek the good," says most admirably,—

> "'Tis that compels the elements, *and wrings*
>
> *A human music from the indifferent air.*"

When the Prior pronounces Fedalma's blood "unchristian as the leopard's," Don Silva retorts with,—

"Unchristian as the Blessed Virgin's blood.

Before the angel spoke the word, 'All hail!'"

Zarca qualifies his daughter's wish to maintain her faith to her lover, at the same time that she embraces her father's fortunes, as

"A woman's dream,—who thinks by smiling well

To ripen figs in frost."

This happy brevity of expression is frequently revealed in those rich descriptive passages and touches in which the work abounds. Some of the lines taken singly are excellent:—

"And bells make Catholic the trembling air";

and,

"Sad as the twilight, all his clothes ill-girt";

and again

"Mournful professor of high drollery."

Here is a very good line and a half:—

"The old rain-fretted mountains in their robes

Of shadow-broken gray."

Here, finally, are three admirable pictures:—

"The stars thin-scattered made the heavens large,

Bending in slow procession; in the east,

Emergent from the dark waves of the hills,

Seeming a little sister of the moon,

Glowed Venus all unquenched."

"Spring afternoons, when delicate shadows fall

Pencilled upon the grass; high summer morns,

When white light rains upon the quiet sea,

And cornfields flush for ripeness."

"Scent the fresh breath of the height-loving herbs,

That, trodden by the pretty parted hoofs

Of nimble goats, sigh at the innocent bruise,

And with a mingled difference exquisite

Pour a sweet burden on the buoyant air."

But now to reach the real substance of the poem, and to allow the reader to appreciate the author's treatment of human character and passion, I must speak briefly of the story. I shall hardly misrepresent it, when I say that it is a very old one, and that it illustrates that very common occurrence in human affairs,—the conflict of love and duty. Such, at least, is the general impression made by the poem as it stands. It is very possible that the author's primary intention may have had a breadth which has been curtailed in the execution of the work,—that it was her wish to present a struggle between nature and culture, between education and the instinct of race. You can detect in such a theme the stuff of a very good drama,—a somewhat stouter stuff, however, than *The Spanish Gypsy* is made of. George Eliot, true to that didactic tendency for which she has hitherto been remarkable, has preferred to make her heroine's predicament a problem in morals, and has thereby, I think, given herself hard work to reach a satisfactory solution. She has, indeed, committed herself to a signal error, in a psychological sense,—that of making a Gypsy girl with a conscience. Either Fedalma was a perfect Zincala in temper and instinct,—in which case her adhesion to her father and her race was a blind, passionate, sensuous movement, which is almost expressly contradicted,—or else she was a pure and intelligent Catholic, in which case nothing in the nature of a struggle can be predicated. The character of Fedalma, I may say, comes very near being a failure,—a very beautiful one; but in point of fact it misses it.

It misses it, I think, thanks to that circumstance which in reading and criticising *The Spanish Gypsy* we must not cease to bear in mind, the fact that the work is emphatically a *romance*. We may contest its being a poem, but we must admit that it is a romance in the fullest sense of the word. Whether the term may be absolutely defined I know not; but we may say of it, comparing it with the novel, that it carries much farther that compromise with reality which is the basis of all imaginative writing. In the romance this principle of compromise pervades the superstructure as well as the basis. The most that we exact is that the fable be consistent with itself. Fedalma is not a real Gypsy maiden. The conviction is strong in the reader's mind that a genuine Spanish Zincala would have somehow contrived both to follow her tribe and to keep her lover. If Fedalma is not real, Zarca is even less so. He is interesting, imposing, picturesque; but he is very far, I take it, from being a genuine *Gypsy* chieftain. They are both ideal figures,—the offspring of a strong mental desire for creatures well rounded in their elevation and heroism,—creatures who should illustrate the nobleness of human nature divorced from its smallness. Don Silva has decidedly more of the common stuff of human feeling, more charming natural passion and weakness. But he, too, is largely a vision of the intellect; his constitution is adapted to the atmosphere and the climate of romance. Juan, indeed, has one foot well planted on the lower earth; but Juan is only an accessory figure. I have said enough to lead the reader to perceive that the poem should not be regarded as a rigid transcript of actual or possible fact,—that the action goes on in an artificial world, and that properly to comprehend it he must regard it with a generous mind.

Viewed in this manner, as efficient figures in an essentially ideal and romantic drama, Fedalma and Zarca seem to gain vastly, and to shine with a brilliant radiance. If we reduce Fedalma to the level of the heroines of our modern novels, in which the interest aroused by a young girl is in proportion to the similarity of her circumstances to those of the reader, and in which none but the commonest feelings are required, provided they be expressed with energy, we shall be tempted to call her a solemn and cold-blooded jilt. In a novel it would have been next to impossible for the author to make the heroine renounce her lover. In novels we not only forgive that weakness which is common and familiar and human, but we actually demand it. But in poetry, although we are compelled to adhere to the few elementary passions of our nature, we do our best to dress them in a new and exquisite garb. Men and women in a poetical drama are nothing, if not distinguished.

> "Our dear young love,—its breath was happiness!
>
> But it had grown upon a larger life,
>
> Which tore its roots asunder."

These words are uttered by Fedalma at the close of the poem, and in them she emphatically claims the distinction of having her own private interests invaded by those of a people. The manner of her kinship with the Zincali is in fact a very much "larger life" than her marriage with Don Silva. We may, indeed, challenge the probability of her relationship to her tribe impressing her mind with a force equal to that of her love,—her "dear young love." We may declare that this is an unnatural and violent result. For my part, I think it is very far from violent; I think the author has employed her art in reducing the apparently arbitrary quality of her preference for her tribe. I say reducing; I do not say effacing; because it seems to me, as I have intimated, that just at this point her art has been wanting, and we are not sufficiently prepared for Fedalma's movement by a sense of her Gypsy temper and instincts. Still, we are in some degree prepared for it by various passages in the opening scenes of the book,—by all the magnificent description of her dance in the Plaza:—

> "All gathering influences culminate
>
> And urge Fedalma. Earth and heaven seem one,
>
> Life a glad trembling on the outer edge
>
> Of unknown rapture. Swifter now she moves,
>
> Filling the measure with a double beat
>
> And widening circle; now she seems to glow

With more declaréd presence, glorified.

Circling, she lightly bends, and lifts on high

The multitudinous-sounding tambourine,

And makes it ring and boom, then lifts it higher,

Stretching her left arm beauteous."

We are better prepared for it, however, than by anything else, by the whole impression we receive of the exquisite refinement and elevation of the young girl's mind,—by all that makes her so bad a Gypsy. She possesses evidently a very high-strung intellect, and her whole conduct is in a higher key, as I may say, than that of ordinary women, or even ordinary heroines. She is natural, I think, in a poetical sense. She is consistent with her own prodigiously superfine character. From a lower point of view than that of the author, she lacks several of the desirable feminine qualities,—a certain womanly warmth and petulance, a graceful irrationality. Her mind is very much too lucid, and her aspirations too lofty. Her conscience, especially, is decidedly over-active. But this is a distinction which she shares with all the author's heroines,—Dinah Morris, Maggie Tulliver, Romola, and Esther Lyon,—a distinction, moreover, for which I should be very sorry to hold George Eliot to account. There are most assuredly women and women. While Messrs. Charles Reade and Wilkie Collins, and Miss Braddon and her school, tell one half the story, it is no more than fair that the author of *The Spanish Gypsy* should, all unassisted, attempt to relate the other.

Whenever a story really interests one, he is very fond of paying it the compliment of imagining it otherwise constructed, and of capping it with a different termination. In the present case, one is irresistibly tempted to fancy *The Spanish Gypsy* in prose,—a compact, regular drama: not in George Eliot's prose, however: in a diction much more nervous and heated and rapid, written with short speeches as well as long. (The reader will have observed the want of brevity, retort, interruption, rapid alternation, in the dialogue of the poem. The characters all talk, as it were, standing still.) In such a play as the one indicated one imagines a truly dramatic Fedalma,—a passionate, sensuous, irrational Bohemian, as elegant as good breeding and native good taste could make her, and as pure as her actual sister in the poem,—but rushing into her father's arms with a cry of joy, and losing the sense of her lover's sorrow in what the author has elsewhere described as "the hurrying ardour of action." Or in the way of a different termination, suppose that Fedalma should for the time value at once her own love and her lover's enough to make her prefer the latter's destiny to that represented by her father. Imagine, then, that, after marriage, the Gypsy blood and nature should begin to flow and throb in quicker pulsations,—and that the poor girl should sadly contrast the sunny freedom and lawless joy of her people's lot with the splendid rigidity and formalism of her own. You may conceive at this point that she should pass from sadness to despair, and from despair to revolt. Here the catastrophe may occur in a dozen different ways. Fedalma may die before her husband's eyes, of unsatisfied longing for the fate she has rejected; or she may make an attempt actually to recover her fate, by wandering off and seeking out her people. The cultivated mind, however, it seems to me, imperiously demands, that, on finally overtaking them, she shall die of mingled weariness and shame, as neither a good Gypsy nor a good Christian, but simply a good figure for a tragedy. But there is a degree of levity which almost amounts to irreverence in fancying this admirable performance as anything other than it is.

After Fedalma comes Zarca, and here our imagination flags. Not so George Eliot's: for as simple imagination, I think that in the conception of this impressive and unreal figure it appears decidedly at its strongest. With Zarca, we stand at the very heart of the realm of romance. There is a truly grand simplicity, to my mind, in the outline of his character, and a remarkable air of majesty in his poise and attitude. He is a *père noble* in perfection. His speeches have an exquisite eloquence. In strictness, he is to the last degree unreal, illogical, and rhetorical; but a certain dramatic unity is diffused through his character by the depth and energy of the colours in which he is painted. With a little less simplicity, his figure would be decidedly modern. As it stands, it is neither modern nor mediæval; it belongs to the world of intellectual dreams and visions. The reader will admit that it is a vision of no small beauty, the conception of a stalwart chieftain who distils the cold exaltation of his purpose from the utter loneliness and obloquy of his race:—

"Wanderers whom no God took knowledge of,

To give them laws, to fight for them, or blight

Another race to make them ampler room;

A people with no home even in memory,

No dimmest lore of giant ancestors

To make a common hearth for piety";

242

a people all ignorant of

"The rich heritage, the milder life,

Of nations fathered by a mighty Past."

Like Don Silva, like Juan, like Sephardo, Zarca is decidedly a man of intellect.

Better than Fedalma or than Zarca is the remarkably beautiful and elaborate portrait of Don Silva, in whom the author has wished to present a young nobleman as splendid in person and in soul as the dawning splendour of his native country. In the composition of his figure, the real and the romantic, brilliancy and pathos, are equally commingled. He cannot be said to stand out in vivid relief. As a piece of painting, there is nothing commanding, aggressive, brutal, as I may say, in his lineaments. But they will bear close scrutiny. Place yourself within the circumscription of the work, breathe its atmosphere, and you will see that Don Silva is portrayed with a delicacy to which English story-tellers, whether in prose or verse, have not accustomed us. There are better portraits in Browning, but there are also worse; in Tennyson there are none as good; and in the other great poets of the present century there are no attempts, that I can remember, to which we may compare it. In spite of the poem being called in honour of his mistress, Don Silva is in fact the central figure in the work. Much more than Fedalma, he is the passive object of the converging blows of Fate. The young girl, after all, did what was easiest; but he is entangled in a network of agony, without choice or compliance of his own. It is an admirable subject admirably treated. I may describe it by saying that it exhibits a perfect aristocratic nature (born and bred at a time when democratic aspirations were quite irrelevant to happiness), dragged down by no fault of its own into the vulgar mire of error and expiation. The interest which attaches to Don Silva's character revolves about its exquisite human weakness, its manly scepticism, its antipathy to the trenchant, the absolute, and arbitrary. At the opening of the book, the author rehearses his various titles:—

"Such titles with their blazonry are his

Who keeps this fortress, sworn Alcaÿde,

Lord of the valley, master of the town,

Commanding whom he will, himself commanded

By Christ his Lord, who sees him from the cross,

And from bright heaven where the Mother pleads;

By good Saint James, upon the milk-white steed,

Who leaves his bliss to fight for chosen Spain;

By the dead gaze of all his ancestors;

And by the mystery of his Spanish blood,

Charged with the awe and glories of the past."

Throughout the poem, we are conscious, during the evolution of his character, of the presence of these high mystical influences, which, combined with his personal pride, his knightly temper, his delicate culture, form a splendid background for passionate dramatic action. The finest pages in the book, to my taste, are those which describe his lonely vigil in the Gypsy camp, after he has failed in winning back Fedalma, and has pledged his faith to Zarca. Placed under guard, and left to his own stern thoughts, his soul begins to react against the hideous disorder to which he has committed it, to proclaim its kinship with "customs and bonds and laws," and its sacred need of the light of human esteem:—

"Now awful Night,

Ancestral mystery of mysteries, came down

Past all the generations of the stars,

And visited his soul with touch more close

Than when he kept that closer, briefer watch,

Under the church's roof, beside his arms,

And won his knighthood."

To be appreciated at their worth, these pages should be attentively read. Nowhere has the author's marvellous power of expression, the mingled dignity and pliancy of her style, obtained a greater triumph. She has reproduced the expression of a mind with the same vigorous distinctness as that with which a great painter represents the expression of a countenance.

The character which accords best with my own taste is that of the minstrel Juan, an extremely generous conception. He fills no great part in the drama; he is by nature the reverse of a man of action; and, strictly, the story could very well dispense with him. Yet, for all that, I should be sorry to lose him, and lose thereby the various excellent things which are said of him and by him. I do not include his songs among the latter. Only two of the lyrics in the work strike me as good: the song of Pablo, "The world is great: the birds all fly from me"; and, in a lower degree, the chant of the Zincali, in the fourth book. But I do include the words by which he is introduced to the reader:—

> "Juan was a troubadour revived,
>
> Freshening life's dusty road with babbling rills
>
> Of wit and song, living 'mid harnessed men
>
> With limbs ungalled by armour, ready so
>
> To soothe them weary and to cheer them sad.
>
> Guest at the board, companion in the camp,
>
> A crystal mirror to the life around:
>
> Flashing the comment keen of simple fact
>
> Defined in words; lending brief lyric voice
>
> To grief and sadness; hardly taking note
>
> Of difference betwixt his own and others';
>
> But, rather singing as a listener
>
> To the deep moans, the cries, the wildstrong joys
>
> Of universal Nature, old, yet young."

When Juan talks at his ease, he strikes the note of poetry much more surely than when he lifts his voice in song:—

> "Yet if your graciousness will not disdain
>
> A poor plucked songster, shall he sing to you?
>
> *Some lay of afternoons,—some ballad strain*
>
> *Of those who ached once, but are sleeping now*
>
> *Under the sun-warmed flowers?"*

Juan's link of connection with the story is, in the first place, that he is in love with Fedalma, and, in the second, as a piece of local colour. His attitude with regard to Fedalma is indicated with beautiful delicacy:—

> "O lady, constancy has kind and rank.
>
> One man's is lordly, plump, and bravely clad,
>
> Holds its head high, and tells the world its name:
>
> Another man's is beggared, must go bare,
>
> And shiver through the world, the jest of all,
>
> But that it puts the motley on, and plays
>
> Itself the jester."

Nor are his merits lost upon her, as she declares, with no small force,—

> "No! on the close-thronged spaces of the earth
>
> A battle rages; Fate has carried me

'Mid the thick arrows: I will keep my stand,—

Nor shrink, and let the shaft pass by my breast

To pierce another. O, 'tis written large,

The thing I have to do. But you, dear Juan,

Renounce, endure, are brave, unurged by aught

Save the sweet overflow of your good-will."

In every human imbroglio, be it of a comic or a tragic nature, it is good to think of an observer standing aloof, the critic, the idle commentator of it all, taking notes, as we may say, in the interest of truth. The exercise of this function is the chief ground of our interest in Juan. Yet as a man of action, too, he once appeals most irresistibly to our sympathies: I mean in the admirable scene with Hinda, in which he wins back his stolen finery by his lute-playing. This scene, which is written in prose, has a simple realistic power which renders it a truly remarkable composition.

Of the different parts of *The Spanish Gypsy* I have spoken with such fullness as my space allows: it remains to add a few remarks upon the work as a whole. Its great fault is simply that it is not a genuine poem. It lacks the hurrying quickness, the palpitating warmth, the bursting melody of such a creation. A genuine poem is a tree that breaks into blossom and shakes in the wind. George Eliot's elaborate composition is like a vast mural design in mosaic-work, where great slabs and delicate morsels of stone are laid together with wonderful art, where there are plenty of noble lines and generous hues, but where everything is rigid, measured, and cold,—nothing dazzling, magical, and vocal. The poem contains a number of faulty lines,—lines of twelve, of eleven, and of eight syllables,—of which it is easy to suppose that a more sacredly commissioned versifier would not have been guilty. Occasionally, in the search for poetic effect, the author decidedly misses her way:—

"All her being paused

In resolution, *as some leonine wave,*" etc.

A "leonine" wave is rather too much of a lion and too little of a wave. The work possesses imagination, I think, in no small measure. The description of Silva's feelings during his sojourn in the Gypsy camp is strongly pervaded by it; or if perchance the author achieved these passages without rising on the wings of fancy, her glory is all the greater. But the poem is wanting in passion. The reader is annoyed by a perpetual sense of effort and of intellectual tension. It is a characteristic of George Eliot, I imagine, to allow her impressions to linger a long time in her mind, so that by the time they are ready for use they have lost much of their original freshness and vigour. They have acquired, of course, a number of artificial charms, but they have parted with their primal natural simplicity. In this poem we see the landscape, the people, the manners of Spain as through a glass smoked by the flame of meditative vigils, just as we saw the outward aspect of Florence in *Romola*. The brightness of colouring is there, the artful chiaroscuro, and all the consecrated properties of the scene; but they gleam in an artificial light. The background of the action is admirable in spots, but is cold and mechanical as a whole. The immense rhetorical ingenuity and elegance of the work, which constitute its main distinction, interfere with the faithful, uncompromising reflection of the primary elements of the subject.

The great merit of the characters is that they are marvellously well *understood*,— far better understood than in the ordinary picturesque romance of action, adventure, and mystery. And yet they are not understood to the bottom; they retain an indefinably factitious air, which is not sufficiently justified by their position as ideal figures. The reader who has attentively read the closing scene of the poem will know what I mean. The scene shows remarkable talent; it is eloquent, it is beautiful; but it is arbitrary and fanciful, more than unreal,—untrue. The reader silently chafes and protests, and finally breaks forth and cries, "O for a blast from the outer world!" Silva and Fedalma have developed themselves so daintily and elaborately within the close-sealed precincts of the author's mind, that they strike us at last as acting not as simple human creatures, but as downright *amateurs* of the morally graceful and picturesque. To say that this is the ultimate impression of the poem is to say that it is not a great work. It is in fact not a great drama. It is, in the first place, an admirable study of character,—an essay, as they say, toward the solution of a given problem in conduct. In the second, it is a noble literary performance. It can be read neither without interest in the former respect, nor without profit for its signal merits of style,—and this in spite of the fact that the versification is, as the French say, as little *réussi* as was to be expected in a writer beginning at a bound with a kind of verse which is very much more difficult than even the best prose,—the author's own prose. I shall indicate most of its merits and defects, great and small, if I say it is a romance,—a romance written by one who is emphatically a thinker.

II. THE LEGEND OF JUBAL AND OTHER POEMS

When the author of *Middlemarch* published, some years since, her first volume of verse, the reader, in trying to judge it fairly, asked himself what he should think of it if she had never published a line of prose. The question, perhaps, was not altogether a help to strict fairness of judgment, but the author was protected from illiberal conclusions by the fact that, practically, it was impossible to answer it. George Eliot belongs to that class of pre-eminent writers in relation to whom the imagination comes to self-consciousness only to find itself in subjection. It was impossible to disengage one's judgment from the permanent influence of *Adam Bede* and its companions, and it was necessary, from the moment that the author undertook to play the poet's part, to feel that her genius was all of one piece.

People have often asked themselves how they would estimate Shakespeare if they knew him only by his comedies, Homer if his name stood only for the *Odyssey*, and Milton if he had written nothing but "Lycidas" and the shorter pieces. The question of necessity, inevitable though it is, leads to nothing. George Eliot is neither Homer nor Shakespeare nor Milton; but her work, like theirs, is a massive achievement, divided into a supremely good and a less good, and it provokes us, like theirs, to the fruitless attempt to estimate the latter portion on its own merits alone.

The little volume before us gives us another opportunity; but here, as before, we find ourselves uncomfortably divided between the fear, on the one hand, of being bribed into favour, and, on the other, of giving short measure of it. The author's verses are a narrow manifestation of her genius, but they are an unmistakeable manifestation. *Middlemarch* has made us demand even finer things of her than we did before, and whether, as patented readers of *Middlemarch*, we like "Jubal" and its companions the less or the more, we must admit that they are characteristic products of the same intellect.

We imagine George Eliot is quite philosopher enough, having produced her poems mainly as a kind of experimental entertainment for her own mind, to let them commend themselves to the public on any grounds whatever which will help to illustrate the workings of versatile intelligence,—as interesting failures, if nothing better. She must feel they are interesting; an exaggerated modesty cannot deny that.

We have found them extremely so. They consist of a rhymed narrative, of some length, of the career of Jubal, the legendary inventor of the lyre; of a short rustic idyl in blank verse on a theme gathered in the Black Forest of Baden; of a tale, versified in rhyme, from Boccaccio; and of a series of dramatic scenes called "Armgart,"—the best thing, to our sense, of the four. To these are added a few shorter pieces, chiefly in blank verse, each of which seems to us proportionately more successful than the more ambitious ones. Our author's verse is a mixture of spontaneity of thought and excessive reflectiveness of expression and its value is generally more in the idea than in the form. In whatever George Eliot writes you have the comfortable certainty, infrequent in other quarters, of finding an idea, and you get the substance of her thought in the short poems, without the somewhat rigid envelope of her poetic diction.

If we may say, broadly, that the supreme merit of a poem is in having warmth, and that it is less and less valuable in proportion as it cools by too long waiting upon either fastidious skill or inefficient skill, the little group of verses entitled "Brother and Sister" deserve our preference. They have extreme loveliness, and the feeling they so abundantly express is of a much less intellectualised sort than that which prevails in the other poems. It is seldom that one of our author's compositions concludes upon so simply sentimental a note as the last lines of "Brother and Sister":—

"But were another childhood-world my share,

I would be born a little sister there!"

This will be interesting to many readers as proceeding more directly from the writer's personal experience than anything else they remember. George Eliot's is a personality so enveloped in the mists of reflection that it is an uncommon sensation to find one's self in immediate contact with it. This charming poem, too, throws a grateful light on some of the best pages the author has written,—those in which she describes her heroine's childish years in *The Mill on the Floss*. The finest thing in that admirable novel has always been, to our taste, not its portrayal of the young girl's love-struggles as regards her lover, but those as regards her brother. The former are fiction,—skilful fiction; but the latter are warm reality, and the merit of the verses we speak of is that they are coloured from the same source.

In "Stradivarius," the famous old violin-maker affirms in every pregnant phrase the supreme duty of being perfect in one's labour, and lays down the dictum, which should be the first article in every artist's faith:—

"'Tis God gives skill,

But not without men's hands: He could not make

Antonio Stradivari's violins

Without Antonio."

This is the only really inspiring working-creed, and our author's utterance of it justifies her claim to having the distinctively artistic mind, more forcibly than her not infrequent shortcomings in the direction of an artistic *ensemble*.

Many persons will probably pronounce "A Minor Prophet" the gem of this little collection, and it is certainly interesting, for a great many reasons. It may seem to characterise the author on a number of sides. It illustrates vividly, in the extraordinary ingenuity and flexibility of its diction, her extreme provocation to indulge in the verbal licence of verse. It reads almost like a close imitation of Browning, the great master of the poetical grotesque, except that it observes a discretion which the poet of *Red-Cotton Night-caps* long ago threw overboard. When one can say neat things with such rhythmic felicity, why not attempt it, even if one has at one's command the magnificent vehicle of the style of *Middlemarch*?

The poem is a kindly satire upon the views and the person of an American vegetarian, a certain Elias Baptist Butterworth,—a gentleman, presumably, who under another name, as an evening caller, has not a little retarded the flight of time for the author. Mr. Browning has written nothing better than the account of the Butterworthian "Thought Atmosphere":—

"And when all earth is vegetarian,

When, lacking butchers, quadrupeds die out,

And less Thought-atmosphere is re-absorbed

251

By nerves of insects parasitical,

Those higher truths, seized now by higher minds,

But not expressed (the insects hindering),

Will either flash out into eloquence,

Or, better still, be comprehensible,

By rappings simply, without need of roots."

The author proceeds to give a sketch of the beatific state of things under the vegetarian *régime* prophesied by her friend in

"Mildly nasal tones,

And vowels stretched to suit the widest views."

How, for instance,

"Sahara will be populous

With families of gentlemen retired

From commerce in more Central Africa,

Who order coolness, as we order coal,

And have a lobe anterior strong enough

To think away the sand-storms."

Or how, as water is probably a non-conductor of the Thought-atmosphere,

"Fishes may lead carnivorous lives obscure,

But must not dream of culinary rank

Or being dished in good society."

Then follows the author's own melancholy head-shake and her reflections on the theme that there can be no easy millennium, and that

"Bitterly

I feel that every change upon this earth

Is bought with sacrifice";

and that, even if Mr. Butterworth's axioms were not too good to be true, one might deprecate them in the interest of that happiness which is associated with error that is deeply familiar. Human improvement, she concludes, is something both larger and smaller than the vegetarian bliss, and consists less in a realised perfection than in the sublime dissatisfaction of generous souls with the shortcomings of the actual. All this is unfolded in verse which, if without the absolute pulse of spontaneity, has at least something that closely resembles it. It has very fine passages.

Very fine, too, both in passages and as a whole, is "The Legend of Jubal." It is noteworthy, by the way, that three of these poems are on themes connected with music; and yet we remember no representation of a musician among the multitudinous figures which people the author's novels. But George Eliot, we take it, has the musical sense in no small degree, and the origin of melody and harmony is here described in some very picturesque and sustained poetry.

Jubal invents the lyre and teaches his companions and his tribe how to use it, and then goes forth to wander in quest of new musical inspiration. In this pursuit he grows patriarchally old, and at last makes his way back to his own people. He finds them, greatly advanced in civilisation, celebrating what we should call nowadays his centennial, and making his name the refrain of their songs. He goes in among them and declares himself, but they receive him as a lunatic, and buffet him, and thrust him out into the wilderness again, where he succumbs to their unconscious ingratitude.

"The immortal name of Jubal filled the sky,

While Jubal, lonely, laid him down to die."

253

In his last hour he has a kind of metaphysical vision which consoles him, and enables him to die contented. A mystic voice assures him that he has no cause for complaint; that his use to mankind was everything, and his credit and glory nothing; that being rich in his genius, it was his part to give, gratuitously, to unendowed humanity; and that the knowledge of his having become a part of man's joy, and an image in man's soul, should reconcile him to the prospect of lying senseless in the tomb. Jubal assents, and expires.

"A quenched sun-wave,

The all-creating Presence for his grave."

This is very noble and heroic doctrine, and is enforced in verse not unworthy of it for having a certain air of strain and effort; for surely it is not doctrine that the egoistic heart rises to without some experimental flutter of the wings. It is the expression of a pessimistic philosophy which pivots upon itself only in the face of a really formidable ultimatum. We cordially accept it, however, and are tolerably confident that the artist in general, in his death-throes, will find less repose in the idea of a heavenly compensation for earthly neglect than in the certainty that humanity is really assimilating his productions.

"Agatha" is slighter in sentiment than its companions, and has the vague aroma of an idea rather than the positive weight of thought. It is very graceful. "How Lisa loved the King" seems to us to have, more than its companions, the easy flow and abundance of prime poetry; it wears a reflection of the incomparable naturalness of its model in the *Decameron*. "Armgart" we have found extremely interesting, although perhaps it offers plainest proof of what the author sacrifices in renouncing prose. The drama, in prose, would have been vividly dramatic, while, as it stands, we have merely a situation contemplated, rather than unfolded, in a dramatic light. A great singer loses her voice, and a patronising nobleman, who, before the calamity, had wished her to become his wife, retire from the stage, and employ her genius for the beguilement of private life, finds that he has urgent business in another neighbourhood, and that he has not the mission to espouse her misfortune. Armgart rails tremendously at fate, often in very striking phrase. The Count of course, in bidding her farewell, has hoped that time will soften her disappointment:—

"That empty cup so neatly ciphered, 'Time,'

Handed me as a cordial for despair.

Time—what a word to fling in charity!

Bland, neutral word for slow, dull-beating pain,—

Days, months, and years!"

We must refer the reader to the poem itself for knowledge how resignation comes to so bitter a pain as the mutilation of conscious genius. It comes to Armgart because she is a very superior girl; and though her outline, here, is at once rather sketchy and rather rigid, she may be added to that group of magnificently generous women,—the Dinahs, the Maggies, the Romolas, the Dorotheas,—the representation of whom is our author's chief title to our gratitude. But in spite of Armgart's resignation, the moral atmosphere of the poem, like that of most of the others and like that of most of George Eliot's writings, is an almost gratuitously sad one.

It would take more space than we can command to say how it is that at this and at other points our author strikes us as a spirit mysteriously perverted from her natural temper. We have a feeling that, both intellectually and morally, her genius is essentially of a simpler order than most of her recent manifestations of it. Intellectually, it has run to epigram and polished cleverness, and morally to a sort of conscious and ambitious scepticism, with which it only half commingles. The interesting thing would be to trace the moral divergence from the characteristic type. At bottom, according to this notion, the author of *Romola* and *Middlemarch* has an ardent desire and faculty for positive, active, constructive belief of the old-fashioned kind, but she has fallen upon a critical age and felt its contagion and dominion. If, with her magnificent gifts, she had been borne by the mighty general current in the direction of passionate faith, we often think that she would have achieved something incalculably great.

THE LIMITATIONS OF DICKENS

OUR Mutual Friend is, to our perception, the poorest of Mr. Dickens's works. And it is poor with the poverty not of momentary embarrassment, but of permanent exhaustion. It is wanting in inspiration. For the last ten years it has seemed to us that Mr. Dickens has been unmistakeably forcing himself. *Bleak House* was forced; *Little Dorrit* was laboured; the present work is dug out as with a spade and pickaxe.

Of course—to anticipate the usual argument—who but Dickens could have written it? Who, indeed? Who else would have established a lady in business in a novel on the admirably solid basis of her always putting on gloves and tying a handkerchief around her head in moments of grief, and of her habitually addressing her family with "Peace! hold!" It is needless to say that Mrs. Reginald Wilfer is first and last the occasion of considerable true humour. When, after conducting her daughter to Mrs. Boffin's carriage, in sight of all the envious neighbours, she is described as enjoying her triumph during the next quarter of an hour by airing herself on the doorstep "in a kind of splendidly serene trance," we laugh with as uncritical a laugh as could be desired of us. We pay the same tribute to her assertions, as she narrates the glories of the society she enjoyed at her father's table, that she has known as many as three copper-plate engravers exchanging the most exquisite sallies and retorts there at one time. But when to these we have added a dozen more happy examples of the humour which was exhaled from every line of Mr. Dickens's earlier writings, we shall have closed the list of the merits of the work before us.

To say that the conduct of the story, with all its complications, betrays a long-practised hand, is to pay no compliment worthy the author. If this were, indeed, a compliment, we should be inclined to carry it further, and congratulate him on his success in what we should call the manufacture of fiction; for in so doing we should express a feeling that has attended us throughout the book. Seldom, we reflected, had we read a book so intensely *written*, so little seen, known, or felt.

In all Mr. Dickens's works the fantastic has been his great resource; and while his fancy was lively and vigorous it accomplished great things. But the fantastic, when the fancy is dead, is a very poor business. The movement of Mr. Dickens's fancy in Mr. Wilfer and Mr. Boffin and Lady Tippins, and the Lammles and Miss Wren, and even in Eugene Wrayburn, is, to our mind, a movement lifeless, forced, mechanical. It is the letter of his old humour without the spirit. It is hardly too much to say that every character here put before us is a mere bundle of eccentricities, animated by no principle of nature whatever.

In former days there reigned in Mr. Dickens's extravagances a comparative consistency; they were exaggerated statements of types that really existed. We had, perhaps, never known a Newman Noggs, nor a Pecksniff, nor a Micawber; but we had known persons of whom these figures were but the strictly logical consummation. But among the grotesque creatures who occupy the pages before us, there is not one whom we can refer to as an existing type. In all Mr. Dickens's stories, indeed, the reader has been called upon, and has willingly consented, to accept a certain number of figures or creatures of pure fancy, for this was the author's poetry. He was, moreover, always repaid for his concession by a peculiar beauty or power in these exceptional characters. But he is now expected to make the same concession, with a very inadequate reward.

What do we get in return for accepting Miss Jenny Wren as a possible person? This young lady is the type of a certain class of characters of which Mr. Dickens has made a specialty, and with which he has been accustomed to draw alternate smiles and tears, according as he pressed one spring or another. But this is very cheap merriment and very cheap pathos. Miss Jenny Wren is a poor little dwarf, afflicted as she constantly reiterates, with a "bad back" and "queer legs," who makes doll's dresses, and is for ever pricking at those with whom she converses in the air, with her needle, and assuring them that she knows their "tricks and their manners." Like all Mr. Dickens's pathetic characters, she is a little monster; she is deformed, unhealthy, unnatural; she belongs to the troop of hunchbacks, imbeciles, and precocious children who have carried on the sentimental business in all Mr. Dickens's novels; the little Nells, the Smikes, the Paul Dombeys.

Mr. Dickens goes as far out of the way for his wicked people as he does for his good ones. Rogue Riderhood, indeed, in the present story, is villainous with a sufficiently natural villainy; he belongs to that quarter of society in which the author is most at his ease. But was there ever such wickedness as that of the Lammles and Mr. Fledgeby? Not that people have not been as mischievous as they; but was any one ever mischievous in that singular fashion? Did a couple of elegant swindlers ever take such particular pains to be aggressively inhuman?—for we can find no other word for the gratuitous distortions to which they are subjected. The word *humanity* strikes us as strangely discordant, in the midst of these pages; for, let us boldly declare it, there is no humanity here.

Humanity is nearer home than the Boffins, and the Lammles, and the Wilfers, and the Veneerings. It is in what men have in common with each other, and not what they have in distinction. The people just named have nothing in common with each other, except the fact that they have nothing in common with mankind at large. What a world were this world if the world of *Our Mutual Friend* were an honest reflection of it! But a community of eccentrics is impossible. Rules alone are consistent with each other; exceptions are inconsistent. Society is maintained by natural sense and natural feeling. We cannot conceive a society in which these principles are not in some manner represented. Where in these pages are the depositaries of that intelligence without which the movement of life would cease? Who represents nature?

Accepting half of Mr. Dickens's persons as intentionally grotesque, where are those examplars of sound humanity who should afford us the proper measure of their companions' variations? We ought not, in justice to the author, to seek them among his weaker—that is, his mere conventional—characters; in John Harmon, Lizzie Hexam, or Mortimer Lightwood; but we assuredly cannot find them among his stronger—that is, his artificial creations.

Suppose we take Eugene Wrayburn and Bradley Headstone. They occupy a half-way position between the habitual probable of nature and the habitual impossible of Mr. Dickens. A large portion of the story rests upon the enmity borne by Headstone to Wrayburn, both being in love with the same woman. Wrayburn is a gentleman, and Headstone is one of the people. Wrayburn is well-bred, careless, elegant, sceptical, and idle: Headstone is a high-tempered, hard-working, ambitious young schoolmaster. There lay in the opposition of these two characters a very good story. But the prime requisite was that they should *be* characters: Mr. Dickens, according to his usual plan, has made them simply figures, and between them the story that was to be, the story that should have been, has evaporated. Wrayburn lounges about with his hands in his pockets, smoking a cigar, and talking nonsense. Headstone strides about, clenching his fists and biting his lips and grasping his stick.

There is one scene in which Wrayburn chaffs the schoolmaster with easy insolence, while the latter writhes impotently under his well-bred sarcasm. This scene is very clever, but it is very insufficient. If the majority of readers were not so very timid in the use of words we should call it vulgar. By this we do not mean to indicate the conventional impropriety of two gentlemen exchanging lively personalities; we mean to emphasise the essentially small character of these personalities. In other words, the moment, dramatically, is great, while the author's conception is weak. The friction of two *men*, of two characters, of two passions, produces stronger sparks than Wrayburn's boyish repartees and Headstone's melodramatic commonplaces.

Such scenes as this are useful in fixing the limits of Mr. Dickens's insight. Insight is, perhaps, too strong a word; for we are convinced that it is one of the chief conditions of his genius not to see beneath the surface of things. If we might hazard a definition of his literary character, we should, accordingly, call him the greatest of superficial novelists. We are aware that this definition confines him to an inferior rank in the department of letters which he adorns; but we accept this consequence of our proposition. It were, in our opinion, an offence against humanity to place Mr. Dickens among the greatest novelists. For, to repeat what we have already intimated, he has created nothing but figure. He has added nothing to our understanding of human character. He is master of but two alternatives: he reconciles us to what is commonplace, and he reconciles us to what is odd. The value of the former service is questionable; and the manner in which Mr. Dickens performs it sometimes conveys a certain impression of charlatanism. The value of the latter service is incontestable, and here Mr. Dickens is an honest, an admirable artist.

But what is the condition of the truly great novelist? For him there are no alternatives, for him there are no oddities, for him there is nothing outside of humanity. He cannot shirk it; it imposes itself upon him. For him alone, therefore, there is a true and a false; for him alone, it is possible to be right, because it is possible to be wrong. Mr. Dickens is a great observer and a great humourist, but he is nothing of a philosopher.

Some people may hereupon say, so much the better; we say, so much the worse. For a novelist very soon has need of a little philosophy. In treating of Micawber, and Boffin, and Pickwick, *et hoc genus omne*, he can, indeed, dispense with it, for this—we say it with all deference—is not serious writing. But when he comes to tell the story of a passion, a story like that of Headstone and Wrayburn, he becomes a moralist as well as an artist. He must know *man* as well as *men*, and to know man is to be a philosopher.

The writer who knows men alone, if he have Mr. Dickens's humour and fancy, will give us figures and pictures for which we cannot be too grateful, for he will enlarge our knowledge of the world. But when he introduces men and women whose interest is preconceived to lie not in the poverty, the weakness, the drollery of their natures, but in their complete and unconscious subjection to ordinary and healthy human emotions, all his humour, all his fancy, will avail him nothing if, out of the fullness of his sympathy, he is unable to prosecute those generalisations in which alone consists the real greatness of a work of art.

This may sound like very subtle talk about a very simple matter. It is rather very simple talk about a very subtle matter. A story based upon those elementary passions in which alone we seek the true and final manifestation of character must be told in a spirit of intellectual superiority to those passions. That is, the author must understand what he is talking about. The perusal of a story so told is one of the most elevating experiences within the reach of the human mind. The perusal of a story which is not so told is infinitely depressing and unprofitable.

TENNYSON'S DRAMA

I. QUEEN MARY

ANEW poem by Mr. Tennyson is certain to be largely criticised, and if the new poem is a drama, the performance must be a great event for criticism as well as for poetry. Great surprise, great hopes, and great fears had been called into being by the announcement that the author of so many finely musical lyrics and finished, chiselled specimens of narrative verse, had tempted fortune in the perilous field of the drama.

Few poets seemed less dramatic than Tennyson, even in his most dramatic attempts—in "Maud," in "Enoch Arden," or in certain of the *Idyls of the King*. He had never used the dramatic form, even by snatches; and though no critic was qualified to affirm that he had no slumbering ambition in that direction, it seemed likely that a poet who had apparently passed the meridian of his power had nothing absolutely new to show us. On the other hand, if he had for years been keeping a gift in reserve, and suffering it to ripen and mellow in some deep corner of his genius, while shallower tendencies waxed and waned above it, it was not unjust to expect that the consummate fruit would prove magnificent.

On the whole, we think that doubt was uppermost in the minds of those persons who to a lively appreciation of the author of "Maud" added a vivid conception of the exigencies of the drama. But at last *Queen Mary* appeared, and conjecture was able to merge itself in knowledge. There was a momentary interval, during which we all read, among the cable telegrams in the newspapers, that the London *Times* affirmed the new drama to contain more "true fire" than anything since Shakespeare had laid down the pen. This gave an edge to our impatience; for "fire," true or false, was not what the Laureate's admirers had hitherto claimed for him. In a day or two, however, most people had the work in their hands.

Every one, it seems to us, has been justified—those who hoped (that is, expected), those who feared, and those who were mainly surprised. *Queen Mary* is both better and less good than was to have been supposed, and both in its merits and its defects it is extremely singular. It is the least Tennysonian of all the author's productions; and we may say that he has not so much refuted as evaded the charge that he is not a dramatic poet. To produce his drama he has had to cease to be himself. Even if *Queen Mary*, as a drama, had many more than its actual faults, this fact alone—this extraordinary defeasance by the poet of his familiar identity—would make it a remarkable work.

We know of few similar phenomena in the history of literature—few such examples of rupture with a consecrated past. Poets in their prime have groped and experimented, tried this and that, and finally made a great success in a very different vein from that in which they had found their early successes. But the writers in prose or in verse are few who, after a lifetime spent in elaborating and perfecting a certain definite and extremely characteristic manner, have at Mr. Tennyson's age suddenly dismissed it from use and stood forth clad from head to foot in a disguise without a flaw. We are sure that the other great English poet—the author of "The Ring and the Book,"—would be quite incapable of any such feat. The more's the pity, as many of his readers will say!

Queen Mary is upward of three hundred pages long; and yet in all these three hundred pages there is hardly a trace of the Tennyson we know. Of course the reader is on the watch for reminders of the writer he has greatly loved; and of course, vivid signs being absent, he finds a certain eloquence in the slightest intimations. When he reads that

——"that same tide

Which, coming with our coming, seemed to smile

And sparkle like our fortune as thou saidest,

Ran sunless down and moaned against the piers,"

he seems for a moment to detect the peculiar note and rhythm of "Enoch Arden" or "The Princess." Just preceding these, indeed, is a line which seems Tennysonian because it is in a poem by Tennyson:

"Last night I climbed into the gate-house, Brett,

And scared the gray old porter and his wife."

262

In such touches as these the Tennysonian note is faintly struck; but if the poem were unsigned, they would not do much toward pointing out the author. On the other hand, the fine passages in *Queen Mary* are conspicuously deficient in those peculiar cadences—that exquisite perfume of diction—which every young poet of the day has had his hour of imitating. We may give as an example Pole's striking denial of the charge that the Church of Rome has ever known trepidation:

"What, my Lord!

The Church on Petra's rock? Never! I have seen

A pine in Italy that cast its shadow

Athwart a cataract; firm stood the pine—

The cataract shook the shadow. To my mind

The cataract typed the headlong plunge and fall

Of heresy to the pit: the pine was Rome.

You see, my Lords,

It was the shadow of the Church that trembled."

This reads like Tennyson doing his best not to be Tennyson, and very fairly succeeding. Well as he succeeds, however, and admirably skilful and clever as is his attempt throughout to play tricks with his old habits of language, and prove that he was not the slave but the master of the classic Tennysonian rhythm, I think that few readers can fail to ask themselves whether the new gift is of equal value with the old. The question will perhaps set them to fingering over the nearest volume of the poet at hand, to refresh their memory of his ancient magic. It has rendered the present writer this service, and he feels as if it were a considerable one. Every great poet has something that he does supremely well, and when you come upon Tennyson at his best you feel that you are dealing with poetry at its highest. One of the best passages in *Queen Mary*—the only one, it seems to me, very sensibly warmed by the "fire" commemorated by the London *Times*—is the passionate monologue of Mary when she feels what she supposes to be the intimations of maternity:

"He hath awaked, he hath awaked!

He stirs within the darkness!

Oh Philip, husband! how thy love to mine

Will cling more close, and those bleak manners thaw,

That make me shamed and tongue-tied in my love.

The second Prince of Peace—

The great unborn defender of the Faith,

Who will avenge me of mine enemies—

He comes, and my star rises.

The stormy Wyatts and Northumberlands

And proud ambitions of Elizabeth,

And all her fiercest partisans, are pale

Before my star!

His sceptre shall go forth from Ind to Ind!

His sword shall hew the heretic peoples down!

His faith shall clothe the world that will be his,

Like universal air and sunshine! Open,

Ye everlasting gates! The King is here!—

My star, my son!"

That is very fine, and its broken verses and uneven movement have great felicity and suggestiveness. But their magic is as nothing, surely, to the magic of such a passage as this:

"Yet hold me not for ever in thine East;

How can my nature longer mix with thine?

Coldly thy rosy shadows bathe me, cold

Are all thy lights, and cold my wrinkled feet

Upon thy glimmering thresholds, where the stream

Floats up from those dim fields about the homes

Of happy men that have the power to die,

And grassy barrows of the happier dead.

Release me and restore me to the ground;

Thou seëst all things, thou wilt see my grave;

Thou wilt renew thy beauty morn by morn;

I, earth in earth, forget these empty courts,

And thee returning on thy silver wheels."

In these beautiful lines from "Tithonus" there is a purity of tone, an inspiration, a something sublime and exquisite, which is easily within the compass of Mr. Tennyson's usual manner at its highest, but which is not easily achieved by any really dramatic verse. It is poised and stationary, like a bird whose wings have borne him high, but the beauty of whose movement is less in great ethereal sweeps and circles than in the way he hangs motionless in the blue air, with only a vague tremor of his pinions. Even if the idea with Tennyson were more largely dramatic than it usually is, the immobility, as we must call it, of his phrase would always defeat the dramatic intention. When he wishes to represent movement, the phrase always seems to me to pause and slowly pivot upon itself, or at most to move backward. I do not know whether the reader recognizes the peculiarity to which I allude; one has only to open Tennyson almost at random to find an example of it:

"For once when Arthur, walking all alone,

Vext at a rumour rife about the Queen,

Had met her, Vivien being greeted fair,

Would fain have wrought upon his cloudy mood

With reverent eyes mock-loyal, shaken voice,

And fluttered adoration."

That perhaps is a subtle illustration; the allusion to Teolin's dog in "Aylmer's Field" is a franker one:

——"his old Newfoundlands, when they ran

To lose him at the stables; for he rose,

Two-footed, at the limit of his chain,

Roaring to make a third."

What these pictures present is not the action itself, but the poet's complex perception of it; it seems hardly more vivid and genuine than the sustained posturings of brilliant *tableaux vivants*. With the poets who are natural chroniclers of movement, the words fall into their places as with some throw of the dice, which fortune should always favour. With Scott and Byron they leap into the verse *à pieds joints*, and shake it with their coming; with Tennyson they arrive slowly and settle cautiously into their attitudes, after having well scanned the locality. In consequence they are generally exquisite, and make exquisite combinations; but the result is intellectual poetry and not passionate—poetry which, if the term is not too pedantic, one may qualify as static poetry. Any scene of violence represented by Tennyson is always singularly limited and compressed; it is reduced to a few elements—refined to a single statuesque episode. There are, for example, several descriptions of tournaments and combats in the *Idyls of the King*. They are all most beautiful, but they are all curiously delicate. One gets no sense of the din and shock of battle; one seems to be looking at a bas relief of two contesting knights in chiselled silver, on a priceless piece of plate. They belong to the same family as that charming description, in Hawthorne's *Marble Faun*, of the sylvan dance of Donatello and Miriam in the Borghese gardens. Hawthorne talks of the freedom and frankness of their mirth and revelry; what we seem to see is a solemn frieze in stone along the base of a monument. These are the natural fruits of geniuses who are of the brooding rather than the impulsive order. I do not mean to say that here and there Tennyson does not give us a couplet in which motion seems reflected without being made to tarry. I open "Enoch Arden" at hazard, and I read of Enoch's ship that

　　　　　　　　——"at first indeed

　　Thro' many a fair sea-circle, day by day,

　　Scarce rocking, her full-busted figure-head

　　Stared o'er the ripple feathering from her bows."

I turn the page and read of

　　"The myriad shriek of wheeling ocean fowl,

　　The league-long roller thundering on the reef,

　　The moving whisper of huge trees that branched

　　And blossomed in the zenith";

of

　　"The sunrise broken into scarlet shafts

　　Among the palms and ferns and precipices;

　　The blaze upon the waters to the east;

　　The blaze upon his island overhead;

　　The blaze upon the waters to the west;

　　Then the great stars that globed themselves in Heaven,

　　The hollower-bellowing Ocean, and again

　　The scarlet shafts of sunrise."

These lines represent movement on the grand natural scale—taking place in that measured, majestic fashion which, at any given moment, seems identical with permanence. One is almost ashamed to quote Tennyson; one can hardly lay one's hand on a passage that does not form part of the common stock of reference and recitation. Passages of the more impulsive and spontaneous kind will of course chiefly be found in his lyrics and rhymed verses (though rhyme would at first seem but another check upon his freedom); and passages of the kind to which I have been calling attention, chiefly in his narrative poems, in the *Idyls* generally, and especially in the later ones, while the words strike one as having been pondered and collated with an almost miserly care.

But a man has always the qualities of his defects, and if Tennyson is what I have called a static poet, he at least represents repose and stillness and the fixedness of things, with a splendour that no poet has surpassed. We all of this generation have lived in such intimacy with him, and made him so much part of our regular intellectual meat and drink, that it requires a certain effort to hold him off at the proper distance for scanning him. We need to cease mechanically murmuring his lines, so that we may hear them speak for themselves.

Few persons who have grown up within the last forty years but have passed through the regular Tennysonian phase; happy few who have paid it a merely passive tribute, and not been moved to commit their emotions to philosophic verse, in the metre of "In Memoriam"! The phase has lasted longer with some persons than with others; but it will not be denied that with the generation at large it has visibly declined. The young persons of twenty now read Tennyson (though, as we imagine, with a fervour less intense than that which prevailed twenty years ago); but the young persons of thirty read Browning and Dante Rossetti, and Omar Kheyam—and are also sometimes heard to complain that poetry is dead and that there is nothing nowadays to read.

We have heard Tennyson called "dainty" so often, we have seen so many allusions to the "Tennysonian trick," we have been so struck, in a certain way, with M. Taine's remarkable portrait of the poet, in contrast to that of Alfred de Musset, that every one who has anything of a notion of keeping abreast of what is called the "culture of the time" is rather shy of making an explicit, or even a serious profession of admiration for his earlier idol. It has long been the fashion to praise Byron, if one praises him at all, with an apologetic smile; and Tennyson has been, I think, in a measure, tacitly classed with the author of "Childe Harold" as a poet whom one thinks most of while one's taste is immature.

This is natural enough, I suppose, and the taste of the day must travel to its opportunity's end. But I do not believe that Byron has passed, by any means, and I do not think that Tennyson has been proved to be a secondary or a tertiary poet. If he is not in the front rank, it is hard to see what it is that constitutes exquisite quality. There are poets of a larger compass; he has not the passion of Shelley nor the transcendent meditation of Wordsworth; but his inspiration, in its own current, is surely as pure as theirs. He depicts the assured beauties of life, the things that civilisation has gained and permeated, and he does it with an ineffable delicacy of imagination. Only once, as it seems to me (at the close of "Maud"), has he struck the note of irrepressible emotion, and appeared to say the thing that must be said at the moment, at any cost. For the rest, his verse is the verse of leisure, of luxury, of contemplation, of a faculty that circumstances have helped to become fastidious; but this leaves it a wide province—a province that it fills with a sovereign splendour.

When a poet is such an artist as Tennyson, such an unfaltering, consummate master, it is no shame to surrender one's self to his spell. Reading him over here and there, as I have been doing, I have received an extraordinary impression of talent—talent ripened and refined, and passed, with a hundred incantations, through the crucible of taste. The reader is in thoroughly good company, and if the language is to a certain extent that of a coterie, the coterie can offer convincing evidence of its right to be exclusive. Its own tone is exquisite; listen to it, and you will desire nothing more.

Tennyson's various *Idyls* have been in some degree discredited by insincere imitations, and in some degree, perhaps, by an inevitable lapse of sympathy on the part of some people from what appears their falsetto pitch. That King Arthur, in the great ones of the series, is rather a prig, and that he couldn't have been all the poet represents him without being a good deal of a hypocrite; that the poet himself is too monotonously unctuous, and that in relating the misdeeds of Launcelot and Guinevere he seems, like the lady in the play in "Hamlet," to "protest too much" for wholesomeness—all this has been often said, and said with abundant force. But there is a way of reading the *Idyls*, one and all, and simply enjoying them. It has been, just now, the way of the writer of these lines; he does not exactly know what may be gained by taking the other way, but he feels as if there were a pitiful loss in not taking this one. If one surrenders one's sense to their perfect picturesqueness, it is the most charming poetry in the world. The prolonged, delicate, exquisite sustentation of the pictorial tone seems to me a marvel of ingenuity and fancy. It appeals to a highly cultivated sense, but what enjoyment is so keen as that of the cultivated sense when its finer nerve is really touched? The *Idyls* all belong to the poetry of association; but before they were written we had yet to learn how finely association could be analysed, and how softly its chords could be played upon. When Enoch Arden came back from his desert island,

> "He like a lover down through all his blood
>
> Drew in the dewy, meadowy morning breath
>
> Of England, blown across her ghostly wall."

Tennyson's solid verbal felicities, his unerring sense of the romantic, his acute perception of everything in nature that may contribute to his fund of exquisite imagery, his refinement, his literary tone, his aroma of English lawns and English libraries, the whole happy chance of his selection of the Arthurian legends—all this, and a dozen minor graces which it would take almost his own "daintiness" to formulate, make him, it seems to me, the most charming of the *entertaining* poets. It is as an entertaining poet I chiefly think of him; his morality, at moments, is certainly importunate enough, but elevated as it is, it never seems to me of so fine a distillation as his imagery. As a didactic creation I do not greatly care for King Arthur; but as a fantastic one he is infinitely remunerative. He is doubtless not, as an intellectual conception, massive enough to be called a great figure; but he is, picturesquely, so admirably self-consistent, that the reader's imagination is quite willing to turn its back, if need be, on his judgment, and give itself up to idle enjoyment.

As regards Tennyson's imagery, anything that one quotes in illustration is, as I have said, certain to be extremely familiar; but even familiarity can hardly dull the beauty of such a touch as that about Merlin's musings:

> "So dark a forethought rolled about his brain,
>
> As on a dull day in an Ocean cave
>
> The blind wave feeling round his long sea-hall
>
> In silence."

Or of that which puts in vivid form the estrangement of Enid and Geraint:

"The two remained

Apart by all the chamber's width, and mute

As creatures voiceless through the fault of birth,

Or two wild men, supporters of a shield,

Painted, who stare at open space, nor glance

The one at other, parted by the shield."

Happy, in short, the poet who can offer his heroine for her dress

———"a splendid silk of foreign loom,

Where, like a shoaling sea, the lovely blue

Played into green."

I have touched here only upon Tennyson's narrative poems, because they seemed most in order in any discussion of the author's dramatic faculty. They cannot be said to place it in an eminent light, and they remind one more of the courage than of the discretion embodied in *Queen Mary*. Lovely pictures of things standing, with a sort of conscious stillness, for their poetic likeness, measured speeches, full of delicate harmonies and curious cadences—these things they contain in plenty, but little of that liberal handling of cross-speaking passion and humour which, with a strong constructive faculty, we regard as the sign of a genuine dramatist.

The dramatic form seems to me of all literary forms the very noblest, I have so extreme a relish for it that I am half afraid to trust myself to praise it, lest I should seem to be merely rhapsodizing. But to be really noble it must be quite itself, and between a poor drama and a fine one there is, I think, a wider interval than anywhere else in the scale of success. A sequence of speeches headed by proper names—a string of dialogues broken into acts and scenes—does not constitute a drama; not even when the speeches are very clever and the dialogue bristles with "points."

The fine thing in a real drama, generally speaking, is that, more than any other work of literary art, it needs a masterly structure. It needs to be shaped and fashioned and laid together, and this process makes a demand upon an artist's rarest gifts. He must combine and arrange, interpolate and eliminate, play the joiner with the most attentive skill; and yet at the end effectually bury his tools and his sawdust, and invest his elaborate skeleton with the smoothest and most polished integument. The five-act drama—serious or humourous, poetic or prosaic—is like a box of fixed dimensions and inelastic material, into which a mass of precious things are to be packed away. It is a problem in ingenuity and a problem of the most interesting kind. The precious things in question seem out of all proportion to the compass of the receptacle; but the artist has an assurance that with patience and skill a place may be made for each, and that nothing need be clipped or crumpled, squeezed or damaged. The false dramatist either knocks out the sides of his box, or plays the deuce with the contents; the real one gets down on his knees, disposes of his goods tentatively, this, that, and the other way, loses his temper but keeps his ideal, and at last rises in triumph, having packed his coffer in the one way that is mathematically right. It closes perfectly, and the lock turns with a click; between one object and another you cannot insert the point of a penknife.

To work successfully beneath a few grave, rigid laws, is always a strong man's highest ideal of success. The reader cannot be sure how deeply conscious Mr. Tennyson has been of the laws of the drama, but it would seem as if he had not very attentively pondered them. In a play, certainly, the subject is of more importance than in any other work of art. Infelicity, triviality, vagueness of subject, may be outweighed in a poem, a novel, or a picture, by charm of manner, by ingenuity of execution; but in a drama the subject is of the essence of the work—it *is* the work. If it is feeble, the work can have no force; if it is shapeless, the work must be amorphous.

Queen Mary, I think, has this fundamental weakness; it would be very hard to say what its subject is. Strictly speaking, the drama has none. To the statement, "It is the reign of the elder daughter of Henry VIII.," it seems to me very nearly fair to reply that that is not a subject. I do not mean to say that a consummate dramatist could not resolve it into one, but the presumption is altogether against it. It cannot be called an intrigue, nor treated as one; it tends altogether to expansion; whereas a genuine dramatic subject should tend to concentration.

Madame Ristori, that accomplished tragédienne, has for some years been carrying about the world with her a piece of writing, punctured here and there with curtain-falls, which she presents to numerous audiences as a tragedy embodying the history of Queen Elizabeth. The thing is worth mentioning only as an illustration; it is from the hand of a prolific Italian purveyor of such wares, and is as bad as need be. Many of the persons who read these lines will have seen it, and will remember it as a mere bald sequence of anecdotes, roughly cast into dialogue. It is not incorrect to say that, as regards form, Mr. Tennyson's drama is of the same family as the historical tragedies of Signor Giacometti. It is simply a dramatised chronicle, without an internal structure, taking its material in pieces, as history hands them over, and working each one up into an independent scene—usually with rich ability. It has no shape; it is cast into no mould; it has neither beginning, middle, nor end, save the chronological ones.

A work of this sort may have a great many merits (those of *Queen Mary* are numerous), but it cannot have the merit of being a drama. We have, indeed, only to turn to Shakespeare to see how much of pure dramatic interest may be infused into an imperfect dramatic form. *Henry IV.* and the others of its group, *Richard III.*, *Henry VIII.*, *Antony and Cleopatra*, *Julius Cæsar*, are all chronicles in dialogue, are all simply Holinshed and Plutarch transferred into immortal verse. They are magnificent because Shakespeare could do nothing weak; but all Shakespearian as they are, they are not models; the models are *Hamlet* and *Othello*, *Macbeth* and *Lear*. Tennyson is not Shakespeare, but in everything he had done hitherto there had been an essential perfection, and we are sorry that, in the complete maturity of his talent, proposing to write a drama, he should have chosen the easy way rather than the hard.

He chose, however, a period out of which a compact dramatic subject of the richest interest might well have been wrought. For this, of course, considerable invention would have been needed, and Mr. Tennyson had apparently no invention to bring to his task. He has embroidered cunningly the groundwork offered him by Mr. Froude, but he has contributed no new material. The field offers a great stock of dramatic figures, and one's imagination kindles as one thinks of the multifarious combinations into which they might have been cast. We do not pretend of course to say in detail what Mr. Tennyson might have done; we simply risk the affirmation that he might have wrought a somewhat denser tissue. History certainly would have suffered, but poetry would have gained, and he is writing poetry and not history. As his drama stands, we take it that he does not pretend to have deepened our historic light.

Psychologically, picturesquely, the persons in the foreground of Mary's reign constitute a most impressive and interesting group. The imagination plays over it importunately, and wearies itself with scanning the outlines and unlighted corners. Mary herself unites a dozen strong dramatic elements—in her dark religious passion, her unrequited conjugal passion, her mixture of the Spanish and English natures, her cruelty and her conscience, her high-handed rule and her constant insecurity. With her dark figure lighted luridly by perpetual martyr-fires, and made darker still by the presence of her younger sister, radiant with the promise of England's coming greatness; with Lady Jane Grey groping for the block behind her; her cold fanatic of a husband beside her, as we know him by Velasquez (with not a grain of fanaticism to spare for her); with her subtle ecclesiastical cousin Pole on the other side, with evil counsellors and dogged martyrs and a threatening people all around her, and with a lonely, dreary, disappointed and unlamented death before her, she is a subject made to the hand of a poet who should know how to mingle cunningly his darker shades. Tennyson has elaborated her figure in a way that is often masterly; it is a success—the greatest success of the poem. It is compounded in his hands of very subtle elements, and he keeps them from ever becoming gross.

The Mary of his pages is a complex personage, and not what she might so easily become—a mere picturesque stalking-horse of melodrama. The art with which he has still kept her sympathetic and human, at the same time that he has darkened the shadows in her portrait to the deepest tone that he had warrant for, is especially noticeable. It is not in Mr. Tennyson's pages that Mary appears for the first time in the drama; she gives her name to a play of Victor Hugo's dating from the year 1833—the prime of the author's career. I have just been reading over *Marie Tudor*, and it has suggested a good many reflections. I think it probable that many of the readers of *Queen Mary* would be quite unable to peruse Victor Hugo's consummately unpleasant production to the end; but they would admit, I suppose, that a person who had had the stomach to do so might have something particular to say about it.

If one had an eye for contrasts, the contrast between these two works is extremely curious. I said just now that Tennyson had brought no invention to his task; but it may be said, on the other side, that Victor Hugo has brought altogether too much. If Tennyson has been unduly afraid of remodelling history, the author of *Marie Tudor* has known no such scruples; he has slashed into the sacred chart with the shears of a *romantique* of 1830. Although Tennyson, in a general way, is an essentially picturesque poet, his picturesqueness is of an infinitely milder type than that of Victor Hugo; the one ends where the other begins. With Victor Hugo the horrible is always the main element of the picturesque, and the beautiful and the tender are rarely introduced save to give it relief. In *Marie Tudor* they cannot be said to be introduced at all; the drama is one masterly compound of abominable horror; horror for horror's sake—for the sake of chiaroscuro, of colour, of the footlights, of the actors; not in the least in any visible interest of human nature, of moral verity, of the discrimination of character.

What Victor Hugo has here made of the rigid, strenuous, pitiable English queen seems to me a good example of how little the handling of sinister passions sometimes costs a genius of his type—how little conviction or deep reflection goes with it. There was a Mary of a far keener tragic interest than the epigrammatic Messalina whom he has portrayed; but her image was established in graver and finer colours, and he passes jauntily beside it, without suspecting its capacity. Marie Tudor is a lascivious termagant who amuses herself, first, with caressing an Italian adventurer, then with slapping his face, and then with dabbling in his blood; but we do not really see why the author should have given his heroine a name which history held in her more or less sacred keeping; one's interest in the drama would have been more comfortable if the persons, in their impossible travesty, did not present themselves as old friends. It is true that the "Baron of Dinasmonddy" can hardly be called an old friend; but he is at least as familiar as the Earl of Clanbrassil, the Baron of Darmouth in Devonshire, and Lord South-Repps.

Marie Tudor, then has little to do with nature and nothing with either history or morality; and yet, without a paradox, it has some very strong qualities. It is at any rate a genuine drama, and it succeeds thoroughly well in what it attempts. It is moulded and proportioned to a definite scenic end, and never falters in its course. To read it just after you have read *Queen Mary* brings out its merits, as well as its defects; and if the contrast makes you inhale with a double satisfaction the clearer moral atmosphere of the English work, it leads you also to reflect with some gratitude that dramatic tradition, in our modern era, has not remained solely in English hands.

Mr. Tennyson has very frankly fashioned his play upon the model of the Shakespearian "histories." He has given us the same voluminous list of characters; he has made the division into acts merely arbitrary; he has introduced low-life interlocutors, talking in archaic prose; and whenever the fancy has taken him, he has culled his idioms and epithets from the Shakespearian vocabulary. As regards this last point, he has shown all the tact and skill that were to be expected from so approved a master of language. The prose scenes are all of a quasi-humourous description, and they emulate the queer jocosities of Shakespeare more successfully than seemed probable; though it was not to be forgotten that the author of the "Palace of Art" was also the author of

275

the "Northern Farmer." These few lines might have been taken straight from *Henry IV.* or *Henry VIII.*:

"No; we know that you be come to kill the Queen, and we'll pray for you all on our bended knees. But o' God's mercy, don't you kill the Queen here, Sir Thomas; look ye, here's little Dickon, and little Robin, and little Jenny—though she's but a side cousin—and all, on our knees, we pray you to kill the Queen farther off, Sir Thomas."

The poet, however, is modern when he chooses to be:

"Action and reaction,

The miserable see-saw of our child-world,

Make us despise it at odd hours, my Lord."

That reminds one less of the Elizabethan than of the Victorian era. Mr. Tennyson has desired to give a general picture of the time, to reflect all its leading elements and commemorate its salient episodes. From this point of view England herself—England struggling and bleeding in the clutches of the Romish wolf, as he would say—is the heroine of the drama. This heroine is very nobly and vividly imaged, and we feel the poet to be full of a retroactive as well as a present patriotism. It is a plain Protestant attitude that he takes; there is no attempt at analysis of the Catholic sense of the situation; it is quite the old story that we learned in our school-histories as children. We do not mean that this is not the veracious way of presenting it; but we notice the absence of that tendency to place it in different lights, accumulate *pros* and *cons*, and plead opposed causes in the interest of ideal truth, which would have been so obvious if Mr. Browning had handled the theme. And yet Mr. Tennyson has been large and liberal, and some of the finest passages in the poem are uttered by independent Catholics. The author has wished to give a hint of everything, and he has admirably divined the anguish of mind of many men who were unprepared to go with the new way of thinking, and yet were scandalised at the license of the old—who were willing to be Catholics, and yet not willing to be delivered over to Spain.

Where so many episodes are sketched, few of course can be fully developed; but there is a vivid manliness of the classic English type in such portraits as Lord William Howard and Sir Ralph Bagenhall—poor Sir Ralph, who declares that

"Far liefer had I in my country hall

Been reading some old book, with mine old hound

Couch'd at my hearth, and mine old flask of wine

    Beside me,"

than stand as he does in the thick of the trouble of the time; and who finally is brought to his account for not having knelt with the commons to the legate of Charles V. We have a glimpse of Sir Thomas Wyatt's insurrection, and a portrait of that robust rebel, who was at the same time an editor of paternal sonnets—sonnets of a father who loved

"To read and rhyme in solitary fields,

The lark above, the nightingale below,

And answer them in song."

We have a very touching report of Lady Jane Grey's execution, and we assist almost directly at the sad perplexities of poor Cranmer's eclipse. We appreciate the contrast between the fine nerves and many-sided conscience of that wavering martyr, and the more comfortable religious temperament of Bonner and Gardiner—Bonner, apt "to gorge a heretic whole, roasted, or raw;" and Gardiner, who can say,

"I've gulpt it down; I'm wholly for the Pope,

Utterly and altogether for the Pope,

The Eternal Peter of the changeless chair,

Crowned slave of slaves and mitred king of kings.

God upon earth! What more? What would you have?"

Elizabeth makes several appearances, and though they are brief, the poet has evidently had a definite figure in his mind's eye. On a second reading it betrays a number of fine intentions. The circumspection of the young princess, her high mettle, her coquetry, her frankness, her coarseness, are all rapidly glanced at. Her exclamation—

> "I would I were a milkmaid,
>
> To sing, love, marry, churn, brew, bake, and die,
>
> And have my simple headstone by the church,
>
> And all things lived and ended honestly"—

marks one limit of the sketch; and the other is indicated by her reply to Cecil at the end of the drama, on his declaring, in allusion to Mary, that "never English monarch dying left England so little":

> "But with Cecil's aid
>
> And others', if our person be secured
>
> From traitor stabs, we will make England great!"

The middle term is perhaps marked by her reception of the functionary who comes to inform her that her sister bids her know that the King of Spain desires her to marry Prince Philibert of Savoy:

> "I thank you heartily, sir,
>
> But I am royal, tho' your prisoner,
>
> And God hath blessed or cursed me with a nose—
>
> Your boots are from the horses."

The drama is deficient in male characters of salient interest. Philip is vague and blank, as he is evidently meant to be, and Cardinal Pole is a portrait of a character constitutionally inapt for breadth of action. The portrait is a skilful one, however, and expresses forcibly the pangs of a sensitive nature entangled in trenchant machinery. There is a fine scene near the close of the drama in which Pole and the Queen—cousins, old friends, and for a moment betrothed (Victor Hugo characteristically assumes Mary to have been her cousin's mistress)—confide to each other their weariness and disappointment. Mary endeavours to console the Cardinal, but he has only grim answers for her:

> "Our altar is a mound of dead men's clay,
>
> Dug from the grave that yawns for us beyond;
>
> And there is one Death stands beside the Groom,
>
> And there is one Death stands beside the Bride."

Queen Mary, I believe, is to be put upon the stage next winter in London. I do not pretend to forecast its success in representation; but it is not indiscrete to say that it will suffer from the absence of a man's part capable of being made striking. The very clever Mr. Henry Irving has, we are told, offered his services, presumably to play either Philip or Pole. If he imparts any great relief to either figure, it will be a signal proof of talent. The actress, however, to whom the part of the Queen is allotted will have every reason to be grateful. The character is full of colour and made to utter a number of really dramatic speeches. When Renard assures her that Philip is only waiting for leave of the Parliament to land on English shores she has an admirable outbreak:

> "God change the pebble which his kingly foot
>
> First presses into some more costly stone
>
> > Than ever blinded eye. I'll have one mark it
>
> And bring it me. I'll have it burnished firelike;
>
> I'll set it round with gold, with pearl, with diamond.

Let the great angel of the Church come with him,

Stand on the deck and spread his wings for sail!"

Mary is not only vividly conceived from within, but her physiognomy, as seen from without, is indicated with much pictorial force:

"Did you mark our Queen?

The colour freely played into her face,

And the half sight which makes her look so stern

Seemed, through that dim, dilated world of hers,

To read our faces."

In the desolation of her last days, when she bids her attendants go to her sister and

"Tell her to come and close my dying eyes

And wear my crown and dance upon my grave,"

Mary, to attest her misery, seats herself on the ground, like Constance in "King John"; and the comment of one of her women hereupon is strikingly picturesque:

"Good Lord! how grim and ghastly looks her Grace,

With both her knees drawn upward to her chin.

There was an old-world tomb beside my father's,

And this was opened, and the dead were found

Sitting, and in this fashion; she looks a corpse."

The great merit of Mr. Tennyson's drama, however, is not in the quotableness of certain passages, but in the thoroughly elevated spirit of the whole. He desired to make us feel of what sound manly stuff the Englishmen of that Tudor reign of terror needed to be, and his verse is pervaded by the echo of their deep-toned refusal to abdicate their manhood. The temper of the poem, on this line, is so noble that the critic who has indulged in a few strictures as to matters of form feels as if he had been frivolous and niggardly. I nevertheless venture to add in conclusion that *Queen Mary* seems to me a work of rare ability rather than great inspiration; a powerful *tour de force* rather than a labour of love. But though it is not the best of a great poet's achievement, only a great poet could have written it.

II. HAROLD

The author of *Queen Mary* seems disposed to show us that that work was not an accident, but rather, as it may be said, an incident of his literary career. The incident has just been repeated, though *Harold* has come into the world more quietly than its predecessor.

It is singular how soon the public gets used to unfamiliar notions. By the time the reader has finished *Harold* he has almost contracted the habit of thinking of Mr. Tennyson as a writer chiefly known to fame by "dramas" without plots and dialogues without point. This impression it behooves him, of course, to shake off if he wishes to judge the book properly. He must compare the author of "Maud" and the earlier *Idyls* with the great poets, and not with the small. *Harold* would be a respectable production for a writer who had spent his career in producing the same sort of thing, but it is a somewhat graceless anomaly in the record of a poet whose verse has, in a large degree, become part of the civilisation of his day.

Queen Mary was not, on the whole, pronounced a success, and *Harold*, roughly speaking, is to *Queen Mary* what that work is to the author's earlier masterpieces. *Harold* is not in the least bad: it contains nothing ridiculous, unreasonable, or disagreeable; it is only decidedly weak, decidedly colourless, and tame. The author's inspiration is like a fire which is quietly and contentedly burning low. The analogy is perfectly complete. The hearth is clean swept and the chimney-side is garnished with its habitual furniture; but the room is getting colder and colder, and the occasional little flickers emitted by the mild embers are not sufficient to combat the testimony of the poetical thermometer. There is nothing necessarily harsh in this judgment. Few fires are always at a blaze, and the imagination, which is the most delicate machine in the world, cannot be expected to serve longer than a good gold repeater. We must take what it gives us, in every case, and be thankful. Mr. Tennyson is perfectly welcome to amuse himself with listening to the fainter tick of his honoured time-piece; it is going still, unquestionably; it has not stopped. Only we may without rudeness abstain from regulating our engagements by the indications of the instrument.

Harold seems at first to have little, in form, that is characteristic of the author— little of the thoroughly familiar Tennysonian quality. Nevertheless, there is every now and then a line which arrests the ear by the rhythm and cadence which have always formed the chief mystery in the art of imitating the Laureate.

Meeting in the early pages such a line as

"What, with this flaming horror overhead?"

we should suspect we were reading Tennyson if we did not know it; and our suspicion would he amply confirmed by half a dozen other lines:

"Taken the rifted pillars of the wood."

"My greyhounds fleeting like a beam of light."

"Suffer a stormless shipwreck in the pools."

"That scared the dying conscience of the king."

Harold is interesting as illustrating, in addition to *Queen Mary*, Mr. Tennyson's idea of what makes a drama. A succession of short scenes, detached from the biography of a historical character, is, apparently, to his sense sufficient; the constructive side of the work is thereby reduced to a primitive simplicity. It is even more difficult to imagine acting *Harold* than it was to imagine acting *Queen Mary*; and it is probable that in this case the experiment will not be tried. And yet the story, or rather the historical episode, upon which Mr. Tennyson has here laid his hand is eminently interesting.

Harold, the last of the "English," as people of a certain way of feeling are fond of calling him—the son of Godwin, masterful minister of Edward the Confessor, the wearer for a short and hurried hour of the English crown, and the opponent and victim of William of Normandy on the field of Hastings—is a figure which combines many of the elements of romance and of heroism. The author has very characteristically tried to accentuate the moral character of his hero by making him a sort of distant relation of the family of Galahad and Arthur and the other moralising gallants to whom his pages have introduced us. Mr. Tennyson's Harold is a warrior who talks about his "better self," and who alludes to

"Waltham, my foundation

For men who serve their neighbour, not themselves,"

—a touch which transports us instantly into the atmosphere of the Arthurian Idyls. But Harold's history may be very easily and properly associated with a moral problem, inasmuch as it was his unhappy fortune to have to solve, practically, a knotty point which might have been more comfortably left to the casuists. Shipwrecked during Edward's life upon the coast of Normandy, he is betrayed into the hands of Duke William, who already retains as hostage one of his brothers (the sons of Godwin were very numerous, and they all figure briefly, but with a certain attempt at individual characterisation, in the drama). To purchase his release and that of his brother, who passionately entreats him, he consents to swear by certain unseen symbols, which prove afterwards to be the bones of certain august Norman saints, that if William will suffer him to return to England, he will, on the Confessor's death, abstain from urging the claim of the latter's presumptive heir and do his utmost to help the Norman duke himself to the crown.

This scene is presented in the volume before us. Harold departs and regains England, and there, on the king's death, overborne by circumstances, but with much tribulation of mind, violates his oath, and himself takes possession of the throne. The interest of the drama is in a great measure the picture of his temptation and remorse, his sense of his treachery and of the inevitableness of his chastisement. With this other matters are mingled: Harold's conflict with his disloyal brother Tostig, Earl of Northumberland, who brings in the King of Norway to claim the crown, and who, with his Norwegian backers, is defeated by Harold in battle just before William

283

comes down upon him. Then there is his love-affair with Edith, ward of the Confessor, whom the latter, piously refusing to hear of his violation of his oath, condemns him to put away, as penance for the very thought. There is also his marriage with Aldwyth, a designing person, widow of a Welsh king whom Harold has defeated, and who, having herself through her parentage, strong English interests, inveigles Harold into a union which may consolidate their forces.

Altogether, Harold is, for a hero, rather inclined to falter and succumb. It is to his conscience, however, that he finally succumbs; he loses heart and goes to meet William at Hastings with a depressing presentiment of defeat. Mr. Tennyson, however, as we gather from a prefatory sonnet, which is perhaps finer than anything in the drama itself, holds that much can be said for the "Norman-slandered hero," and declares that he has nothing to envy William if

"Each stands full face with all he did below."

Edith, Harold's repudiated lady-love, is, we suppose, the heroine of the story, inasmuch as she has the privilege of expiring upon the corpse of the hero. Harold's defeat is portrayed through a conversation between Edith and Stigand, the English and anti-papal Archbishop of Canterbury, who watches the fight at Senlac from a tent near the field, while the monks of Waltham, outside, intone a Latin invocation to the God of Battles to sweep away the Normans.

The drama closes with a scene on the field, after the fight, in which Edith and Aldwyth wander about, trying to identify Harold among the slain. On discovering him they indulge in a few natural recriminations, then Edith loses her head and expires by his side. William comes in, rubbing his hands over his work, and intimates to Aldwyth that she may now make herself agreeable to *him*. She replies, hypocritically, "My punishment is more than I can bear"; and with this, the most dramatic speech, perhaps in the volume, the play terminates. Edith, we should say, is a heroine of the didactic order. She has a bad conscience about Harold's conduct, and about her having continued on affectionate terms with him after his diplomatic marriage with Aldwyth. When she prays for Harold's success she adds that she hopes heaven will not refuse to listen to her because she loves "the husband of another"; and after he is defeated she reproaches herself with having injured his prospects—

"For there was more than sister in my kiss."

Though there are many persons in the poem it cannot be said that any of them attains a very vivid individuality. Indeed, their great number, the drama being of moderate length, hinders the unfolding of any one of them.

Mr. Tennyson, moreover, has not the dramatic touch; he rarely finds the phrase or the movement that illuminates a character, rarely makes the dialogue strike sparks. This is generally mild and colourless, and the passages that arrest us, relatively, owe their relief to juxtaposition rather than to any especial possession of the old Tennysonian energy. Now and then we come upon a few lines together in which we seem to catch an echo of the author's earlier magic, or sometimes simply of his earlier manner. When we do, we make the most of them and are grateful. Such, for instance, is the phrase of one of the characters describing his rescue from shipwreck. He dug his hands, he says, into

"My old fast friend the shore, and clinging thus

Felt the remorseless outdraught of the deep

Haul like a great strong fellow at my legs."

Such are the words in which Wulfnoth, Harold's young brother, detained in Normandy, laments his situation:

"Yea, and I

Shall see the dewy kiss of dawn no more

Make blush the maiden-white of our tall cliffs,

Nor mark the sea-bird rouse himself and hover

Above the windy ripple, and fill the sky

With free sea-laughter."

In two or three places the author makes, in a few words, a picture, an image, of considerable felicity. Harold wishes that he were like Edward the Confessor,

> "As holy and as passionless as he!
>
> That I might rest as calmly! Look at him—
>
> The rosy face, and long, down-silvering beard,
>
> The brows unwrinkled as a summer mere."

We may add that in the few speeches allotted to this monarch of virtuous complexion this portrait is agreeably sustained. "Holy, is he?" says the Archbishop, Stigand, of him to Harold—

> "A conscience for his own soul, not his realm;
>
> A twilight conscience lighted thro' a chink;
>
> Thine by the sun."

And the same character hits upon a really vigorous image in describing, as he watches them, Harold's exploits on the battle-fields:

> "Yea, yea, for how their lances snap and shiver,
>
> Against the shifting blaze of Harold's axe!
>
> War-woodman of old Woden, how he fells
>
> The mortal copse of faces!"

We feel, after all, in Mr. Tennyson, even in the decidedly minor key in which this volume is pitched, that he has once known how to turn our English poetic phrase as skilfully as any one, and that he has not altogether forgotten the art.

CONTEMPORARY NOTES ON WHISTLER VS. RUSKIN

I. THE SUIT FOR LIBEL

THE London public is never left for many days without a *cause célèbre* of some kind. The latest novelty in this line has been the suit for damages brought against Mr. Ruskin by Mr. James Whistler, the American painter, and decided last week. Mr. Whistler is very well known in the London world, and his conspicuity, combined with the renown of the defendant and the nature of the case, made the affair the talk of the moment. All the newspapers have had leading articles upon it, and people have differed for a few hours more positively than it had come to be supposed that they could differ about anything save the character of the statesmanship of Lord Beaconsfield. The injury suffered by Mr. Whistler resides in a paragraph published more than a year ago in that strange monthly manifesto called *Fors Clavigera*, which Mr. Ruskin had for a long time addressed to a partly edified, partly irritated, and greatly amused public. Mr. Ruskin spoke at some length of the pictures at the Grosvenor Gallery, and, falling foul of Mr. Whistler, he alluded to him in these terms:

"For Mr. Whistler's own sake, no less than for the protection of the purchaser, Sir Coutts Lindsay ought not to have admitted works into the gallery in which the ill-educated conceit of the artist so nearly approached the aspect of wilful imposture. I have seen and heard much of cockney impudence before now, but never expected to hear a coxcomb ask 200 guineas for flinging a pot of paint in the public's face."

Mr. Whistler alleged that these words were libellous, and that, coming from a critic of Mr. Ruskin's eminence, they had done him, professionally, serious injury; and he asked for £1,000 damage. The case had a two days' hearing, and it was a singular and most regrettable exhibition. If it had taken place in some Western American town, it would have been called provincial and barbarous; it would have been cited as an incident of a low civilisation. Beneath the stately towers of Westminster it hardly wore a higher aspect.

A British jury of ordinary tax-payers was appealed to decide whether Mr. Whistler's pictures belonged to a high order of art, and what degree of "finish" was required to render a picture satisfactory. The painter's singular canvases were handed about in court, and the counsel for the defence, holding one of them up, called upon the jury to pronounce whether it was an "accurate representation" of Battersea Bridge. Witnesses were summoned on either side to testify to the value of Mr. Whistler's productions, and Mr. Ruskin had the honour of having his estimate of them substantiated by Mr. Frith. The weightiest testimony, the most intelligently, and apparently the most reluctantly delivered, was that of Mr. Burne Jones, who appeared to appreciate the ridiculous character of the process to which he had been summoned (by the defence) to contribute, and who spoke of Mr. Whistler's performance as only in a partial sense of the word pictures—as being beautiful in colour, and indicating an extraordinary power of representing the atmosphere, but as being also hardly more than beginnings, and fatally deficient in finish. For the rest the crudity and levity of the whole affair were decidedly painful, and few things, I think, have lately done more to vulgarise the public sense of the character of artistic production.

The jury gave Mr. Whistler nominal damages. The opinion of the newspapers seems to be that he has got at least all he deserved—that anything more would have been a blow at the liberty of criticism. I confess to thinking it hard to decide what Mr. Whistler ought properly to have done, while—putting aside the degree of one's appreciation of his works—I quite understand his resentment. Mr. Ruskin's language quite transgresses the decencies of criticism, and he has been laying about him for some years past with such promiscuous violence that it gratifies one's sense of justice to see him brought up as a disorderly character. On the other hand, he is a chartered libertine—he has possessed himself by prescription of the function of a general scold. His literary bad manners are recognised, and many of his contemporaries have suffered from them without complaining. It would very possibly, therefore, have been much wiser on Mr. Whistler's part to feign indifference. Unfortunately, Mr. Whistler's productions are so very eccentric and imperfect (I speak here of his paintings only; his etchings are quite another affair, and altogether admirable) that his critic's denunciation could by no means fall to the ground of itself. I wonder that before a British jury they had any chance whatever; they must have been a terrible puzzle.

The verdict, of course, satisfies neither party; Mr. Ruskin is formally condemned, but the plaintiff is not compensated. Mr. Ruskin too, doubtless, is not gratified at finding that the fullest weight of his disapproval is thought to be represented by the sum of one farthing.

II. MR. WHISTLER'S REJOINDER

I may mention as a sequel to the brief account of the suit Whistler v. Ruskin, which I sent you a short time since, that the plaintiff has lately published a little pamphlet in which he delivers himself on the subject of art-criticism.

This little pamphlet, issued by Chatto & Windus, is an affair of seventeen very prettily-printed small pages; it is now in its sixth edition, it sells for a shilling, and is to be seen in most of the shop-windows. It is very characteristic of the painter, and highly entertaining; but I am not sure that it will have rendered appreciable service to the cause, which he has at heart. The cause that Mr. Whistler has at heart is the absolute suppression and extinction of the art-critic and his function. According to Mr. Whistler the art-critic is an impertinence, a nuisance, a monstrosity—and usually, into the bargain, an arrant fool.

Mr. Whistler writes in an off-hand, colloquial style, much besprinkled with French—a style which might be called familiar if one often encountered anything like it. He writes by no means as well as he paints; but his little diatribe against the critics is suggestive, apart from the force of anything that he specifically urges. The painter's irritated feeling is interesting, for it suggests the state of mind of many of his brothers of the brush in the presence of the bungling and incompetent disquisitions of certain members of the fraternity who sit in judgment upon their works.

"Let work be received in silence," says Mr. Whistler, "as it was in the days to which the penman still points as an era when art was at its apogee." He is very scornful of the "penman," and it is on the general ground of his being a penman that he deprecates the existence of his late adversary, Mr. Ruskin. He does not attempt to make out a case in detail against the great commentator of pictures; it is enough for Mr. Whistler that he is a "littérateur," and that a littérateur should concern himself with his own business. The author also falls foul of Mr. Tom Taylor, who does the reports of the exhibitions in the *Times*, and who had the misfortune, fifteen years ago, to express himself rather unintelligently about Velasquez.

"The Observatory at Greenwich under the direction of an apothecary," says Mr. Whistler, "the College of Physicians with Tennyson as president, and we know what madness is about! But a school of art with an accomplished littérateur at its head disturbs no one, and is actually what the world receives as rational, while Ruskin writes for pupils and Colvin holds forth at Cambridge! Still, quite alone stands Ruskin, whose writing is art and whose art is unworthy his writing. To him and his example do we owe the outrage of proffered assistance from the unscientific—the meddling of the immodest—the intrusion of the garrulous. Art, that for ages has hewn its own history in marble and written its own comments on canvas, shall it suddenly stand still and stammer and wait for wisdom from the passer-by?—for guidance from the hand that holds neither brush nor chisel? Out upon the shallow conceit! What greater sarcasm can Mr. Ruskin pass upon himself than that he preaches to young men what he cannot perform? Why, unsatisfied with his conscious power, should he choose to become the type of incompetency by talking for forty years of what he has never done?"

Mr. Whistler winds up by pronouncing Mr. Ruskin, of whose writings he has perused, I suspect, an infinitesimally small number of pages, "the Peter Parley of Painting." This is very far, as I say, from exhausting the question; but it is easy to understand the state of mind of a London artist (to go no further) who skims through the critiques in the local journals. There is no scurrility in saying that these are for the most part almost incredibly weak and unskilled; to turn from one of them to a critical *feuilleton* in one of the Parisian journals is like passing from a primitive to a very high civilisation. Even, however, if the reviews of pictures were very much better, the protest of the producer as against the critic would still have a considerable validity.

Few people will deny that the development of criticism in our day has become inordinate, disproportionate, and that much of what is written under that exalted name is very idle and superficial. Mr. Whistler's complaint belongs to the general question, and I am afraid it will never obtain a serious hearing, on special and exceptional grounds. The whole artistic fraternity is in the same boat—the painters, the architects, the poets, the novelists, the dramatists, the actors, the musicians, the singers. They have a standing, and in many ways a very just, quarrel with criticism; but perhaps many of them would admit that, on the whole, so long as they appeal to a public laden with many cares and a great variety of interests, it gratifies as much as it displeases them. Art is one of the necessities of life; but even the critics themselves would probably not assert that criticism is anything more than an agreeable luxury—something like printed talk. If it be said that they claim too much in calling it "agreeable" to the criticised, it may be added in their behalf that they probably mean agreeable in the long run.

A NOTE ON JOHN BURROUGHS

THIS is a very charming little book. We had noticed, on their appearance in various periodicals, some of the articles of which it is composed, and we find that, read continuously, they have given us even more pleasure. We have, indeed, enjoyed them more perhaps than we can show sufficient cause for. They are slender and light, but they have a real savour of their own.

Mr. Burroughs is known as an out-of-door observer—a devotee of birds and trees and fields and aspects of weather and humble wayside incidents. The minuteness of his observation, the keenness of his perception of all these things, give him a real originality which is confirmed by a style sometimes indeed idiomatic and unfinished to a fault, but capable of remarkable felicity and vividness. Mr. Burroughs is also, fortunately for his literary prosperity in these days, a decided "humourist"; he is essentially and genially an American, without at all posing as one, and his sketches have a delightful oddity, vivacity, and freshness.

The first half of his volume, and the least substantial, treats of certain rambles taken in the winter and spring in the country around Washington; the author is an apostle of pedestrianism, and these pages form a prolonged rhapsody upon the pleasures within the reach of any one who will take the trouble to stretch his legs. They are full of charming touches, and indicate a real genius for the observation of natural things. Mr. Burroughs is a sort of reduced, but also more humourous, more available, and more sociable Thoreau. He is especially intimate with the birds, and he gives his reader an acute sense of how sociable an affair, during six months of the year, this feathery lore may make a lonely walk. He is also intimate with the question of apples, and he treats of it in a succulent disquisition which imparts to the somewhat trivial theme a kind of lyrical dignity. He remarks, justly, that women are poor apple-eaters.

But the best pages in his book are those which commemorate a short visit to England and the rapture of his first impressions. This little sketch, in spite of its extreme slightness, really deserves to become classical. We have read far solider treatises which contained less of the essence of the matter; or at least, if it is not upon the subject itself that Mr. Burroughs throws particularly powerful light, it is the essence of the ideal traveller's spirit that he gives us, the freshness and intensity of impression, the genial bewilderment, the universal appreciativeness. All this is delightfully *naïf*, frank, and natural.

"All this had been told, and it pleased me so in the seeing that I must tell it again," the author says; and this is the constant spirit of his talk. He appears to have been "pleased" as no man was ever pleased before; so much so that his reflections upon his own country sometimes become unduly invidious. But if to be appreciative is the traveller's prime duty, Mr. Burroughs is a prince of travellers.

"Then to remember that it was a new sky and a new earth I was beholding, that it was England, the old mother at last, no longer a faith or a fable but an actual fact, there before my eyes and under my feet—why should I not exult? Go to! I will be indulged. These trees, those fields, that bird darting along the hedge-rows, those men and boys picking blackberries in October, those English flowers by the roadside (stop the carriage while I leap out and pluck them), the homely domestic look of things, those houses, those queer vehicles, those thick-coated horses, those big-footed, coarsely-clad, clear-skinned men and women; this massive, homely, compact architecture—let me have a good look, for this is my first hour in England, and I am drunk with the joy of seeing! This house-fly let me inspect it, and that swallow skimming along so familiarly."

One envies Mr. Burroughs his acute relish of the foreign spectacle even more than one enjoys his expression of it. He is not afraid to start and stare; his state of mind is exactly opposed to the high dignity of the *nil admirari*. When he goes into St. Paul's, "my companions rushed about," he says, "as if each one had a search-warrant in his pocket; but I was content to uncover my head and drop into a seat, and busy my mind with some simple object near at hand, while the sublimity that soared about me stole into my soul." He meets a little girl carrying a pail in a meadow near Stratford, stops her and talks with her, and finds an ineffable delight in "the sweet and novel twang of her words. Her family had emigrated to America, failed to prosper, and come back; but I hardly recognise even the name of my own country in her innocent prattle; it seemed like a land of fable—all had a remote mythological air, and I pressed my enquiries as if I was hearing of this strange land for the first time."

Mr. Burroughs is unfailingly complimentary; he sees sermons in stones and good in everything; the somewhat dusky British world was never steeped in so intense a glow of rose-colour. Sometimes his optimism rather interferes with his accuracy—as when he detects "forests and lakes" in Hyde Park, and affirms that the English rural landscape does not, in comparison with the American, appear highly populated. This latter statement is apparently made apropos of that long stretch of suburban scenery, pure and simple, which extends from Liverpool to London. It does not strike us as felicitous, either, to say that women are more kindly treated in England than in the United States, and especially that they are less "leered at." "Leering" at women is happily less common all the world over than it is sometimes made to appear for picturesque purposes in the magazines; but we should say that if there is a country where the art has not reached a high stage of development, it is our own.

It must be added that although Mr. Burroughs is shrewd as well as *naïf*, the latter quality sometimes distances the former. He runs over for a week to France. "At Dieppe I first saw the wooden shoe, and heard its dry, senseless clatter upon the pavement. How suggestive of the cramped and inflexible conditions with which human nature has borne so long in these lands!" But in Paris also he is appreciative—singularly so for so complete an outsider as he confesses himself to be—and throughout he is very well worth reading. We heartily commend his little volume for its honesty, its individuality, and, in places, its really blooming freshness.

MR. KIPLING'S EARLY STORIES

IT would be difficult to answer the general question whether the books of the world grow, as they multiply, as much better as one might suppose they ought, with such a lesson of wasteful experiment spread perpetually behind them. There is no doubt, however, that in one direction we profit largely by this education: whether or not we have become wiser to fashion, we have certainly become keener to enjoy. We have acquired the sense of a particular quality which is precious beyond all others—so precious as to make us wonder where, at such a rate, our posterity will look for it, and how they will pay for it. After tasting many essences we find freshness the sweetest of all. We yearn for it, we watch for it and lie in wait for it, and when we catch it on the wing (it flits by so fast) we celebrate our capture with extravagance. We feel that after so much has come and gone it is more and more of a feat and a *tour de force* to be fresh. The tormenting part of the phenomenon is that, in any particular key, it can happen but once—by a sad failure of the law that inculcates the repetition of goodness. It is terribly a matter of accident; emulation and imitation have a fatal effect upon it. It is easy to see, therefore, what importance the epicure may attach to the brief moment of its bloom. While that lasts we all are epicures.

This helps to explain, I think, the unmistakeable intensity of the general relish for Mr. Rudyard Kipling. His bloom lasts, from month to month, almost surprisingly— by which I mean that he has not worn out even by active exercise the particular property that made us all, more than a year ago, so precipitately drop everything else to attend to him. He has many others which he will doubtless always keep; but a part of the potency attaching to his freshness, what makes it as exciting as a drawing of lots, is our instinctive conviction that he cannot, in the nature of things, keep that; so that our enjoyment of him, so long as the miracle is still wrought, has both the charm of confidence and the charm of suspense. And then there is the further charm, with Mr. Kipling, that this same freshness is such a very strange affair of its kind—so mixed and various and cynical, and, in certain lights, so contradictory of itself. The extreme recentness of his inspiration is as enviable as the tale is startling that his productions tell of his being at home, domesticated and initiated, in this wicked and weary world. At times he strikes us as shockingly precocious, at others as serenely wise. On the whole, he presents himself as a strangely clever youth who has stolen the formidable mask of maturity and rushes about, making people jump with the deep sounds, and sportive exaggerations of tone, that issue from its painted lips. He has this mark of a real vocation, that different spectators may like him—must like him, I should almost say—for different things; and this refinement of attraction, that to those who reflect even upon their pleasures he has as much to say as to those who never reflect upon anything. Indeed there is a certain amount of room for surprise in the fact that, being so much the sort of figure that the hardened critic likes to meet, he should also be the sort of figure that inspires the multitude with confidence—for a complicated air is, in general, the last thing that does this.

By the critic who likes to meet such a bristling adventurer as Mr. Kipling I mean, of course, the critic for whom the happy accident of character, whatever form it may take, is more of a bribe to interest than the promise of some character cherished in theory—the appearance of justifying some foregone conclusion as to what a writer or a book "ought," in the Ruskinian sense, to be; the critic, in a word, who has, *à priori*, no rule for a literary production but that it shall have genuine life. Such a critic (he gets much more out of his opportunities, I think, than the other sort) likes a writer exactly in proportion as he is a challenge, an appeal to interpretation, intelligence, ingenuity, to what is elastic in the critical mind—in proportion indeed as he may be a negation of things familiar and taken for granted. He feels in this case how much more play and sensation there is for himself.

Mr. Kipling, then, has the character that furnishes plenty of play and of vicarious experience—that makes any perceptive reader foresee a rare luxury. He has the great merit of being a compact and convenient illustration of the surest source of interest in any painter of life—that of having an identity as marked as a window-frame. He is one of the illustrations, taken near at hand, that help to clear up the vexed question in the novel or the tale, of kinds, camps, schools, distinctions, the right way and the wrong way; so very positively does he contribute to the showing that there are just as many kinds, as many ways, as many forms and degrees of the "right," as there are personal points in view. It is the blessing of the art he practises that it is made up of experience conditioned, infinitely, in this personal way—the sum of the feeling of life as reproduced by innumerable natures; natures that feel through all their differences, testify through their diversities. These differences, which make the identity, are of the individual; they form the channel by which life flows through him, and how much he is able to give us of life—in other words, how much he appeals to us—depends on whether they form it solidly.

This hardness of the conduit, cemented with a rare assurance, is perhaps the most striking idiosyncrasy of Mr. Kipling; and what makes it more remarkable is that incident of his extreme youth which, if we talk about him at all, we cannot affect to ignore. I cannot pretend to give a biography or a chronology of the author of "Soldiers Three," but I cannot overlook the general, the importunate fact that, confidently as he has caught the trick and habit of this sophisticated world, he has not been long of it. His extreme youth is indeed what I may call his window-bar—the support on which he somewhat rowdily leans while he looks down at the human scene with his pipe in his teeth; just as his other conditions (to mention only some of them), are his prodigious facility, which is only less remarkable than his stiff selection; his unabashed temperament, his flexible talent, his smoking-room manner, his familiar friendship with India—established so rapidly, and so completely under his control; his delight in battle, his "cheek" about women—and indeed about men and about everything; his determination not to be duped, his "imperial" fibre, his love of the inside view, the private soldier and the primitive man. I must add further to this list of attractions the remarkable way in which he makes us aware that he has been put up to the whole thing directly by life (miraculously, in his teens), and not by the communications of others. These elements, and many more, constitute a singularly robust little literary character (our use of the diminutive is altogether a note of endearment and enjoyment) which, if it has the rattle of high spirits and is in no degree apologetic or shrinking, yet offers a very liberal pledge in the way of good faith and immediate performance. Mr. Kipling's performance comes off before the more circumspect have time to decide whether they like him or not, and if you have seen it once you will be sure to return to the show. He makes us prick up our ears to the good news that in the smoking-room too there may be artists; and indeed to an intimation still more refined—that the latest development of the modern also may be, most successfully, for the canny artist to put his victim off his guard by imitating the amateur (superficially, of course) to the life.

These, then, are some of the reasons why Mr. Kipling may be dear to the analyst as well as, M. Renan says, to the simple. The simple may like him because he is wonderful about India, and India has not been "done"; while there is plenty left for the morbid reader in the surprises of his skill and the *fioriture* of his form, which are so oddly independent of any distinctively literary note in him, any bookish association. It is as one of the morbid that the writer of these remarks (which doubtless only too shamefully betray his character) exposes himself as most consentingly under the spell. The freshness arising from a subject that—by a good fortune I do not mean to underestimate—has never been "done," is after all less of an affair to build upon than the freshness residing in the temper of the artist. Happy indeed is Mr. Kipling, who can command so much of both kinds. It is still as one of the morbid, no doubt—

that is, as one of those who are capable of sitting up all night for a new impression of talent, of scouring the trodden field for one little spot of green—that I find our young author quite most curious in his air, and not only in his air, but in his evidently very real sense, of knowing his way about life. Curious in the highest degree and well worth attention is such an idiosyncrasy as this in a young Anglo-Saxon. We meet it with familiar frequency in the budding talents of France, and it startles and haunts us for an hour. After an hour, however, the mystery is apt to fade, for we find that the wondrous initiation is not in the least general, is only exceedingly special, and is, even with this limitation, very often rather conventional. In a word, it is with the ladies that the young Frenchman takes his ease, and more particularly with the ladies selected expressly to make this attitude convincing. When they have let him off, the dimnesses too often encompass him. But for Mr. Kipling there are no dimnesses anywhere, and if the ladies are indeed violently distinct they are not only strong notes in a universal loudness. This loudness fills the ears of Mr. Kipling's admirers (it lacks sweetness, no doubt, for those who are not of the number), and there is really only one strain that is absent from it—the voice, as it were, of the civilised man; in whom I of course also include the civilised woman. But this is an element that for the present one does not miss—every other note is so articulate and direct.

It is a part of the satisfaction the author gives us that he can make us speculate as to whether he will be able to complete his picture altogether (this is as far as we presume to go in meddling with the question of his future) without bringing in the complicated soul. On the day he does so, if he handles it with anything like the cleverness he has already shown, the expectation of his friends will take a great bound. Meanwhile, at any rate, we have Mulvaney, and Mulvaney is after all tolerably complicated. He is only a six-foot saturated Irish private, but he is a considerable pledge of more to come. Hasn't he, for that matter, the tongue of a hoarse siren, and hasn't he also mysteries and infinitudes almost Carlylese? Since I am speaking of him I may as well say that, as an evocation, he has probably led captive those of Mr. Kipling's readers who have most given up resistance. He is a piece of portraiture of the largest, vividest kind, growing and growing on the painter's hands without ever outgrowing them. I can't help regarding him, in a certain sense, as Mr. Kipling's tutelary deity—a landmark in the direction in which it is open to him to look furthest. If the author will only go as far in this direction as Mulvaney is capable of taking him (and the inimitable Irishman is like Voltaire's Habakkuk, *capable de tout*) he may still discover a treasure and find a reward for the services he has rendered the winner of Dinah Shadd. I hasten to add that the truly appreciative reader should surely have no quarrel with the primitive element in Mr. Kipling's subject-matter, or with what, for want of a better name, I may call his love of low life. What is that but essentially a part of his freshness? And for what part of his freshness are we exactly more thankful than for just this smart jostle that he gives the old stupid superstition that the amiability of a story-teller is the amiability of the people he represents—that their vulgarity, or depravity, or gentility, or fatuity are tantamount to the same qualities in the painter itself? A blow from which, apparently, it will not easily recover is dealt this infantine philosophy by Mr. Howells when, with the most distinguished dexterity and all the detachment of a master, he handles some of the clumsiest, crudest, most human things in life—answering surely thereby the play-goers in the sixpenny gallery who howl at the representative of the villain when he comes before the curtain.

Nothing is more refreshing than this active, disinterested sense of the real; it is doubtless the quality for the want of more of which our English and American fiction has turned so wofully stale. We are ridden by the old conventionalities of type and small proprieties of observance—by the foolish baby-formula (to put it sketchily) of the picture and the subject. Mr. Kipling has all the air of being disposed to lift the whole business off the nursery carpet, and of being perhaps even more able than he is disposed. One must hasten of course to parenthesise that there is not, intrinsically, a bit more luminosity in treating of low life and of primitive man than of those whom civilisation has kneaded to a finer paste: the only luminosity in either case is in the intelligence with which the thing is done. But it so happens that, among ourselves, the frank, capable outlook, when turned upon the vulgar majority, the coarse, receding edges of the social perspective, borrows a charm from being new; such a charm as, for instance, repetition has already despoiled it of among the French—the hapless French who pay the penalty as well as enjoy the glow of living intellectually so much faster than we. It is the most inexorable part of our fate that we grow tired of everything, and of course in due time we may grow tired even of what explorers shall come back to tell us about the great grimy condition, or, with unprecedented items and details, about the gray middle state which darkens into it. But the explorers, bless them! may have a long day before that; it is early to trouble about reactions, so that we must give them the benefit of every presumption. We are thankful for any boldness and any sharp curiosity, and that is why we are thankful for Mr. Kipling's general spirit and for most of his excursions.

Many of these, certainly, are into a region not to be designated as superficially dim, though indeed the author always reminds us that India is above all the land of mystery. A large part of his high spirits, and of ours, comes doubtless from the amusement of such vivid, heterogeneous material, from the irresistible magic of scorching suns, subject empires, uncanny religions, uneasy garrisons and smothered-up women—from heat and colour and danger and dust. India is a portentous image, and we are duly awed by the familiarities it undergoes at Mr. Kipling's hand and by the fine impunity, the sort of fortune that favours the brave, of *his* want of awe. An abject humility is not his strong point, but he gives us something instead of it—vividness and drollery, the vision and the thrill of many things, the misery and strangeness of most, the personal sense of a hundred queer contacts and risks. And then in the absence of respect he has plenty of knowledge, and if knowledge should fail him he would have plenty of invention. Moreover, if invention should ever fail him, he would still have the lyric string and the patriotic chord, on which he plays admirably; so that it may be said he is a man of resources. What he gives us, above all, is the feeling of the English manner and the English blood in conditions they have made at once so much and so little their own; with manifestations grotesque enough in some of his satiric sketches and deeply impressive in some of his anecdotes of individual responsibility.

His Indian impressions divide themselves into three groups, one of which, I think, very much outshines the others. First to be mentioned are the tales of native life, curious glimpses of custom and superstition, dusky matters not beholden of the many, for which the author has a remarkable *flair*. Then comes the social, the Anglo-Indian episode, the study of administrative and military types, and of the wonderful rattling, riding ladies who, at Simla and more desperate stations, look out for husbands and lovers; often, it would seem, and husbands and lovers of others. The most brilliant group is devoted wholly to the common soldier, and of this series it appears to me that too much good is hardly to be said. Here Mr. Kipling, with all his off-handedness, is a master; for we are held not so much by the greater or less oddity of the particular yarn—sometimes it is scarcely a yarn at all, but something much less artificial—as by the robust attitude of the narrator, who never arranges or glosses or falsifies, but makes straight for the common and the characteristic. I have mentioned the great esteem in which I hold Mulvaney—surely a charming man and one qualified to adorn a higher sphere. Mulvaney is a creation to be proud of, and his two comrades stand as firm on their legs. In spite of Mulvaney's social possibilities, they are all three finished brutes; but it is precisely in the finish that we delight. Whatever Mr. Kipling may relate about them forever will encounter readers equally fascinated and unable fully to justify their faith.

Are not those literary pleasures after all the most intense which are the most perverse and whimsical, and even indefensible? There is a logic in them somewhere, but it often lies below the plummet of criticism. The spell may be weak in a writer who has every reasonable and regular claim, and it may be irresistible in one who presents himself with a style corresponding to a bad hat. A good hat is better than a bad one, but a conjuror may wear either. Many a reader will never be able to say what secret human force lays its hand upon him when Private Ortheris, having sworn "quietly into the blue sky," goes mad with homesickness by the yellow river and raves for the basest sights and sounds of London. I can scarcely tell why I think "The Courting of Dinah Shadd" a masterpiece (though, indeed, I can make a shrewd guess at one of the reasons), nor would it be worth while perhaps to attempt to defend the same pretension in regard to "On Greenhow Hill"—much less to trouble the tolerant reader of these remarks with a statement of how many more performances in the nature of "The End of the Passage" (quite admitting even that they might not represent Mr. Kipling at his best) I am conscious of a latent relish for. One might as well admit while one is about it that one has wept profusely over "The Drums of the Fore and Aft," the history of the "Dutch courage" of two dreadful dirty little boys, who, in the face of Afghans scarcely more dreadful, saved the reputation of their regiment and perished, the least mawkishly in the world, in a squalor of battle incomparably expressed. People who know how peaceful they are themselves and have no bloodshed to reproach themselves with needn't scruple to mention the glamour that Mr. Kipling's intense militarism has for them, and how astonishing and contagious they find it, in spite of the unromantic complexion of it—the way it bristles with all sorts of ugliness and technicalities. Perhaps that is why I go all the way even with "The Gadsbys"—the Gadsbys were so connected (uncomfortably, it is true) with the army. There is fearful fighting—or a fearful danger of it—in "The Man Who Would be King"; is that the reason we are deeply affected by this extraordinary tale? It is one of them, doubtless, for Mr. Kipling has many reasons, after all, on his side, though they don't equally call aloud to be uttered.

One more of them, at any rate, I must add to these unsystematised remarks— it is the one I spoke of a shrewd guess at in alluding to "The Courting of Dinah Shadd." The talent that produces such a tale is a talent eminently in harmony with the short story, and the short story is, on our side of the Channel and of the Atlantic, a mine which will take a great deal of working. Admirable is the clearness with which Mr. Kipling perceives this—perceives what innumerable chances it gives, chances of touching life in a thousand different places, taking it up in innumerable pieces, each a specimen and an illustration. In a word, he appreciates the episode, and there are signs to show that this shrewdness will, in general, have long innings. It will find the detachable, compressible "case" an admirable, flexible form; the cultivation of which may well add to the mistrust already entertained by Mr. Kipling, if his manner does not betray him, for what is clumsy and tasteless in the time-honoured practice of the "plot." It will fortify him in the conviction that the vivid picture has a greater communicative value than the Chinese puzzle. There is little enough "plot" in such a perfect little piece of hard representation as "The End of the Passage," to cite again only the most salient of twenty examples.

But I am speaking of our author's future, which is the luxury that I meant to forbid myself—precisely because the subject is so tempting. There is nothing in the world (for the prophet) so charming as to prophesy, and as there is nothing so inconclusive the tendency should be repressed in proportion as the opportunity is good. There is a certain want of courtesy to a peculiarly contemporaneous present even in speculating, with a dozen differential precautions, on the question of what will become in the later hours of the day of a talent that has got up so early. Mr. Kipling's actual performance is like a tremendous walk before breakfast, making one welcome the idea of the meal, but consider with some alarm the hours still to be traversed. Yet if his breakfast is all to come, the indications are that he will be more active than ever after he has had it. Among these indications are the unflagging character of his pace and the excellent form, as they say in athletic circles, in which he gets over the ground. We don't detect him stumbling; on the contrary, he steps out quite as briskly as at first, and still more firmly. There is something zealous and craftsman-like in him which shows that he feels both joy and responsibility. A whimsical, wanton reader, haunted by a recollection of all the good things he has seen spoiled; by a sense of the miserable, or, at any rate, the inferior, in so many continuations and endings, is almost capable of perverting poetic justice to the idea that it would be even positively well for so surprising a producer to remain simply the fortunate, suggestive, unconfirmed and unqualified representative of what he has actually done. We can always refer to that.

About Author

Henry James OM (15 April 1843 – 28 February 1916) was an American-British author regarded as a key transitional figure between literary realism and literary modernism, and is considered by many to be among the greatest novelists in the English language. He was the son of Henry James Sr. and the brother of renowned philosopher and psychologist William James and diarist Alice James.

He is best known for a number of novels dealing with the social and marital interplay between émigré Americans, English people, and continental Europeans. Examples of such novels include The Portrait of a Lady, The Ambassadors, and The Wings of the Dove. His later works were increasingly experimental. In describing the internal states of mind and social dynamics of his characters, James often made use of a style in which ambiguous or contradictory motives and impressions were overlaid or juxtaposed in the discussion of a character's psyche. For their unique ambiguity, as well as for other aspects of their composition, his late works have been compared to impressionist painting.

His novella The Turn of the Screw has garnered a reputation as the most analysed and ambiguous ghost story in the English language and remains his most widely adapted work in other media. He also wrote a number of other highly regarded ghost stories and is considered one of the greatest masters of the field.

James published articles and books of criticism, travel, biography, autobiography, and plays. Born in the United States, James largely relocated to Europe as a young man and eventually settled in England, becoming a British subject in 1915, one year before his death. James was nominated for the Nobel Prize in Literature in 1911, 1912 and 1916.

Life

Early years, 1843–1883

James was born at 2 Washington Place in New York City on 15 April 1843. His parents were Mary Walsh and Henry James Sr. His father was intelligent and steadfastly congenial. He was a lecturer and philosopher who had inherited independent means from his father, an Albany banker and investor. Mary came from a wealthy family long settled in New York City. Her sister Katherine lived with her adult family for an extended period of time. Henry Jr. had three brothers, William, who was one year his senior, and younger brothers Wilkinson (Wilkie) and Robertson. His younger sister was Alice. Both of his parents were of Irish and Scottish descent.

The family first lived in Albany, at 70 N. Pearl St., and then moved to Fourteenth Street in New York City when James was still a young boy. His education was calculated by his father to expose him to many influences, primarily scientific and philosophical; it was described by Percy Lubbock, the editor of his selected letters, as "extraordinarily haphazard and promiscuous." James did not share the usual education in Latin and Greek classics. Between 1855 and 1860, the James' household traveled to London, Paris, Geneva, Boulogne-sur-Mer and Newport, Rhode Island, according to the father's current interests and publishing ventures, retreating to the United States when funds were low. Henry studied primarily with tutors and briefly attended schools while the family traveled in Europe. Their longest stays were in France, where Henry began to feel at home and became fluent in French. He was afflicted with a stutter, which seems to have manifested itself only when he spoke English; in French, he did not stutter.

In 1860 the family returned to Newport. There Henry became a friend of the painter John La Farge, who introduced him to French literature, and in particular, to Balzac. James later called Balzac his "greatest master," and said that he had learned more about the craft of fiction from him than from anyone else.

In the autumn of 1861 Henry received an injury, probably to his back, while fighting a fire. This injury, which resurfaced at times throughout his life, made him unfit for military service in the American Civil War.

In 1864 the James family moved to Boston, Massachusetts to be near William, who had enrolled first in the Lawrence Scientific School at Harvard and then in the medical school. In 1862 Henry attended Harvard Law School, but realised that he was not interested in studying law. He pursued his interest in literature and associated with authors and critics William Dean Howells and Charles Eliot Norton in Boston and Cambridge, formed lifelong friendships with Oliver Wendell Holmes Jr., the future Supreme Court Justice, and with James and Annie Fields, his first professional mentors.

His first published work was a review of a stage performance, "Miss Maggie Mitchell in Fanchon the Cricket," published in 1863. About a year later, A Tragedy of Error, his first short story, was published anonymously. James's first payment was for an appreciation of Sir Walter Scott's novels, written for the North American Review. He wrote fiction and non-fiction pieces for The Nation and Atlantic Monthly, where

Fields was editor. In 1871 he published his first novel, Watch and Ward, in serial form in the Atlantic Monthly. The novel was later published in book form in 1878.

During a 14-month trip through Europe in 1869–70 he met Ruskin, Dickens, Matthew Arnold, William Morris, and George Eliot. Rome impressed him profoundly. "Here I am then in the Eternal City," he wrote to his brother William. "At last—for the first time—I live!" He attempted to support himself as a freelance writer in Rome, then secured a position as Paris correspondent for the New York Tribune, through the influence of its editor John Hay. When these efforts failed he returned to New York City. During 1874 and 1875 he published Transatlantic Sketches, A Passionate Pilgrim, and Roderick Hudson. During this early period in his career he was influenced by Nathaniel Hawthorne.

In 1869 he settled in London. There he established relationships with Macmillan and other publishers, who paid for serial installments that they would later publish in book form. The audience for these serialized novels was largely made up of middle-class women, and James struggled to fashion serious literary work within the strictures imposed by editors' and publishers' notions of what was suitable for young women to read. He lived in rented rooms but was able to join gentlemen's clubs that had libraries and where he could entertain male friends. He was introduced to English society by Henry Adams and Charles Milnes Gaskell, the latter introducing him to the Travellers' and the Reform Clubs.

In the fall of 1875 he moved to the Latin Quarter of Paris. Aside from two trips to America, he spent the next three decades—the rest of his life—in Europe. In Paris he met Zola, Alphonse Daudet, Maupassant, Turgenev, and others. He stayed in Paris only a year before moving to London.

In England he met the leading figures of politics and culture. He continued to be a prolific writer, producing The American (1877), The Europeans (1878), a revision of Watch and Ward (1878), French Poets and Novelists (1878), Hawthorne (1879), and several shorter works of fiction. In 1878 Daisy Miller established his fame on both sides of the Atlantic. It drew notice perhaps mostly because it depicted a woman whose behavior is outside the social norms of Europe. He also began his first masterpiece, The Portrait of a Lady, which would appear in 1881.

In 1877 he first visited Wenlock Abbey in Shropshire, home of his friend Charles Milnes Gaskell whom he had met through Henry Adams. He was much inspired by the darkly romantic Abbey and the surrounding countryside, which features in his essay Abbeys and Castles. In particular the gloomy monastic fishponds behind the Abbey are said to have inspired the lake in The Turn of the Screw.

While living in London, James continued to follow the careers of the "French realists", Émile Zola in particular. Their stylistic methods influenced his own work in the years to come. Hawthorne's influence on him faded during this period, replaced by George Eliot and Ivan Turgenev. 1879–1882 saw the publication of The Europeans, Washington Square, Confidence, and The Portrait of a Lady. He visited America in 1882–1883, then returned to London.

The period from 1881 to 1883 was marked by several losses. His mother died in 1881, followed by his father a few months later, and then by his brother Wilkie. Emerson, an old family friend, died in 1882. His friend Turgenev died in 1883.

Middle years, 1884–1897

In 1884 James made another visit to Paris. There he met again with Zola, Daudet, and Goncourt. He had been following the careers of the French "realist" or "naturalist" writers, and was increasingly influenced by them. In 1886, he published The Bostonians and The Princess Casamassima, both influenced by the French writers he'd studied assiduously. Critical reaction and sales were poor. He wrote to Howells that the books had hurt his career rather than helped because they had "reduced the desire, and demand, for my productions to zero". During this time he became friends with Robert Louis Stevenson, John Singer Sargent, Edmund Gosse, George du Maurier, Paul Bourget, and Constance Fenimore Woolson. His third novel from the 1880s was The Tragic Muse. Although he was following the precepts of Zola in his novels of the '80s, their tone and attitude are closer to the fiction of Alphonse Daudet. The lack of critical and financial success for his novels during this period led him to try writing for the theatre. (His dramatic works and his experiences with theatre are discussed below.)

In the last quarter of 1889, he started translating "for pure and copious lucre" Port Tarascon, the third volume of Alphonse Daudet adventures of Tartarin de Tarascon. Serialized in Harper's Monthly Magazine from June 1890, this translation praised as "clever" by The Spectator was published in January 1891 by Sampson Low, Marston, Searle & Rivington.

After the stage failure of Guy Domville in 1895, James was near despair and thoughts of death plagued him. The years spent on dramatic works were not entirely a loss. As he moved into the last phase of his career he found ways to adapt dramatic techniques into the novel form.

In the late 1880s and throughout the 1890s James made several trips through Europe. He spent a long stay in Italy in 1887. In that year the short novel The Aspern Papers and The Reverberator were published.

Late years, 1898–1916

In 1897–1898 he moved to Rye, Sussex, and wrote The Turn of the Screw. 1899–1900 saw the publication of The Awkward Age and The Sacred Fount. During 1902–1904 he wrote The Ambassadors, The Wings of the Dove, and The Golden Bowl.

In 1904 he revisited America and lectured on Balzac. In 1906–1910 he published The American Scene and edited the "New York Edition", a 24-volume collection of his works. In 1910 his brother William died; Henry had just joined William from an unsuccessful search for relief in Europe on what then turned out to be his (Henry's) last visit to the United States (from summer 1910 to July 1911), and was near him, according to a letter he wrote, when he died.

In 1913 he wrote his autobiographies, A Small Boy and Others, and Notes of a Son and Brother. After the outbreak of the First World War in 1914 he did war work. In 1915 he became a British subject and was awarded the Order of Merit the following year. He died on 28 February 1916, in Chelsea, London. As he requested, his ashes were buried in Cambridge Cemetery in Massachusetts.

Biographers

James regularly rejected suggestions that he should marry, and after settling in London proclaimed himself "a bachelor". F. W. Dupee, in several volumes on the James family, originated the theory that he had been in love with his cousin Mary ("Minnie") Temple, but that a neurotic fear of sex kept him from admitting such affections: "James's invalidism ... was itself the symptom of some fear of or scruple against sexual love on his part." Dupee used an episode from James's memoir A Small Boy and Others, recounting a dream of a Napoleonic image in the Louvre, to exemplify James's romanticism about Europe, a Napoleonic fantasy into which he fled.

Dupee had not had access to the James family papers and worked principally from James's published memoir of his older brother, William, and the limited collection of letters edited by Percy Lubbock, heavily weighted toward James's last years. His account therefore moved directly from James's childhood, when he trailed after his older brother, to elderly invalidism. As more material became available to scholars, including the diaries of contemporaries and hundreds of affectionate and sometimes erotic letters written by James to younger men, the picture of neurotic celibacy gave way to a portrait of a closeted homosexual.

Between 1953 and 1972, Leon Edel authored a major five-volume biography of James, which accessed unpublished letters and documents after Edel gained the permission of James's family. Edel's portrayal of James included the suggestion he was celibate. It was a view first propounded by critic Saul Rosenzweig in 1943. In 1996 Sheldon M. Novick published Henry James: The Young Master, followed by Henry James: The Mature Master (2007). The first book "caused something of an uproar in Jamesian circles" as it challenged the previous received notion of celibacy, a once-familiar paradigm in biographies of homosexuals when direct evidence was non-existent. Novick also criticised Edel for following the discounted Freudian interpretation of homosexuality "as a kind of failure." The difference of opinion erupted in a series of exchanges between Edel and Novick which were published by the online magazine Slate, with the latter arguing that even the suggestion of celibacy went against James's own injunction "live!"—not "fantasize!"

A letter James wrote in old age to Hugh Walpole has been cited as an explicit statement of this. Walpole confessed to him of indulging in "high jinks", and James wrote a reply endorsing it: "We must know, as much as possible, in our beautiful art, yours & mine, what we are talking about — & the only way to know it is to have lived & loved & cursed & floundered & enjoyed & suffered — I don't think I regret a single 'excess' of my responsive youth".

The interpretation of James as living a less austere emotional life has been subsequently explored by other scholars. The often intense politics of Jamesian scholarship has also been the subject of studies. Author Colm Tóibín has said that Eve Kosofsky Sedgwick's Epistemology of the Closet made a landmark difference to Jamesian scholarship by arguing that he be read as a homosexual writer whose desire to keep his sexuality a secret shaped his layered style and dramatic artistry. According to Tóibín such a reading "removed James from the realm of dead white males who wrote about posh people. He became our contemporary."

James's letters to expatriate American sculptor Hendrik Christian Andersen have attracted particular attention. James met the 27-year-old Andersen in Rome in 1899, when James was 56, and wrote letters to Andersen that are intensely emotional: "I hold you, dearest boy, in my innermost love, & count on your feeling me—in every throb of your soul". In a letter of 6 May 1904, to his brother William, James referred to himself as "always your hopelessly celibate even though sexagenarian Henry".

How accurate that description might have been is the subject of contention among James's biographers,   but the letters to Andersen were occasionally quasi-erotic: "I put, my dear boy, my arm around you, & feel the pulsation, thereby, as it were, of our excellent future & your admirable endowment." To his homosexual friend Howard Sturgis, James could write: "I repeat, almost to indiscretion, that I could live with you. Meanwhile I can only try to live without you."

His numerous letters to the many young gay men among his close male friends are more forthcoming. In a letter to Howard Sturgis, following a long visit, James refers jocularly to their "happy little congress of two" and in letters to Hugh Walpole he pursues convoluted jokes and puns about their relationship, referring to himself as an elephant who "paws you oh so benevolently" and winds about Walpole his "well meaning old trunk". His letters to Walter Berry printed by the Black Sun Press have long been celebrated for their lightly veiled eroticism.

He corresponded in almost equally extravagant language with his many female friends, writing, for example, to fellow novelist Lucy Clifford: "Dearest Lucy! What shall I say? when I love you so very, very much, and see you nine times for once that I see Others! Therefore I think that—if you want it made clear to the meanest intelligence—I love you more than I love Others." To his New York friend Mary Cadwalader Jones: "Dearest Mary Cadwalader. I yearn over you, but I yearn in vain; & your long silence really breaks my heart, mystifies, depresses, almost alarms me, to the point even of making me wonder if poor unconscious & doting old Célimare [Jones's pet name for James] has 'done' anything, in some dark somnambulism of the spirit, which has ... given you a bad moment, or a wrong impression, or a 'colourable pretext' ... However these things may be, he loves you as tenderly as ever; nothing, to the end of time, will ever detach him from you, & he remembers those Eleventh St. matutinal intimes hours, those telephonic matinées, as the most romantic of his life ..." His long friendship with American novelist Constance Fenimore Woolson, in whose house he lived for a number of weeks in Italy in 1887, and his shock and grief over her suicide in 1894, are discussed in detail in Edel's biography and play a central role in a study by Lyndall Gordon. (Edel conjectured that Woolson was in love with James and killed herself in part because of his coldness, but Woolson's biographers have objected to Edel's account.)

Works

Style and themes

James is one of the major figures of trans-Atlantic literature. His works frequently juxtapose characters from the Old World (Europe), embodying a feudal civilisation that is beautiful, often corrupt, and alluring, and from the New World (United States), where people are often brash, open, and assertive and embody the virtues—freedom and a more highly evolved moral character—of the new American society. James explores this clash of personalities and cultures, in stories of personal relationships in which power is exercised well or badly. His protagonists were often young American women facing oppression or abuse, and as his secretary Theodora Bosanquet remarked in her monograph Henry James at Work:

> When he walked out of the refuge of his study and into the world and looked around him, he saw a place of torment, where creatures of prey perpetually thrust their claws into the quivering flesh of doomed, defenseless children of light ... His novels are a repeated exposure of this wickedness, a reiterated and passionate plea for the fullest freedom of development, unimperiled by reckless and barbarous stupidity.

Critics have jokingly described three phases in the development of James's prose: "James I, James II, and The Old Pretender." He wrote short stories and plays. Finally, in his third and last period he returned to the long, serialised novel. Beginning in the second period, but most noticeably in the third, he increasingly abandoned direct statement in favour of frequent double negatives, and complex descriptive imagery. Single paragraphs began to run for page after page, in which an initial noun would be succeeded by pronouns surrounded by clouds of adjectives and prepositional clauses, far from their original referents, and verbs would be deferred and then preceded by a series of adverbs. The overall effect could be a vivid evocation of a scene as perceived by a sensitive observer. It has been debated whether this change of style was engendered by James's shifting from writing to dictating to a typist, a change made during the composition of What Maisie Knew.

In its intense focus on the consciousness of his major characters, James's later work foreshadows extensive developments in 20th century fiction. Indeed, he might have influenced stream-of-consciousness writers such as Virginia Woolf, who not only read some of his novels but also wrote essays about them. Both contemporary and modern readers have found the late style difficult and unnecessary; his friend Edith Wharton, who admired him greatly, said that there were passages in his work that were all but incomprehensible. James was harshly portrayed by H. G. Wells as a hippopotamus laboriously attempting to pick up a pea that had got into a corner of its cage. The "late James" style was ably parodied by Max Beerbohm in "The Mote in the Middle Distance".

More important for his work overall may have been his position as an expatriate, and in other ways an outsider, living in Europe. While he came from middle-class and provincial beginnings (seen from the perspective of European polite society) he worked very hard to gain access to all levels of society, and the settings of his fiction range from working class to aristocratic, and often describe the efforts of middle-class Americans to make their way in European capitals. He confessed he got some of his best story ideas from gossip at the dinner table or at country house weekends. He worked for a living, however, and lacked the experiences of select schools, university, and army service, the common bonds of masculine society. He was furthermore a man whose tastes and interests were, according to the prevailing standards of Victorian era Anglo-American culture, rather feminine, and who was shadowed by the cloud of prejudice that then and later accompanied suspicions of his homosexuality. Edmund Wilson famously compared James's objectivity to Shakespeare's:

> One would be in a position to appreciate James better if one compared him with the dramatists of the seventeenth century—Racine and Molière, whom he resembles in form as well as in point of view, and even Shakespeare, when allowances are made for the most extreme differences in subject and form. These poets are not, like Dickens and Hardy, writers of melodrama—either humorous or pessimistic, nor secretaries of society like Balzac, nor prophets like Tolstoy: they are occupied simply with the presentation of conflicts of moral character, which they do not concern themselves about softening or averting. They do not indict society for these situations: they regard them as universal and inevitable. They do not even blame God for allowing them: they accept them as the conditions of life.

It is also possible to see many of James's stories as psychological thought-experiments. In his preface to the New York edition of The American he describes the development of the story in his mind as exactly such: the "situation" of an American, "some robust but insidiously beguiled and betrayed, some cruelly wronged, compatriot..." with the focus of the story being on the response of this wronged man. The Portrait of a Lady may be an experiment to see what happens when an idealistic young woman suddenly becomes very rich. In many of his tales, characters seem to exemplify alternative futures and possibilities, as most markedly in "The Jolly Corner", in which the protagonist and a ghost-doppelganger live alternative American and European lives; and in others, like The Ambassadors, an older James seems fondly to regard his own younger self facing a crucial moment.

Major novels

The first period of James's fiction, usually considered to have culminated in The Portrait of a Lady, concentrated on the contrast between Europe and America. The style of these novels is generally straightforward and, though personally characteristic, well within the norms of 19th-century fiction. Roderick Hudson (1875) is a Künstlerroman that traces the development of the title character, an extremely talented sculptor. Although the book shows some signs of immaturity—this was James's first serious attempt at a full-length novel—it has attracted favourable comment due to the vivid realisation of the three major characters: Roderick Hudson, superbly gifted but unstable and unreliable; Rowland Mallet, Roderick's limited but much more mature friend and patron; and Christina Light, one of James's most enchanting and maddening femmes fatales. The pair of Hudson and Mallet has been seen as representing the two sides of James's own nature: the wildly imaginative artist and the brooding conscientious mentor.

In The Portrait of a Lady (1881) James concluded the first phase of his career with a novel that remains his most popular piece of long fiction. The story is of a spirited young American woman, Isabel Archer, who "affronts her destiny" and finds it overwhelming. She inherits a large amount of money and subsequently becomes the victim of Machiavellian scheming by two American expatriates. The narrative is set mainly in Europe, especially in England and Italy. Generally regarded as the masterpiece of his early phase, The Portrait of a Lady is described as a psychological novel, exploring the minds of his characters, and almost a work of social science, exploring the differences between Europeans and Americans, the old and the new worlds.

The second period of James's career, which extends from the publication of The Portrait of a Lady through the end of the nineteenth century, features less popular novels including The Princess Casamassima, published serially in The Atlantic Monthly in 1885–1886, and The Bostonians, published serially in The Century Magazine during the same period. This period also featured James's celebrated Gothic novella, The Turn of the Screw.

The third period of James's career reached its most significant achievement in three novels published just around the start of the 20th century: The Wings of the Dove (1902), The Ambassadors (1903), and The Golden Bowl (1904). Critic F. O. Matthiessen called this "trilogy" James's major phase, and these novels have certainly received intense critical study. It was the second-written of the books, The Wings of the Dove (1902) that was the first published because it attracted no serialization. This novel tells the story of Milly Theale, an American heiress stricken with a serious disease, and her impact on the people around her. Some of these people befriend Milly with honourable motives, while others are more self-interested. James stated in his autobiographical books that Milly was based on Minny Temple, his beloved cousin who died at an early age of tuberculosis. He said that he attempted in the novel to wrap her memory in the "beauty and dignity of art".

Shorter narratives

James was particularly interested in what he called the "beautiful and blest nouvelle", or the longer form of short narrative. Still, he produced a number of very short stories in which he achieved notable compression of sometimes complex subjects. The following narratives are representative of James's achievement in the shorter forms of fiction.

- "A Tragedy of Error" (1864), short story
- "The Story of a Year" (1865), short story
- A Passionate Pilgrim (1871), novella
- Madame de Mauves (1874), novella
- Daisy Miller (1878), novella
- The Aspern Papers (1888), novella
- The Lesson of the Master (1888), novella
- The Pupil (1891), short story
- "The Figure in the Carpet" (1896), short story
- The Beast in the Jungle (1903), novella
- An International Episode (1878)
- Picture and Text
- Four Meetings (1885)
- A London Life, and Other Tales (1889)
- The Spoils of Poynton (1896)
- Embarrassments (1896)
- The Two Magics: The Turn of the Screw, Covering End (1898)

- A Little Tour of France (1900)

- The Sacred Fount (1901)

- Views and Reviews (1908)

- The Wings of the Dove, Volume I (1902)

- The Wings of the Dove, Volume II (1909)

- The Finer Grain (1910)

- The Outcry (1911)

- Lady Barbarina: The Siege of London, An International Episode and Other Tales (1922)

- The Birthplace (1922)

Plays

At several points in his career James wrote plays, beginning with one-act plays written for periodicals in 1869 and 1871 and a dramatisation of his popular novella Daisy Miller in 1882. From 1890 to 1892, having received a bequest that freed him from magazine publication, he made a strenuous effort to succeed on the London stage, writing a half-dozen plays of which only one, a dramatisation of his novel The American, was produced. This play was performed for several years by a touring repertory company and had a respectable run in London, but did not earn very much money for James. His other plays written at this time were not produced.

In 1893, however, he responded to a request from actor-manager George Alexander for a serious play for the opening of his renovated St. James's Theatre, and wrote a long drama, Guy Domville, which Alexander produced. There was a noisy uproar on the opening night, 5 January 1895, with hissing from the gallery when James took his bow after the final curtain, and the author was upset. The play received moderately good reviews and had a modest run of four weeks before being taken off to make way for Oscar Wilde's The Importance of Being Earnest, which Alexander thought would have better prospects for the coming season.

After the stresses and disappointment of these efforts James insisted that he would write no more for the theatre, but within weeks had agreed to write a curtain-raiser for Ellen Terry. This became the one-act "Summersoft", which he later rewrote into a short story, "Covering End", and then expanded into a full-length play, The High Bid, which had a brief run in London in 1907, when James made another concerted effort to write for the stage. He wrote three new plays, two of which were in production when the death of Edward VII on 6 May 1910 plunged London into mourning and theatres closed. Discouraged by failing health and the stresses of theatrical work, James did not renew his efforts in the theatre, but recycled his plays as successful novels. The Outcry was a best-seller in the United States when it was published in 1911. During the years 1890–1893 when he was most engaged with the theatre, James wrote a good deal of theatrical criticism and assisted Elizabeth Robins and others in translating and producing Henrik Ibsen for the first time in London.

Leon Edel argued in his psychoanalytic biography that James was traumatised by the opening night uproar that greeted Guy Domville, and that it plunged him into a prolonged depression. The successful later novels, in Edel's view, were the result of a kind of self-analysis, expressed in fiction, which partly freed him from his fears. Other biographers and scholars have not accepted this account, however; the more common view being that of F.O. Matthiessen, who wrote: "Instead of being crushed by the collapse of his hopes [for the theatre]... he felt a resurgence of new energy."

Non-fiction

Beyond his fiction, James was one of the more important literary critics in the history of the novel. In his classic essay The Art of Fiction (1884), he argued against rigid prescriptions on the novelist's choice of subject and method of treatment. He maintained that the widest possible freedom in content and approach would help ensure narrative fiction's continued vitality. James wrote many valuable critical articles on other novelists; typical is his book-length study of Nathaniel Hawthorne, which has been the subject of critical debate. Richard Brodhead has suggested that the study was emblematic of James's struggle with Hawthorne's influence, and constituted an effort to place the elder writer "at a disadvantage." Gordon Fraser, meanwhile, has suggested that the study was part of a more commercial effort by James to introduce himself to British readers as Hawthorne's natural successor.

When James assembled the New York Edition of his fiction in his final years, he wrote a series of prefaces that subjected his own work to searching, occasionally harsh criticism.

At 22 James wrote The Noble School of Fiction for The Nation's first issue in 1865. He would write, in all, over 200 essays and book, art, and theatre reviews for the magazine.

For most of his life James harboured ambitions for success as a playwright. He converted his novel The American into a play that enjoyed modest returns in the early 1890s. In all he wrote about a dozen plays, most of which went unproduced. His costume drama Guy Domville failed disastrously on its opening night in 1895. James then largely abandoned his efforts to conquer the stage and returned to his fiction. In his Notebooks he maintained that his theatrical experiment benefited his novels and tales by helping him dramatise his characters' thoughts and emotions. James produced a small but valuable amount of theatrical criticism, including perceptive appreciations of Henrik Ibsen.

With his wide-ranging artistic interests, James occasionally wrote on the visual arts. Perhaps his most valuable contribution was his favourable assessment of fellow expatriate John Singer Sargent, a painter whose critical status has improved markedly in recent decades. James also wrote sometimes charming, sometimes brooding articles about various places he visited and lived in. His most famous books of travel writing include Italian Hours (an example of the charming approach) and The American Scene (most definitely on the brooding side).

James was one of the great letter-writers of any era. More than ten thousand of his personal letters are extant, and over three thousand have been published in a large number of collections. A complete edition of James's letters began publication in 2006, edited by Pierre Walker and Greg Zacharias. As of 2014, eight volumes have been published, covering the period from 1855 to 1880. James's correspondents included celebrated contemporaries like Robert Louis Stevenson, Edith Wharton and Joseph Conrad, along with many others in his wide circle of friends and acquaintants. The letters range from the "mere twaddle of graciousness" to serious discussions of artistic, social and personal issues.

Very late in life James began a series of autobiographical works: A Small Boy and Others, Notes of a Son and Brother, and the unfinished The Middle Years. These books portray the development of a classic observer who was passionately interested in artistic creation but was somewhat reticent about participating fully in the life around him.

Reception

Criticism, biographies and fictional treatments

James's work has remained steadily popular with the limited audience of educated readers to whom he spoke during his lifetime, and has remained firmly in the canon, but, after his death, some American critics, such as Van Wyck Brooks, expressed hostility towards James for his long expatriation and eventual naturalisation as a British subject. Other critics such as E. M. Forster complained about what they saw as James's squeamishness in the treatment of sex and other possibly controversial material, or dismissed his late style as difficult and obscure, relying heavily on extremely long sentences and excessively latinate language. Similarly Oscar Wilde criticised him for writing "fiction as if it were a painful duty". Vernon Parrington, composing a canon of American literature, condemned James for having cut himself off from America. Jorge Luis Borges wrote about him, "Despite the scruples and delicate complexities of James, his work suffers from a major defect: the absence of life." And Virginia Woolf, writing to Lytton Strachey, asked, "Please tell me what you find in Henry James. ... we have his works here, and I read, and I can't find anything but faintly tinged rose water, urbane and sleek, but vulgar and pale as Walter Lamb. Is there really any sense in it?" The novelist W. Somerset Maugham wrote, "He did not know the English as an Englishman instinctively knows them and so his English characters never to my mind quite ring true," and argued "The great novelists, even in seclusion, have lived life passionately. Henry James was content to observe it from a window." Maugham nevertheless wrote, "The fact remains that those last novels of his, notwithstanding their unreality, make all other novels, except the very best, unreadable." Colm Tóibín observed that James "never really wrote about the English very well. His English characters don't work for me."

Despite these criticisms, James is now valued for his psychological and moral realism, his masterful creation of character, his low-key but playful humour, and his assured command of the language. In his 1983 book, The Novels of Henry James, Edward Wagenknecht offers an assessment that echoes Theodora Bosanquet's:

> "To be completely great," Henry James wrote in an early review, "a work of art must lift up the heart," and his own novels do this to an outstanding degree ... More than sixty years after his death, the great novelist who sometimes professed to have no opinions stands foursquare in the great Christian humanistic and democratic tradition. The men and women who, at the height of World War II, raided the secondhand shops for his out-of-print books knew what they were about. For no writer ever raised a braver banner to which all who love freedom might adhere.

William Dean Howells saw James as a representative of a new realist school of literary art which broke with the English romantic tradition epitomised by the works of Charles Dickens and William Makepeace Thackeray. Howells wrote that realism found "its chief exemplar in Mr. James... A novelist he is not, after the old fashion, or after any fashion but his own." F.R. Leavis championed Henry James as a novelist of "established pre-eminence" in The Great Tradition (1948), asserting that The Portrait of a Lady and The Bostonians were "the two most brilliant novels in the language." James is now prized as a master of point of view who moved literary fiction forward by insisting in showing, not telling, his stories to the reader. (Source: Wikipedia)

NOTABLE WORKS

NOVELS

Watch and Ward (1871)

Roderick Hudson (1875)

The American (1877)

The Europeans (1878)

Confidence (1879)

Washington Square (1880)

The Portrait of a Lady (1881)

The Bostonians (1886)

The Princess Casamassima (1886)

The Reverberator (1888)

The Tragic Muse (1890)

The Other House (1896)

The Spoils of Poynton (1897)

What Maisie Knew (1897)

The Awkward Age (1899)

The Sacred Fount (1901)

The Wings of the Dove (1902)

The Ambassadors (1903)

The Golden Bowl (1904)

The Whole Family (collaborative novel with eleven other authors, 1908)

The Outcry (1911)

The Ivory Tower (unfinished, published posthumously 1917)

The Sense of the Past (unfinished, published posthumously 1917)

SHORT STORIES AND NOVELLAS

A Tragedy of Error (1864)

The Story of a Year (1865)

A Landscape Painter (1866)

A Day of Days (1866)

My Friend Bingham (1867)

Poor Richard (1867)

The Story of a Masterpiece (1868)

A Most Extraordinary Case (1868)

A Problem (1868)

De Grey: A Romance (1868)

Osborne's Revenge (1868)

The Romance of Certain Old Clothes (1868)

A Light Man (1869)

Gabrielle de Bergerac (1869)

Travelling Companions (1870)

A Passionate Pilgrim (1871)

At Isella (1871)

Master Eustace (1871)

Guest's Confession (1872)

The Madonna of the Future (1873)

The Sweetheart of M. Briseux (1873)

The Last of the Valerii (1874)

Madame de Mauves (1874)

Adina (1874)

Professor Fargo (1874)

Eugene Pickering (1874)

Benvolio (1875)

Crawford's Consistency (1876)

The Ghostly Rental (1876)

Four Meetings (1877)

Rose-Agathe (1878, as Théodolinde)

Daisy Miller (1878)

Longstaff's Marriage (1878)

An International Episode (1878)

The Pension Beaurepas (1879)

A Diary of a Man of Fifty (1879)

A Bundle of Letters (1879)

The Point of View (1882)

The Siege of London (1883)

Impressions of a Cousin (1883)

Lady Barberina (1884)

Pandora (1884)

The Author of Beltraffio (1884)

Georgina's Reasons (1884)

A New England Winter (1884)

The Path of Duty (1884)

Mrs. Temperly (1887)

Louisa Pallant (1888)

The Aspern Papers (1888)

The Liar (1888)

The Modern Warning (1888, originally published as The Two Countries)

A London Life (1888)

The Patagonia (1888)

The Lesson of the Master (1888)

The Solution (1888)

The Pupil (1891)

Brooksmith (1891)

The Marriages (1891)

The Chaperon (1891)

Sir Edmund Orme (1891)

Nona Vincent (1892)

The Real Thing (1892)

The Private Life (1892)

Lord Beaupré (1892)

The Visits (1892)

Sir Dominick Ferrand (1892)

Greville Fane (1892)

Collaboration (1892)

Owen Wingrave (1892)

The Wheel of Time (1892)

The Middle Years (1893)

The Death of the Lion (1894)

The Coxon Fund (1894)

The Next Time (1895)

Glasses (1896)

The Altar of the Dead (1895)

The Figure in the Carpet (1896)

The Way It Came (1896, also published as The Friends of the Friends)

The Turn of the Screw (1898)

Covering End (1898)

In the Cage (1898)

John Delavoy (1898)

The Given Case (1898)

Europe (1899)

The Great Condition (1899)

The Real Right Thing (1899)

Paste (1899)

The Great Good Place (1900)

Maud-Evelyn (1900)

Miss Gunton of Poughkeepsie (1900)

The Tree of Knowledge (1900)

The Abasement of the Northmores (1900)

The Third Person (1900)

The Special Type (1900)

The Tone of Time (1900)

Broken Wings (1900)

The Two Faces (1900)

Mrs. Medwin (1901)

The Beldonald Holbein (1901)

The Story in It (1902)

Flickerbridge (1902)

The Birthplace (1903)

The Beast in the Jungle (1903)

The Papers (1903)

Fordham Castle (1904)

Julia Bride (1908)

The Jolly Corner (1908)

The Velvet Glove (1909)

Mora Montravers (1909)

Crapy Cornelia (1909)

The Bench of Desolation (1909)

A Round of Visits (1910)

OTHER

Transatlantic Sketches (1875)

French Poets and Novelists (1878)

Hawthorne (1879)

Portraits of Places (1883)

A Little Tour in France (1884)

Partial Portraits (1888)

Essays in London and Elsewhere (1893)

Picture and Text (1893)

Terminations (1893)

Theatricals (1894)

Theatricals: Second Series (1895)

Guy Domville (1895)

The Soft Side (1900)

William Wetmore Story and His Friends (1903)

The Better Sort (1903)

English Hours (1905)

The Question of our Speech; The Lesson of Balzac. Two Lectures (1905)

The American Scene (1907)

Views and Reviews (1908)

Italian Hours (1909)

A Small Boy and Others (1913)

Notes on Novelists (1914)

Notes of a Son and Brother (1914)

Within the Rim (1918)

Travelling Companions (1919)

Notebooks (various, published posthumously)

The Middle Years (unfinished, published posthumously 1917)

A Most Unholy Trade (1925, published posthumously)

The Art of the Novel : Critical Prefaces (1934)

CPSIA information can be obtained
at www.ICGtesting.com
Printed in the USA
LVHW041215150920
666054LV00001B/65

9 781662 723285